Twisted

Linda Riel-Bourgon

Twisted

Cover © Dan Burgess
"Heartland" reproduced with permission.
Dan Burgess The Artist on Facebook

A very special mention must go to a few people in particular....

My sister, Debbie Antonopoulos began this project as an editor and quickly established she could contribute so much more. Debbie helped breathe life into these characters on each page.

Karen Graham, I can't say enough. What a wonderful, generous person. You have sincerely been a joy to work with and have the patience of a saint!

Kaitlin Bourgon, thank you for taking from what little extra time you had to complete the final proof read. You are my perfect daughter and as always you make me so proud.

I would also like to thank my family and friends for their much needed encouragement and wisdom while writing this, especially:

Shirley Hamilton, Debbie Sherry, Susie Robidoux, Tracy McCartney, Rosie deVries, Diane Bourgon, Debbie Harding-Roberston and the late Alain Kieffer, for his technical help.

Nathalie Theriault, BFF through thick and thin, love you!

Elzear O'Connor, yes, you made it in to the book!

Enormous gratitude to the superbly talented artist Dan Burgess for this amazing cover, absolutely love it!

*This novel is dedicated to Kaitlin, Kenneth and Marc,
you are the lights that guide me on this path called life.*

L.R.B.

Twisted

- Chapter 1 –

Well established equestrian center seeks a qualified full time Hunter/ Jumper trainer/instructor/manager. Job description includes training of horses for both the program and for sale. Working with students from beginner to advanced levels. Must be available to compete and accompany students to rated competitions. Forward resumes to Jarod Kingsley, Kingsley Ranch.......

Dana nervously toyed with the small frayed classified clutched in her hand. She had come across the advertisement a little over a month ago in a national equestrian publication. At the time it seemed like a godsend, an answer to her prayers. But now, as she stood waiting in the New Mexico train station for someone to come and collect her, a flurry of doubts attacked her already crumbling confidence.

She was a stranger in a strange land. The train station was much busier than she had anticipated and Dana felt increasingly conspicuous standing there as people hurried around her, jostling her as they passed her by.

A loud, large man in the midst of a heated argument with his companion abruptly stopped in front of Dana, effectively blocking her view. The couple appeared oblivious to Dana's immediate presence and as a result, Dana saw no other option but to lift her saddle across one bent arm and drag her suitcase along with the other to a different location.

As she awkwardly struggled with her belongings, the tattered slip of paper fluttered away and she watched with dismay as it escaped her reach only to be trampled in the hectic thoroughfare.

She sighed deeply, hoping it was not a sign of things to come. She checked her wristwatch once more; it was too late to turn back now.

Dana noticed an older man of average stature approaching her with an inquisitive look.

"Miss Northington?" He asked in a raspy voice as he briefly raised the tan western hat from his head.

Dana nodded to the man. "Hello."

"G'day, I'm Ben Strothers. Mr. Kingsley sent me to come gather you and your things, if that's okay with you?" Ben looked down to the bulky suitcase at her feet with the saddle sitting squarely atop and then glanced curiously over her shoulder. "Is that all you got with you?"

Dana nodded once more. "I thought if I was missing anything I could just pick it up here."

"Are you?" Ben stood patiently, a grin lighting his weathered face.

"Am I what?" Dana, tired from her journey, tried to look composed.

"Missing anything." Ben's grin widened.

Dana's attractive features broke into an easy smile. "I don't know yet," she said suddenly aware of the honesty in her answer.

She discreetly contemplated Ben. He must have been close to his sixties and there was a definite sweetness in his worn face that the years and the sun had not managed to steal from him. Dana had seen this face many times before, in artists' renditions that hung in the western gear area of almost every tack shop. Ben epitomized the word 'cowboy' and Dana's interest in what the other people at the ranch would be like grew.

"Well, I guess we'll get a move on." Ben handed Dana her saddle as he reached for her suitcase.

They made their way through the populated station and once outside, loaded Dana's possessions into the back of the truck that was parked nearby.

"It's a fine day for travel, Miss Northington. You just missed a real windy spell."

"Please call me Dana," she smiled in Ben's direction.

Ben dusted his hands on the faded denim of his jeans and offered one to Dana. "Well, I got no problem callin' you Dana so long's you call me Ben. That mister stuff just makes a man old before his time." Ben opened the passenger door to the truck. "Hop in."

Dana found herself taking an immediate liking to Ben, he had a relaxed manner about him that allowed her to feel at ease.

"Why don't you tell me something about Kingsley Ranch," Dana invited as they drove through the city.

"Kingsley Ranch is a couple thousand acres of the most beautiful land you'll see here in New Mexico," Ben informed her, his voice filled with pride. "Got everything on it; hills, flat land and a river running through the east corner. There's a big main house and a bunk house, two barns, indoor arena and the outdoor rings. Of course you'll be staying at the main house. In about an hour and a half we'll be home and you can see it for yourself."

They were putting Santa Fe behind them now and Ben reached for the stub of a half-finished cigar that sat in an overfilled ashtray. He glanced across at Dana and changed his mind.

"So what would make a girl like you travel all the way across country like this?"

Dana realized it was merely idle curiosity, and that some questions were going to be inevitable.

"I guess it was time for a change in scenery and by the looks of things I would say I've achieved that." Dana gazed through the window of the moving vehicle. Everything had become unfamiliar now, and in an odd sense she found comfort in that. Travelling through the remarkable countryside of New Mexico was like a breath of fresh air and with each breath she took, it seemed a fragment of her soul returned to her.

Dana sighed lightly and placed her head back against the seat. Today she was taking control of her destiny back into her own hands.

Control had always been a deciding factor in her young life. At twenty-eight years of age, Dana felt as if she was starting all over. Although she was not certain of what lay ahead, she would meet it willingly, determined to find a way to fit as a newcomer in this rugged land.

Born in Maine to a middle-class family, the only child of Carol and Paul, Dana had never felt alone, until now.

Paul and Carol had surrounded Dana with love and support. Her parents had encouraged her from an early age to discover her talent in life and regardless of what that might be, to pursue it and dedicate herself to it in hopes that in return, she would experience the satisfaction of self-accomplishment and find lasting happiness in whatever it was she chose to undertake.

Dana could remember her parents' stunned expressions when at the tender age of thirteen, she rushed headlong through the front door of their home announcing she planned on making a career for herself working with horses. Having not come from a family of equestrians, it was all quite unexpected. However, her parents indulged her young dream, even if it was not taken seriously at the time. Eventually they came to realize it was an earnest endeavor.

Dana's best friend Emma was the daughter of local stable owners and true to her ambition, Dana spent the next years working at their stable in exchange for riding lessons. Her days consisted of early morning feedings and muck-outs in return for late afternoon riding lessons. Her daily schedule fit together neatly with little time to spare and Dana thrived on her self-imposed regimen.

During those years she was aware that she had inadvertently caused her mother a certain amount of worry. Dana always knew that her parents were proud of her, but she could sense her mother's growing reservations towards Dana's disciplined lifestyle. Her mother found it difficult to understand why Dana chose to remain on such a demanding time table, while her classmates were out enjoying social activities and having a good time. Her mother viewed it all as too huge a sacrifice.

Dana did not see it as a sacrifice, but rather a wonderful opportunity.

A smile crossed Dana's face as she recalled the discussion concerning her high school prom, which she had flatly refused to attend.

Dana had patiently explained to her mother that she would be competing the following morning and attending a dance was the last thing she needed to be doing on the eve of such an important show. The ensuing debate had gone on for days, but in the end, Dana refused to be detoured from her priority.

After her graduation, Dana's parents brought her to the stable where she was now spending a good portion of her time and presented her with Pepper. He was a beautiful mount of 16.2 hands high, a four year old dappled gray thoroughbred gelding. Tears cascaded down Dana's cheeks; she could hardly believe this precious horse was her own or that her parents had gone to such lengths for her.

An immediate rapport was struck between horse and rider and at the time no one could've foretold the impact Pepper would have on Dana's life.

Over the next few years Dana and Pepper, as a team, went from participating in local horse shows to becoming state champions. It was a grueling program and Dana's life was moving at a rapid pace.

Although initially disappointed in Dana's lack of interest in college, her parents could not deny her success. They had raised her to believe in her dreams and in herself and they were quick to assure Dana she had not let them down.

Dana and Emma had remained the best of friends through their youth. They supported each other in everything and the years together had bonded them as sisters; if not by blood, certainly by affection and when the time had come for Dana to try life on her own it seemed only natural for Emma to do the same. They found a simple apartment and moved into it.

During that time Dana dated occasionally, but the relationships remained casual. Riding had always come first to her and her time was at a premium. The possibility of making the U.S. Equestrian Team was becoming more and more of a reality and she worked diligently towards that goal.

She was twenty-six when she first met Sonny. He was handsome, charming and intelligent and their relationship together gave credence to the theory that opposites attract. Sonny didn't know the first thing about horses, yet for the first time in Dana's life things were becoming serious.

Dana suddenly shook herself and straightened up in her seat. She turned her attention to Ben, realizing she had been poor company so far.

"I'm sorry, Ben. I haven't made for a very entertaining travel companion," she apologized.

He cleared his throat. "It's been a long trip for you, don't be worrying about me. I like a girl who doesn't prattle on and on about nothin'." Ben grinned.

For the remainder of the trip, Ben occasionally pointed out various landmarks as he described New Mexico and some of its colorful history.

Suddenly he announced. "We're here."

Dana glanced around her, feeling somewhat bewildered.

Ben noticed her look of confusion. "We're on Kingsley land now, the buildings are just over this hill," he explained as the pick-up climbed the expanse easily and then slowed to a stop. Ben gestured with an open hand. "That's Kingsley Ranch."

Dana was speechless.

Perched on the edge of the butte, the view before them was amazing. The ranch buildings sprawled below them, but other than that there was no sign of civilization for as far as the eye could see.

"You can call it home now." Ben was smiling as he slid the truck into gear. "We best get on, Jarod'll be waiting on us."

He turned the pick-up back down to the road and soon found the lane to the ranch. Dana understood that Ben had purposefully chosen that particular spot to give Dana her first look at Kingsley Ranch.

The big, main house was obviously older, but completely restored. It was a two-storey building with a generous verandah that extended across the entire face of the house and down each side.

Ben hoisted Dana's suitcase out of the truck. "I'll bring your saddle to the tack room later. Come on in, Jarod's most likely in his office."

Dana closed her eyes for a moment and drew a deep, steadying breath. This was it, she thought, a new beginning. She followed Ben into the house.

"We're home June," Ben called out.

A heavyset woman in her early fifties came to greet them.

"Hello, hello. Ben, I see you managed to get home in one piece." She turned and smiled at Dana. "And you, my dear, must be exhausted. We'll take you straight up to your room and you can freshen up. I'll bring you up a nice glass of iced tea, it'll give you a chance to catch your breath before you meet Mr. Kingsley."

The woman made a motion towards the wide staircase and abruptly stopped.

"Oh, where are my manners? My name is June and I'm very happy you'll be staying with us."

Dana returned the introduction.

"Thank you for your thoughtfulness, June. A shower and a drink would be much appreciated, it's been a long trip."

"Don't I know it." They began to ascend a wide, polished staircase as June continued. "I get myself in such a state when I have to travel, always have."

They made their way down a long hall until June turned and opened a door. "This will be your room, Dana. Through the door there," June pointed to the left of the room. "It's a full bath, linens and such should all be there. If there's anything missing, you just let me know. It's going to be wonderful to finally have another girl in this big house." June patted Dana's shoulder. "I'll go get your tea now."

Dana turned her attention to her room. The floor and furniture were made of pine and two decorative Native prints depicting wild horses hung from walls that were painted a quiet sage green. In the corner of the room reposed a big, brass bed covered with a handmade quilt. A vase filled with freshly cut wildflowers stood on the dresser. Ben had already been there and Dana's suitcase sat at the foot of the bed.

She lifted her suitcase onto the bed, opened it and removed a change of clothing. The atmosphere of the room was soothing and Dana was suddenly exhausted. She firmly told herself that what she needed was a brisk shower. Turning her back on the welcoming bed, she headed towards the bathroom.

When Dana returned to her room she felt refreshed and as she towel dried her hair she noticed that June was true to her word. On her nightstand stood a tall, frosty glass. There was a note propped up against the lamp, it read: Meet Mr. Kingsley in his office whenever you are ready. It's the door to the right at the bottom of the staircase, June.

Dana took a few minutes to appreciate June's hospitality and to finish getting ready and then made her way to the office. She stood at the door for a moment and before gently knocking.

"Come in," a deep voice responded from within the room.

Dana entered the office, closing the door behind her.

"I'll just be a second." The same voice continued from the vicinity of a massive wooden desk that was literally covered in paperwork.

He needs a secretary more than a stable manager, Dana thought to herself as she waited patiently, taking the opportunity to study her new employer. All she could see of the man with his head bent was his sun-streaked hair and his hands as he finished writing on a document...strong hands.

"Sorry to keep you waiting." He lifted piercing blue eyes to meet her. His gold ballpoint pen fell noisily from his fingers onto the desk.

During the brief moment that followed, there was only silence as Jarod took in the image of her standing silhouette against the door.

She was tall and slender, her long hair curling slightly and playing over her shoulders and about her face which was fair, a true ivory against the dark brilliance. Her features were delicate other than a generous bottom lip giving her the faintest suggestion of a pout. Her eyes, which were neither blue nor green, seemed to change color with each blink she took and those amazing eyes were framed by thick lashes and wide sculptured eyebrows.

"I'm sorry," Jarod repeated for a second time as he struggled to bring himself to the business at hand. This woman was definitely not what he had anticipated. He stood and introduced himself.

"I'm Jarod Kingsley, and you must be Miss Northington." Jarod smiled. "Please take a seat." He indicated a leather chair.

"Thank you," Dana answered politely as they shook hands. "Please call me Dana."

"You have to excuse me," Jarod said as he retrieved his pen. "You're...you look younger than I had expected," he added lamely.

And so do you, Dana thought to herself. Her new employer was probably in his mid-thirties, she judged as she sat into the deep chair. He was a striking man, his frame large but lean and muscular, his jaw square.

"Call me Jarod. I'm not big on formalities. June is the only one who insists on Mr., she seems to be quite set on that for some reason. Has she shown you to your room? Is everything to your satisfaction?"

"My room is lovely, you have a beautiful home," she assured him.

"I hope your trip was uneventful and that you didn't have any problems. Ben found you at the station easily enough?"

"Yes." Dana nodded. "He seems like a nice man."

"He's his own man." Jarod's face broke into a smile. "Ben does a great job around here. He's a serious horseman with years of experience behind him and he's also a dependable friend."

"Is the staff here large?" Dana asked with curiosity.

"Ideally there should be one manager for each barn, which would be Adam and yourself. There are two hands and Ben fills in on days off." Jarod paused. "You must be hungry and tired. I'm sure June has prepared us something special. She does love to fuss," he said fondly.

"Actually, I'm a little of both," Dana admitted.

Jarod smiled warmly. "Well, let's go and eat. We'll save talk of work until tomorrow, but you won't be starting for a couple of days. That'll give you a chance to get settled and become acquainted with everyone."

They stood and he guided her to the dining room.

The dining room carried the same unpretentious solid style as the other rooms that Dana had seen. Whoever had decorated the house had kept in mind that this was a man's abode. There was a simple beauty throughout the home and the house was furnished with strong pieces crafted by hand before the introduction of mass production. It filled the house with a sense of history, of having always been there. Every now and then Dana's eye came across subtle surprises of a woman's influence; splashes of wild flowers, a linen table cloth, an enormous clay pot resting in the corner of the room.

June, Dana thought to herself. June's presence could also be evidenced by the delicious aroma coming from what could only be the kitchen.

Jarod motioned Dana to take her seat and once she was comfortable, he took his chair.

June bustled in serving them their meal, then left the room only to return with a decanter of wine.

Jarod laughed as he poured two glasses. "You must have made an impression on June," he remarked. "She's not too fond of the wine cellar."

June chuckled as she wiped her hands across her apron. "There, there now. That'll be enough out of you, Mr. Kingsley. Eat up while it's still hot," she gently commanded as she departed to the kitchen.

Dana had not realized how hungry she was or how quickly she had eaten until she placed her fork down beside an empty plate. She noticed Jarod's food was still half uneaten.

"Well, there's nothing wrong with your appetite, that's always a good sign." Jarod reached for his wine glass. "You'll need a hearty appetite to keep up with things around here."

Dana could feel her cheeks redden.

Jarod immediately noted her discomfort.

"I'm sorry Dana," he apologized awkwardly. "I didn't mean to embarrass you. You had me worried a bit, you have the look of a fussy eater...what I meant was...," Jarod stumbled to a halt.

Dana's color was high as she continued to stare at him blankly.

"Why don't you tell me about yourself?" Jarod prompted, anxious to change the subject. "You've been very quiet."

Dana directed him a level stare. "I suppose I was too busy eating," she countered pointedly.

There was a moment of dead silence.

Her lips quivered as she attempted to conceal a smile and they both broke into laughter.

"Touché!" Jarod threw his hand over his heart in mock expression. "I think I deserved that. A stable manager with spirit, I see I'm going to have my hands full." He grinned.

Dana took a sip of wine and began to describe herself, elaborating little on any personal details of her life. Most of what she related Jarod was already well aware of from her resume and what articles he had come across. She was a young woman with talent who had been well on her way to glory.

As Dana spoke, Jarod caught himself studying her full lips. They were the only give away in her quiet, reserved manner and they had an expressiveness all of their own that she appeared to be unaware of. He was at a loss to understand his irrational behavior, this attractive woman both captivated and unnerved him. Suddenly he realized Dana was looking at him expectantly.

"It's your turn," she repeated.

Jarod pulled his thoughts together.

"Let's see," he began as he sat back in his chair. "I've always lived in New Mexico, other than my time at university. I had just finished school, where I majored in business, when my father passed away. It was a heart attack, Dad was a corporate mogul, he worked hard and played hard too. He just never knew when to quit, and I guess in the end, that's what did him in." Jarod paused.

Dana watched Jarod as he spoke with seeming indifference about his father's death, his manner calm and unhurried.

"That must've been very difficult for you," Dana said quietly. She was very close to her own father and she could not imagine having to cope with such a loss.

"That was some time ago." Jarod looked across the room, unable to understand why he had brought the subject up to begin with.

"I vowed to myself that I wouldn't end up like that," he continued slowly. "So, I bought this ranch. It is my sanctuary. I've ridden most of my life and have always found something truly special in the nobility of the horse. But I'm only one man, I still have a lot of business that takes me away and that's part of the reason you're here. That, and the fact that I'm certain you are more of a trainer than I will ever be." Jarod smiled at Dana and she was acutely aware of his penetrating blue eyes.

"Unless I'm mistaken, you were long-listed for the team. That seems like a lot to give up. I can't understand what would cause you to leave that to come and work for me. I'm proud of my ranch and the success we have achieved here, but I'm not falsely conceited. You had a lot of promise in your future."

Jarod leaned forward in his chair, an unasked question apparent in his countenance.

Dana drew a measured breath and her delicate chin lifted ever so slightly. Unconsciously she had drawn a line and Jarod instinctively recognized that he was not welcomed to cross it.

"I had some personal problems." She faced him squarely, sedately drawing her hands together in her lap. "I would prefer not to go into the details, but I want to assure you that this will in no way affect my performance or ability to do my job." Her expression softened. "I apologize if I sound rude."

"No, you are definitely qualified to do this job and I feel fortunate to have you here." Jarod felt her tension and he flashed her an easy smile. "I'm willing to take my chances."

Dana nodded slightly averting her gaze.

"Look, you must be exhausted and I still have a mountain of paperwork. Why don't we call it a night?" Jarod suggested, picking up on her cue.

They stood up from the table. "I want you to make yourself at home. Before you turn in, feel welcomed to poke around and find out where things are, or I can have June show you about if you prefer," he offered and then continued. "Feel free to sleep in tomorrow, whenever you're ready I'll show you around the ranch. We'll go for a ride, if you are up to it."

"That sounds fine, thank you. There's no need to bother June. I'll find my way."

They said goodnight and Jarod retreated to his office. Dana was too tired to investigate the house, she optioned to go straight to bed.

Making her way back to her room she found herself looking forward to the next day.

A trace of a smile hovered on her lips, it had been a long time since she last felt she would sleep soundly. Her new employer had said earlier that this ranch was his sanctuary and as Dana got into her bed she found herself feeling much the same way. She drifted into a deep sleep.

Jarod massaged his eyes with his fingertips. Stifling a yawn, he checked the time, eleven-thirty. He closed the folder on his desk and stretched his body as he stood. He switched off his desk lamp and the room was engulfed in darkness.

Climbing the stairs to his room, he took a shower and then turned in. Although he was tired, sleep would not come to him. He couldn't erase the picture of Dana standing against his office door from his mind.

This was sheer craziness! Yes, she was beautiful, but Jarod had encountered a number of attractive women during his lifetime. What made Dana different? Jarod ran his hand through his hair. Was it her laughter? Her sensuous mouth? Or that level gaze she delivered with teasing eyes?

Rolling over Jarod punched his pillow into shape. Was it her mystery? What was she not telling him? He cursed himself. He was losing sleep over a woman he didn't even know. She was an employee and this was highly unprofessional. It had to stop. He was acting completely out of character and none of it made any sense.

His eyes ached from the hours of paperwork and fatigue. He'd tossed most of the covers free and he swore irritably as he got up.

Walking over to his window he stopped and pulled it open. As he stood there, his muscular body tensed against the brisk night air, he breathed in deeply allowing the scent from the earth below to assail his senses. The yard light was customarily left on at night and Jarod was able to survey a good section of the immediate ranch. This always brought him a feeling of calm satisfaction.

After a time he realized his skin was chilled. He closed the window and went back to his bed. The last time he checked, the light on his clock read 3:20.

- *Chapter 2* -

Dana opened her eyes to sunlight peeking through her lace curtains. It took her only a second to register where she was. She had slept peacefully in the unfamiliar bed and she was eager to start her day. She quickly dressed in her riding breeches and a light sweater, anticipating her first ride on Kingsley soil.

It had been much too long a time between rides and she felt overdue for the sense of serenity only a horse could provide. For Dana, nothing had ever compared to the magical time when horse and rider became one in spirit, when her horse's brute strength succumbed willingly to each direction her body commanded and everything else was pushed to the outside by a calm certainty that every single movement was a freeze-frame of perfection. It was a therapy that could carry Dana away to a place where the past and the future had no relevance.

She lifted her thick hair into a ponytail and left her room, allowing her sense of smell to guide her down a narrow back-stairway that led straight into the kitchen.

"Good morning, June. It smells wonderful," Dana said cheerfully as she entered the room.

"Well, good morning. How did you sleep?" June asked, pouring a steamy mug of freshly perked coffee and setting it in front of Dana.

"Fine, my bed was very comfortable," Dana replied. "Can I give you a hand with something?"

"I'm just finishing up these eggs. Why don't you pop your bread into the toaster?" June pointed over to the breakfast counter.

The kitchen was generously proportioned. The floor was a terra cotta ceramic tile and numerous pots of herbs grew in the windows of the room. June worked back and forth from a double oven to a large well-worn butcher's block. The walls of the kitchen were cream in color and gleaming copper utensils hung from one of the exposed wooden beams that was part of the original structure of the house. There was a minimum of appliances; no microwave, no dishwasher. Plastics and microchips had not found their way into June's domain. This room had been created from sand, stone and sun.

"I'm looking forward to going riding this morning." Dana made light conversation as she buttered her toast. "The weather looks like it's cooperating."

"Yes, I see you're dressed for it. Mr. Kingsley will like that. Where can he be now?" June placed a platter of eggs, ham and bacon on the counter next to Dana. "Help yourself, dear. He's usually up bright and early, I'm sure I heard him before."

"Did I hear my name? It had better been in good context," Jarod teased as he entered the room and kissed June on the cheek. He pulled up a stool next to Dana and began serving himself. "Good morning, Dana. I trust you slept well. I see you're dressed to get going this morning."

Last night, Jarod had considered having someone else show Dana about and take her riding this morning. As he watched her now, fresh and vibrant, he reconsidered the idea and decided against it.

"Yes, I am. In fact, June and I were just talking about that."

They conversed pleasantly over breakfast, as it turned out June had a sister who lived in Vermont. She occasionally went to visit her there and they were soon jokingly debating the benefits of New Mexico's arid climate versus the variable weather conditions of New England.

Dana glanced over at Jarod. He appeared quite casual in his denim shirt with his sleeves rolled, jeans and leather boots. It was difficult to imagine this man in a stuffy office, wearing a tie. He was definitely a handsome man, but right now his blond hair was not combed into any particular style, seeming to fall naturally into place by its own will. He just didn't appear the business type and she could see why this ranch meant so much to him.

As if sensing her attention, Jarod felt her eyes on him and turned his head to face her. "Ready?"

Outside the sky was clear above and the brilliant sunlight radiated strongly across the ground beneath them. Dana shielded her eyes for a second as they adjusted to the brightness.

[15]

The land continued on an even plane in front of them until it hit up against a barrier of mountainous jagged rock. In the distance lay snow-capped peaks dotted by evergreens. It was a stunning view.

A big golden labrador dog came running to join them, tail wagging.

"Hey there, Jesse Dog, what kind of trouble have you been into?" Jarod rubbed the dog's head, to its obvious enjoyment.

"What a great dog!" Dana exclaimed.

"He is great and he's an ever better companion. He'll follow you anywhere if you let him. Remember that if you're nervous in the dark."

Dana felt the color leave her face and she purposely strode ahead of Jarod.

"I can't wait to see the horses," she said.

Jarod caught up with her and began to explain the set-up of the barns, the larger of the two being for broodmares and foals, the other for working horses.

They entered the smaller of the two barns. It was impressive, housing approximately twenty horses. At the far end of the structure was an attached indoor riding hall and the barn itself included grooming areas, a shower for the horses and a well-appointed tack room where Dana noticed her saddle already perched on a rack.

Jarod carefully studied Dana's silent evaluation.

"I like the way you're set up." She turned to face him and he was once again fascinated by the pout in her smile and eyes that seemed to dance with excitement. "You have good use of your space and I like the roominess of stalls and the wide aisles."

Jarod nodded in acknowledgement. "The majority of these horses are rideable, so look around and choose one for yourself. Except this guy," he added, walking over to a sorrel with a flaxen mane. "Dana, meet Goldrush."

The horse extended his large head over the lower half of his door as Dana rubbed his forehead. "He's a huge animal. Quarter horse?"

"The only one on the ranch. I've had him for two years now," Jarod explained as he stood beside Dana. "I didn't care for the way he was being handled and I bought him on the spot. There was something I liked in his spirit and he's never shown me any reason to doubt my decision." Jarod slipped a halter over the horse's head, unlatched the stall door and led him to a pair of cross-ties in the wide barn aisle. The horse was in superb condition and responded easily to Jarod. He turned to Dana. "I'll just be a minute," Jarod said before disappearing into the tack room.

Ben entered the barn followed by a younger, pleasant looking man.

"Well, g'day. It's gonna be another fine one. Dana, this is Adam." Ben made the introduction. "He's been with us goin' on three years now. Knows his stuff."

"Good morning, Ben. I'm pleased to meet you Adam." Dana smiled.

"Likewise Ma'am." Adam nodded his dark head and offered Dana an open hand.

"Just Dana will do." She shook his hand.

"Good morning, gentlemen." Jarod returned holding a large western saddle by the horn and a breastplate hung over his shoulder. "Dana, I see you've met Adam. Have you had a chance to choose a horse?"

Dana had been standing in front of an elegant bay with a narrow blaze that ran the length of its head. "What about this horse?"

"This particular horse was bought off the track, she was never quite fast enough to cut it there. She's eight years old and her name is Paska's Arrow. Originally we were going to use her in the breeding program but we liked the way she moved. I think she has a lot of potential here in our competitive program. Actually, I'm hoping Paska will be one of your main projects."

"Now you've aroused my curiosity." Dana put the mare's halter on and brought her out to an empty set of cross-ties. "Let's see what she can do."

Ben and Adam had moved down the barn and were busy with daily chores. Once Dana and Jarod finished tacking up their horses they led them outdoors. The morning had already begun to warm.

Paska did a small dance as Dana placed her left foot into the stirrup iron and swung her right leg over the mare's hindquarters. Dana stood in the stirrups for a second and adjusted her saddle as she stroked Paska's neck. She looked over to Jarod who was already mounted on Goldrush.

"So, which way?" Dana secured the chin-strap on her black riding helmet as her eyes scanned the land surrounding them.

Jarod tipped his tan Stetson closer to his brow and eased Goldrush into a jog. Paska smoothly came alongside at a trot. The earth was hard and dry beneath them and for the most part even the vegetation was unwelcoming. Dana had spent her life in a place that was vastly different.

There were no lush carpets of green grass here, no soft rolling hills or fat, leafy trees. Still, the rugged beauty of this country left her in awe of it. Before her lay a land of stark contrasts; flat lands broken by arrogant mountains. Where water could be found, there was a celebration of flora but where there was none, the cactus, yucca and juniper bush tenaciously struggled to survive. This land had little to spare for the weak or the sickly.

Paska was responding readily to Dana's direction. Earlier Dana had sensed a degree of distrust in the horse in the tension of the reins, but as they progressed into the ride Paska became more relaxed, her rhythm evened out and Dana could feel the horse rounding up beneath her. This horse was full of heart and Dana agreed with Jarod, the mare had great potential. They rode without mishap for a good part of the morning, working the horses through a variety of gaits.

Jarod brought Goldrush to a halt and dismounted. "I thought we could use a break."

Dana eased herself down from Paska and walked over to where Jarod stood, reins in hand. He lifted a canteen from the horn of his saddle and offered it to her.

"You are right about Paska. Has anyone put her over fences?" Dana asked him, declining the water.

"She's clearing 3'6" easily." He took off his hat, wiping his brow with the back of hand before replacing it. "You're a remarkable horseman Dana, you have a natural instinct. I had some high expectations and I don't think I'm going to be disappointed."

"Horses are my life," Dana replied simply as she focussed on the distant peaks. In the sunlight her eyes were a brilliant sea green accentuated by her dark curling lashes. "It's always been that way since childhood. I'm just fortunate enough to have been able to make a career doing something that I enjoy so much."

Jarod nodded in understanding.

"What happened with that big gray you had? I came across an article on the two of you, there was a photo. An impressive looking horse."

Dana turned to face him with a pained level gaze. He had caught her unguarded and now he watched as she struggled to regain her

[18]

composure. She had tremendous force of will and there was only the smallest catch in her voice as she answered.

"Pepper was a wonderful horse. He was seriously injured," she hesitated and drew in a breath. "I had no choice but to have him put down. It was the hardest thing I have ever done."

"I'm so sorry, Dana. I had no idea." He reached out to place a comforting hand on her shoulder. She stiffened and turned away, rejecting his gesture of sympathy. Jarod realized that once again she had placed an invisible barrier between them and he knew it was time to move on.

"Look, let's go back and grab some lunch. This afternoon I'll finish showing you around."

They rode back in silence. Jarod knew he had touched a raw nerve and he could have kicked himself for it. He wanted Dana to stay on at the ranch and he was quickly realizing that any personal questions were unwelcomed. Yet the more she withdrew from him, the more intrigued he found himself. No woman had ever made such a strong impression on him in such a short space of time. He felt unsettled and frustrated as he reminded himself that this was a professional relationship and that Dana's private life was her own.

Dana noticed little of the scenery on the return home, barely conscious of the ride at all as she allowed her well-trained reflexes to command the horse. Her mind was filled with the image of Pepper as he lay dying, his head on her lap. She knew she would always feel responsible for what had led to that tragedy. Dana questioned how she had ever imagined that by coming to New Mexico she would just be able to start a new life. Some things were far too painful to simply leave behind.

Paska started to play up and Dana was grateful for the demand of her attention. The barn was now in view. Upon arriving there, Jarod and Dana unsaddled the horses and rubbed them down before returning them to their stalls.

Dana felt the perceptible distance between them as they walked to the house and she made an effort to bridge it. "It was a good ride. Paska will go a long way for you. I'll get her started on a training program tomorrow." She smiled tentatively at Jarod.

"I thought you were supposed to take a few days to get adjusted!" Jarod followed her lead, joking with her lightly as if nothing was amiss.

"Seriously though, I know June was looking forward to going into town with you tomorrow, to do some shopping."

They entered the house and after washing up, met in the kitchen. June was nowhere to be found but she'd prepared two cold plates. As they ate they discussed the ranch, Jarod elaborating on a few of his short and long term goals. He eventually wanted to become a respected breeder of championship class jumpers.

He put his napkin down and pushed back his chair. "I have some calls to make. Later on, say around three o'clock, you can come by my office and we can get into the specifics of your position here." Jarod stood. "Is that okay with you?"

"That'll be fine. It'll give me a chance to look around the place."

"Alright, three o'clock it is." Jarod gave her a quick smile and left the room.

Dana cleared off the table and went outside where she was joined by Jesse Dog. When she reached the big open doors of the barn the dog turned back towards the house. Dana entered its shady recess and instinctively she checked each horse briefly. Paska was munching on a cake of hay as Dana walked into her stall.

"You having lunch too?" She stroked the mare's neck a few times before running her hands down the horse's legs, everything was fine. Dana left the mare to eat undisturbed.

Goldrush banged heavily on his stall door, demanding the same attention.

"Hey, big guy. What's your problem? Are you jealous?"

Goldrush pushed his amber colored head into Dana's arms and she rubbed his cheeks, his eyes closing in pleasure.

Dana heard a noise coming from the tack room and her hand suspended in mid-air as she realized she was not alone in the barn.

Ben came out of the room and paused in the barn aisle noticing Dana. He touched the brim of his hat in greeting. "Hello Dana, how was your ride this morning?"

"I enjoyed it," she replied with an outward calmness. "I thought I'd just come in here and start familiarizing myself with the horses."

"Good." Ben gestured with a nod of his head. "Don't know if anyone showed you yet, there's an office in here." Dana followed Ben back through the tack room to a small room that was furnished with a desk, phone and computer. "This is your office now. You'll find files on every horse; blacksmith and vetting schedules, show schedules and so on. You make yourself at home now. If you need me, I'll be in Barn Two with Adam." He made his way to leave.

"Thank you, Ben."

The office was well equipped. Dana sat behind the desk and turned on the computer, accessing the horses' files. She soon lost track of time, immersed in folders detailing every aspect of the management of the ranch.

Jarod quietly walked into the room. Dana was as yet unaware of his presence. He took the opportunity to study her. Wisps of hair had escaped her ponytail and curled softly around her delicate face. Her eyes were narrowed in concentration and her perfect white teeth gently pulled at her bottom lip. Once again Jarod was surprised by an unfamiliar feeling that he seemed to have little control over.

He cleared his throat. "Hey," he said lightly. "I'm not used to being stood up for a meeting this early on. People usually get to know me better first."

Dana's head shot up and her face blanched.

"Please, don't ... don't sneak up on me like that," she managed, obviously shaken. "'I'm sorry," she added lamely as she turned off the computer and checked the time on her watch. It was almost four o'clock.

"I'm the one who should apologize. I didn't mean to startle you," he said calmly, soothingly. He paused for a full minute. "I saw Ben, he told me I might find you here," Jarod explained.

"I was just going through the files." Dana turned the conversation towards work. "This is an impressive group of horses. Your breeding program seems quite successful and from what I can tell you have a working student program."

"You've been pretty busy since I saw you last." Jarod smiled.

"It's a comprehensive program," she replied, at ease now. Jarod sat on the couch and bent forward, his hands cupped together between open knees.

"I liked the student program," he explained. "It seemed to be the perfect solution. There were too many horses to exercise, train and show. There are three girls between the ages of fifteen and twenty-four, and Darren is twenty-one. They're all talented. Natasha and Darren alternate days with Emily and Sue. That schedule will start up next Monday. They will become part of your responsibility. Adam's been handling most of it up to now," Jarod continued. "It's too much for one person. So he'll manage Barn Two and concentrate his efforts on the breeding program and you will manage this barn."

Dana nodded. "Maybe you could give me a typical day. You know, just how an ordinary day runs."

"Okay, the horses are on four feedings a day: 7:00 am, noon, 4:00 pm and 8:30 pm. Have you met Kent or Annie yet? No? Okay, I'll introduce you later. They are my regular employees. They handle the feedings, mucking out and they also train. I'll let you set up your own exercise and training program inside that framework. There are a few horses I'm particularly interested in, Paska being one of them. There's also Goliath, a black gelding and a bay mare, Masquerade. I think a lot of these three and I believe they're ready for you. As I mentioned earlier, you'll be in charge of the students, also Kent and Annie, as far as their work in Barn One goes." Jarod gave her a moment to digest the information. "It's a big job, you can go to Ben or Adam for advice, but you have the final authority in the management of this barn. Have I discouraged you?" Jarod watched for her reaction.

"Jarod, I didn't come all this way to run off before I've even begun." Dana stated with determination, smiling. "I'm not afraid of work."

"Good." Jarod checked the time. "Let's take a walk around. I can show you the layout of the buildings. How would you like to see Barn Two?"

"I'd like that," Dana agreed as she stood from the desk.

They took a leisurely tour of the ranch, Jarod describing improvements he had already made and some changes that were still to come. Dana listened intently, gaining an understanding for the place and what was expected from her. She felt she could be an asset to this operation.

Jarod took simple pleasure in just watching her. There was a warm breeze coming from the west and it gently swept her mahogany hair across her face. Even Jesse Dog seemed enchanted by this elusive creature, following Dana faithfully from place to place. Occasionally Dana would reach over to pat his golden head.

They arrived at Barn Two to discover they had just missed Annie and Kent. The horses were eating contentedly. Adam was completing his work for the day and he and Jarod discussed a mare that was overdue while Dana watched a gangly young foal suckling on its mother. She was making her way from stall to stall, interestedly observing the horses when Jarod lightly touched her elbow.

"Hungry?"

She nodded.

"Good, let's go and wash up. June should have supper ready. We can confirm your day out tomorrow."

"I think I like a boss who gives me a day out before I've even begun work!" She laughed softly, her dark head coyly tilted to the side. Jarod stood just inches from her. He had a glimpse of her completely relaxed and he was loathe to break the spell.

"Come on, let's go back to the house."

The wind had picked up and was coming down off the mountains in a steady sweep as they made their way back to the main house. Dust was drifting across the open plains in the distance.

"Maybe we'll get some rain," Jarod commented hopefully.

After Dana showered and changed, she stopped in the kitchen to say hello to June. They made informal plans for the next day, then Dana headed towards the dining room, leaving June to her work.

Jarod was already seated when Dana walked in and joined him at the table.

"It looks like it's cajun chicken tonight. I was told 'it's Mr. Kingsley's favorite'. That woman thinks the world of you," Dana remarked, referring to June.

"It's a mutual feeling," Jarod replied. "June does more here than cooking and cleaning. She's the heart of Kingsley Ranch, a mom to anyone who needs one." He smiled fondly as June carried their supper in. "Isn't that right, June?"

June blushed, her face breaking into a lovely smile. "There, there now, Mr. Kingsley. You'll have me tripping over my own feet, my nose'll be so high in the air." She laid their steaming plates in front of them. "Take care now," she cautioned Dana. "It's not too spicy, all the same it takes getting used to. I'll be back later with the coffee," she added as she left the room.

"Last night you mentioned your father. Does your mother live in New Mexico?" Dana asked as she sampled her chicken, finding it to be delicious.

Jarod's words came slowly, in careful concentration. "I don't really remember her. She passed away when I was only six. I have the odd memory of her, but that's about it. It devastated my father at the time and he was never very close to anyone after that, including me. That's when June came to take care of me." Jarod smiled and shrugged his shoulders slightly. "Life has an odd way of working itself out."

"I suppose that's true. Some things are difficult to comprehend. Pain can do strange things to people... it's often hard to see your way when your world's been turned upside down." Dana stopped herself, she was close to a door she didn't want to open. "You were lucky to have June," she said, turning her back on that threshold.

If Jarod had noticed her hesitation, he was careful not to show it.

"I'm sure you'll enjoy her company tomorrow," he said lightly as he reached for his coffee. "So, Dana tell me, are you comfortable with the set up?" Jarod paused. "If you have any concerns I want you to feel free to discuss them with me. I have learnt through life almost anything is fixable," he smiled casually.

"You have put a lot of thought behind the layout of this ranch and its operation." Dana assured him. "I'm really looking forward to contributing here."

June came at that minute to clear the table and offer them more coffee, which they politely declined.

"June, you always spoil me before I have to leave." Jarod smiled fondly at the woman.

"If I had it my way, you wouldn't be taking so many of these trips. A man should be able to sleep in his own bed." June imparted before leaving the room.

"You're leaving?" Dana was surprised not only by the fact that he was going, but also that she was disappointed by it.

"I've got business in Dallas. As I told you, duty tends to call me away every so often. It's a short trip. I should be back late Saturday."

Dana nodded. She hadn't realized until then how much she had enjoyed his companionship that day.

As if mirroring her own thoughts, Jarod got up from the table and said, "I enjoyed myself today. I think this is going to work Dana. My flight is quite early tomorrow and I haven't packed yet, so I'll say goodnight."

"Thank you, Jarod. You've made me feel very welcomed. It means a lot to me and I hope I'll fit in here as well as everyone else seems to have," Dana spoke sincerely.

Jarod went into the kitchen to find June and kissed her on the cheek.

"I'm going to bed now 'mom'," he teased her affectionately.

She had been busy washing up but now she turned to him, wiping her hands on her apron. "That's very sweet."

She gave him a probing look as she waited expectantly. He shook his head back and forth. "June, you could always read me like a book."

"Yes, that's true dear," she told him calmly as she continued to wait, knowing there was something he wanted to say.

"Take care of that girl while I'm gone. I can't help but be a little worried about her," he said finally, his face sober.

"Don't you worry about a thing." June assured him. "Off with you now, I've got work to do." She shooed him out of the kitchen before turning back to the sink. She caught herself humming as she worked.

- Chapter 3 -

Dana crossed her room to the window, the rain Jarod had hoped for had never realized, the day was clear. Dana dressed casually in khakis and a crisp cotton shirt. She brushed her hair then braided it.

She found June having her coffee in the kitchen.

"Good morning, June. Are we still on for today?"

"Good morning, dear. I certainly hope so, I think we'll have a grand time. I've been putting off going to town for awhile, I'm not very brave driving by myself, I'd much rather have some company. I'll get your breakfast." June started to get up.

"I'll just have toast. Sit down June, I'll fix my own, if that's alright? Enjoy your coffee." Dana prepared a simple breakfast. 'There are a few things I need to get, so this works out wonderfully for me."

Dana volunteered to drive, while June gave directions and June seemed delighted with the arrangement. The closest town was about thirty minutes from the ranch. As they drove, June reminisced about her life and eventually the conversation turned to the time when she had come to care for Jarod as a little boy.

'I've never married or had children of my own," she said. "It wasn't long before I loved him as if he was my own son."

"Jarod told me last night that his mother died when he was quite young, it must've been hard."

"Yes, poor wee thing. That's when the first Mr. Kingsley brought me in. He had no clue how to care for the boy."

They reached their destination and June indicated a convenient parking space.

Dana turned to June with a puzzled frown. "Do you mind if I ask something that is none of my business?"

"That all depends," June smiled. "What is it?"

"The two of you are so close, yet you always call Jarod 'Mr. Kingsley'. I don't understand, have you always called him that?"

"Oh my, no. I used to call him Jarod, and I do still every now and then, but when his father died, he was overwhelmed with grief. There was a lot of unfinished business between them and his father had so many business dealings to contend with. Jarod had no living relatives to speak of, he took it hard.

One night he was sitting at the table, his head in his hands. I happened into the room, he lifted those blue eyes up to me and asked me how was he going to manage? I said to him, 'Jarod, now you are Mr. Kingsley. There isn't anything you can't manage. You are a fine young man and you'll live up to that name.' From that time on, I've called him Mr. Kingsley. It's only proper."

Dana nodded, slowly digesting June's intuitive logic. "He seems happy and successful, you must be very proud of him."

"I couldn't be prouder if he was my own flesh and blood. Well, let's get busy. We could sit here and talk all day long, but we'd look pretty sad going home empty-handed."

Dana and June spent an enjoyable day shopping. They picked up the things that they needed and ate lunch at a little Mexican eatery. By the time they arrived back at the ranch, it was late afternoon.

Ben saw them return and came over to the car to help them unload their purchases.

"How do you ladies find so much stuff every time you go shopping?" He faked a complaint.

"I guess we got carried away." Dana laughed, trying to determine which bags were hers.

Once they got everything into the house, June invited Ben to stay for supper. "We're just having something simple in the kitchen."

Ben quickly replied that he'd be honored to have supper with the ladies and he'd be back as soon as he had a chance to wash up.

After their meal, the three of them sat and visited over coffee. Eventually Ben reached for his hat as he got up to leave.

"Thank you ladies for the nice meal. I gotta tell you, you young ladies are prettier company than Adam." Ben winked at June and Dana was surprised to see June blush. Ben turned his attention to Dana. "Dana,

Jarod thought I should shadow you tomorrow, in case you needed anything."

Ben's choice of words sent a chill through Dana. When she answered, her words sounded flat even to her own ears.

"Thanks Ben, I'm sure I can use your help. I'll see you tomorrow around 7:00 in Barn One." Dana got up from the table. "June, it was a lovely day, I really enjoyed myself. I've got a big day tomorrow so I'm going to head upstairs. Goodnight."

Dana crawled into her comfortable bed and curled up with her oversized pillows.

In the darkness she allowed the tears to come. She was angry with herself for getting upset so easily. The simplest thing would spook her when she least expected it. The past few months had been so difficult, and they had taken their toll. Dana realized she was overly sensitive and she consoled herself with knowing that she had good reason to be. She missed Emma and her family, she missed her home and most of all she missed her horse, Pepper, because that loss was a final one and with Pepper had disappeared her desire to ever make the Olympic team.

Thankfully, she felt good about the ranch. The people were nice, everyone was considerate and welcoming and her duties as manager looked challenging enough to keep her busy. Things would get better, she thought to herself and for once she believed it could be true. Tomorrow she would phone home and let her parents know she was okay. The last thought before she drifted asleep was how much her mom would like June.

Dana had set her alarm for 6:00 a.m. She rolled back over in bed and her face touched a pillow that was still slightly damp. She padded barefoot to her bathroom and looked in the mirror. Her reddened eyes were a telltale reminder of the previous night and she bathed her face in icy cold water.

As she dressed, Dana realized she felt a lot better. She had kept up a brave front for so long, a good cry had helped to relieve her sadness. She looked forward to the day ahead of her. It was her first official day on the job, and that gave her a stronger sense of belonging. She hurried down the stairs.

"Good morning, June."

"Good morning, dear." June was ready with Dana's breakfast. She laid a plate of flapjacks, fresh fruit and cheese in front of Dana and poured her mug of coffee. June obviously believed that breakfast was the most important meal of the day.

"This is beautiful June. You're spoiling me."

"And I'm happy to do it. No one ever leaves my table hungry." June said with pride.

Dana ate quickly and bidding June goodbye she left for the barn with Jesse Dog in tow. At the barn she came across Ben grooming Goldrush.

"Jarod usually does this every day, so when he's off doin' business, I like to make sure this guy gets his brushing anyway," Ben explained. "So Dana, are you lookin' forward to your first day of work?"

"Yes, I am. I'm going in the office to go over a few files, it shouldn't take too long. After that, I think I'd like to meet Kent and Annie, we must've just missed them yesterday."

Once in the office, Dana pulled the files on Paska, Goliath and Masquerade. She planned to take the three of them out for a workout sometime during the course of the day and she wanted to check their histories beforehand. Everything appeared to be in order.

Dana rose from her chair and headed back into the barn.

"Kent, Annie," Ben called out. "Your new boss lady's here. Pull up your boots and get over here on the double." Ben chuckled to himself, quite amused.

Dana smiled at him. "Very funny, Ben."

Kent and Annie advanced towards them from opposite sides of the barn. Dana guessed they were close to her own age. Kent was tall and husky, a powerful looking man and Annie was a friendly looking young woman with short, strawberry blond hair and a round face, dimpled with freckles.

Ben made the introductions.

Dana knew how she wanted to begin. "Kent, Annie, at this stage you obviously have more experience working in this barn than I do. Before I go and make any changes, I'd like to have a clear picture of your routine. It would be a great help to me if you could keep a written journal of when and what you normally do, for the next couple of days. You know, things like when which horse is usually exercised, which ones are turned out and so on. I'll need this information to make up my schedule. I know it's a bit of a nuisance, but I believe it will make for a smoother transition in the long run."

"Sure, that's no problem," Annie offered agreeably.

"Wait a minute. Annie, slow down." Kent cut in arrogantly and Dana immediately sensed the resentment in his tone. He turned to face Dana with an irritated expression. "I've got a lot of work to do here. Do you really expect me to run around with a little notepad and pencil and write down everything I do?"

"If it has to do with the horses and the ranch's time, yes. If that's the only way you can manage it, then that's what I expect," Dana insisted calmly. She was not a pushover and if Kent was testing the water, he might as well get wet. She allowed a few seconds for her intention to be understood. "This is the best way for me to make informed decisions and unless you want me standing over you for the next few days, you'd better keep that record." Kent was looking hot under the collar and Dana considered that she'd pushed him hard enough. "Look, I know it's a pain, but we all want the same thing here: horses that are in prime condition and showing successfully. It's only for a few days." Dana watched for Kent's reaction.

Kent was still far from co-operative, but he had the sense to keep his disparaging comments to a minimum. "I'm just not crazy about paperwork and changes. I don't see what's wrong with what we've been doing up to now," he grumbled.

"I feel you're taking this personally. We all have a job to do. It's because I value your input that I'm asking for this." Dana's tone was considerate, yet final. "Okay. Are we done here?" Dana looked at Kent and Annie inquiringly.

Kent nodded and returned to his work. Annie hesitated, obviously uncomfortable with the situation.

"What is it, Annie?" Dana invited quietly, not rushing her.

"Kent is really a good guy and he's good with the horses." Annie defended her co-worker. "Everyone almost expected he would be managing this barn, but Jarod didn't offer him the position and now here you are. I know he didn't make a good first impression, but give him a chance, he'll come around."

"Don't worry Annie, everything will work itself out." Dana decided it was time to change the subject. "Has Goliath been fed?"

"Goliath and the others were fed at seven, they always are."

Dana checked her watch. It was 8:45.

"Okay then. I'm going to take him out, he's had plenty of time to digest his breakfast." She smiled reassuringly at Annie. "Thanks for your help, we'll talk again later." Dana turned and noticed Ben leaning up against the stall with a satisfied grin on his face.

"You look like the cat that swallowed the cream," Dana observed. Ben tipped his hat to her. It suddenly dawned on her that Ben had instigated the whole episode.

"You knew that would happen," she said slowly.

"I'm an old man, Dana. I've met a lot of people in my time, after a bit you get wise to their ways. He's a good kid but his nose is outta joint, you comin' in here all polite and polished like. I just wanted to make sure you could handle it."

Dana was dumbfounded. "And?"

"You're a spitfire." Ben's grin widened.

"You're terrible!" Dana shook her head, breaking into quiet laughter. She started to walk away then stopped and turned around. "Ben, it seems like Kent would've been the obvious choice for this job. Why didn't Jarod offer it to him?"

"I told Jarod that Kent tries too hard. He still has to learn to hear the horse when it speaks to him. Sometimes, it's only a whisper. He's strong, he's confident and that's got him to where he's at, now he's gotta learn how to listen. You can't always make things happen just 'cause you want them bad enough."

Dana had a new found respect for Ben and she felt closer to him. She made her way to Goliath's stall.

She unlatched his door and led him to the cross-ties. She stood back for a second and looked him over; he was truly a stunning specimen of a horse, coal black without a speck of white. She judged he had to be close to seventeen hands high. She saddled him up and led him into the riding hall.

She worked Goliath for approximately an hour, putting him through all his paces. Towards the end of the session the big gelding was responding to Dana's legs and hands easily.

"You're a good man." She bent forward and patted his neck, then dismounted. Dana loosened Goliath's girth and proceeded to cool him down.

Ben rejoined her. "He's our best prospect right now."

Dana nodded. "I think now that I'm warmed up, I'll take Paska out. I'd like to try the outdoor ring. What do you think, Ben?"

"The temperature's good for a morning ride. I gotta soft spot for that mare and if I wasn't such an old man, I'd be tempted to get on her myself. I'd like to watch, if you don't mind?"

Dana absently scratched the horse's chin. When she stopped, the horse nudged her arm, looking for more.

"That's fine by me, Ben. I'd value your opinion. I'm just going to bring this big guy back to his stall. I'll meet you outside as soon as I have Paska ready."

The sun was bright and warm as Dana led Paska out of the barn. Paska repeated the same dance she had done the previous day as Dana mounted. She directed the horse down the path on a loose rein, checking her in every so often.

Dana noticed Ben waiting for them, his arms crossed over the top of the railing. He closed the gate after they entered the riding ring.

Dana spent the first forty-five minutes doing flat work until she was satisfied that the horse was completely relaxed. Until now they had ignored the two fences that were set up: one at three feet, the other at three and a half. Dana decided it was time to give them a try.

She cued Paska to take up a canter and once the rhythm felt right, Dana encouraged her towards the jump. Paska's body tightened and there was some hesitation. Dana's legs instinctively urged the mare forward. Paska responded but her timing was lost, causing her to abruptly hop over the small fence. Dana pulled Paska together and cantered on to the next fence. Paska sailed over the higher fence with grace. Dana slowed Paska to a trot and then to a walk, stroking her warm moist neck.

"So, Ben. What do you think of your girl?" Dana called to him. Ben could hear the delight in her voice.

"She's a fine animal and you look good together."

Dana brought the horse around to Ben.

"Paska doesn't have any patience with them small fences. Nah, she just wants to take on the big ones. She'll never make a hunter, but we got ourselves one heck of a jumper. If you don't mind Dana, I'd like to cool her off. I could use the exercise." He looked affectionately at the mare.

"She's all yours, Ben. I'll meet up with you in the barn later." Dana placed the reins in Ben's aged hand and checked the time. Realizing she was getting hungry, she headed to the main house. June was busy putting out the wash.

"Your lunch is laid out on the table, Dana, I'll just be a bit..."

Dana interrupted her, noticing the basket of wet laundry. "Don't worry, June, I'll make myself at home. Go ahead with what you were doing."

Dana ate in solitude. She felt wonderful. After all these years, her enjoyment of the sport still never ceased to amaze her. This afternoon she would take out Masquerade. She did a quick mental review of what she had learned from the file that morning. Masquerade was a Kingsley Ranch offspring. She was five years old and had successfully shown at the preliminary levels, but something had gone wrong, she seemed to have difficulty advancing from there. Dana had purposefully kept her workout for the last.

By the time Dana got back to the barn it was almost one-thirty. All was quiet as Dana found Masquerade's stall. She quickly checked the bay horse over, tacked her up and led her into the riding hall.

For the most part the lesson went well. Masquerade's basic performance was brilliant, yet when Dana attempted to ask for something more challenging, the mare would panic, throwing her legs up and out behind her in protest.

Dana would have to get to know the horse better. She was deep in thought as she led Masquerade back into the barn. Ben met up with them at the door.

"How did it go?" He asked casually.

"Is she always so...so...feisty?" Dana answered his question with one of her own.

"Hmm," Ben sighed. "Yeah, she started playing up 'bout a year ago. She was doin' fine before that. Jarod had big plans for that mare. Something must've spooked her somehow and instead of easin' her over it, I figure she got pushed too hard. Kent was doin' most of her training and he knew how much she meant to Jarod. He was just determined to prove he could get the job done. Some things can't be rushed." Ben lifted his hat off his head and ran the back of his wrist across his brow. Masquerade eyed him uneasily. "Now when she feels pressured, she bucks. She's not a mean horse, she's just lost her trust, that's all. A mean horse'd be easier to fix," he added.

Dana took off Masquerade's tack and returned her to her stall. She paused there for a moment, watching the mare chewing on her hay.

Dana tried to imagine how confusing it must be for a horse when it simply didn't understand the language of the aid. To try again and again, only to continually get it wrong, to feel the rider on its back become more tense and agitated with each attempt.

It all came together, Ben was probably right. Masquerade had lost her confidence.

Dana left the mare and headed to the office where she placed a call to her parents. On the east coast, afternoon was already drawing to a close and her parents were just getting ready to eat. It was good to hear the sound of their voices. She reassured them that she was happy and well, keeping her answers light and easy, promising them more details once she had the chance to become more settled.

She was halfway through updating the files on Paska, Goliath and Masquerade when she was interrupted by a knock at the door.

"Come in."

Kent stepped into the room, closing the door behind him. He stood there, ill at ease, uncertain how to begin.

"I heard you tried out Masquerade this afternoon." He spoke finally, avoiding looking at Dana directly. "You know, she's always had a crazy streak in her. I don't know why Jarod liked her so much in the first place. She's too unreliable to ever do well in the show ring."

Dana remained silent. Kent shuffled his feet and continued on a different tack. "Anyways, I thought about that journal you wanted and I guess it's okay. I wanted to apologize about this morning, I was out of line."

Dana considered her words carefully. If Kent had any horse sense at all, he had to already know that he may have ruined this horse permanently. Dana did not feel she was in any position to draw that assumption conclusively, but if it was true, it would be a very difficult thing to accept. It's terribly hard for a trainer to admit that he's soured a horse. The only positive outcome from a mistake like that was experience gained for the next time, but first he had to be honest with himself. Kent didn't look ready yet. He was still somewhere between knowing it and accepting it.

Dana's compassion tempered her response. "I appreciate your apology, Kent. I'm looking forward to working with you, but you're going to have to meet me halfway on this. Try not to be too quick in judging me. Allow me the benefit of a doubt and I'll try to do the same for you. Is it a deal?"

"Deal." Kent agreed. "Well, I guess I'll get back to my work. Thanks for your time, Dana." Kent left the room.

Dana sat for awhile, deep in thought. Bringing Masquerade around would require a lot of ground work, if she could be brought around at all.

As far as the issue with Kent went, it was much too early to form any valid opinion. As manager, her ability to guide and advance her trainers was as important as her ability to train horses. To be ultimately successful, they would need to work as a collective force, tuning their talents towards the same objective.

Dana finished up her paperwork and looked in on the horses one last time before calling it a day. As she approached Goldrush's stall, he stretched out his neck in Dana's direction.

"Hey, big guy. Coming to say goodnight?" She rubbed his cheeks. "Jarod will be home tomorrow. Sleep well."

Dana made her way to the main house. She especially loved this time of the day when peace settled over the ranch and everything was still. The sun's redness cast a glow across the warm baked earth. The windmill stood tall and foreboding, its gentle breeze for once absent. The ponderosa pine and quaking aspen stood motionless in the distance, starkly etched, dark against light on the mountainside as the sun traveled westward. For all its strangeness, Dana was overwhelmed by the power of the beauty surrounding her, and she felt she had made her way to where she was intended to be.

She smiled to herself upon entering the main house. June was hard at work, as was evident by the aroma that greeted her. It brought back fond memories of an earlier time when Dana would hurry home famished after working in the stables in Maine.

She popped her head into the kitchen. "Hi, June, how was your day?"

"Hello dear. My day was good, thank you. Will you be wanting your supper?"

"Well, I was wondering if I'd have time to shower and change."

"Sure you will. I was thinking we'd just eat in the kitchen tonight, you know, just us girls."

"That's fine by me." Dana hurried up to her room.

When Dana returned downstairs June noticed she had changed into a loose fitting pair of charcoal gray sweats, she had on slippers and her hair was lifted off her shoulders in a ponytail.

"That must feel better," June commented. "Come and eat, dear."

They took their time over supper, there was no reason to hurry. June asked about Dana's day and Dana shared it with her gladly, deliberately omitting the episode involving Kent. During the conversation June told Dana that Jarod had phoned and he would be catching an earlier flight, probably arriving at the ranch sometime after noon tomorrow.

"He asked about you," June added with an innocent smile.

As they relaxed over their coffee, June suggested a movie. "We have quite the movie library here. If you aren't too tired I thought we might watch one"

"That sounds like fun." Dana was agreeable to the suggestion. She gave June a hand clearing up and then accompanied her to the den.

It was a very spacious room made on the long. As in the kitchen, the ceiling was framed with dark wooden beams. There was an expansive stone fireplace at one end of the room, the mantle adorned with riding trophies and in the far corner, tucked neatly in its crevice, someone had cleverly engineered a well-stocked bar. At the opposite end of the room stood a solid oak entertainment center complete with television and various other state-of-the-art electronics. In the center of the room sat twin leather sofas, back-to-back, each one facing an opposite end. The curtains were drawn on the two windows that sat on the exterior wall. A large portrait resided between them, its subject bearing a close resemblance to Jarod.

"It's the first Mr. Kingsley," June explained following Dana's gaze.

Dana nodded. "It's an unusual room."

"Yes it is. Mr. Kingsley said it was too big for one room, yet too small for two, so the only thing to be done was to make two rooms in one." June laughed, her dark eyes sparkling in the lamp light.

Dana realized that was it, apart from the odd easy chair, one half of the room almost mirrored the other.

"Occasionally he likes to entertain his business associates and it works well this way, and yet it's cozy enough to relax in." June crossed over to the entertainment center and opened a door to reveal a variety of movies. They reviewed the selection and decided on a comedy.

Dana curled up on the couch, tucking her feet underneath her. June chose an upholstered rocker chair. It was very comfortable. The girls became relaxed and almost giddy, encouraged by the hilarious escapades of the film. About half way through, June put the movie on pause and excused herself. When she returned she brought in a tray with a bowl of popcorn and two glasses of soda.

"We even have intermission!" June teased.

"So, June. Has Ben never married?" Dana recalled his wink the night before. June's round face creased into a large smile.

"Oh, that old coot! He's had his share of tom-catting in his younger days, if you know what I mean." June gave Dana a knowing look. "He was too charming to settle on one sweetheart, as far as I can tell." June's hand unconsciously tidied her salt and pepper hair. Dana couldn't help but smile, seeing Ben from a whole different perspective. "He's got a bad leg to show for it, thanks to a bar fight where he got caught messing with a married woman. Let me think, that happened shortly after Jarod bought this ranch. I remember he was laid up for days, licking his wounds. That slowed him down." June said, looking indignant. "Imagine! He must've been close to fifty at the time." June shook her head in disbelief and Dana hid her amusement by sipping on her soda. Her cheeks were sore from the effort as she tried to keep a straight face. It was sweet to see that romance came in a variety of colors and ages.

"Maybe after you came to the ranch, he no longer cared for it," Dana said subtly. It took June a moment to register Dana's meaning.

"Oh, go away with you now!" June protested blushing. "He's just an old flirt that can't help himself, that's all. Anyway, listen to me gossiping about other people. I hold no stock in gossip and here I am, guilty of it myself." June pressed a button on the remote control and the movie resumed.

They thoroughly enjoyed the remainder of the feature and the climax made them laugh until their eyes watered. June turned off the television as she tried to stifle a yawn.

"That was a great idea, June." Dana also began to yawn. "We'll have to do that again. I guess it's time to go to bed. Goodnight."

"I'll see you tomorrow morning dear, sleep well."

The next morning Dana found June looking a little tired, but they both had a good laugh over how silly they had been the night before. Dana could tell June truly enjoyed having some female companionship and Dana would be lying if she said she had not enjoyed June's company as well.

Dana decided to follow the same agenda as the previous day and worked Goliath and Paska during the morning. Both horses performed smoothly and as she was finishing up she noticed Annie and Kent preparing to begin the noon feeding. She joined them and offered to give them a hand.

"Kent, Annie, I'd like to do the hay, if you don't mind. It's time I get to know the other horses in the barn."

Annie looked to Kent and he shrugged his shoulders. "Sure, if that's what you want. We were just about to start watering." Kent's attitude towards Dana was still cool but definitely an improvement from yesterday. His wide arms flexed as he unhooked the coils of water hose from the support.

"It's fine with me," Annie piped in. "We'll be done all the sooner."

Dana sensed a whim of peacemaker in Annie's gentle nature.

Dana had always enjoyed doing the daily chores. It was the one constant with horses. She broke for lunch once she was finished and then returned to work.

She had been carefully contemplating Masquerade all morning and as she walked back to the barn she settled on her course of action. In order to teach Masquerade language, it would require beginning with the alphabet. Dana would bring Masquerade back to square one and advance her at the mare's own pace. It could be a long process and the outcome was never guaranteed, but Dana believed it to be the surest plan.

[38]

Decisively, Dana tacked Masquerade and once again led her into the riding hall. She had been working the mare through a repetition of uncomplicated commands for some time, a composition of walk and trot work with some simple bends when she became aware of Jarod leaning against the gate that separated the hall from the barn. She trotted Masquerade over to where he stood.

"Hi, Jarod. Have you been watching us for long?"

Jarod made an unsuccessful attempt to disguise the disappointment in his tone. "Hello, Dana. Long enough," he answered. "She's a beautiful example of everything a horse should be. I had hoped by now she would've been much further along than she is." He looked away from Masquerade and up at Dana. "So, what do you think?" Jarod asked her doubtfully.

"I've always chosen to believe a person has the ability to improve almost anything. If it's not working, then it's time to figure out a different way. It's just a matter of faith and a little patience." Dana shifted in her saddle. "The qualities you once saw in Masquerade are still there, it's just to find the key to unlock them. I think she has a definite future in the show ring, it's just going to take longer than you planned. It's a setback but I'm sure you won't regret the extra effort involved." Dana's tone was calm and unhurried.

"I hope you're right." Jarod spoke sincerely. He looked tired.

"How was your trip?" Dana asked.

"Successful. I did what needed doing and now I'm happy to be home," he explained briefly. "So much can be accomplished by computer now, I don't have to leave as often and that suits me just fine. Some things still require a personal touch, you know, face-to-face deals." Jarod smiled his easy grin and Dana thought he must be a fairly persuasive person to do business with. "Handshakes still go a long way in this part of the country."

Jarod did not bother to tell Dana that his time away had felt like an eternity, for more than the usual reasons. How he had looked forward to this trip as an opportunity to retrieve his common sense, but it had only achieved the contrary.

He had been preoccupied by thoughts of her during every idle moment.

"How did everything go here while I was away?"

Dana recalled the incident with Kent and decided against bringing it up, satisfied that she had dealt with it on her own. "Everything went well, although I do believe Goldrush missed you!"

Jarod laughed aloud. "Don't tell me, you fell for that act of his! He plays for attention and he knows how to get it. I'm taking him out tomorrow, I have some fencing that needs checking. Maybe you'd like to tag along?"

"Actually, that sounds like a good idea. I'll take Masquerade out and see how she does in an open setting."

Jarod nodded and took his leave. Dana pulled lightly on Masquerade's reins and continued her session.

Dana had finished riding and was exiting the tack room when Adam came through the barn's main doors. He rapidly scanned the recess of the barn before noticing her.

"Dana, come give me a hand," he called over to her. "I've got a mare foaling and it looks like a breach. The vet's on his way but I need some help." He disappeared out of the door and Dana quickly headed to Barn Two.

"I'm over here."

Dana followed the sound of Adam's voice. She hesitated for a moment, unsure, then she gently entered the roomy box stall. A gray mare lay on the thickly bedded floor, her body straining in a contraction. It was clear at a glance that she was in pain and not doing well.

"Adam, I've never done anything like this before," Dana warned him nervously.

"It's okay Dana. You just do what I say. Take a deep breath." Adam looked at Dana steadily as he reassured her. "I want you to gently sit on her head and whatever you do, don't let her get her head up. Her name is Venture. Talk to her, keep her calm. I'm going to have to try and turn the foal, there's no time for the vet."

Dana felt the color drain from her face, unconsciously she looked towards the stall door. She stood immobile.

"Dana," Adam recalled her with the same even tone. "You can do this."

She mutely nodded. Bending down slowly, she seated herself across the horse's cheekbone. She was able to feel the horse's heat and the mare's silky coat was damp with sweat. Venture was too exhausted to protest.

"Hey, Venture, that a girl. You'll be fine," Dana spoke softly to the mare, hardly noticing what she said. Adam pulled on a long pair of sterile gloves. Dana focussed on what she was told to do, remaining steady as the mare groaned in pain and attempted to pull up. Adam cursed under his breath, struggling in the awkward enclosure. It took all of his force, working against the horse, his eyes squeezed shut as he tried to push the foal back to a position where he had more space to turn it. The horse's contractions squeezed his arm until it was numb.

Dana was terrified, but she kept her sentry, trying to soothe the horse as best she could.

"Here we go baby," Adam spoke with quiet excitement. Dana could just barely see a dark head and what looked like a hoof. Adam waited for the horse's next contraction and helped her expel the foal.

Adam was rubbing the little body down with some dry, soft hay. The little black foal was all gangly legs and already attempting to stand.

Dana slowly got up, her knees weak and her legs unsteady as she gripped the side of the stall for support.

Venture also made it to her feet, her maternal instinct guiding her to her newborn. She nuzzled the filly and began to lick it. Dana's eyes misted. She had never seen the birth of a foal and she was overcome with emotion. Adam stood back, removed his gloves inside out and massaged his arm. His dark hair fell damp in his face, his shirt soaked with perspiration.

"Alright," was all he said, his face breaking into a smile.

The barn door swung open. Kent quickly entered, followed by the vet.

"Is there a problem? I was out in the field when I saw the vet's pickup pulling into the yard."

They reached the box stall and the vet set his kit on the barn floor. They laid their arms across the stall railing and looked in to see the filly already nursing on shaky, outspread legs.

"I don't know what you called me all the way here for, Adam. Everything appears to be under control." The vet joked, tipping his hat to the back of his head.

Adam placed a hand on Dana's shoulder and safely guided her out of the stall.

"Well, you're late like always," he kidded back. Adam could feel Dana tremble and he kept a protective arm around her.

"Dana, you okay? You're not going to pass out on me, are you?" Adam teased her.

"Of course I'm okay!" Dana insisted.

"This is Dr. Winslow. Things got pretty tight there for a while, Doc. It would be a good idea to check that mare over. Dana here was a great help. I think it was her first time around."

"Are they going to be okay?" Dana was concerned.

"She looks great, nice bone, good muscle. She'll be a grey like her mom." Adam said enthusiastically. Dana remembered all gray horses were black at birth.

"I'll check them over to be sure, but they're both standing and that's always a good sign with my patients." The vet had a good laugh, although Dana failed to see what was so funny.

"Kent, I'm going to give Doc a hand. I think Dana's seen enough for one day. Why don't you just walk her to the house?" Adam suggested.

"I'm fine." Dana protested. "Really, I'm okay."

"Most likely you are fine," Dr. Winslow agreed. "Just indulge us a little. I've seen vet students pass out from less than this. Let Kent walk you to the house and we'll all feel better."

Dana grudgingly allowed Kent to walk her to the house. She held her head high, annoyed with their old-fashioned, chauvinistic attitudes. Upon reaching the steps to the verandah she found she couldn't help but turn around and face Kent. "See, I told you I'm okay."

Kent held up his hands in front of himself. "Okay, I believe you. Good work, Dana." He smiled, tipped his hat and returned to the barn.

Jarod was coming out of his office as Dana walked into the house.

"Dana, are you okay?" He took in her disheveled appearance.

"Jarod, I just witnessed the most incredible thing!" Dana cried excitedly. "It was absolutely amazing."

"Whoa, slow down, Dana." Jarod chuckled. She looked like a child, her face shining with excitement. It was different to see her without that careful reserve she usually wore. "What happened?"

"Venture had a foal and I was there! In all the years that I've been riding, I've never seen a mare give birth...it was a breach and Adam had to turn the foal, he worked so hard..." Suddenly she swayed.

Jarod grabbed her by the arm, steadying her and led her into the office.

"Okay, here, sit down for a minute." Jarod went behind his desk and pulled out a bottle of bourbon. He poured two stiff shots and handed one of them to Dana. "Come on, try it."

Dana found it tasted wretched, but it did manage to steady her nerves. Jarod smiled at her warmly.

"Are you okay?"

"I'm so sorry, I feel foolish."

"There's no need to feel foolish. I'm surprised you've never seen this kind of thing before. And you're right, it is amazing. The night Masquerade was born, there were problems and I still think she's a miracle every time I see her." They sat for a minute, quietly.

"Oh, God," Dana moaned. "Please don't tell the guys about this. They were all teasing and making fun. Adam insisted that Kent walk me to the house. I don't want to lose face."

"There's nothing to tell."

"Thank you, Jarod." Dana set down her empty glass and got up from her chair. "I'm going to shower and then I'll be down for supper." Dana excused herself.

When Dana returned downstairs to the dining room Jarod was pouring wine. She took her place at the table.

"I thought we'd celebrate tonight." Jarod explained. "So, Dana. Seeing as how you sort of acted as midwife to this little foal and it's your first experience with this kind of thing, I think it's only fitting that you have the honor of choosing a name."

"You're going to let me name her?" Dana was pleased. "She's stunning...Can I have a couple of days to come up with something?"

"Actually, we can take up to a couple of months before sending in her registration form, so don't feel rushed."

They ate their meal while Dana described her day in general and in particular the arrival of the new filly.

"What do you think about Goliath and Paska?" Jarod asked her.

"Goliath is a gentle giant, predictable, dependable. He's the perfect hunter and I think he's ready for the show ring. I took him over some jumps this morning and he was very smooth. Paska is quite different, she's high-strung, brave and a true jumper. She's not ready yet, but it's not going to take long and she's going to be fun to work with." Dana's cheeks were flushed and suddenly she was very tired. The wine and the excitement of the day were catching up on her.

"Jarod, what time did you want to head out in the morning?"

"Sometime mid-morning. Maybe we can look in on that filly before we take off." Jarod suggested with a smile.

"I'd like that. I'm looking forward to the morning. I'm really tired, Jarod, so if you don't mind I'll turn in." Dana rose from her chair.

"You sleep well, Dana. I'll see you in the morning."

"Good night, Jarod."

Jarod felt the room become empty as she left. There was a difference in her since he'd returned. She seemed softer and more at ease. He heaved a sigh, rubbing his hand across his face. Jarod decided to call it a night and made his way to his room.

The next day Jarod found Dana in the tack room.

"So, have you checked in on that filly yet?" He kidded her from the doorway.

She smiled in return. "No, I was waiting for you. I thought it would be fun to go together." She said it simply but she could tell he was pleased.

They made their way to Barn Two accompanied by Jesse Dog and found Adam hard at work.

"So, Adam, I hear you had some excitement here yesterday."

"Hey Boss. Good morning, Dana, come to check up on the little gal?" Adam leaned his pitchfork against a beam and dusted his hands on his pants.

Adam was light on his feet, his movement deliberate and his tone of voice steady. She remembered he was the same even in the midst of foaling the day before. His straight dark hair was in an elastic and she noticed for the first time the angular outline of his features. He was an excellent choice for this barn, a calming influence for the horses.

Adam joined them and they headed towards Venture's stall.

Dana peered in over the doorway and a wide smile crossed her face as she gazed at the sight before her. The black filly was trotting around her mother with ease, a picture much different from yesterday when Dana had watched her struggle to stand.

She turned to Jarod, her face glowing. "What do you think?"

Jarod took a long scrutinizing look at the foal who was now starting to nurse. "I think your description last night was pretty on the mark, she is stunning." He turned to Adam. "Did the mare check out all right?"

"Doc and I checked them both over, Doc says they're just fine. Venture was a real trooper and so was Dana." Adam smiled at her.

"I thought we'd give Dana the privilege of naming this little filly," Jarod said.

Dana slowly thought of her life this past week as she quietly watched the filly. It had been a good move to come to New Mexico. Her life was regaining its sense of sanity. She was starting to look forward to being herself again.

"Blue Serenity." Dana said out loud and smiled feeling the name was very fitting.

- Chapter 4 -

The room was in complete darkness other than the eerie glow coming from the screen of the computer.

"This shouldn't take long." He spoke out loud, even though he was alone in the room.

"Come on, come on." He typed furiously at his keyboard, his breathing came heavily.

After a few moments he yelled out. "Bingo! You're mine now." Beads of perspiration formed on his brow. "You can run, but you can't hide, Dana." His voice had a perverted pitch to it. He hit some more keys on the computer and a map of New Mexico flashed across the screen.

Laughter filled the room.

- Chapter 5 -

Spring smoothly slipped into an early summer at Kingsley Ranch. June's garden bloomed into a cascade of colors under her careful nurturing: bold red and brilliant white blossoms abounded, resplendent in the abundant sunlight. Jesse Dog, growing bored with basking in the sun's glory, indolently sauntered to a shadier spot under an accommodating lean-to, dropping effortlessly to the ground with an irritated groan. A warm breeze lazily stirred the dry air, its presence just barely existent.

Dana enjoyed a sense of peace and contentment within these surroundings. Just a little over six weeks had elapsed since her arrival at the ranch and gradually her life was shaping into a comforting routine and familiarity. She eagerly threw herself into her work. It was a habit she had practiced for a lifetime.

The people here were forthright and without guile and Dana found herself forming a positive relationship with everyone on the ranch. Even Kent had gotten past his initial resentment of her.

Each of the four working students showed promise, and Natasha in particular had a God given gift for riding. Dana had begun teaching her on Goliath. The combination of horse and rider was a suitable match, both being calm and sure by nature.

Paska showed marked progress, jumping courses at 4'6" rarely touching a rail. She relished in the challenge of a difficult course.

It was working Masquerade that gave Dana the greatest sense of accomplishment. The mare had taken her first fence without hesitation or rebuke a fortnight earlier. Dana had diligently worked with this horse almost daily, practicing in measured steps and establishing a strong bond of trust between them. Her patience and determination were finally being rewarded. Masquerade was beginning to progress at a remarkable pace. Dana had developed a special fondness for this animal and she was confident the mare's schooling was rapidly reaching a level comparable to the other horses.

Dana was occupied soaping her saddle when Kent came across her in the barn. He made his way by her, reaching for a lead line.

"Hey, Dana. Did Jarod mention anything to you about our big staff party yet?"

Dana brushed an errant lock of hair out of her eyes with the back of her wrist.

"Staff party? No, what are you talking about?"

"Wow, I don't believe it! It's an annual event here at Kingsley. We had a wild time last year," he explained to her. "Jarod throws this great party with all the trimmings, you know: tent, music, food, drinks."

"Yes, I know what a party is." Dana rolled her eyes at Kent's teasing attitude.

Kent laughed, amused at his own joke. "Anyway, we party-hardy all night and Jarod does the chores the next day."

"You're kidding, right?" Dana stopped what she was doing and looked at Kent doubtfully. "Why would he want to do that?" She sounded skeptical.

Kent shrugged his broad shoulders. "Because it's fun. Lighten up, Dana. You'll finally have an opportunity to have a good time, instead of work, work, work. You know what they say about all work and no play." Kent warned her. "We party and it keeps us human; Jarod does chores and it keeps him humble. It's got all the makings of a great trade-off. I'm happy." Kent did indeed sound enthused. "Next weekend was just about the only open weekend with the show season underway. It's a real dress up thing, just so you know," Kent added as he left the tack room, whistling.

Dana checked her watch, she had a lesson to teach. She finished up and was replacing her saddle on its rack when Emily and Sue entered.

"Hi, girls. Are you ready to get going?"

Emily at twenty-four was closer to Dana's age than Sue who was only fifteen, but there was a lot about Sue that reminded Dana of herself, thirteen years ago. She was a pretty girl. Short on experience, but with time and training, Dana was certain she would make a talented rider. Dana caught herself smiling wistfully.

"Okay, let's get to work. Emily, you can get Apollo ready and Sue, I'd like you to try Mayday. I'll meet you in the riding hall."

The girls got their tack together and left to ready their respective horses. Dana spent a few minutes tidying up. The more she thought about the staff party on Saturday, the more she found herself looking forward to it. She smiled, this was something only Jarod would think of. In the past few weeks Dana had come to know him quite well. He expected a lot from his employees, but he gave a lot in return. He was open-minded and fair in his judgement which made for a positive and efficient working environment. Dana was surprised by how much she had grown to enjoy his company. They dined together most evenings and rode together often. He had a calm, attentive manner and Dana found herself looking forward to the time they spent together.

Dana went to the riding hall and taught her lesson. Sue experienced a few problems with Mayday, which was to be expected on a strange horse. Dana carefully studied Sue's reactions, giving her some brief instructions. Emily's workout with Apollo was very competent. It was a good session and Dana was pleased with the progress being made.

"Okay, girls. Let's call it a day," Dana informed them. "Good work."

She was reviewing the lesson in depth with Emily and Sue as the girls untacked their horses when Dana noticed Ben coming into the barn with the feed supplement that he had gone to pick up in town. "That should wrap things up for now, we'll continue with those techniques next time," Dana ended.

"Hello, Ben. Did you have a safe trip?" Dana asked.

"Tried not to hit too many a them roadrunners." Ben let go of a hearty laugh. "Thought you'd be gone for supper by now. You could use some meat on those bones."

"Don't worry about my appetite. And by the way, I like my bones fine the way they are." Dana quipped with Ben.

"I like my women rounder, more..." Ben gestured in the air with a sly wink.

"I think I get the drift." Dana interrupted, hurriedly avoiding any further description. "Actually, I was just going to close up the office and then head out." She made her way through the tack room, checking over the equipment they had used.

Dana noticed the computer screen was on as she entered the office. She was certain she had shut everything off when she was finished working with it earlier that day.

"Hmm, you're getting forgetful," Dana said aloud to herself. She crossed the room and went behind the desk, raising her hand to turn the computer off. Her hand arrested in mid-air. A chill ran through her as she read the screen: **MISS YOU DANA. SEE YOU SOON.** She froze for a second, stunned, then bracing herself against the desk, she slid into the chair.

"Dana, how many bags of feed did you order?" Ben called to her as he came into the office. "Dana? What's wrong?"

Dana's eyes were glued to the screen. She slowly lifted them to meet Ben's concerned expression.

"Who's been in the office? Has anyone been in the office?" There was alarm in her tone.

"I don't know, I just got here. Calm down Dana, tell me what's wrong."

Dana got up from her chair, trembling. "Someone's been playing with my computer. Who would do that?"

Ben walked over to her and put an arm around her. He read the message on the screen. "Well, Dana, looks like someone might have a little crush on you. Ain't nothin' for you to be gettin' so upset over. You look like you seen a ghost." Ben patted her arm. Dana's face was white with dread. She hesitated considering what he said. It could make sense, maybe it was just an innocent joke. It could've been Kent teasing like he always did. Ben was worriedly watching her.

"Ben, I'm so sorry. I just over-reacted." Dana deliberately convinced herself that Ben must be right.

Her color was slowly returning, but Ben could tell she was still unsure. "I've put a lot of work into some of those files. I'd hate to lose that by someone playing around and erasing it by accident." They both realized it was a weak excuse, but Ben let it go at that.

"You feelin' better now?"

"I'm fine, really," Dana attempted a smile, struggling between fear and reason. "Ben, do you mind if we just keep this between ourselves? I'm embarrassed about the whole thing. I think I acted foolishly." Her voice was still a little shaky.

Ben hesitated. Something had scared the wits out of this girl, but for the life of him, he couldn't figure out what it was. She was a proud woman and he respected her for it. "Sure, if that's what you're wantin' then I won't be tellin' anyone. Nobody's business anyways. Com'on, I'll walk you to the main house."

"I'd appreciate that," Dana said genuinely. "Ben, you're a good friend, thanks." Ben acted as if nothing had happened as he walked with Dana. She paused as she reached the steps and turned to face him. "Thanks again, Ben. I'm sorry about causing such a commotion. I'll see you in the morning."

"Don't worry about nothin', Dana. You get yourself a good night's sleep." He touched his fingers to the brim of his hat and made his way back towards the bunkhouse.

Dana thought a few minutes of fresh air would do her good. She lowered herself into a sitting position on the steps of the porch. Jesse Dog quickly took advantage of this quiet interlude and joined Dana, laying his golden head in her lap. She absently scratched behind his ears as she sat deep in thought, her chin resting in her free hand.

It was a good idea to take the time to collect herself before facing Jarod, he always seemed to have the ability to read her mood. Dana was still uneasy about the computer incident but she continued to remind herself that it was probably easily explained.

She turned her thoughts to the show schedule which was fast approaching. Dana decided Natasha would show Goliath, and she was eager to give Natasha the news tomorrow. One of Dana's priorities was to have each of her students competing on a regular basis during the course of the summer.

The early evening air was beginning to cool. Dana placed her two hands on each side of Jesse Dog's head. "Thanks for the company, you big mooch. I've got to go in now and get washed up for supper. It's getting late."

Jarod was coming down the staircase as Dana walked through the front door.

"Dana, I was just about to go check on you. You're not in the habit of being late, especially when it comes to meals!" Jarod flashed her a smile accompanied by a wink.

"I had a lesson that ran a little late." More lies, she thought with a sigh. "How was your day? I didn't notice you in the barn."

"Same old, same old. Hey, I've got something I want to talk to you about. We can discuss it over supper."

"Sure," Dana replied. "I'll just get cleaned up and I'll meet you in the dining room." She hurried up the stairs.

When Dana returned she found Jarod waiting for her with his elbows resting on the table, his hands closed together in a fist, looking pensive.

"Am I interrupting you? You look like you're miles away."

"No, actually you're saving me from boring myself." Jarod laughed just as June came into the room with the supper plates. "June, it smells like another great meal."

"Now, now, Mr. Kingsley, flattery will get you everywhere," June said, obviously pleased. Dana also smiled to herself; it was a variation on a theme that these two practiced every night. Jarod making a big fuss over June's supper and her appreciating his effort.

Jarod turned his attention to Dana. "Dana, has anyone mentioned the staff party to you?"

"Yes," she replied. "Kent did earlier today. I didn't take him seriously at first. He's always pulling my leg." Dana looked perplexed. "I thought you would've told me yourself."

"I wasn't holding out on you, I swear. I've been preoccupied with this business merger that just went through and when I finally got around to checking the show schedule, there weren't a lot of weekends open. So, next Saturday it is. I think you'll enjoy yourself. Last year's party was a resounding success." Jarod massaged his square jaw, laughing to himself. "Well, we did have to collect a couple of dead soldiers off the front yard. They must've lost their way."

"Maybe I should wear my cowboy boots with spurs and carry a pistol come Saturday. Seriously though, what is the dress code?"

"Dress as you would for an important dinner date. You have done that before?" Jarod gave her a charmingly pointed smile.

"Everybody's a comedian around here today. This party really does have you excited," Dana observed.

"I've got a great staff and I like to show my appreciation once in a while."

"Well, don't tell anyone," Dana dropped her voice to a conspiratorial whisper. "I get the impression everyone thinks I'm a little stiff, but I'm starting to get excited about this party, too." Dana noticed Jarod's mock expression of disbelief. "Really," she added. "And you're right about this being our last free weekend. I plan to keep those students and the horses busy."

"By the way, who are we bringing to our first show? Have you made any decisions yet?" Jarod questioned.

"Yes, I have. I'm entering Paska in the open jump division, Natasha on Goliath in novice hunter and Darren will ride Empire also in the hunter division for the first show. Then I'll probably rotate turns having Emily on Apollo and Sue competing on Mayday in the flat classes for the following weekend. Do you approve?"

"It sounds like you have everything under control. I like the idea of Natasha riding Goliath," Jarod agreed.

"So do I. She's got a lot of talent. Well, it's getting late, I'm going to turn in." She was just about to leave the room when as an afterthought, Dana asked, "Jarod, are you really doing the chores the day after the party?"

"I certainly am," Jarod answered with a grin.

"No wonder everybody's so thrilled with this deal. Sleep well, Jarod."

"You too, Dana," Jarod answered softly.

Dana slept fitfully that night, tossing in her bed, the computer message nagging at her subconscious. **MISS YOU DANA, MISS YOU, MISS YOU. SEE YOU SOON**. Followed by peels of manic laughter. She was lost in a barn. Then she was on Masquerade bucking and charging, sailing over fences so high Dana's stomach was in her throat, and as the horse's hooves came down to hit the hard earth, Dana woke with a start.

The unrelenting sound of rain drumming against her windowpane pulled Dana from a heavy sleep. She rubbed her eyes with her knuckles, feeling disoriented. It took a few minutes for her to shake it off. Perhaps the change of weather had something to do with her rotten night, she thought curiously. It was odd that in Maine she would have cursed waking to the sound of rain, but in New Mexico it was almost a cause for celebration. Dana sighed and dragged herself out of bed. She checked the time and decided a good hot shower would help turn her morning around.

Feeling somewhat better, Dana promptly dressed and hurried down to the kitchen. The aroma of freshly perked coffee and the sizzle of frying bacon greeted her at the doorway.

"Oh, June, you can't begin to know how good this feels this morning." Dana smiled as she poured coffee into her favorite mug. "I see we finally have rain."

"It's a blessing, dear. How are you this morning?" June served Dana her breakfast.

"I'm good." Dana pressed the corner of her toast into her egg yolk.

"Do you have a busy day?" June wiped out the heavy cast-iron skillet before she hung it against the wall.

"Diego is going to be here for the next few days, doing the horses' feet. He always adds a little spice to the flavor of the day." Dana smiled, remembering the last time the blacksmith had been there, shortly after her arrival.

In the morning, he would begin trimming and shoeing the horses, pleasant and polite; then usually by mid-afternoon, he could be heard swearing to himself in Spanish, bent over some horse's foot, while the horse refused to stand still on the cross ties. Diego's work was physically demanding and Dana could well understand his irritability, spending hours bent in an unnatural position with horses leaning their weight lazily against him. Diego was occasionally short-tempered, yet he never took it out on the horses, regardless of how frustrated he became.

"Good morning, ladies." Jarod entered the kitchen. He pulled up his chair. "I have to go into town to pick up some things and make some arrangements for the party. Anyone need anything while I'm there?"

"Just the usual fare," June said. It was standard practice that anyone going to town would pick up milk, bread, eggs and butter and as a rule that routine worked pretty well.

Dana drained her coffee cup and stood.

"Time to get rolling. Diego is probably already at work. I'd like him to do Masquerade this morning. She's been overreaching a bit."

Jarod laughed. "That's right, Diego's here today." He helped himself to a generous serving of home fries, along with his bacon and eggs.

"I'll try and get back early enough to give him a hand this afternoon." Obviously, Jarod had seen Diego work in the afternoon before.

"You have a good morning, Dana. I'll catch up with you later." Dana returned their good-byes and headed to the barn.

Jarod considered how much more complete his life felt these days, as if something crucial had been absent from it before Dana's arrival. He struggled to keep his attitude on a professional level, but he admitted to himself that his feelings toward her were more than that.

By the time Dana arrived at the barn she was saturated from the downpour. She hurried into the tack room and grabbed a clean towel to dry her face. Peeling off her navy mackintosh, she hung it on an empty bridle hook. Diego already had Empire on the cross-ties in the barn aisle.

"Well hallo, Miss Dana, how is it going with you?" He spoke with a strong Mexican accent.

"I'm fine Diego, how is your family? On your last visit, Tomas was not well. Is he feeling better?" Dana inquired courteously.

"Okay, he is better now, thank you. You know kids, nothing keeps them down for long."

Dana didn't really know kids, having no siblings or young cousins. Even her best friend Emma had been the youngest of four, coming after a considerable gap. It had never really occurred to her before now, but her experience with youngsters was quite deficient.

"And how is their schooling going?"

Diego grunted as he straightened his thick, muscular form and flexed his back in a side-to-side motion, pulling his shoulders back.

"Tomas has good respect for the book. He reads and reads, in English, in Spanish. His teacher is very proud," Diego said noncommittally. "Luis will live like his father and his father's father. It is not the book that gives you life, it is the land. My family has lived by our craft: our tools, the fire. My grandfather was a great silversmith and his name will live on for years. He was a respected man, his work admired by many." Diego paused, running his hand fondly across the length of the horse. "My work is not as famous. I did not have the patience. My hands were not gifted for fine work, but there is a beauty in what I create." Diego stood for a second, staring at the magnificent gelding in front of him, lost in thought. Dana quietly considered the validity of his words, remembering her parents' disappointment when she had informed them she would not be attending college. She watched him, realizing that in an odd way, they had more in common than one would have imagined.

Diego reached for a pick lying on the barn floor and continued. "The Anglo have a great love for the school, the book, but they plunder the land. A book will not teach me my work." Diego laughed, looking up at Dana. "Someone must care to the needs of these spirited creatures."

Dana studied the gleaming chestnut.

"If only they were all like this beast, my work would be a lot easier." Diego allowed the horse's foot to slide to the barn floor and gave him an affectionate slap on the hindquarter. "He is done."

"Good. Do you mind if we do Masquerade next? She's been overreaching and I'd like to see what you think."

Diego was leading Empire back to his stall and he called back. "Get her out, I will look her over."

Dana put Masquerade on a lead line and brought her into the riding hall as Diego followed.

"Okay." He instructed her with a nod. Dana trotted the mare up and down the hall a few times as Diego squatted down and studied the horse's movement.

"That is enough," he called out. "She needs a good trim and I will put a lighter shoe on her in front. Bring her back in."

After Diego had completed the necessary adjustments they returned to the riding hall and repeated the same procedure.

"Good," he said, satisfied with the result.

Dana was impressed, Diego was a master at his trade. "That's great Diego. Annie should be almost finished in Barn Two. She'll give you a hand this morning and Jarod said he'd try to help you this afternoon." Dana stroked Masquerade's forehead. "I'm going to ride this girl for a bit and try out her new shoes."

Dana rode to the sound of the rain hitting on the tin roof of the riding hall. It echoed loudly in the open structure. Masquerade was edgy throughout the session, the noise distracting her, but Dana persisted, achieving a degree of success. It was important that Masquerade become conditioned to changes in her working environment.

Dana ended the lesson on a positive note and dismounted.

"You did good, baby," she talked softly in the horse's ear. Masquerade turned her head and rubbed it against Dana's shoulder. Dana smiled, happy with the horse's token of trust.

Dana led the mare back to the barn and found Annie and Diego working on one of the geldings.

"Hi there, how did your ride go?" Annie asked her as Dana removed the saddle from the horse.

"It was challenging. It's amazing how loud it can get in the hall." Dana latched Masquerade's door and walked over to join them. "So, how are things going here?"

"I save the hard ones for last," Diego grunted. "For now it goes good."

"Has Paska been done?"

"Diego did her while you were on Masquerade." Annie steadied her charge. "I figured you would probably want to work her next, so we got her ready." It was not the first time that Dana had noticed Annie's subtle attention to detail. She was a gentle-natured, unassuming girl, happy to please.

"Good thinking, Annie," Dana said as she reached for her saddle once more.

Paska rode well after she became accustomed to the sound of the rain. Dana had just about finished cooling Paska down when she noticed Ben leaning against the gate.

"Hi, Ben." She walked with the horse to meet him.

"Hello, Dana. How are you?" Ben deliberately kept his tone casual but she knew he was still concerned about the way she had behaved yesterday.

"I'm fine, really. Thanks for asking. I'm sorry if I made you uncomfortable in any way yesterday, don't worry about me." Dana assured him.

Ben hesitated for a moment. The rain had finally let up to a musical patter above them.

"Dana, I hope you know by now, I'm good to my word. I haven't said anything and I won't, but you gotta promise me, if you need anything, don't be too proud to ask."

Dana lightly laid a hand on his arm. She was touched by his concern.

"I promise. You're a sweet man." She led Paska by him into the barn. Ben's expression was inscrutable as he quietly watched them go.

The afternoon had a few colorful moments to it. It appeared that Jarod spoke fluent Spanish and even though Dana did not, she was able to understand most of what transpired, thanks to Diego's very expressive manner. He would curse rapidly, a long string of strange words that sounded almost melodious to Dana's ears, then he would stomp across the barn aisle and spit into the gutter.

Diego had just picked up Mascot's third foot when the horse suddenly shifted his center of gravity, conveniently finding Diego's hunched back. He forcibly resisted the horse's weight and rapidly moved away, yelling explosively.

"Buenos Dias!" He raised his head to the barn rafters and rolled his eyes, waving his hands over his head in an exaggerated prayer. "This beast has four legs, I have only two. Why does he think I am here to hold him up? Can he not count?"

Dana quickly turned her head away, covering the smile that sprang to her lips. Diego's theatrics were entertaining if somewhat draining. She did not envy Jarod. Diego definitely did his best work in the morning and it was probably his pious sense of justice that entreated him to save the ornery horses for the afternoon.

Later, after supper was over, Jarod invited Dana to join him on the verandah to have their coffee. They sat side by side trading anecdotes from the day. Jarod leaned back in his seat, stretching his long legs in front of him. He closed his eyes, enjoying the smell of the earth. The rain had ended, leaving everything cleansed and refreshed.

"I thought it was pretty amusing when Diego eyeballed Karat square in the face and said, 'And if you break my back, who will put your pretty shoes on then, eh? Estupido!'"

"I know," Dana said. "I had to keep ducking and hiding. I was sure he'd catch me laughing and use me for a ring toss! How do you think I'd look with a horseshoe collar?"

Jarod turned his head and thoughtfully looked her over." "I think you'd look pretty good, no matter what you had on," he said deliberately.

Dana's turquoise eyes opened wide. She shifted uncomfortably and quickly looked down, feeling uncertain. She changed the subject.

"How are your preparations going for the party?"

Jarod recalled himself with effort. "Hmmm, I think everything's been taken care of. Even the weather seems to be co-operating."

"Everyone is so looking forward to it, I guess I can understand why you enjoy doing it so much," Dana spoke quietly as she studied Jarod. He seemed different tonight. "Jarod, I'm beginning to get cold and tired. I think I'm going to turn in." For reasons unknown even to herself, Dana laid her hand over his as she paused in passing.

Jarod's surprise showed as he lifted his face to hers.

"Good night, Dana," his voice was barely audible.

She hurried into the house feeling bewildered. Dana closed her bedroom door and sat on her bed, momentarily confused. What had she just done? She undressed for bed, replaying what had happened.

Would Jarod misunderstand a trivial platonic gesture to mean something more than what it was? The circumstances of her employment were quite intimate with her living in the main house and she didn't want to complicate that. They spent a lot of time together by necessity, and it would be difficult if those boundaries became unclear. That was the last thing she needed, or wanted. Dana persuaded herself to listen to that fine logic, turning a deaf ear to the whisper of doubt that troubled her. They were friends, that was all, no more, no less. She slid her slender body under the sheets.

Jarod remained on the porch for some time. His thoughts were filled with Dana, of the past two months and of how her touch had startled him. He had always been so careful not to give anything away, to keep his personal feelings private and his demeanor professional. He'd definitely slipped tonight. Apart from a small touch, she had never indicated to him that she desired anything more than the relationship they had.

He sighed, staring into the darkness over the plains. Coyotes howled in the distance as the moon slipped out from behind the cover of clouds.

- *Chapter 6* -

It was late in the day and the sun lay over the unyielding terrain in a sharp slice of pale apricot. Although the air shimmered in a listless repose, the mood at the ranch was one of giddiness and anticipation. The talk of the day had been filled with the upcoming party, starting casually and steadily gaining momentum, almost feeding on itself. It included various recollections of past years, one story spurring on another or a different version of the same. The one common factor shared by all accounts was that everyone had enjoyed themselves immensely.

June had been busy during the week, turning out the guest rooms in the main house and preparing the bunk house shared by Adam and Ben, for visitors. People who may have indulged in a liberal consumption of alcohol were persuaded to spend the night, a standing invitation that was extended to all. Singing to herself, June depleted the linen cupboard of its contents, generously stocking the bathrooms and making certain all the beds were available. Like a mother preparing for her family's homecoming at Christmas, June was in her element. Dana would occasionally come across Jarod assisting her with the heavier tasks, patiently awaiting June's instruction. It was a sight that Dana found touching.

In the barn, the last feeding of the day had been moved up an hour earlier in order to allow everyone ample time to get showered and changed and Dana gave Kent and Annie a hand. In no time, the horses were bedded down for the night. They exited the side door of the barn leading to where Kent's car was parked. He removed two garment bags from the back seat and handed one of them to Annie.

"Are you coming up to the main house to get ready?" Annie asked Kent.

"No way! With three women in the house, I'd never get a free bathroom. I've seen how you girls work, 'Should I wear this pink lipstick or the orange one?'" He moaned in a comical falsetto.

"Oh, get outta here. We're not that bad!" They laughingly protested.

"Yeah, well, maybe not. All the same, I think I'd rather take my chances in the bunk house. I'll catch you girls later." He directed them a wink and headed off, whistling.

The girls made their way around the side of the barn towards the yard in front of the main house.

Dana stopped in her tracks, momentarily stunned and then burst into laughter. The entire yard had been transformed.

"My God! Jarod does know how to throw a party."

Smartly outfitted waiters attired in blue tuxedos were hard at work under a massive blue and white tent, completing the task at hand. A long table was laid out, dressed in a gleaming, starched tablecloth with centerpieces of red and white carnations. Navy and silver iridescent balloons framed the two bars that had been set up: one under the tent, the other on the verandah.

A delicious smoked aroma drifted lightly through the air, originating from the pit where two attendants were slowly roasting a selection of meats over an open fire.

"My God," Dana repeated.

"Come on, let's get ready," Annie urged, giving her a nudge.

The house appeared vacant as they entered.

"Everybody must be busy getting dressed," Annie remarked.

"Annie, why don't you come upstairs to my room and we can get ready together?"

Annie gladly accepted Dana's offer.

While Annie showered, Dana opened the doors to her scantily furnished wardrobe. She had brought only three dresses with her: one being a casual cotton print, another a black fitted blazer with matching slitted skirt and lastly, a short, lightweight velvet dress with long sheer sleeves. It was also black, but had a dark, coppery brown shimmer to it; the dress was very elegant and with its low cut neckline and fitted bodice, quite seductive. She hesitated, considering the last two choices, unable to reach a decision, when Annie came out of the bathroom, clad in a robe that Dana had lent her.

"Wow, go for the little velvet number. It's gorgeous and it will really bring out the highlights in your hair."

Dana looked uncertain. "You don't think it's too much?"

"I think it's perfect. Anyway, you just wait and see what I'm planning to wear," Annie added mischievously. She selected the dress from the closet and handed it over to Dana.

"Go get showered and changed, and by the time you're done, I'll be dressed."

"Okay, decision made. Make yourself at home, Annie."

After showering, Dana dried her dark, thick hair and arranged it loosely on top of her head, securing it with an antique rhinestone clasp that had belonged to her grandmother. She artfully left a few strands of hair to curl softly around her face and down the nape of her long, slender neck. She applied shadow and blush very lightly, pencilling her full lips and painting them a cinnamon hue. She carefully outlined her brilliant eyes, darkening her thick lashes and enhancing the contrast that nature had already given her.

Dana gently eased the dress over her head until it softly fell into place, then reaching behind to zip it up, she stood back to study her reflection. Dana had always appreciated the subtle coloring of this dress and Annie was right, it indeed complimented the rich highlights in her hair. She slipped her feet into a pair of strapless pumps and stepped from the bathroom into the bedroom.

Annie looked up from the mirror where she was putting on the final touches to her makeup. Annie had chosen to wear a sapphire blue body-hugging dress that was cut mid-thigh and although the dress had long sleeves and a high collar, it left little to the imagination. Annie's normally fair complexion was drawn in a dramatic fashion and her short exuberant hair was styled sleekly against her head. She looked sensational and Dana was quick to tell her so.

"Well, thank you. Hopefully somebody's going to stand up and take notice."

Dana reached for a matched set of delicate diamond and emerald earrings and necklace.

"Here, I'll help you with that," Annie offered. Dana looked at Annie's reflection in the mirror as she turned her back to her.

"Take notice? What do you mean by that?"

"Well, I shouldn't really say," Annie hesitated, as she concentrated on fastening the necklace. "There you go." Annie sat back carefully on Dana's bed. "Ever since I've laid eyes on Kent, I thought he was such a babe, you know?"

Dana laughed softly at the description and turned around to face her, taken aback by Annie's words.

"What? You don't think so?" Annie was incredulous.

"No, no. I mean, yes, I think he's...a good looking man," Dana was mildly surprised. "I just had no idea..."

"Well, you're not the only one. He can be so thick-headed." Annie shook her head, discouraged. "No matter what kind of hint I drop, he jokes around with me like I'm one of the guys."

Dana tilted her head coyly to the side. "If he thinks you're just 'one of the guys' after tonight, I'd say he's more than thick-headed."

The girls burst into laughter.

Dana double-checked her teardrop earrings and patted the necklace that fell daintily just below her throat, emphasizing the pearly softness of her ivory skin.

The girls stood to leave. "It's a beautiful set." Annie complimented, indicating Dana's jewelry.

"Thanks, it was a twenty-first birthday gift from my parents." Dana recalled fondly. "Ready?"

They left the bedroom. Jarod was leaving his room just as they were approaching. He looked debonair in a black dinner jacket and tie and his light blue eyes glittered against his tanned skin which was freshly shaven and smooth. He looked impressive in a suit, having the height and breadth of shoulder to carry it handsomely. His blond hair was neatly trimmed, with just the slightest suggestion of a wave in it. He pulled sharply at his cuffs, straightening his shirt sleeves inside the jacket. Dana's heart almost skipped a beat as his attention focussed on her. She felt as if she was meeting him for the first time.

"Ladies, I must say you are a vision of loveliness."

Annie stepped up to Jarod and patted down his tie. "Boss, you don't look too bad yourself. I think I'm going to check out the other local characters." Annie proceeded down the stairs leaving Dana and Jarod alone.

"Dana, you take my breath away."

She shyly looked down under his intense gaze. "Thank you," she answered softly.

Jarod cleared his throat. "Let me escort you to the dinner table"

He offered her his elbow, which she accepted and they descended down the stairs. Immediately upon leaving the main house, a loud vocal cheer burst forth from under the canopy.

"They're already on a roll!" Jarod laughed as they made their way to the table.

June hurried over to greet them. She was beautiful in a deep pink dress, accented by a floral print silk scarf that she wore draped over one shoulder. Delight radiated in her soft round features. Jarod bent down and lightly kissed June's cheek. The two women graciously traded compliments. With an arm casually around each, Jarod guided June and Dana to the table and attentively seated them. Adam was arriving at the same time with his date, a petite blonde woman. He quickly introduced Leanne to the group and found two empty chairs.

Jarod was just about to seat himself when everyone began shouting: "Speech, speech!" He slowly straightened back up and stood for a moment acknowledging the boisterous group before him.

"As I look out at all of you," he began. "I can't help but feel blessed to be surrounded by your collective talent and expertise. The people gathered under this tent tonight help make this ranch what it is. Without each and every one of you, this ranch, which is so close to my heart, would not be the same."

"Nah, it would probably be a helluva lot better!" Dr. Winslow interrupted with a catcall. Thankfully his veterinary skills surpassed his social graces, Dana thought to herself, once again at a loss to understand his sense of humor. There was a round of laughter and then everyone settled back down.

"Tonight," Jarod continued, becoming serious. "I give thanks to the Lord for bringing all of you here." Jarod looked at Dana for an instant, catching her eye. "I want to thank each of you for your individual contribution to the success of this ranch. Now, let's have one helluva show season!"

Loud clapping and cheering erupted, as Jarod sat down.

"You spoke eloquently," Dana told him with a smile.

"It was easy. I meant every word of it."

"I know. That's what made it special."

As if on cue, waiters appeared, filling wine glasses and serving the appetizer. The table was alive with activity. Dana looked around. Her students were all present, she noticed Sue sitting with her parents and a younger boy that she assumed to be her brother. Darren, Natasha and Adam had each brought dates with them. Emily sat amongst them, her young husband worked evenings as an E.M.T. and had been unable to attend. Diego and his wife, Consuela, were seated at the opposite end of the table and Dana smiled to herself, noticing that Consuela gestured as freely as her husband, a habit probably learned through years of marriage. They seemed to be enjoying themselves. Dr. Winslow's florid face was thrown back in an uninhibited guffaw as he joked with his partner, Dr. Hernandez. It was a curious partnership, Dr. Hernandez being very reserved in character. Their wives conversed pleasantly together, oblivious to their men. Ben sat next to June, pulling uncomfortably on his tie, but looking quite pleased with himself. Dana was unable to see Kent and Annie clearly from where she was seated, but they were together. She wished she had been present to see Kent's reaction when he first saw Annie so smartly attired. He still appeared to be in shock, from what Dana was able to determine.

The atmosphere was festive and very sophisticated, a far cry from the daily routine. Jarod had spared little expense on this lavish event and the party celebrants had co-operated whole-heartedly, taking full advantage of the opportunity to show an entirely different side of themselves.

Adam and Jarod were discussing the filly Serenity, when Jarod interrupted turning to Dana.

"Dana, has Adam told you that Serenity is officially registered? Her papers came in yesterday."

"That's wonderful. Do you know what your intentions are for her?" Dana asked.

"Well, Adam and I were just talking about that." As if reading her thoughts, Jarod continued. "We've pretty much decided that we won't be selling her in the fall sale. We'll see how she matures and keep her here in one of our programs."

Serenity had come to mean a lot to Dana, inexplicably becoming a symbol of her new life and she was pleased to know they would be keeping the filly.

"Now, now, that's enough talk of business," June admonished them. "Tonight is a special night, let's enjoy ourselves."

"Agreed." Jarod said, smiling as he sampled a portion of his meal.

Twilight enveloped the tent and its occupants. A multitude of miniature light bulbs hung suspended from the blue underside of the canopy, twinkling like silver stars above them. The food was delicious, having been cooked in the fresh, open air and Dana realized with wonder how attached she had grown to the people gathered here.

"Ben, you stop talking like that!" June loudly scolded, drawing everyone's attention.

"Ah, com'on, no need to get in a dither. A beautiful, mature woman like yourself deserves some sweet words now and then." Ben complained in exaggerated innocence, his hands spread before him.

"Who are you calling mature? You old coot!" The group burst into laughter, heightening June's already apparent blush. Ben appeared undaunted by her rebuff, in fact he looked quite smug with a grin spread across his weathered features.

The waiters began clearing the table and returned with the dessert accompanied by tall, clear glasses dressed in napkins, brimming with whipped cream. Jarod noticed Dana staring at the drink in front of her, uncertain.

"It's a Spanish coffee. Have you never had one?" Jarod asked. Dana shook her head, slightly embarrassed. "Go ahead, you'll like it," he encouraged. Dana lifted the warm glass to her lips, took a tentative sip and then another.

"Oh, so good," she agreed.

"Hey, Jarod," Dr. Winslow called from across the table. "Diego here is trying to sell me on your Thoroughbreds. For the life of me, I can't figure out your fascination with all these highstrung beasts when you could have a couple of barns full of Quarter horses. Now, there's an honest horse!"

Jarod laughed lightly. "I think you'd have a difficult time promoting that opinion amongst this crowd, Bob." There followed a thunderous applause. "I guess beauty lies in the eyes of the beholder," Jarod finished.

"That's an interesting point," Dana commented. "Why did you choose to breed Thoroughbreds? I would've thought living in New Mexico, well…," Dana hesitated, shrugging her delicate shoulders. "Quarter horses would've been a more likely choice. Goldrush is a Quarter horse, so you obviously like them."

"The Thoroughbred is an amazing animal to watch and there's so much history behind them. Show me anyone, equestrian or not, who doesn't know of Man-O-War or Secretariat. In my opinion, there is a spirit in the Thoroughbred that is finer than anything I've seen in any other horse, including all the warmbloods. All that energy bundled up into such a beautiful package." He deliberately paused before continuing. "How could anyone resist? Some things are simply appreciated for the intelligence and the beauty they have to offer." Jarod looked directly into Dana's eyes, his tone of voice had deepened and his point was perfectly clear. Dana's lips parted as she drew in a quivering breath, feeling her heart beating rapidly. Soft music played in the background and she was more beautiful than he had ever seen her before. Since the moment he had met her, he had struggled with a growing desire and being in such close proximity to her now only added to his torment. The stones of her delicate jewelry caught and reflected the lights from above, sparkling ever so softly about her lovely face. Without realizing it, his gaze travelled down her slender neck towards her tightly robed bodice, her breasts swelling gently against its embrace with each breath she took.

Dana was caught unaware by the unexpected turn in the conversation. She felt confused and looked towards the makeshift dance floor where people had begun to dance, trying to gather her thoughts.

There was an awkward silence.

"Do you dance, Dana?" Jarod asked her casually, recognizing that look of escape in her wide eyes. He pulled back slightly.

"Not well," Dana answered honestly. She spoke slowly in a preoccupied manner. "In the years that everyone else was busy learning those skills, I was far more interested in polishing my riding technique and competing."

Jarod noticed her glass was empty.

"I could use a drink, can I get you something?"

"Sure, I'll have the same. Thank you," she answered, her thoughts elsewhere.

Jarod rose from the table and made his way to the bar. He made a mental effort to bring his emotions under control. For months he had tried to deny the growing attraction he felt for Dana. It was a struggle that became more difficult with each passing day. There were times when he wondered that she might feel the same, moments when she had sensed the energy between them.

Dana watched Jarod's tall figure as he stood at the bar conversing with Emily. She could not ignore the powerful emotion she was feeling at that moment. He had a way of making her feel cared for and special, a deliberate manner of movement and speech that was very, very seductive.

She just wasn't ready for any of this.

"I'm sorry it took so long, Dana." Jarod bent down and placed her drink in front of her. "These take a little time to make."

"Thanks."

"We could do a little mingling, what do you think?" Jarod suggested. "I shouldn't be keeping you to myself all night."

"I'd like that," Dana complied as Jarod helped her with her chair. Jarod handed her her drink and picking up his own, they joined a group of people just as Dr. Winslow was saying: "Read my lips, P-O-S-S-E!" The group erupted into laughter. Dr. Winslow was at his best with an audience.

Kent noticed them and leaving Annie's side, he moved over to them.

"Jarod, it's a great party, as usual," Kent commented, his dark features alive with excitement. "Dana, there's something I wanted to talk to you about, I was wondering... Jarod, you don't mind if...?" Kent hesitated.

"Of course not," Jarod answered.

Kent guided her to a secluded corner.

"Where's your date, Kent? What's her name again? Lucy?" Dana couldn't help but ask, desperately trying to keep a straight face, but the word 'Babe' kept popping into her thoughts.

"Maggie." Kent absentmindedly corrected her. She followed his gaze towards Annie, who looked in need of rescuing from yet another of Dr. Winslow's attempts at humor. "Maggie couldn't make it, she came down with a stomach flu yesterday. She's really not feeling well." Strangely enough, Kent didn't sound at all disappointed. He managed to draw his eyes from Annie and focussed on Dana. He shifted his weight, uncomfortable with what he was about to say.

"Look, Dana, there's something I've wanted to tell you for some time," he began slowly. "I...I just didn't know when...or how." He drew a deep breath.

"When you first came here, I had a real problem with it. I thought I was getting that job, that I deserved that job." Kent ran his hand through his hair. "I wasn't fair to you, and I wasn't fair to Masquerade either. I knew Jarod expected a lot from that mare, and he had good reason to. She's a helluva horse." Kent shook his head. "Well, she was until I got to her. I pushed her and pushed her until she got all tied up inside. I was so convinced in my mind that if I could prove myself with that horse, I'd be a shoe-in for the job." Kent sighed heavily. "I was so wrong, about a lot of things," he added.

"I just wanted to come clean, and apologize. Dana, I think you're a great manager and you fill those boots better than I ever could."

Dana had remained silent during the time Kent spoke. She was deeply affected by his confession.

"It took a lot of courage for you to do what you just did. I didn't expect this." She laid a hand on his arm. "Kent, you have a genuine talent with horses, don't let one mistake undermine that. We've all made mistakes, it's the lesson they teach us that makes us stronger and smarter the next time around." Dana squeezed his hand briefly and smiled. "Thank you," she said sincerely. "Hey, I think there's a party underway, somewhere around here."

Kent smiled at Dana and they went to rejoin the others. As they walked back, Dana felt a new closeness to Kent and she admired his honesty. She could not help but feel there was a lesson for her in all of this.

"Let me get you a drink," he offered.

Dana looked at her empty glass and decided against it. "No, thanks. I've had enough for now."

"Come on," he pleaded. "It's a peace offering. Have your tried an authentic New Mexican Marguerita?"

Dana had to admit that she hadn't.

"Great, let me get you one, just give me a minute." He hurried towards the bar. Dana understood that Kent was anxious to make amends.

She waited for him to return as she watched Jarod dancing with June, along with Emily and Darren and Sue's parents.

"Cheers." Kent said, as he handed Dana a lime colored drink.

"Cheers," she replied taking a sip. "Oh, God!" She pulled the glass away from her lips, making a face. It tasted quite sour after her Spanish coffee.

"What's wrong?"

"Nothing," she laughed at herself. "I just assumed the glass rimmed with sugar, like my coffee. It's salt."

"Yeah, I'm sorry, maybe I should've told you. Do you want something else instead?"

"No, it's good." Dana nodded her reassurance. "It just took me by surprise."

The song came to an end. Jarod thanked June for the dance and made his way over to them. "Your turn is coming soon." Jarod warned Dana.

"Well, I hope your boots have steel toes!" Dana teased him.

Kent fidgeted impatiently. "I think I'll go find Annie, I'm kinda in a dancing mood myself. Catch you guys later." Kent nodded and smiled, taking his leave.

"He seems awfully pleased, was it something you said?" Jarod asked with a grin.

"I think he just enjoys a good party."

They stood companionably, watching the activity. Kent had indeed found Annie, and she secretly winked over at Dana.

"I see you've changed your poison," Jarod commented.

"Pardon me?"

He indicated the glass in her hand.

"Oh, that. Kent insisted. It's very refreshing after the sweet coffees. I like it." To Jarod's astonishment, she drained her glass.

"I'd say so," he agreed with a chuckle. "And to think I was worried you were a picky eater!"

A slow song started.

"Okay, young lady." Jarod took Dana's hand and led her to the dance floor, where he slipped his other hand lightly across the small of her back. There was a moment of awkwardness.

"The secret of dancing is simple. I lead and you follow. It's not a wrestling match." Jarod explained with humor. A tone of self-confidence underscored his words.

"Who thought up these rules? They sound archaic to me." Dana's upturned face was smiling.

"Cavemen. Will you be quiet and dance?" He pulled her in closer and soon they were effortlessly moving to the rhythm of the music.

"I think you've been holding out on me. You dance beautifully," Jarod said softly.

"Not usually," she answered. She looked into his intense eyes, feeling a little lightheaded, unsure if it was from the effects of the alcohol or the closeness of him. She closed her eyes and enjoyed the security of his arm around her, the warmth of him. It had been a long time since she had felt the presence of a man and the intimacy of Jarod's strong presence was overwhelming. They danced in silence.

When the song came to its end Jarod was slow to let her go.

"Could we take a little walk?" Dana suggested, hoping the quiet would help clear her head.

"Sure."

The moon was bright and lit their path as they walked. It was pleasant as the clamor of the party faded behind them. They reached a tall tree and stopped for awhile, appreciating the reprieve. The night air had started to cool and Dana shivered slightly.

"You're cold." Jarod removed his dinner jacket and carefully placed it around Dana's shoulders, letting his hands rest on the lapels.

A small voice inside of her warned to turn back, before it would be too late, but Dana turned a deaf ear. The temptation was too great for her to resist. Instinctively she had known all along that somehow the evening would find its way to this moment.

She didn't pull away. The moonlight played in her shining hair. Dana looked into his eyes steadfast, unwavering. Unable to help himself, Jarod slowly lifted his hand and gently traced the contour of her face, her skin was soft and cool to his touch. He cupped her face in his two hands, never daring to look away, hardly believing she was before him.

Still, she did not protest. He hesitated, then his lips brushed her forehead, her eyes closed and he softly kissed her lids. His blond head bent down deliberately, the side of his cheek making contact with hers. He could barely feel the wisps of her hair, the smell of her perfume.

Still, she did not resist. His lips sought hers and her head tilted in willing acquiescence. His lips scarcely brushed the petals of her mouth before he pulled back. She opened her eyes, faintly surprised.

She read his questioning look and moved into his embrace. Jarod kissed her once again, softly, and closed his arms around her, never wanting to let go. It seemed as though he had waited forever. Their kisses became intense. Dana abandoned her defenses, succumbing to her desire...yearning for him...lost in him.

Abruptly, she pulled away.

"Oh, God! What have I done?" Dana's voice trembled with fear. "I'm so sorry." She held her hand to her mouth and Jarod saw that it was shaking.

"Dana," he said taking a step towards her. Panic rose in her eyes and he stopped.

"Oh, Dana, please don't do this. I'm not sorry and you shouldn't be either." He said it slowly, in a choked voice. "I've wanted this almost from the moment I laid eyes on you. And just now, well, I thought you wanted it too. I don't understand why you're pulling away from me," he pleaded.

Her eyes grew moist, a tear welled up and gently spilled down her cheek.

"I don't know how to make you understand!" She turned away, deeply upset. "It's not about you, it's about me. I can't do this. You're an attractive man, Jarod. A wonderful, good-hearted man. I was overcome. But this never should've happened. I'm so sorry," she repeated, pulling his jacket around her tighter. "It's my fault."

"It's not your fault," he said, distraught. "It's not anybody's fault. Dana, know this, I would never intentionally hurt you. You must be able to feel how much I care for you." Jarod sighed heavily. "Look, we can forget about all of this, if that's what you want." Even as he spoke the words, he doubted them. He would never be able to forget the way she had responded to his touch.

"But everything has changed!" Dana cried.

"Everything will be fine, you'll see," he tried to sooth her. "Nothing has to change."

Inwardly he accepted what he knew to be the truth. For a brief interlude Dana had dropped her defenses and Jarod carried with him the certainty that at the moment she had wanted him as much as he had wanted her.

- Chapter 7 -

His body was cramped and stiff. He had been motionless for a long time, not daring to take his eyes off her. It was incredible what a little technology could accomplish. Even though she was almost a mile away, he felt he could reach out and touch her as he watched through the telescope lens.

He straightened up and flexed his fingers, curling them into a tight fist.

"Bitch!" He spat, seething. "You belong to me!"

Dana laughing, Dana flirting, Dana kissing, having the time of her life.

"How dare you make a fool of me this way. You think you're clever, but you should know better. No, you always had to learn the hard way."

She could've saved herself a whole lot of grief.

No more chances. No more crying and begging for her forgiveness, no more Mr. Nice Guy. He was going to have what was rightfully his.

He kicked furiously at the telescope, he'd seen enough of her disgusting tricks for one night.

- Chapter 8 -

Dana slowly made her way to the barn, examining the dry earth beneath her feet as she walked. She felt terrible. She had awoken to an immediate feeling of guilt accompanied by a throbbing headache, and neither one had abated any during the time she had been up.

As she crossed the yard, she noticed the truck. Men were busily dismantling the tent and picking up the equipment that had been used at the party. She pushed her hands deeper into her jean pockets as she entered the barn. All was quiet, other than the steady, chewing sounds made by the horses contentedly munching on their breakfast. Obviously, Jarod had already been there.

Dana leaned her back against a supporting beam, her hands still resting in her pockets and closed her eyes. She was tired and confused. Last night had been a big mistake. She was usually so disciplined, so in control of herself, she still couldn't believe she had allowed herself to yield to the pleasure and the passion of the moment. Even as she thought of it, feelings stirred within her, begging to be acknowledged. Alright, she argued with herself, it was more than just a fleeting moment of weakness. She had never intended to become involved with Jarod and tried so hard to resist it. She wiped a tear from her eye. Life could be so complicated, so hard. Where would all this lead? She had found true happiness in this enchanted land of contrasts and in just a few months she had become a member of this, this family of people. Now she was putting that all in jeopardy.

There were so many things he did not know about her, and her past. She was in no position to offer herself to anyone, it was so wrong of her to even hope for such a thing. She had made her way to the barn with the intention of clearing things up with Jarod, to repair what had happened, before it went any further, but now she felt her resolve seeping away from her.

Goldrush banged on his stall door. Dana walked over to him.

"Hey, big guy. What am I to do? Huh?" Goldrush eagerly pushed his head towards her. Dana rested her forehead against his and gently stroked his cheeks.

"That would make a beautiful picture." Jarod stood at the barn door. He had caught Dana by surprise and she felt a rush of emotion flood through her as she saw him there, looking tanned and strong, his sun-streaked hair in its usual informal disarray. Although he wore a smile, it didn't quite reach his weary eyes. There was a moment of awkward silence as she struggled with the turmoil flourishing inside of her, striving to accomplish what she had set out to do.

"Jarod," she said quietly, "I thought I might find you here."

"You should still be in bed." He moved closer to where she stood. "Did you come to make sure I was doing my job?" Jarod strove for some humor and they both recognized it was a frail attempt.

Dana drew a staggered breath, she felt weak. "No, I came because I wanted to apologize."

The smile ebbed from Jarod's face, he stood silently still. This was going to be very difficult, Dana thought to herself. She dropped her gaze to the floor, unable to look at him. "I could make up several excuses, but in the end there is no excuse for the way I behaved."

"The way we behaved, Dana." Jarod underlined. "You make it sound like I wasn't even there." There was a quiet undertone of disappointment in his words. "I told you last night there was nothing to be sorry about." He could've reached out and touched her, but he didn't. "What happened last night was perfectly natural. The only regret I have is that you have been so upset by it all. Dana, I've told you where I stand in all of this. I don't understand all that's going on here, what's going on with you, but I can live with it. We can just let it be... I told you, things don't have to change."

He wished with all his heart that she would look at him and move into his arms, telling him that it was not so. He willed it to happen. The urge to take her, to kiss her and make it happen was overwhelming.

She finally brought herself to look at him. "Thank you," she said softly. "For being so kind."

Jarod looked away, his jaw tight. "Dana, why don't you go back to bed and get some sleep," he said evenly, managing to contain his frustration. There was another stilted silence. "Well, I've got a lot of work to do."

"Let me give you a hand," she offered.

"If you give me a hand I'll never live it down. These guys like the idea of me doing the chores almost as much as the party itself." He lightly made a valid excuse. He needed time alone. "Don't worry about anything, Dana. Get some sleep and I'll see you later." Jarod spoke with a tone of finality and she was unable to read the closed expression in his eyes.

Dana nodded and left the barn, she still had a dull ache in her head, and her feelings of quilt had not subsided. Jarod had remained calm, almost indifferent. She didn't know what she had expected and she didn't understand why she felt so disappointed now.

Dana noticed a mare and foal in one of the paddocks and was drawn in that direction. She rested her arms across the top rail of the fence and planted her right foot on the bottom rung, watching the colt run freely around his mother.

Last night had seemed like a different lifetime. She slowly went over the evening in her mind. Everything had begun innocently enough, or maybe not, she thought as she remembered dancing with Jarod. She could not deny the powerful attraction she felt then. What had she been thinking of, suggesting going for a walk? Dana closed her eyes, almost breathless as she relived the moments leading to the kiss. She had never experienced that kind of passion before, an unbridled urgency overcoming her. It was almost frightening.

"I'm so confused," Dana said aloud. "I wish I could scream."

The fatigue she had been fighting all morning was suddenly too much; she decided to give in to her exhaustion and made her way back to the main house.

Dana rolled over and checked the time. She had slept for almost two hours. She decided to have a bite to eat and then take out Masquerade. Dressing into her riding clothes, she checked her appearance in the mirror. She was glad to see that some of the color had returned to her face.

June was in the kitchen, standing over a steaming pot. She greeted Dana warmly.

"Hello, dear. How are you feeling?"

"A little better than before," she replied smiling at June. June always had a way of comforting her without having to do much at all, her mere presence was enough. Dana longed to sit down and pour her heart out to the woman and ask for her advice, but it would have been a very long story. What purpose would it serve? She watched June's mildly plump form, happily preparing her meal and thought, how would June ever begin to understand the things she had gone through? Dana sighed, suddenly missing Emma.

June placed a bowl of homemade soup in front of Dana and cut her a thick slice of bread. There was a cold plate of freshly prepared vegetables and cheese already on the table. June sat down with her, pouring them each a tall glass of iced tea.

"June, you seemed to enjoy yourself last night," Dana said, realizing talk of the party would be inevitable.

"It was a beautiful party. I think I could say the same for you and Mr. Kingsley. I can't remember the last time I've seen him so happy." June glowed as she spoke.

"Is he not coming in for lunch?" Dana appeared to be preoccupied with her food, deliberately avoiding June's probing look.

"He's already come in and asked for a packed lunch. He said he had some things to check in the south corner and he would be back in a couple of hours. For a man who's barely had any sleep, he's putting in a big day," June replied. "Emily spent the night upstairs. She didn't want to drive home in the dark, but she left while you were asleep. I haven't checked in the bunkhouse."

"Ben was in fine form," Dana teased, a sparkle coming into her green-blue eyes.

"Oh! That Ben, going on the way he does!" June shook her head.

Dana laughed and rose from the table. "Well, June, you just keep him in line. I'll see you at supper."

Dana returned to the barn. It was different to see things so quiet, without the habitual commotion of people and horses coming and going. She took her time, enjoying the silence and the peace. She made her way up and down the barn aisle, checking in on each horse, some of them had already been turned out. Jarod had been very busy. She eventually found her way to the tack room where she selected what she needed to take out Masquerade.

The mare seemed to excel in the open air and after she was saddled up, Dana directed her to the outdoor jumping ring. Masquerade was responding very smoothly. They worked for some time doing ground work, concentrating mainly on lead changes.

The wind was picking up and Dana loved the sensation of it against her.

"Well, girl, I think you're ready for something a little more exciting." Dana stroked the horse's neck. She squeezed Masquerade into an easy canter, the mares ears twitched back and forth attentively as Dana lined her up to the first fence and then onto the second, Masquerade completing the entire course with only one rail down. There had been no hesitation in the mare's approach to any of the ten jumps that Dana had put her over. They had sailed easily through the wind: up, over and down in a fluid motion, time after time.

"Way to go, girl. You know how to lift my spirits," Dana spoke to the horse, exhilarated with her performance.

"I can't believe it's the same horse." Jarod stood at the gate to the ring, his enthusiasm apparent in his voice. Ever since the week following Dana's arrival at the ranch, Jarod had purposefully stayed away from Masquerade's training sessions. Jarod had always had faith in Dana's capabilities as a trainer, but what she had accomplished with this horse was truly amazing.

Dana slid effortlessly to the ground and loosened Masquerade's girth. "I'm so proud of her, she's a wonderful horse!" She said delighted as she led the mare around the ring, cooling her down.

"You should be proud of yourself. You've done a helluva job with this horse." His words were sincere and Dana noted that he seemed to be his usual self. "The clouds are coming in, Dana. I don't care for the look of them."

Dana raised her eyes toward the mountains and realized what he meant. Big, dark puffs of angry looking clouds swirled and churned in the distance. She became uneasy.

"Are we going to get a tornado?"

Jarod couldn't help but laugh at her stricken expression.

"I doubt we're in for anything that serious. I've sent Ben and Adam out to the eastern pasture, maybe you can give me a hand here. It's the hailstorms that give us more problems. I want to bring the horses into the barn, to be on the safe side. It's just a precaution, Dana. You've never seen hail in New Mexico, it can bruise horseflesh."

"Okay. Tell me what you want me to do."

They worked together, quickly bringing in the horses that were in the nearby paddocks. The wind had picked up again, blowing dust and sagebrush around them, whipping the words from their mouths. Adam and Ben returned to the ranch, having rounded up over a dozen horses that had been turned out to graze in the eastern pasture earlier. The horses stood impatiently at the gate, instinctively nervous. They had just completed securing the animals in the barns when the first drops of rain began to fall. Adam and Ben made sure the horses had adequate food and water in Barn Two, while Dana and Jarod tended to the animals in Barn One.

They then made a dash to the main house, escaping into its interior.

"Your weather is just like your landscape!" Dana said breathlessly, running her fingers through her windswept hair, attempting to return it to some kind of order. "It knows no compromise."

True to Jarod's prediction, the hail began to fall, slamming and ricocheting across the earth's unyielding surface. Dana recalled a dust storm that had occurred not long after her arrival. The unrelenting winds had spent their fury over the course of almost three full days, making the working life at the ranch miserable. And when the winds were done, a layer of dust had permeated into every nook and cranny imaginable. Even Dana had had to admit it was one of the more adverse aspects of life in New Mexico; yet she still believed it was a small price to pay for the grandiose beauty it offered.

That evening at dinner, Dana was relieved to find that Jarod was still his personable self. Inevitably, the subject of the party came up and Dana couldn't help but cringe in her chair, but her anxiety was unfounded. Jarod kept the conversation entertaining and she soon found that she was enjoying herself. True to his word, it was as if nothing had changed between them. Dana deliberately repressed an emotion that almost felt like regret.

"How did you find your day in the barn?" Dana asked as she picked up her coffee cup.

"I loved it," he replied smiling. "Of course that's easy enough for me to say, because I'm not in there every day. I should do it more often. Mother Nature was very kind today, speeding my work right along! I was lucky to have been out on Goldrush this afternoon. If I had been working inside the barn I would've never noticed the storm coming in."

The storm had been intense, unleashing a wild torrent of rain and hail and then as if by magic, abruptly ceasing. It was indeed fortunate that they had collected the horses in time.

Jarod pushed his plate away as he rubbed his eyes. He leaned back in his chair and Dana noticed the faint lines of tiredness on his handsome features. Once again, she was made aware of his even disposition, his lack of temper or moodiness. His demeanor was always patient and calm, a quality she had come to admire. He carried a natural, quiet force that came from within.

"I still can't believe the improvement I saw in Masquerade today." He broke the silence that had fallen over the table.

"Hmm," Dana looked at him and smiled, momentarily taken aback by the unexpected feeling of intimacy that had welled up in her.

"I wanted to talk to you about her," Dana hesitated. "I'd like to bring her with us to the show in two weeks." Dana studied Jarod's reaction of mild surprise.

"To compete?"

"Jarod, I'd just be putting her into one or two low hunter classes. I know she can do it. The courses would be smaller than what you saw her do today."

Jarod looked away for a moment, then slowly turned to face her.

"I don't want you to feel you have to prove anything to me." The ambiguity of his words were not lost on Dana. "You are not being pressured in here."

"I am doing this because I know she's ready for it." Dana was very definite in her tone. "I would never feel pressured into making this kind of decision."

Jarod hesitated for a second, considering where they were going with this conversation.

"It's your call." He shook his head decisively. "You've done a great job with this horse and I don't think it's my place to tell you whether she's ready or not," he said with a noticeable emphasis.

"Good," Dana smiled at Jarod, unsure of herself, wondering if she was imagining something that wasn't even there. "I'll make the entries for her tomorrow. We won't let you down."

Jarod nodded, attempting a smile. "I'm still running on two hours sleep, and I think it's catching up with me." He excused himself, as he rose from the table. "Good night, Dana, I'll see you in the morning."

"Good night, Jarod."

Jarod stretched his long body before getting into bed. It had been a full day and he was very tired. He lay on his back, cupping his hands behind his head. When Dana had come to find him that morning in the barn, he had not known what to expect from her. For a fraction of a second he had feared that she had come to tell him she would be leaving the ranch. So, he supposed, he had something to be thankful for.

She was still a puzzle to him; she would show a small piece of herself and then hide it away again. He considered for a minute that Dana was playing with him, but he quickly discounted the idea. Dana was not manipulative or conniving by nature. Lord knows, he thought, he'd seen enough of the world to recognize that when he met it. Last night her fear had been genuine.

Why was she so frightened? Why couldn't she help him to understand instead of always shutting him out every time he came too close?

She was going to drive him crazy. He rolled over and closed his eyes, bidding the questions in his mind to stop. The picture of her standing before him with the moonlight playing in her hair engulfed him. He remembered the return of her passion when they had come together.

It would be alright, he told himself. Sooner or later she would come back to him. It was probably the only thing he was certain of when it came to Dana. He could wait. He rolled over again, exhausted, and fell asleep.

By the next morning, things had returned to their usual routine and the feeling of normalcy was welcomed by Dana. The atmosphere in the barn was upbeat, with everyone fully recovered from the party and anticipating the first show of the season.

Dana felt well prepared for it. Natasha and Darren were looking good and the three horses: Paska, Goliath and Empire were all performing consistently. This week, she would concentrate on polishing their delivery, paying particular attention to small detail. Dana found comfort in the knowledge that she would be too occupied to concentrate on anything other than the task at hand. This was the milieu in which Dana excelled, confident and focussed, eagerly awaiting the challenge of competition.

Natasha and Darren felt her intensity and couldn't help but be affected by it, though they each reacted somewhat differently. Natasha was a tall young woman with dark eyes and high cheekbones. She had been raised on horses and had competed in local shows ever since she could remember. As a youngster she had ridden Western, eventually participating in rodeos as a teenager. Later, she had been introduced to English riding, where she had truly struck a connection. Natasha's strength lay in her versatility; there was nothing she couldn't accomplish on a horse. Dana often teased her, telling Natasha she had missed her calling in life, she was actually born to be a stunt rider. Natasha was at ease in either saddle, Western or English, the latter being her personal preference.

One time Dana had come across Natasha giving Sue a mock lesson in grand style, her back primly arched, her riding crop cocked at an angle from her extended hand to the toe of her riding boot.

"There are three ways to dismount, grasshopper. Simply put: the first is to get off, the second is to fall off and the third...is to be thrown off, the only difference separating your options is how hard you hit the ground."

Sue, sitting on horseback, had looked down at Natasha's serious pose and burst into a fit of giggles. Having experienced all three options countless times, it was no surprise that Natasha was immune to pre-show jitters.

Darren, on the other hand, was a very serious contender. His background was greatly opposite to that of Natasha's and he lacked the vast experience that she brought with her. This was his first year competing and as the actual event drew closer, his anxiety grew. When Dana watched Darren on horseback, the old adage 'practice makes perfect' was never far from her thoughts. He would repeatedly perform the same routine, over and over, until it was right or better than right. He was a sweet guy, driven by some invisible force.

When Natasha had once jokingly called him 'an ulcer waiting to happen', he had been the first to agree with her. Although they were like day and night in personality, Darren and Natasha had managed to form a solid friendship and could often be found helping each other out.

Dana turned off the computer and checked the time. Natasha and Darren would be there shortly. She had just enough time to phone in Masquerade's entry into the Santa Rosa show. With that done, Dana left the office in search of her students.

Empire and Goliath were already in the grooming area their coats gleaming and now being tacked by their respective riders.

"When you're ready, you can both meet me outside in the hunter ring," Dana called out to them.

The summer sun blazed in the desert sky. The air was hot and dry. Dana could see that she would have to keep today's lesson short. Fortunately, yesterday's precipitation would help to keep the dust down to a minimum. The temperature would be hopefully more tolerable on Saturday.

Natasha and Darren rode out to the ring, looking uncomfortable in the heat.

"Look, guys. I know it's not fun, but we won't be able to pick the weather on Saturday either. We have to be conditioned for anything. On the rail," Dana commanded.

The horses were sluggish, Darren and Natasha were forced to work hard in an effort to keep them in an even rhythm and after approximately forty minutes, Dana decided to call the session to a halt.

Natasha dismounted and led Goliath over to Dana.

"What do you think, Dana? Are we ready?" She took off her riding helmet, her dark hair clung to her scalp and she shook it loose.

"You were born ready. Don't forget to pay particular attention to Goliath's lead changes. Listen," she addressed them both. "I think you should give these horses a shower before you put them away. Okay, let's go." They started back towards the barn. Dana noticed that Darren had been especially quiet.

"Darren, is something bothering you?" Dana asked him, as she patted at her brow with the top of her wrist.

"My Dad's coming to watch me at the show on Saturday…as if I wasn't nervous enough to start with. It's going to mean extra pressure, he expects a lot from me." Darren shrugged his broad shoulders.

Natasha had motioned silently to Dana from behind Darren, pointedly raising her eyebrows as he was speaking.

"Darren, you are an extremely conscientious rider. If I didn't believe that you had talent, I wouldn't be wasting my time and yours." Dana chose her words carefully. "Saturday is just another day. Hopefully it will go really well, but even if it doesn't, that doesn't make you any less talented. It's going to be your first time out there, try and enjoy yourself and everything else will fall into place."

Natasha came forward, giving him a friendly shove. "Come on, Bucko. How many mustangs has your old man broken in?"

Darren shook his head, laughing at the mental picture of his father on horseback. "My Dad's not really what you could call cowboy material."

"Well, there you go. You remember that on Saturday." Natasha had a habit of twirling her riding crop and Goliath snorted his displeasure. "No sweat. Let's get these horses showered and shaved." She continued to joke with Darren as they led the horses to the showers.

Dana watched them go, deep in thought. She decided it was time for Paska's workout, now that her students had been taken care of. On her way to the tack room to get her saddle, she came across Annie and Kent laughing in the feed room. Dana had observed them on and off throughout the day and she wondered if it was only her imagination, but they seemed different with each other. Dana smiled, remembering them dancing together at the party. Maybe Annie had been granted her wish, after all.

The next few days passed speedily. They were fairly uneventful, other than the odd fit of nerves brought on by last minute adjustments in the final preparations. Friday quickly rolled around and basically all that was left to be done was to review the equipment in the tack boxes and to braid the horses. It was a long, tedious job, plaiting up to forty small, evenly matched braids in each horse's mane.

Natasha and Darren had finished up with Goliath and Empire. Dana looked at her watch. She still had about an hour's work left on Paska. It would be a late night. Dana left Paska momentarily, and went over to check in on her students.

"Good work! You've both done a great job." She told them as she critically surveyed the horses. "Let's bed down these guys, then you two can go home and get yourselves to bed. Get a good night's sleep. Tomorrow's the big day." She smiled at them. Together, they settled Empire and Goliath in their stalls, keeping the conversation light. Natasha's not-so-subtle influence over Darren was evident. She had deliberately encouraged him throughout the week with her off-hand manner and he was looking confident. Dana had expected him to be quite anxious by this time, but she had misjudged him. Mentally, she thanked her lucky stars for having paired these two students together this weekend. Natasha was very nurturing and protective about any person or animal that she chose to bring in under her wing. It was hard to understand, because she never gave the impression of being overly sensitive or sympathetic. In fact, her manner appeared to be anything but that.

They said their good-byes and Dana returned to complete Paska's braids.

Sometime later, she heard someone entering the barn.

"Hello?" Dana called out from the grooming area.

"It's just me." Jarod answered, as he walked over to where Dana stood on a wooden crate, working on Paska's mane.

"June was worried about you, she sent me over with a care package."

"I've just got three braids left, it won't take long. I'm famished."

"That comes as a big surprise." Jarod laughed. "What can I do?"

"Each of the three horses has a tack box near the barn entrance. You'll see a checklist taped to them. I've already checked them this afternoon, but it wouldn't hurt to have you look through the boxes and make sure everything is in order," Dana suggested, as her hands deftly wove through the horse's coarse hair.

"Say no more." Jarod set down June's basket on an empty spot on the shelf and walked away. They each completed their jobs at about the same time and decided to enjoy June's snack in the office.

"Are you excited?" Jarod asked her, as he poured coffee from a thermos.

"Hmm," Dana thought about it. "I'm a lot of things, mostly tired right now. I've never been...a full-fledged teacher before. Do you know what I mean? There's always been someone higher up instructing me. In fact it often seemed that the better I became, the more involved my trainers became."

Jarod sat quietly, just listening to her talk. It was one of the rare pictures he got of her personal life, her life before she came to Kingsley Ranch.

"I think it's the first time that I can remember being more concerned with someone else's performance than my own. Well, that didn't sound right." Dana made a wry face.

"No, I know what you mean."

"I don't know how to explain it. Emma and I often competed together and it was important to me, how well she did... but it was something we shared. I worried about her, she worried about me. Not like now, with Darren and Natasha, it's not the same. I feel..." Dana searched for the right word. "I don't know, responsible?"

Jarod nodded. "Is Emma your sister?"

It struck Dana how little Jarod really knew about her.

"Almost," she smiled fondly. "No, Emma Fisher. She's my best friend. We've known each other forever." Dana shrugged her shoulders and changed the subject, talking of Emma only made Dana miss her. "Darren is worried about his father being there tomorrow, something about added pressure, high expectations. I don't know."

Jarod had the mental picture of a shutter closing and opening on a new image.

"I can relate to that. It's hard enough learning how to deal with one's own successes and failures without the added pressure from a parent." Jarod stared ahead unseeingly.

"Was your father domineering?" Dana asked softly.

Jarod laughed. "Only with every single thing in his life, including me. It was his idea of parenting, and it was always some else's fault: a coach, a teacher, a doctor, June, me. I guess it's easy to lay blame when you're never personally involved. Once I was able to see past my resentment, I came to realize I had learnt a lot about myself in those years." Jarod looked across the desk at Dana. "It wasn't all bad. Some good things came out of those learning experiences. What about your parents?"

Jarod was never sure what to expect when bringing up Dana's personal life and he hoped his question was a safe one.

Dana was carefully peeling an orange.

[87]

"My parents are amazing people. I owe everything to the fact that they have always supported me." She brushed her hair from her forehead with the back of her hand. "When I started riding, we didn't even own a horse," she smiled. "They didn't know much about it, but they were always there for me. They taught me how to believe in myself." She looked down at her lap. "It is a lesson I've used often in life."

"They sound like wonderful people." Jarod stood, unsure of whether he should take the conversation any further. "Are you ready to come up to the main house?"

"No, you go on ahead. I just have a couple of last minute details to take care of. Then I'll close up."

"Well, I'll give you a hand," he offered.

"I'll be fine. Really."

"Okay, don't be too long." Jarod paused for a second, but she didn't change her mind. She picked up the remains of their impromptu meal and handed the basket to Jarod.

After he had left the barn, Dana realized she felt homesick. It was too late to phone home now. With the difference in time, her parents would already be fast asleep and phoning this late would only cause them to worry.

She placed a call to Emma.

"Hello?" The voice on the end of the line was drowsy.

"Emma. Were you sleeping?"

"Dana? Is that you?"

Dana laughed, smiling to herself. She settled back in her chair, pulling her legs up in front of her.

"Hey kiddo. How's everything going? My God, I can't believe it's you." Emma's voice was awake now. "How are you?"

"I'm fine, really I am. I've missed you."

"I miss you too, girl. Are you ever coming home to visit?"

"Yeah, but not yet. It's still too early." Dana's voice was subdued.

"I know," Emma said with understanding. "Things have been very quiet here," she said meaningfully. "I can't really talk, Mike's spending the night," Emma explained.

"That's good to hear." Dana squeezed her eyes shut. She wiped a tear from her cheek. "So, what's new with you?"

"Hmm, I'm not riding as much. It's not the same without you here. You know, life gets busy. There's Mike, the job. Hey! Guess what? My sister's pregnant."

"Who? Kimberly?"

"Lindsay. The doctor thinks it might be twins. The whole family is going crazy."

"I can imagine. When will she know for sure?" It felt so good to hear Emma's voice, it was just like old times.

"I'm not sure, pretty soon I guess. She's going for an ultrasound next week. Dana, are you sure you're okay?"

"Yes, I'm sure I'm okay. It's a wonderful set-up here. I'm busy doing work I love. I'm teaching a lot now. It's not like competing to make the Olympics, but it's good. June takes care of me and keeps me fed..." The girls started to laugh together.

"I swear, it's amazing how some skinny people can put their food away! It's not going to be so funny when you're fifty, girl! The metabolism's not the same."

"Ha, ha." Dana smiled. "Anyway, everybody here is really nice. I'm starting to feel at home."

"I'm happy for you. I'm not happy for me..." Emma kidded her. "I'm just teasing you."

"I know." Dana could hear a man's voice in the background. "Look, I'm going to let you go now. It's getting late."

"There's no rush," Emma protested.

"No, it's late. I'm showing tomorrow. I'll phone again soon, I promise."

"I'm going to hold you to that, kiddo. You can wake me up anytime. It's so good to hear you, I wish I could see you!" Emma lamented.

"We'll get together," Dana promised again. "I've got to go now."

"Bye, Dana. Take care of yourself." Emma's voice was artificially bright.

"You too."

The receiver clicked to a dial tone and Dana replaced it on the jacket.

Dana drew in a breath and rose from her chair. She flicked off the main lights in the barn and left for the house. Jesse Dog came running down the lane to meet her.

"You are such a good dog." Dana patted the golden labrador's head.

Something fell behind the barn, making a loud noise. Dana's heart jumped and Jesse Dog began barking furiously. She could feel her pulse racing.

"Is anyone there?" She called out over the dog's barking. Dana paused, she could hear her heart pounding in her ears. There was no answer.

Holding the dog's collar, she quickly made her way to the house and was relieved when she reached the front door.

She stepped into the house, still shaken. The office door was open and she saw Jarod working at his desk.

"Jarod?"

He looked up at her. She was pale and trembling. He got up and came over to her.

"What's the matter?"

"I don't know, there was a noise outside and the dog was barking. Do you think coyotes would come up to the barn?"

"It's not likely. I'll go take a look." He calmly went to the hall closet and got out a flash light and his rifle. Dana was startled by the rifle, but quickly recognized the logic in it. Jarod reached up into a box and pulled out two bullets and proceeded to load them.

"Are you going out alone?" She asked him apprehensively.

"I'll be fine. This kind of thing happens every once in awhile. Nothing ever comes of it. I won't be long, I want you to wait here. "He smiled at Dana reassuringly. "I'll be fine, don't worry so much," he repeated as he left.

Dana nervously paced the floor. She detested feeling scared. Her stomach was upset and she could not control her trembling.

Finally, Dana heard Jarod returning and she quickly hurried to meet him.

"Is everything okay?"

"Whatever you heard was long gone by the time I got there. I checked outside and inside the barns. Everything's alright." He unloaded the rifle. "Dana, there's nothing to worry about." He put a hand on her shoulder. "Hey."

"I'm sorry. I can't stop shaking. I tried, but I think I'm just overtired."

"Dana, you should get some sleep, it's late. I'm sorry, I should've waited for you at the barn. I keep forgetting that you're not really used to big country." He smiled at her. "What? No armadillos in Maine?"

"Not the last time I checked," she returned with a faint smile, beginning to calm down. "That reminds me, I made a long-distance call. When the bill comes in, let me know how much it was."

"Don't worry about your long-distance calls. I've told you that before." Jarod gently reminded her. "You get yourself up to bed. You've got a big day tomorrow."

"Are you coming to the show?"

"I thought I'd drive the horses."

"Great. Okay." Dana suddenly yawned. "I'll see you in the morning. Good night, Jarod."

"Sleep well, Dana."

It had been a long evening, and relaxing in a steamy hot bath eased her tension. Dana crawled into her bed and turned off her lamp. Jarod was so brave and reasonable. She couldn't help but admire his steady calmness. She would've had to be made of stone not be attracted to such a man, she rationalized, but there was a lot more to a relationship than attraction...like honesty. She had made some serious mistakes in the past, and she was living the consequences of them. It was so tempting to just throw caution to the wind and let things lead where they may, but she had issues that were still unresolved. Not everybody's life was easy, she thought. She wrapped her arms around her pillow and fell asleep.

- Chapter 9 -

Dana reached for the black garment bag containing her show clothes and hurried down the stairs to the kitchen, where Jarod was already seated at the table with a steaming mug of coffee in his hands. June was in the midst of serving him his breakfast.

"Good morning, everyone," Dana said briskly. She carefully laid the garment bag over the back of a vacant chair and pulled another up to the table. "June, I can't believe you're up this early."

June gave her a look of exaggerated dismay. "As if I would be sending the two of you off on empty stomachs!"

"Are Annie and Kent bandaging the horses' legs for transport, or should we leave for the barn early?" Jarod asked Dana. He looked weary, as if he had had little sleep and Dana realized that it was not just this morning, he had been looking this way for some time now.

"Kent told me he would load up the tack boxes, the feed and pails while Annie bandaged, so we should be fine. June is right, eat your breakfast, everything is under control." Dana reassured him as she sat down with her coffee.

Jarod looked Dana over and smiled. "You seem quite spry this morning."

"Is it that obvious?" She laughed. "I can't help myself. I've been working hard to get to this day and I plan on enjoying it." Dana's voice was filled with enthusiasm. She tucked a stray lock of hair behind her ear as she ate, throwing him an impish look, her eyes alive with energy.

"I can see I don't have to worry about you passing out from nerves today," he teased her. "June, is there any coffee left?" Jarod rubbed his eyes as June replenished his cup.

"Jarod, you're looking tired." June put her hand on his shoulder. Dana's head shot up. It was the first time she'd ever heard June address Jarod by his first name.

"Don't fuss, June. I'm fine." He patted her hand.

Dana looked from one to the other. "Are you okay?" she asked, concerned.

He held up his hands in an exasperated gesture. "I'm fine," he repeated, looking uncomfortable with the sudden attention. "God, I'd hate to see the two of you if there was something really wrong with me. It's nothing a good night's sleep won't fix," he said with an air of finality as he stood and drained his cup. "Will we be bringing Natasha and Darren with us?"

Dana shook her head as she too rose from the table. "No. They will be meeting us on the show grounds. It'll be just you, me and the horses. How long is the drive? Kent suggested we be loaded by 6:45."

"Sounds about right. The drive will take approximately an hour and a half. Are you ready?"

"Ready."

June came over to Dana and kissed her on the cheek. "Good luck today, dear."

Dana blushed, touched by June's show of affection. "Thank you, June. We'll see you later."

"Mr. Kingsley, you take good care of our girl."

"Always, June. You have a good day."

The barn was a hub of activity as they stepped in. Jarod walked over to help Kent, who was struggling with a cumbersome tack box. Dana found Annie in the grooming area, bandaging Empire.

"Good morning, Annie. What's left to be done?"

"Hey there, Dana. They're all done. Well, almost done. We can start loading them anytime. So, are you nervous?" Annie made idle conversation as she finished up with Empire. "That should do it," she said as she stepped back and surveyed her work.

"Super. I think we'll all be fine. We may as well get them into the trailer," Dana indicated.

Annie led Empire out and as Dana went to get Paska, she came across Ben, who was also up bright and early this morning.

[93]

"Is my girl goin' bring home a ribbon, Dana?" Ben grinned, scratching the horses's muzzle.

"We'll do our best Ben," she assured him with a smile.

The three horses loaded easily and Jarod and Dana waved goodbye to the small group as they climbed into the pick-up and they were on their way, the dust curling into thick clouds behind them as they headed out with horse trailer in tow.

"This will be your first opportunity to meet some of the other equestrians. I think you'll be impressed by the level of talent you'll see today. Because we reside in New Mexico, most outsiders seem to assume all we are, are cowboys and rodeos," Jarod told her, checking his rearview from time-to-time as they drove along.

"I must admit, that is basically what I had expected before I came here," Dana confessed. "I just didn't see myself breaking in broncos." She smiled, reflecting for a moment on how things had changed since she had arrived at Kingsley, and how long ago that now seemed. She recalled her first image of Jarod in his office, writing at his desk. Unconsciously, her eyes strayed to where his hand rested as it lay over the stick-shift; a strong, masculine hand, no longer the hand of a stranger.

"Are you familiar with the show grounds?" Dana asked, turning her attention back to the business of the day.

"Mora County? I've been there several times. It's an easy set-up. The barns are close to the show rings. Last year, Adam and Kent did fairly well at this show. It's a pity neither of them have the desire for competition."

"Is that why Adam chose to take over the breeding program?" Dana asked.

"Mainly. It has worked out for the best. Adam is great with the mares and foals. He has a strong sixth sense with horses, claims it is a gift of his native heritage. He is part Navaho, they had a strong horse culture and were excellent herdsmen."

They were making their way through the Sangre De Christo mountain range. It was a panoramic view with mountains challenging the heavens, a kaleidoscope of breathtaking peaks and crevices washed in sharp prisms of radiant sunlight. Dana felt infinitesimal, lost in the powerfully vivid beauty that surrounded her.

"I've watched Adam a few times. He does have a gift," Dana agreed. "It's all very different from what I'm used to. There is so much culture here in New Mexico."

Jarod shifted down as the pick-up engaged in a careful descent, all the while monitoring the progress of the trailer behind them. The horses seemed quiet.

"A lot of what we see today are staged events, an attempt to preserve the spirit of the forty-seventh state of the Union, mostly for the benefit of the tourists. But it's true, New Mexico's history is colorful, unparallel to that of any other state," he said proudly. "The influence of the Native Americans, the Hispanics, even the missionaries and the outlaws is still very visible. They've left their legacy here."

"Do you know how your family came to be here?" Dana asked Jarod, curious.

"My great-great grandfather made his way over the Santa Fe Trail around 1843. He was a merchant by nature, a trader in wool. In those days, a man was pretty much on his own. Primarily, he acted as a broker for the ranchers, and out of necessity he became their store supplier and banker as well, financing and providing for them, from one season to the next. It was a mutually beneficial operation.

He established my family's fortune around that time. He was your quintessential entrepreneur. Unfortunately, my grandfather did not inherit that penchant for opportunity and investment. He scored a few ill-advised deals during his time, but my dad pretty much managed to recoup whatever had been lost, and then some." Jarod said it simply, without boasting. He turned and flashed Dana one of his easy smiles.

"You must be bored to death! As luck would have it, we have arrived. So, you won't have to listen to anymore long-winded tales." They pulled into the show grounds.

"It kept my mind busy," Dana told him appreciatively and she was sincere. Travelling with horses was something she would never take for granted. She had heard too many horror stories of things that had gone wrong, terrible accidents that were impossible to forget. She breathed in a sigh of relief when Jarod finally parked and turned off the ignition.

Dana quickly looked around noticing that the grounds were already very busy. This would be her first New Mexican competition, she thought to herself. The scenery was different, the countryside being comparably barren of vegetation, yet the grandstands and the rush of adrenaline remained the same.

"Dana, which barn are we in?"

She checked through her information sheets and replied. "We're in barn #9."

"Right. Well, if you want to go and register, I'll begin unloading," Jarod directed as he hopped out of the pick-up, stretching his legs. "Do you see that small, square building just over there?" He pointed to his left. "That's the office."

Dana stepped out of the truck. She squared her shoulders and smiled as she stood for a moment, drinking in the scene before her. Riders on horseback were meticulously going over their repertoires in the warm-up ring. The air reverberated with the familiar sound of hooves echoing down the trailer ramps as new-arrivals unloaded. People rapidly made their way to and fro, tending to their horses, equipment and paperwork.

Dana registered, picking up their designated numbers for the show and then found her way to barn #9. The horses were already in their assigned stalls and Natasha and Darren had joined Jarod.

"Good morning. How are you two feeling?" Dana asked, hoping for positive responses as she approached her students.

"Fine," Natasha answered in her typical, unflurried manner. "Goliath looks none the worse for wear. Nothing bothers that horse."

Dana casually looked towards Darren.

"Don't ask." Darren's answer was curt as he shook his head. "Can someone please have my father barred from attending any future shows?" He forced a weak attempt at humor.

"Come on, Darren. Just turn it off. You can do this," Natasha encouraged him.

"Easy for you to say. Nerves of steel." Darren affectionately poked a finger in Natasha's ribs.

"That's the spirit."

"Jarod!" A booming voice rang out. A stout, middle aged man made his way over to them, extending his hand.

"Mr. Cook," Jarod responded, shaking the gentleman's hand.

"Bruce, Bruce," he protested smiling. "Well, how are you, boy?" The short man was forced to look up in order to meet Jarod's gaze.

"I'm doing well, Bruce. How is Mrs. Cook?"

"Oh, she's wonderful, just wonderful. She's at home this weekend. Lisa came down with the youngsters, so I couldn't pull Dorothy away. Husbands seem to take a back seat when the grandchildren are around!" Bruce Cook contentedly chuckled. "Well, I suppose I should be going, you've got plenty to tend to..." He made no motion to leave, pointedly looking at Dana.

"Bruce, this is my trainer and manager, Dana Northington." Jarod introduced them. "And these are two of our students: Natasha, Darren." The man politely made their acquaintances then turned his attention back to Jarod.

"I thought someone would've gotten their hooks into you by now, make an honest man out of you." He teased Jarod, his expression gradually becoming serious. "You know, your father and I went back a long way."

Jarod respectfully shook his head in agreement.

"Your father never got the chance to enjoy grandchildren. They are a wonderful gift. Don't let the same thing happen to you, son."

"No, sir."

"Well," Bruce Cook cleared his throat. "You come visit us, Jarod. I know Dorothy would be as pleased as punch to have you over."

"Yes, sir. I'll try and do that."

The gentleman took his leave. Dana tried to read Jarod's expression as he watched Mr. Cook walk away.

"He seems nice," she offered.

Jarod gave an imperceptible nod of his head.

"He's a good ol' boy," was all he said.

"All right then," Dana turned to her students, who were patiently waiting. ""You will be riding in about forty-five minutes. Saddle up, light warm-up." She instructed them. "Here are your numbers, don't forget to put them on," Dana kidded with them.

Jarod walked over and threw an arm around Darren's shoulders. "Come on, I'll give you a hand with Empire." He turned to Dana and directed her quick wink.

Good, Dana thought. "Okay, Natasha, it looks like you're left with me." They went to get Goliath ready.

Once done, they proceeded to the warm-up area.

"There is only one thing I'm going to tell you," Dana advised Darren and Natasha. "Remember, this is not the time to school. If your horses don't respond to something, work around it. We don't want any confrontations before your class. Keep it light." Dana stood back, a strong feeling of pride overtook her. The two geldings looked stunning, gleaming in the brilliant sunlight and in prime condition. Natasha and Darren were smartly dressed in their sharply colored show attire, entirely in beige and black.

"They're an impressive sight," Jarod commented as he leaned against the fence railing, his eyes narrowing under his broad-brimmed Stetson as he watched intently.

"You did a great job with Darren, he seems much more relaxed." Dana was relieved. Whatever it was that Jarod had said to Darren while they had tacked up Empire, it had definitely taken the edge off him.

"CLASS 101: TO THE HUNTER RING." A voice called over the loudspeaker.

Natasha and Darren trotted their horses over to where Dana and Jarod stood.

"This is it," she told them with confidence. "Ride smooth and you'll do great."

They nodded in agreement, then turning their mounts around, they headed towards the show ring.

Jarod and Dana followed at a slightly slower pace on foot. Jarod scanned the immediate vicinity around the ring railing and found an empty space where they would have a clear view of the course. He guided Dana to the spot, greeting several people as they passed by.

From what Dana could ascertain, there were twenty-two participants in the class which was about to begin. As the riders entered the ring one-by-one, Dana mentally evaluated each performance. Eight horses had each completed the course when Darren's number was announced over the loudspeaker.

Darren trotted into the ring on Empire and inexplicably Dana felt a sudden sweep of nervous anxiety.

"Come on, Darren. You can do it," she whispered under her breath.

On Darren's command, Empire took up an easy canter. The horse's muscles rippled effortlessly under the sun as he moved through the open course, his hooves sounding in perfect cadence as they hit the ground, the beat steady. The rhythm only momentarily suspended as the horse jumped over each obstacle before once again resuming in perfect measure. Dana could've as easily closed her eyes and still known that Darren had completed his course faultlessly.

Dana turned to face Jarod, who was standing just inches from her.

"He made it!" Dana's upturned face was aglow, an uninhibited smile spread across her features.

"He did great." Jarod agreed.

A passerby accidentally stumbled into Dana and Jarod's arm immediately shot around her protectively, as she was pushed into him. She was suddenly aware of the strength of Jarod's form.

"Sorry," the man excused himself, clumsily tipping his hat. "I wasn't watching my step." There was the unmistakable odor of whisky on his breath.

"It's okay. Take it easy." Jarod lightly held Dana until the man moved on before gently releasing her. "Are you alright?"

"Sure, thanks." Dana composed herself, stepping back a pace.

"It doesn't take a genius to figure out what that cowboy has stashed in his saddlebag," Jarod said lightly, as he pulled his hat forward and looked away.

"Natasha's up," he said quietly.

Natasha expertly guided Goliath into the ring. Dana concentrated her complete attention on her second student. Natasha had remained relaxed all morning and Dana did not anticipate any problems. True to his nature, Goliath manoeuvred the course without the slightest hesitation. The pair made it all look so simple. They were clean and evenly paced, a perfected mastery of movement. They executed the course as a sole force, a spontaneous creation of power and grace that was certain to make a favorable impression on any judge.

Dana had had high hopes for the team, and she was not disappointed. She knew they had both fulfilled her expectations.

"You must be pleased." Jarod smiled, looking quite pleased himself. "Darren should make ribbons and Natasha might have made the class."

"We'll see soon enough," Dana replied.

The last of the contestants were completing their turns. Once they had all finished, a ring steward proceeded to select six horses from the group of competitors. These riders would be required to lead their horses into the ring at a trot, in order to be checked for soundness. Natasha and Darren qualified amongst the six. The steward then lined up the contenders in order of their placement in the class.

Natasha took her position first in line and Darren placed a well-deserved third.

Dana's students walked out of the show ring leading their horses, Natasha carrying a plaque and each horse's bridle was adorned with a large rosette. Jarod and Dana quickly made their way through the crowd, Jarod being congratulated by fellow equestrians and acquaintances. They eventually reached Natasha and Darren.

"You guys did a great job out there," Jarod praised them warmly. "You've done the ranch proud."

Natasha held the plaque out to Jarod.

"For your wall of fame," she told him, a satisfied smile on her face.

"I don't think so, Natasha. You keep that one, you've earned it. It was a fantastic ride and I wouldn't dream of stealing your glory." Jarod flatly refused the plaque and Dana could tell that Natasha appreciated the gesture.

"And you, young man," Jarod slapped Darren's shoulder. "That was an impressive debut in the show circuit. You looked like a pro."

"Thank you, sir," Darren replied as Jarod winced.

"God, I feel like Bruce Cook. Darren, drop the sir, okay? Just call me Jarod."

"You both did extremely well. Try and stay focussed, your next class is coming up," Dana reminded them, just as a tall man with salt-and-pepper hair boldly interrupted them.

He nodded curtly at the group and addressed Darren.

"Well, Darren. That was a mediocre round," he said, depreciatingly. "Hopefully you'll show a little more fire in your next class." The man pointedly regarded the plaque in Natasha's arms.

The group was stunned by the man's blunt manner.

Darren's features tensed as he introduced his father to them. "Jarod, Dana, Natasha: this is my father, Michael Stanton."

The man's eyes narrowed as he impatiently acknowledged their presence with another curt nod of his head. He eyed Jarod. "We've already met."

Dana was speechless and she looked to Jarod, hoping he would deal with this abrasive individual. Jarod's expression remained unaltered, but Dana could sense the difference in him by his steady gaze and his deliberate, even tone as he addressed Mr. Stanton, making an effort to diffuse the sudden tension.

"Your son is a very talented rider, we are fortunate to have him on our team, Mr. Stanton."

"I bet you are. I told him, you want to ride? Fine, don't waste your time with sideliners and hobby-horses. He should be in a real program." Mr. Stanton's words were heavily laced with sarcasm.

Darren flinched.

Jarod's jaw tightened, and Darren deliberately cut in between them. "Don't bother, Jarod. He's not listening." His voice was flat as he mounted Empire, turning his back on his father and walked off.

Natasha made a move forward but Dana put a restraining hand on her arm. "Mr. Stanton, no disrespect intended, but now was not the time to be airing your personal opinions, whatever they may be. Darren is competing in a few minutes. A little consideration would have been more appropriate," Dana spoke up defiantly. She was unable to stop herself, the hurt look on Darren's face had been too much for her to remain silent.

Michael Stanton turned to face Dana, contempt evident in his tone.

"My expectations for my son are high. I want the best for him." His implication that Kingsley Ranch and its personnel were somehow less than that was clear. "I don't owe you any explanations. It's really none of your business, young lady…no disrespect intended," he added, abruptly taking his leave.

"What an idiot!" Natasha called after him. She handed her award over to Dana. "I'm going to find Darren."

Dana was having a difficult time trying to control her anger. "What an odious man. I can't believe that's Darren's father."

"Poor kid." Jarod quietly agreed. "Even if Darren would have placed first in the class, the outcome would still have been the same, the push would be on for the next show, the next level. With people like that, everything is just adding fuel to the fire."

"I hope you don't think I was out of line." Dana was upset and struggling to recover her equanimity.

"You handled yourself well," Jarod told her. "There's a lot more here than meets the eye."

Dana looked at him, not understanding the purport of his words.

"I've met Mr. Stanton before," Jarod explained slowly. "The circumstances were less than pleasant. Still, it's no excuse to use your son to further your own gain."

Jarod checked his watch. "Here, I'll put the plaque in the pick-up for now. We'd better get a move on, or we'll be missing their second class." He returned just as the loudspeaker was announcing Darren and Natasha's class.

They reached the show ring as Darren's number was being called up. Dana studied him carefully. He was tight, his mouth pulled in a thin line.

"This is not good." Dana shook her head slowly and looked towards Jarod, who also seemed concerned.

Darren took the first four fences with one rail tapped, although it remained in place. On his approach to the fifth jump, he pulled Empire short.

"Oh, no!" Dana cried in dismay as the gelding stumbled forward through the obstacle with Darren losing his balance, falling hard to the ground. For a second, he lay motionless, Empire's reins still held in his grip.

"Damn it!" Jarod moved in closer to the rail of the ring. Dana instinctively made a motion to run into the ring and Jarod firmly held her arm. "Wait, Dana. Give him the chance to pull himself up."

Darren stood and straightened his helmet, slapping the dust off his beige breeches as the horse circled around him. Darren carefully examined Empire's legs for injury, then re-mounted. Taking up a slow canter, he determinedly completed his course.

The audience gave a loud round of applause as Darren exited the ring.

"Do you want to go to him, or should I?" Jarod asked her.

Dana paused before answering, weighing her decision carefully. "I have to stay for Natasha. You go, Jarod. Tell Darren not to worry. I'll see him after he's had a chance to pull himself together."

Dana could barely bring herself to concentrate on Natasha's ride, she was so furious with Darren's father. She realized she had been right to stay at the ring, she was too emotional right now to have been any help to Darren. Jarod was better suited, he never pushed or pried or judged. If anyone could make Darren feel better about himself, it would be Jarod.

Jarod searched the grounds and finally came across Darren behind one of the barns, cooling down Empire.

"Are you okay?" Jarod almost added 'son' to his words, but stopped himself in time.

"Yeah." Darren looked at the ground. "I look like a coward, hiding away like this, but I just couldn't face another run-in with my dad." Darren was trying hard to control himself. "Not right now, anyways." He lifted his head and looked away.

"Father and son relationships aren't always easy," Jarod said, drawing from experience. "Sometimes it takes a while to be able to accept each other as equals...and as human."

Darren shook his head.

"And for what it's worth," Jarod continued. "I don't think you're a coward. Being brave is not a quality you prove to someone else, it's something you carry from within. It took courage to finish that course, and I don't think you did it for me, or Dana, or...your father. You did it for yourself."

For the first time, Darren looked Jarod in the eye as he considered the truth in what he said.

"At least Empire's not hurt."

"At least you're both not hurt. It's a sport. It's a risk you take every time you enter the ring."

They stood for a while, in silence. Jarod could see Darren was thinking things through and he quietly let him be.

"What did Dana think? I really let her down." Darren said finally.

"Why don't you ask her that question yourself?" Jarod smiled re-assuringly at Darren.

Darren nodded in agreement. "I think I'd like to find out how Natasha did."

They slowly made their way to barn #9.

"Jarod?" Darren turned to face him, just before they entered the barn. "Thanks."

Darren led Empire to the cross-ties and began removing his saddle.

When Dana entered the barn, she found Darren and Jarod relaxing in the aisle. Darren had already changed into jeans and a denim shirt, and Empire was in his stall. She tentatively approached them, setting Natasha's second award on her tack box.

"Is that from her first class or her second?" Darren asked as he went over to examine it.

"It's from her second. The first is in the pick-up," Dana explained, a smile breaking across her pretty face. "She's cooling Goliath down, she'll be in soon."

"Way to go!" Darren came up to Dana. "I'm sorry I messed up, Dana."

"We've all taken falls, Darren. I don't want to trivialize how you must be feeling..." Dana paused, realizing she wasn't quite sure what Darren was feeling. He looked a lot better than she had anticipated. "Just think of it as a form of christening," she said softly.

Natasha entered the barn, leading Goliath. Jarod and Darren went up to greet her, congratulating her on her success. Bypassers looked on and smiled.

"Darren, let's get the plaques into your car, while the girls get Goliath settled. I'm getting hungry. When we're done, we'll take a break and get some lunch," Jarod suggested.

A makeshift restaurant had been set up under a gigantic tent, offering a variety of fast foods. No sooner had they sat down at an available table, when a very stunning blonde came over to them.

"Jarod, honey!" She bent down and kissed his cheek. "I was hoping I'd see you here today."

Jarod stood. "Monica, it's been awhile." He looked over her trim form. Her pale blond hair was beautifully arranged and her face carefully made-up. He smiled warmly at her, then turned his attention to the table. "Everyone, this is Monica Morgan, a friend and an accomplished rider in her own right. Monica: meet Natasha Hustak, Darren Stanton and Dana Northington. Dana's come all the way from Maine and is staying with us, at Kingsley."

"How do you do," Monica replied civilly, as her smoky gray eyes swept across the members of the party. Her gaze settled for a moment on Dana. "Why in heaven would anyone ever leave Maine for this dust bowl? I can't imagine." There was a polished affectation to her tone.

She looked up at Jarod. "Maybe it's not the dust that drew her out here?" Monica punctured her silvery words with a playful wink.

"Give me a break," Natasha murmured under her breath and Dana had to struggle to keep a straight face. Dana attempted to read Jarod's expression and failed. He seemed taken with the attractive woman, was he being polite or pleased?

"Daddy will be ecstatic to see you, Jarod. He's always asking me why you don't stop by anymore." Monica laid a delicate hand on his arm, her upturned face petulant.

"I've been pretty occupied with business and the ranch. Surely your father knows what that's like. Would you care to join us, Monica?" Jarod extended an invitation, politely pulling out a chair.

Dana was dismayed at the prospect of Monica joining them for lunch. She intuitively recognized her immediate dislike of the woman for what it was: jealousy, and she was disconcerted by the fact. She had no right to feel that way.

"I'd love to, honey, but Daddy's waiting for me. You must come by barn #7 and see my new gelding," Monica insisted. "I'll be competing on him this afternoon." She smiled seductively at Jarod.

"I'll try to stop in when we're finished here," Jarod replied, noncommittally. "It's been lovely seeing you again, Monica."

Monica kissed his cheek for a second time and walked away. Jarod sat back down, reaching for his drink.

"She's quite demonstrative, isn't she?" Dana could not resist pointing out and Natasha burst into laughter.

Jarod sat back in his chair, his blue eyes alight with mischief. "Now, now. Monica is an affectionate woman. I don't think it's anything I'd hold against her."

"Obviously," Dana replied shortly with a grin.

This time even Darren had a hard time stifling a laugh. "I wouldn't mind being held against her," he joined in. "That is one good-looking woman."

"That she is." Jarod smiled and continued with his lunch.

Dana checked her watch and realized she would be riding in just over an hour. "I'm going to change and get Paska ready," she said.

"I'll come and give you a hand," Natasha offered, getting up from her chair.

"Dana, I'll find you before it's time for your class." Jarod stood. "Darren, are you coming with me?"

"Sure am."

As the girls made their way to barn #9 and Dana couldn't help but notice that the guys were on route to barn #7.

A feeling of disappointment settled over her as she watched him go and as she struggled with that ache. She realized how wide the chasm was between her fantasy and what was the reality of her life.

She caught Natasha watching her and smiled brightly. "Looks like the guys are going to check out the competition," Dana said lightly, realizing too late her unfortunate choice of words.

Natasha remained silent, shrugging her shoulders as they entered the barn. Dana changed into her riding clothes while Natasha brought Paska out of her stall. Dana felt more in control dressed in her riding attire and with her first class before her, she had little room to worry about things she could not change.

She went to check on Paska and get the horse readied. The mare had traveled well and the strange surroundings caused her little anxiety. Paska had lived at a racetrack and was well adjusted to a hectic environment.

"Well, big girl. Are you ready to show everybody your stuff?" Dana fondly stroked the mare's shining neck.

Natasha saddled her while Dana reached for Paska's supple bridle, placing it over the mare's head, gently inserting the bit into her mouth. She led the magnificent mahogany out into the sunshine. Kingsley Ranch had brought their finest to Mora County and Dana experienced a rush of excitement. There would be no limitations to hamper her in the show ring. She would be free to capture the brass ring, to go for the best.

Dana mounted Paska and the horse did her customary dance, a vestige of her racing days. Dana led the mare to the warm-up area. She deliberately put Paska through repetitive groundwork, loosening the mare up. Before finishing, Dana rode Paska over two 4' verticals, the mare accomplishing the challenge easily. The loudspeaker called Dana's class to the show ring.

Once they arrived there, Dana dismounted, handing her reins over to Natasha. The riders of this class were allotted a brief interval to walk the course, an opportunity to inspect the jumps and familiarize themselves with the variety of obstacles in the ring.

"Natasha, keep her calm and walking," Dana instructed before entering the ring on foot along with some of her co-competitors. She studied the course carefully, examining each jump individually. The only problem she might encounter would be with fences #7 and #8. It was an in-out combination and the turn leading into it would be complicated. Overall, Dana approved of the course.

Jarod was standing by the gate as Dana walked out of the show ring. Monica, seated on a muscular chestnut, was by his side.

"What do you think of the course, Dana?"

"I like it and Paska will certainly enjoy it. It's big and scopey." Dana's tone enthusiastic and confident.

"It appears we are in the same class," Monica said cutely, smiling down from her mount at Jarod. "Carter also favors this genre of course." She patted the gelding.

Dana couldn't help but stare at Monica blankly. Everything about Monica was such a put-on, she thought. She recognized Jarod's look of quiet amusement as he noticed her reaction and she felt her color rise.

"Honey, would you mind checking my girth?" Monica asked sweetly.

"I'd be delighted," he responded in a gentlemanly fashion, all the while a bemused smile hovering on his lips.

"I'm going to find Paska," Dana said. She turned on her heel as Jarod was about to tighten Monica's girth.

Jarod was enjoying this far too much, Dana thought, her temper building. Ever since this woman had made her appearance at lunch she had monopolized Jarod's attention, and he had happily fallen in with every suggestion. Monica was so...so plastic!

Dana drew in a staggered breath. She was taken aback by the intensity of her emotion. She had no claims on this man. What he did with his time, and whom he chose to spend it with was really none of her concern. An image came to her, an image of two figures kissing in the moonlight.

She shook herself. Now was not the time or the place to allow her thoughts to run rampant. She briskly made her way to Natasha and the horse.

"How's Paska doing?" Dana asked as she accepted the reins from Natasha and mounted.

"Great. She's relaxed," Natasha responded.

Dana guided the horse closer to the ring. Her number was called over the loudspeaker.

She closed her eyes and cleared her mind, then rode into the ring. She respectfully bowed her head to the judge in formal acknowledgement and took up a strong canter. Paska responded brilliantly to Dana's command, sailing over her first jump in a heartbeat. Dana pushed the mare onward. They continued in efficient motion to the next fence, Dana leaning forward, in position over the mare's muscular shoulders, her arms close to Paska's outstretched neck. Dana kept the horse tight, precise; mentally counting her strides as they wove through the course. They cleared the water jump and soared over the triple with Paska's forelegs tucked tightly under her powerful form.

Dana sharply guided the mare through the #7 and #8 combination. This horse had heart and feared nothing, and even though each obstacle purposefully differed from the one before, Paska jumped them all alike, brave and clear. They completed the course and crossed the finish line, Dana reaching forward to stroke Paska's neck.

Jarod had closely observed the entire performance and he now walked over to her. Dana was a beautiful sight, sitting tall on her horse, her delicate features glowing with accomplishment. Her hair was tucked away under her helmet and her riding attire, the black jacket and brilliant white breeches, finely sculptured her shapeliness.

"That was spectacular," he complimented.

Dana swung her right leg over Paska and lightly dismounted. Natasha and Darren joined them.

"That was a great round," Darren told her admiringly. "I've counted only two other clear rounds and there are five horses left to jump."

Natasha took the reins from Dana and began walking Paska.

Jarod and Dana moved in closer to the ring. Dana was still caught up in the fire of competition and had little to say. She had just completed a clean course and in a few minutes she would return to a shortened jump-off. She was reluctant to break her spell of concentration.

They watched in silence as Monica entered the ring.

Dana immediately noted the difference between Monica's riding style and her own. Where Dana strived to become one with the horse, Monica rode in a very controlling manner. She was definitely the driver, nevertheless, the big gelding obeyed well and they finished with a clear round.

Jarod surreptitiously watched Dana as she observed the last of the competitors complete the course. Her expression gave nothing away. Once again he felt the power of her self-control, the elusive and understated quality of her character. Whatever she was feeling, she kept it to herself and Jarod was mesmerized by her mystery. Although he had frequently seen her extend a hand to help another, it never seemed to occur to her to accept such comfort from anyone else.

As if suddenly aware of his attention, Dana turned to face him. She read the depth of expression in his eyes and she hesitated.

For a moment in time they were alone amongst a crowd of people.

"I think I'd better get ready," she said slowly. "I'll see you later."

Jarod nodded as she turned away.

The jumps had been raised for the second round. The course was shortened to eight fences and the clock frequently played the deciding factor with fractions of a second dividing two equally well done performances, swiftly separating the winners from the losers. This course was deliberately contrived with the objective that only one individual would stand successful.

Dana's number was the first called. The onus was on her to have a clean round in the best time, she did not have the luxury of knowing how her opponents would perform.

Dana consciously obliterated all else from her mind. All that existed to her now was the jump before her and the horse beneath her. Paska rapidly moved towards each fence, attacking the obstacle with strength and spirit and they finished the course cleanly, to a thunderous applause.

Paska glistened in a fine sweat as they exited the show ring.

Dana dismounted, her lips curved in a wide smile, her radiant eyes dancing with the rush.

Natasha and Darren congratulated her success. Dana made her way to the ring rail and Jarod.

"Now that was a strong performance," Jarod said with feeling.

The following two riders both finished behind Dana: one incurring four faults, the other riding a clean round, but unable to capture Dana's time.

Monica entered the show ring. Dana glanced at Jarod, who was watching intently. Dana also turned her attention to the young blonde woman atop the big coppery gelding. Monica was already at the fifth fence when Carter flattened out over the oxer, tapping the rail with his hind hooves, causing it to fall to the ground loudly.

"Congratulations, Dana! You've won your first class in New Mexico." Jarod gave her a warm hug.

"Thank you. Paska has a lot of power and courage. She deserves most of the credit." Dana smiled, glowing. They made their way to Natasha, Paska and Darren.

The announcer called out a series of numbers and Dana led Paska back into the ring, along with the other horses and riders that had placed in the class.

Jarod watched as Dana graciously accepted her award. He was overcome with pride, and it came to him that it had little to do with the success his horses had achieved today. All of his thoughts began and ended with Dana. The pure joy he was experiencing was unlike anything he had ever felt before. This was more than friendship, more than desire...this was love.

- Chapter 10 -

June contentedly made her way around the spacious ranch kitchen. She hummed under her breath as she busily wiped down surfaces, tidying things as she went along. The kitchen windows were opened wide and a warm. Dry breeze surrounded her, catching her from one side and then the other. It was going to be a hot day, but a beautiful one nonetheless.

Each summer the topic of air conditioners would inevitably come up with Jarod invariably pointing out how one would lighten June's workload, and she would agree that there were times when there seemed to be dust and sand blown into the most uncanny places, but in the end June would decline and it would be put off to another year.

June loved the feel of the breeze and the smell of the earth as it slowly baked by the warmth of the sun, the sounds of the horses outside as they called to each other. Her linen was already out on the line and would be dry in no time, folded and put away before the strong heat of the afternoon. Sun spilled into her kitchen, laying across the tiled floor in columns of light sliding sharply into shadow.

The fragrant scent of fresh herbs wafted throughout the room.

She stood for a second and surveyed her domain, as always feeling fortunate for what God had chosen to send her. June absently wiped her flattened hands across her apron and the crinkle of paper recalled her from her reverie.

Pulling a posted letter from her pocket, she decided to sit at the sturdy wooden table and take a few moments to herself. The letter was postmarked from Vermont and June quickly recognized her sister Diane's script. June's family was scattered across the country from state to state, so many years ago they had begun a chain letter. Each individual would add a personal postscript to the existing letter and then forward its entirety onto the next family member, continually gathering additional news at each stop. Once June's own bit of news had made its journey across the distance and returned to her, she would retrieve it and save it, sending out a sequel. Those letters reposed in a cedar-lined trunk at the foot of her bed, a journal of her life, a continuing diary of her time on this earth.

It was a pleasurable pastime, managing to hold its own against an increasingly competitive long-distance call market.

Of course, June smiled to herself as she read. Some family members were more imaginative and inspired correspondents than others; some by nature and others by design.

She carefully refolded the pages before her and gently tucked them away.

Her sister had been widowed late last fall and was having a difficult time adjusting to the sudden solitude of her life. Diane complained of things that June took for granted, describing them from a wholly different perspective.

June was at a loss to explain why she herself had never married. The opportunity had arisen, but some things were never meant to be, she supposed. She had long since dealt with any feelings of regret, such as they were. She had made her choices freely and her life was a good one, a happy one.

Jarod had been such a young boy when she had come to care for him, an affectionate youngster surrounded by plenty, yet missing so much. June had witnessed first-hand the torture his father had endured with the loss of his beloved partner. June had never experienced that depth of love and in some ways at this point in her life, she was glad of it. Malcolm Kingsley had become a bitter shell of a man, never accepting or understanding the early death of his wife.

At times he had been unbearable to work for and harsh on his son, but June understood his pain for what it was. The joy of his life had been stolen from his embrace and he never recovered from that tragedy, right up to the time of his own demise.

It was only as Malcolm lay dying on his hospital bed, face to face with his own mortality, did he realize that in finally joining his wife he would be leaving his son behind. It was the first and the last time June ever heard Malcolm tell his son that he loved him. He had found his peace at last.

Dana secured the latch on Paska's stall door. She made her way down the barn aisle, instinctively checking the horses as she passed by, carrying the tack she'd used in her lesson back to the tack room, where she found Annie sitting on a trunk.

"Hey there, Annie." Dana replaced her equipment and brushed her hands across her pant legs. She removed her riding helmet and turned to face an unusually quiet Annie. "Is something wrong?"

"No," Annie paused and continued slowly. "Nothing's wrong, I think I'm still just in a state of shock." She smiled shyly.

Dana approached sitting down beside the girl. "What are you talking about?" She tilted her head and sat down beside the girl.

"You're going to be so surprised," Annie answered quietly, her face deepening into a blush as she slowly extended her left hand. An intricate gold band with a solitary diamond encircled her ring finger.

"Oh, my God!" Dana exclaimed. "When did this happen? This is wonderful, congratulations!"

She gave Annie a quick hug.

"Thank you." Annie's blush became even more apparent. "Kent invited me to supper last night, we've sort of been seeing each other since the party... well, dating actually," Annie admitted, almost embarrassed. "Yesterday, he told me he had something important he wanted to talk about. I was in a fit of nerves all day, I didn't dare to hope... he's been acting differently lately, I don't know. I didn't know what to expect."

"Oh, my God!" Dana repeated. "This is so sweet."

Dana thought back to the period of time before the party when the two girls were getting ready in her room. "I guess that outfit must've done the trick," she teased.

"I feel like I've loved him almost from the minute I first saw him. Oh, Dana, I never imagined this would ever happen! I feel so lucky." Annie sighed, her thoughts wandering off to some secret special place and suddenly Dana felt entirely alone.

Dana stood and forced a bright smile on her face. "You are both very lucky," she agreed. "Annie, you will make Kent a wonderful partner in life," she told her sincerely. "Does anyone else know?"

"My parents know, we told them last night." Annie laughed. "We woke them up. We'd like to tell Jarod this afternoon. Do you think he'll be okay with this? It hasn't interfered with our work here... well, just that once..." Annie faltered, blushing once again. "Oh, I don't know if I'll be able to look Jarod straight in the face now."

Dana stared at Annie uncomprehendingly. An amused smile slowly spread across her features.

"Not like that," Annie denied, quickly making a face.

Kent appeared in the doorway, his deep voice startling them both.

"I was wondering where everyone was."

They looked at him in surprise, then quickly looked to each other and crumpled into a fit of giggles.

"What's so funny?" Kent began to shake his head in disbelief as he watched the girls make several unsuccessful attempts to recover themselves. His exasperation slowly gave way to humor. "Have you girls been sniffing shoe polish, or what?"

Dana walked over to him, smiling. She reached out and shook his hand. "Congratulations, Kent. I know you'll be very happy. This is lovely news."

"Thanks, Dana."

"Well, I don't know how I'll get any work done today, with all this romance in the air. I'd better get busy." As she walked by Kent she stopped, giving him a brief hug. She flashed Annie a smile goodbye and made her way to Masquerade's stall.

As Dana put Masquerade through her routine, she kept catching herself falling into a wave of wistful envy as she imagined the happiness that came from finding a true love, one you believed would last a lifetime. She thought of Annie and Kent and how their relationship had evolved. Obviously, once Kent had recognized what his heart desired, there had been little hesitation in his making sure that it would become a reality. Could there really be such a thing as destiny?

Annie had waited patiently and now her dreams were coming true. It was no wonder she was ecstatic, Dana thought to herself, recalling Annie's look of joy.

Once again a feeling of emptiness swept over Dana. A cold ache lay heavy on her heart. When would she feel free again? When would she be able to accept love, to trust someone and to be open, to be vulnerable to another person?

Even as those thoughts crossed her mind, she could feel her habitual defenses fall into place. She scolded herself. Today should be a day of celebration, not an excuse to indulge in self-pity.

She put Masquerade into a hard gallop. As the mare picked up speed, Dana unknowingly attempted to outrun the pain that haunted her. She lined up the mare to three fences that stood sequentially before them and boldly she urged the mare onward, focussing and drawing all her mental energies to that single objective, nearer, nearer, now. Masquerade jumped them one after the other with ease.

Dana gradually brought the horse back to a walk.

The sun was beginning to peak and with midday approaching Dana decided the session had gone on long enough. She rode Masquerade out of the ring and turned her towards the trail. Dana routinely cooled the horses down this way. This trail in particular was quite scenic, following the side of the mountain which was more wooded. Horse and rider would take the path slowly, they were in no hurry.

Dana couldn't help but feel that her life was in a kind of limbo; she was deliberately cut off from her past and unable to move towards her future. Although she was feeling stronger about herself and more confident in her surroundings, there was still a piece of her that played sentry, remaining ever watchful, careful, not giving away too much and accepting even less. It was so hard to let that go.

A heavy sigh escaped her. Masquerade had reached a summit point in the trail and stood awaiting direction. Dana relaxed in the saddle and looked out over the ranch that lay before her. Since her arrival in New Mexico, she'd spent almost each and every day without exception at Kingsley Ranch.

Dana surveyed the wide ranch house in the distance and thought of June and Jarod. When she'd first come here, she'd looked upon this place as exile but eventually she had come to look upon this place as home.

It came over her in a rush, how she loved him and she wasn't even sure when or how it had happened, though part of her was not surprised by the sudden revelation. She thought of the times when they would run into each other unexpectedly and her heart would catch inside her so hard it would hurt.

Was she ready to trust him and greater yet, was she ready to trust herself?

New Mexico was the Land of Enchantment and maybe anything could be possible here, Dana thought as she silently stared at the vastness before her. She was not the first to come to this place seeking a new life.

She pulled on her reins and turned Masquerade back the way they had come.

Dana was in the process of rubbing the horse down in the barn aisle when Kent and Annie approached her.

"Hi," Kent was the first to speak. "Annie and I were talking things over and we thought we'd go up to the main house with you to give Jarod the big news."

"Actually, that's probably a good idea. From what Jarod was saying this morning, I think he's planning to leave for a few days on business. I'll just finish up with Masquerade and then we can be on our way." Dana threw Annie a confident smile. "I'm sure Jarod will be very happy for you both."

Dana unhooked the cross-ties and led the mare into her stall, giving her a final pat before sliding the door closed.

Annie and Kent were waiting for Dana just outside the barn doors. Kent's arms were resting easily over Annie's shoulders and her upturned face was smiling.

"We were hoping you would come in with us, when we talk to Jarod," Annie invited Dana as she joined the couple.

"Me?" Dana was surprised by the request.

"Well, you know Jarod better than we do and it would be reassuring to me to have a friend there." As they started walking to the main house Dana couldn't help but sense their excitement.

Dana was touched by Annie's words, pleased to be considered a friend, but finding it surprising that Annie would assume that Jarod and Dana were that close.

They entered the house. Kent and Annie paused and looked expectantly at Dana. Jarod's office door was ajar and Dana popped her head around the corner as she knocked softly.

"Jarod? Do you have a few minutes?"

Jarod was sitting back in his chair, arms folded across his chest and his eyes narrowed as he studied his computer screen. At the sound of her voice he looked up and sat forward.

"Is there a problem?" he asked.

Dana motioned to Annie and Kent and they followed her into the office.

"Now I know something's wrong." Jarod stood, looking apprehensive.

"Everything is fine, Jarod," Kent looked out of place in the office, his hat in his hands. "Annie and I had something we wanted to tell you."

"Well, that's a relief." a reassuring smile broke across Jarod's face. "What can I do for you?"

Kent nudged Annie who looked mutely at Jarod. Jarod turned his eyes from Kent to Annie.

"Well, is anyone going to let me in on what's going on?" Jarod's voice had the slightest edge in it.

Kent cleared his throat.

"Yes, sir. Annie and I got engaged last night and we just wanted to let you know." Kent rapidly blurted out the words.

There was a moment of complete silence as Jarod digested the information. He abruptly strode over to Annie, embracing her and kissing her cheek as he reached for Kent's hand.

"Congratulations to both of you. I wish you the very best. This is wonderful news." Jarod was genuinely happy for them.

"Have you set a date, or is it still too early?" Dana asked the couple.

"We've both agreed on a spring wedding, but we haven't set any date," Annie replied.

"Well, that allows plenty of time for me to throw you a party, consider it my engagement gift." Jarod proposed.

"Oh, we couldn't accept that..."

"No, that's too much."

"I insist," Jarod continued in his easy manner. "Pick the date. It's not everyday that people come across true love, this is something worth celebrating." Jarod eyes strayed to Dana, their look unfathomable.

She quietly returned his gaze, a smile hovering on her full lips. She dared for once to be bold and she refused to look away.

Kent was thanking Jarod profusely and reluctantly Jarod turned to deal with matter at hand.

"I'll be away for the next couple of days, unfortunately," he explained. "When I get back you can let me know what's agreeable to you.

You've both been at the ranch for quite some time and you're like family. It's only fitting that we have a party here."

"Well, we'd better get back to work." Kent put his arm around Annie's shoulders.

"Thanks for everything, Jarod." Annie added again as they took their leave.

"It's my pleasure." Jarod saw them to the door then abruptly turned, effectively blocking Dana's exit in one smooth motion.

"So, Dana, what do you think of all this?" Jarod asked her quietly.

His face was just inches from hers and his sudden maneuver had taken her by complete surprise. When she spoke she had a difficult time keeping her voice steady. She felt breathless.

"I'm very happy for them. They were lucky to find each other, and now they're planning their future. Everything is working out for them." Dana faltered to a stop, feeling like she was rattling on. It was difficult for her to think sensibly with him immediately before her, with that deliberate way he had. He was so close she could feel the heat coming from his body.

Instinctively she dropped her gaze, her thick lashes carefully hiding her expression. Her breath came quickly now, her heart beating rapidly in her slender frame. A piece of her urged her to flee, yet she made no movement.

From memory, Jarod could recall the velvet touch of her skin beneath his fingers. Her standing there triggered a few other memories as well. After all this time Dana was still if not more of a mystery to him than before.

"Look at me, Dana," he whispered.

Slowly, she lifted her eyes to meet his. She was ready, ready to tell him what he'd waited so long to hear. She swallowed hard and her tender lips parted, but the words choked in her throat.

He reached out to touch her but misread her silence and smoothly opened the door instead.

"Well, take good care of things while I'm gone. I'll be back in few days," he said as he gently propelled her out of the office and closed the door.

Dana barely had time to realize what had happened. Her heart was pounding so loudly it sounded like waves crashing in her ears. At one point she had been certain Jarod was going to kiss her and in the next breath she was standing in the hallway staring at the door.

It took some time for her to collect herself and once she did, she didn't know if she should laugh, curse or cry.

Dana's week sped by rapidly. She had not had the chance to see Jarod, he'd left the ranch while she was in the barn. Doubts began to assail her, maybe he'd left that way deliberately, maybe he'd had a change of heart, maybe she'd read more into the situation than was actually there and maybe Kent and Annie's engagement had foolishly encouraged her to dare to hope that she could have that happiness also.

She was weary of the endless bickering going on inside her head and she wished with all her might that she could ignore the growing hunger in her heart. With a bleak sense of sadness Dana began to appreciate the subtle difference between being lonely and being alone.

All of her life she had determinedly worked towards a goal and she was usually confident and successful at achieving it, with her head and her heart reaching towards the same objective. This raging turmoil inside of her was new and unwelcome and she was hardput to keep it in check.

A lifetime of discipline and reserve stood in her stead and at the ranch, it was business as usual. Her work was physically demanding and the rigors of preparing for competition offered Dana some relief, there could be no second-guessing in the arena and if Dana was under any strain, no one was the wiser.

Annie and Kent were busy making plans for what promised to be a fiesta of celebration and Dana couldn't help but be affected by their excited anticipation. She found herself facing their engagement party with an overwhelming feeling of ambiguity.

Dana awoke the morning of the Rosedale show feeling on edge. She had once again slept fitfully and the fatigue was beginning to take its toll. Jarod had returned from his business trip the day before yesterday and had been conspicuously busy ever since.

She forced herself out of bed in the semi-darkness of predawn and made her way to the bathroom. Turning on the light, she rubbed at her eyes with fingers that trembled slightly.

She ran a hot bath and lowered herself into the steaming bubbles. Today would be a long day, she could tell. Emily and Sue would be looking to her for support, it would be Masquerade's first show under her training and Jarod would be there. More than likely, Monica would also be present she thought as she made a face, sliding deeper into the tub.

Closing her eyes, she mentally pictured herself in the show ring successfully going through the course mounted on Masquerade. She repeated the process a number of times until she was able to visualize the judge placing the rosette on Masquerade's bridle. It was a strategy she had been taught early in training, a simple mental exercise that served to clear her mind.

Feeling more centered, she dressed and calmly made her way downstairs.

They arrived at the show grounds in Rosedale with ample time to spare. Sue and Emily had traveled along with Dana and Jarod, for which Dana was grateful.

The Rosedale show had more of a fair type environment than the last show, with many booths displaying local arts and crafts. Dana promised herself a visit to them if she had the opportunity later on.

Once again Jarod unloaded the horses while Dana registered. Dana, Sue and Emily would all be riding this morning in the same division although in separate classes; novice, junior, and senior.

"Deanna," Monica's well polished accent sounded behind Dana as she was turning to leave the registration building. "Is that you?"

Dana stopped and faced the petite blonde.

"It's Dana," she corrected politely.

"Yes, Dana. Oops! A slight faux pas, please forgive me." Monica tucked her fine hair behind one ear displaying a large pearl stud as she coolly surveyed Dana.

"Will you be exhibiting today?"

This girl is a walking dictionary, Dana thought to herself, once again irritated by the southern belle put-on, the artificial French influence Monica carried with her. In an area where Americans, Natives and Spaniards were so tightly woven, Monica attempted to place herself above that somehow, obliquely alluding to some French ancestry that was not there.

"Carter did not fare favorably the last time we competed together. I was wondering if we would have the opportunity to show his true ability today. We are grand competitors at heart." Monica's eyes narrowed slightly though her smile remained poised.

"I've always found it to be more challenging to compete within myself, to become my personal best," Dana said simply.

"My, my. What a singularly self-serving practice they encourage in New England! That sounds more like an excuse than a raison d'être." Monica laughed prettily. "You'll soon find we don't lend ourselves to such a facade of civility here. Everyone knows why they are in the ring."

"To the contrary, Monica. If either of us is guilty of practicing a facade of civility, it's not me," Dana offered as a parting shot as she turned and took her leave.

Dana arrived at the barn to find the two girls occupied, readying their mounts.

The morning went extremely well, Emily winning her class and Sue placing a strong third.

Everyone's spirits were high and it soon became time for Dana's class. Dana was making the final adjustments to Masquerade's girth when Jarod came over, looking uneasy.

"Are you sure about this, Dana? If something doesn't feel right in the warm-up, it's not too late to scratch the class. I don't want an accident," he added.

"You're worrying for nothing, Jarod. For someone who is usually so calm, this mare can really get you going." Dana laughed lightly, stroking Masquerade's long, gleaming neck.

"She unpredictable," he said shortly, justifying himself.

"Not anymore," Dana replied as she smoothly mounted the mare and trotted off.

During the warm-up Dana could feel Masquerade's attention occasionally stray to the sights and sounds that surrounded them, but a slight squeeze from Dana's legs managed to pull her back without quarrel. Dana had complete faith in Masquerade's ability and the mare sensed it from her, gaining confidence from Dana's consistent direction.

It was time. Dana's number was called into the ring. As she rode the horse in, she quickly scanned the rail and found Jarod watching anxiously. Dana gave him a reassuring nod and commanded the mare into an easy canter.

Timing would mean everything with this horse and it was up to Dana to deliver her commands with a steady hand, clearly but not harshly. Rider and horse would perform in unison, judging distance and speed, each inwardly confidant that the other would not let them down.

Their pace was a lesson in perfection with Masquerade willingly jumping the fences as if somehow understanding it was her moment to shine. Their hours and hours of schooling had paid off. The mare knew what Dana wanted from her and more importantly she perceived when it was that she wanted it.

Dana's heart filled with pride as they finished the course. She exited the ring and alighted from Masquerade as Jarod joined them.

"You did it," he said simply, but the expression on his face told her much more.

"Thank you. You saw it in her all along," Dana answered, looking up into his clear blue eyes.

"You give me credit I don't really deserve, I thought this horse was gone south. It was your persistence that brought her around." Jarod spoke truthfully.

They waited and observed the remainder of the class, but the other competitors were unable to match Dana and Masquerade's performance, the class was their win.

At the barn the mood was one of jubilation.

"I could easily get used to this winning thing," Jarod commented as he regarded the small group. "What about you girls?"

Emily and Sue were also pleased with their performances. Everyone was busy talking as Dana rubbed down the mare. There was a lot of activity going on around them and as they were finished with their competitions, they were now able to relax and enjoy their success.

Monica entered the barn and Dana immediately felt a sense of irritation, she impatiently pushed her hair from her forehead with the back of her arm and watched the woman with disbelief as she made her way toward them.

"Congratulations, Dana." She stressed the name slightly. "Another win, my, my. But, surely you don't win all the time?" Monica possessively laid her hand on Jarod's arm and smiled at Dana with impudence.

"Well, I'm not in the habit of wasting my time and energy unless I have some kind of indication that success is a strong possibility," Dana returned effortlessly, her frustration mounting.

This is ridiculous, Dana thought to herself, rolling her eyes as she led Masquerade into her stall. She had to give the woman credit, she was not easily daunted.

She walked back to where Jarod stood, Monica waiting attentively at his side.

"Daddy's planning a soirée, a little get-together. I was wondering if you had any plans for this evening?" Monica was asking. "That is if you're not too tired to have a good time." She tilted her pretty head to the side, looking quite alluring Dana had to admit.

"Excuse me," Dana interrupted. "I'm just going to look around and check out the vending booths." She moved around the couple.

"I'll come with you," Jarod offered quickly.

"No, no. You're busy. I won't be long." Dana made her escape.

She took her time browsing through the various stands, attempting to unwind and hardly feeling in a hurry to return to the barn. The booths displayed a wide selection of wares for purchase, leather goods, pottery, art and some of the handmade jewelry was quite exquisite, each piece unique in its own way. A particular silver chain caught Dana's attention and she gently held it up to the light, trying to make out the symbols that were engraved on it.

"It is the chain of lasting happiness, it will make your dreams come true," the Hispanic vendor told her, noticing her interest.

Dana nodded, carefully studying the chain. She would not admit that she believed in that kind of thing, but it was ironic that she was drawn to this individual piece. A smile crossed her face as she studied the necklace's detailed workmanship and decided to buy it. As she dropped her hand to her side, she realized in her haste to leave the barn she had not had the opportunity to change out of her riding clothes. Her money lay in the pocket of her jeans.

"I'm sorry. I don't have my money with me."

"That is no problem. I will hold it for you," the vendor suggested.

"I'll be back," Dana agreed.

She made her way back to the barn, cutting around the back of the large grandstand and crossing the dirt roadway that separated the show rings from the barns. As she reached the second barn she was forced to stop and wait while a young man attempted to load a protesting mare into a back-up trailer.

Dana immediately saw it was going to be a difficult maneuver, it was one of the few things that had a better success rate on the first try. The mare was becoming increasingly obstinate by the second as she cleverly manipulated every strategy possible to her own advantage.

Dana shook her head apprehensively as she watched the young man enter into what was rapidly becoming a battle of wits. She wasn't sure who was smarter, the man or the horse but brute strength was definitely in the mare's favor.

The young man noticed Dana as she patiently waited. "I don't have a lot of experience with this kind of thing," he admitted with a smile, looking discouraged.

"Change her mind," Dana suggested from the sidelines.

"What?"

"She has one objective in her head right now, namely she's not getting on that trailer. Give her something else to think about. Walk her around for a bit, cool her off a little. Bribery is always a handy tool. Shake her grain in front of her as you're loading her."

The young man tipped his hat back as a grin spread across his face. "I can't believe I forgot, that's what my brother did with her this morning!"

"No wonder she's not loading!" Dana began to laugh. "She's been trained to treats. Horses are creatures of habit."

"Yeah, my brother spoils her rotten." The young man stared admiringly at the now quiet animal. He led the horse towards the front of the trailer, opened the side door and reached for the bucket of feed.

"She's certainly used to getting her way."

He loaded the horse without further mishap and thanked Dana for her trouble.

Dana nodded and continued on her way. She was surprised when she got to the barn to find Jarod was also loading the horses. She hadn't realized they would be leaving so soon.

She quickly looked around and saw that Monica was nowhere to be found.

"I was just about to go and look for you," he told her as he led Apollo to the trailer.

"Anxious to get a move on, with the big soirée in front of you?" Dana almost snapped at him. The word soiree rolled off her tongue with exaggerated sarcasm.

Jarod stopped in his tracks, looked at the ground for a second then turned to face her. He paused before speaking, almost enjoying watching her discomfort.

"No," he answered slowly, taking his sweet time. "If you really want to know, I'm trying my damnedest to get out of that big soiree. It's not my idea of a good time and I thought you would've figured that out by now." He looked at her pointedly.

Dana's chin rose ever so slightly as she squared her delicate shoulders, furiously trying to think of a good comeback. Unconsciously her boot tapped the hard ground.

"Well, let's not waste all of our time then standing around acting smart." She turned on her heels and stomped into the barn.

Jarod smiled and shaking his head, he finished loading Apollo.

The drive back was quiet. They had the windows rolled down and the breeze was refreshing. It had been a hot day. Music played on the radio and Emily and Sue conversed in the backseat. They were almost home before Dana remembered about the necklace and she was embarrassed to be reminded of how it had come to slip her mind. Oh well, she thought, maybe she would be able to find another one.

Jarod watched Dana from the corner of his eye and he found her looking drawn, she seemed tired. They approached the ranch and it was not long before he stopped in front of the main house.

"Okay, Dana. Take a break, eat something, freshen up. Out you go," he urged, smiling at her.

"Are you sure? I should help..."

"Out," he commanded gently.

Obediently Dana opened the door and stepped down from the pickup. She made her way through the house to the kitchen and sat down on a stool. Dana put her elbows on the table and rested her chin in the palms of her hands.

June bustled out of the pantry, her arms filled with a collection of empty glass jars. "My dear, you're home early. Is everything alright?"

"Sure, everything is fine," Dana replied despondently. "The show went well."

June carefully set the jars on the table as she studied Dana.

"Let me make you a strong tea, dear," she said as she put the kettle on. "Are you feeling sick?"

Dana heaved a sigh. "No... I don't know."

"There, there," June patted Dana's shoulder, uncertain what to do. This was not the Dana she knew. "Nothing's as bad as all that." The whistle on the kettle began to sing and June prepared the tea. June placed the cup of tea in front of Dana and Dana looked up to see June's worried face. She pulled herself together and gave June a smile.

"I'm okay and everything went fine at the show, really," she stressed. "I'm just more tired than I realized, this tea is just what I needed. Thanks June," she reassured the older woman. "I'm going to take it to my room and wash off some of this dust."

Once upstairs, Dana ran a bath for the second time that day. She soaked in the tub and allowed her mind to wander idly until the water started to cool. She climbed out of the tub, wrapping her body in a thick towel.

She brushed out her hair, bringing back its luster and put a little blush on her face. She stared at herself in the mirror and she was pleased to find a semblance of her old self-staring back.

Dana stepped out of the bathroom and crossed the floor to her bed where she had laid out fresh clothes. As she dressed, something glittered on her pillow and caught her eye. She bent down and gently picked it up.

It was the chain.

"How did this get here?" Dana stared at it in bewilderment.

Incredible as it seemed, there was only one explanation, Jarod had to have placed it there. Somehow he must've seen her at the booth at the horseshow. Maybe he had been looking for her after all.

Smiling with pleasure, she walked to her dresser mirror and placed the necklace around her throat. A sudden warmth flowed through her.

She hurried outside to the barn in search of Jarod and found him at Mayday's stall.

"How's it going?" Dana asked as casually as she could.

He turned to face her. Her bright green eyes were dancing and her face was fresh and happy.

"Great, I'm all done and the horses are fine."

"Jarod, I just wanted to thank you for this." She touched her fingertips to the base of her throat to the silver chain that rested across her collarbone. "I don't know how you did it, but I'm very touched."

Jarod ran his hand through his sun-streaked hair, looking puzzled.

"I'd love to take the credit, but if you're talking about that chain, I've never seen it before. It's very nice," he added, not knowing what she expected him to say.

"Come on, you can tell me the truth," Dana urged him, eager to hear the words come from his lips.

"I am telling the truth, I don't know what you're talking about," Jarod denied firmly.

"You didn't buy me this necklace?" Dana asked in a subdued voice, confused.

He shook his head.

Everything seemed to come to her in slow motion. If Jarod had not brought her that chain then how did it come to be in her bedroom? Someone had to have put it there.

Her mind refused to work. Terror gripped her and she began to tremble visibly.

"Dana? What's wrong?" Jarod saw her face blanch as she began to sway. He reached out to catch her.

She struggled against him.

"Don't touch me! Let me go!" Dana cried.

"Okay, okay! I'm letting go," he said soothingly. "Look, I'm not touching you. Dana, talk to me. Tell me what's going on," he pleaded.

She pulled back and wrapped her arms around herself, leaning against the barn wall, tears in her eyes.

"Dana, you're going to have to talk to me eventually. You can't push me away forever." He didn't approach her, but his voice compelled her to listen.

"I can't!" She cried in desperation. "Don't you see? I just can't!"

"I want to help you. You're going to have to trust somebody, Dana. Let it be me," he paused. "What really brought you to New Mexico?" Jarod looked into her frightened eyes, speaking softly.

She turned her head away.

"No." He shook his head, his voice suddenly demanding. "Not this time. I'm telling you I love you, Dana. It's time you tell me the truth." As Jarod took a step towards her Dana flinched and he froze where he stood, unable to believe it.

"I can't take this anymore," his voice deepened with hurt. "And I can't make you let me in."

She remained silent. Tears were now streaming down her face.

"Damn it, Dana. I love you!" Jarod's voice choked with emotion as he held up his opened hands before him. "None of this makes any sense. This is futile!" He dropped his arms to his side in a rapid motion of surrender.

Jarod turned from her and stormed from the barn. She heard the barn door slam with force.

Exhausted and defeated, Dana's body slid slowly down the wall until it crumpled onto the floor. She drew her knees up close to her chest and began sobbing uncontrollably.

She'd lost so much already, she had little left to lose. She'd walked away from everything she'd ever worked for. She'd closed the door on her past and that future and had bravely tried to make a new life. All this time she'd mistakenly believed that she was moving forward, starting over. It was all a lie.

What a fool she had been.

Her tears were spent, she'd cried herself out. Shakily Dana stood and as she did she felt the chain caress her throat. She angrily grabbed at it with her fist and tore it from her neck, forcibly throwing it across the barn floor, to where it slid into the gutter.

-Chapter 11 -

Dana slept poorly that night, twice waking in a cold sweat, tormented by menacing dreams that she was unable to piece together or make any sense of. When morning finally made its debut, the only thing that offered her any solace was her resolution to tell Jarod everything.

There would be no more secrets and no more lies, and regardless of how he would react to what she had to say, she would be able to face him squarely.

With growing determination and a new found sense of direction Dana dressed in her riding breeches and solemnly made her way downstairs.

"Good morning, June." Dana scanned the kitchen, but could find no trace of Jarod. Last night he was nowhere to be found either and Dana realized that June was aware that something was amiss.

June noticed Dana's searching look.

"Good morning, dear. Mr. Kingsley came in quite late last night and I haven't seen him yet this morning," June offered as she began setting a place for Dana.

"No, that's alright, June." Dana forestalled her. "I'm just going to have coffee." She poured herself a mug of freshly perked coffee.

June hesitated momentarily.

"I don't mean to pry, but is there anything I can do?" June's tone was non-judgmental and her concern genuine.

"Thank you, June, but I've got to fix this myself." Dana respected the woman's intuition and appreciated her distaste for meddling. "I'm going to talk to Jarod as soon as I get the chance." She looked towards the doorway, unconsciously willing him to appear. "I guess for now I'll just go for a ride and get some fresh air." Dana hesitated another moment, hoping to hear the sound of Jarod's footstep, but there was only silence. She walked over to June and kissed her cheek. "I won't be too long."

Annie was busy doing chores at the opposite end of the barn when Dana entered. They briefly acknowledged each other before Dana turned into the tack room to gather her riding equipment. Hearing activity, Ben entered from the adjoining office.

"G'morning, Dana," he greeted her as she lifted up her saddle. He was immediately struck by her drawn features. His eyes narrowed as he studied her.

"Hello, Ben." Dana shifted the saddle to a more comfortable position, aware of his scrutiny. She made a motion towards the door.

"Something's going on," Ben said bluntly. "Jarod's nowhere to be found these days it seems, and you look like the cat just dragged you in." His words were curt but his manner was absent of criticism.

Dana gave him a weary smile.

"I know. I'm sorry," she said, feeling responsible. There was an awkward pause. Not knowing what else to say, she changed the subject. "I'm going to take Masquerade out hacking."

Ben considered pushing the matter further but as he looked at Dana's troubled face he decided to let the matter drop. "Here, I'll carry your things," he offered.

"It's okay, I'm fine with them, thanks." Dana carried the tack to Masquerade's stall.

The temperature outside was agreeable as Dana guided Masquerade past the barns and training ring. Preoccupied with her thoughts, she automatically turned the mare towards the wooded trail. Masquerade was quite familiar with this trail and Dana was content to let the mare set her own pace.

A mental image of the silver chain returned to Dana and a chill ran through her body. Forlornly she recalled yesterday's events knowing she had treated Jarod miserably. At the house that morning Dana had been sorely tempted to climb the wide staircase to Jarod's room, bang on his door and unburden her heart and soul. She had chosen instead to be patient, to wait until she was done riding before meeting with Jarod and offering him the truth. She prayed with all her might that he would still be willing to hear it.

[130]

She was desperately afraid she had already destroyed all her chances. Up to now her courage seemed to have the worst habit of deserting her just when she needed it the most. That was behind her now, she was determined that it would not happen again.

Masquerade abruptly came to a halt, refusing to move forward, her head held high and her ears back in protest. Instinctively, Dana quickly inspected the area immediately surrounding them. Her attention was drawn to a black jeep partially camouflaged in the wooded area. "What's that doing there?"

A man stepped out from behind a tree.

"No!" Dana cried.

Masquerade spooked at the stranger's unexpected appearance and Dana's heart leapt to her throat. Her grip stiffened as she frantically pulled up on the reins too sharply, trying to turn the mare around. Masquerade reared up high on her hind legs, her nostrils flaring, her eyes wild.

Dana's world began to spin and suddenly went black as she plunged to the ground.

The horse galloped off, blindly careening down the path.

The man hurried over to Dana's motionless form and paused, pursing his lips. This wasn't the way he had imagined their encounter. He quickly knelt to the ground and lightly ran his hands over the entire length of her body. Thank God, she was in one piece, he thought.

He noticed that her riding helmet must have become dislodged when she had tumbled to the ground. "A lot of good this stupid thing did you." He picked it up and tossed it into the brush, scowling.

She moaned quietly.

He loosened her hair and buried his face into a handful of generous locks.

"Oh Dana, Dana," he repeated absently under his breath.

She began to stir, moaning again. Her dark lashes swept open revealing no sign of recognition in her pained gaze.

"Dana, baby. You're all right," he spoke to her sweetly, closely studying her reaction as he tried to assess the situation.

Her eyes focussed on his face and her expression remained unchanged. She became aware of the ground beneath her and cried out in pain as she attempted to sit up.

He watched her anxiously. "Darling, where does it hurt?"

She put her right hand to the top of her left arm, directly below the shoulder.

"Where am I? Who are you?"

He hedged, avoiding her questions, thinking furiously now.

"Don't you know where you are?"

Her brows creased in concentration and her brilliant green eyes searched for a familiar landmark, but she could find none. Then she tried searching backward in time to figure out how she had come to be there, why her body ached all over, but there was nothing but an empty void.

A cold terror grew inside her as she came to understand her predicament. She turned to the well-dressed man beside her with a sense of urgency. "I don't.....Who am I?"

My poor darling, he thought to himself as he watched the frightened, lost look on her wan face. This definitely called for a change of plans, he thought, quickly adjusting to the opportune turn of events. He wondered how much of her past would she have discussed with those people at Kingsley Ranch? Probably not much. She was too proud, too damn proud. Chances are she'd never mentioned a thing.

If he played his cards right and luck was on his side, he could end up with everything he'd ever wanted. Calculating the risks involved, he arrogantly decided the prize was well worth the gamble.

"Dana, honey. I'm going to get you some help," he comforted her.

He opened the door to the jeep, then returned and carefully picked her up. She moaned as he lifted her into the vehicle.

"I'm sorry, princess," he said with a great show of affection. Shit, he was feeling lucky already.

Ben was inspecting the gate to the training ring when the echoing beat of hooves in the distance caught his attention. He straightened up in time to see Masquerade gallop into the yard and up to the side of the barn, stopping short. With growing dread he rapidly took in every grim detail: her reins trailing along the ground, her heaving flanks glistening with sweat and the alarming but obvious fact that she was without her rider.

He made his way to the agitated animal, taking care to make no sudden movements.

"Here girl. That'a girl," he made soothing noises as he approached her gently. Bending in from the outside corner he reached down and retrieved the reins. Once he had the reins secure in his hands he faced away from the horse, put his fingers to his lips and whistled loudly.

It was a signal at the ranch and anyone within earshot would soon be there.

Adam was the first to arrive, then Jarod.

Everyone was immediately aware of the gravity of the situation as they took in the frightening sight before them.

"Who took her out?" Jarod asked, knowing full well it had to have been Dana. His jaw was tight and his face troubled.

"Dana took her out close to an hour ago," Ben informed him as he and Adam checked the mare over.

"She's favoring her foreleg." Adam ran his hand down Masquerade's leg. "I don't think it's too serious."

Ben pointed to the west trail. "She came in galloping from over there."

Jarod's eyes looked out over the distance.

Kent and Annie had also joined the small group and they stood silently, grimly awaiting instruction.

Jarod turned his focus back to them.

"Okay, Kent saddle up your horse, I'll get Goldrush ready and we'll go out along the trail. Adam, you'd better take care of Masquerade. Ben, you stay put just in case..." Jarod paused, collecting himself before continuing. "In case Dana shows up. Annie, maybe you could go to the main house, let June know..." Once again he faltered.

"I'll take care of it." Annie turned towards the house.

Adam led Masquerade into the barn and Jarod and Kent were just about to follow when Ben drew their attention to a vehicle approaching from over the incline.

"Damn, who can that be?" Stress was evident in Jarod's voice.

The jeep pulled into the yard, stopping in front of the main house.

Jarod ran over as the driver jumped out.

"What happened here?" Jarod demanded, opening the passenger door. Dana leaned limply against the seat, her hair cascading in every direction, her clothes disheveled. "Dana, are you alright?"

She looked at him blankly, the only expression on her features was one of physical pain.

With a growing sense of panic, he turned and faced the dark haired stranger.

"What the hell happened and who are you?" Jarod demanded again impatiently.

"She fell from her horse, but she doesn't seem to remember anything. I think she's hurt," the stranger answered anxiously, inwardly enjoying the drama unfolding before him.

Jarod bent down to Dana's eye level. "I'm going to carry you into the house. Do you think you can manage that?"

She nodded an affirmation, wincing.

"I think Dana needs a doctor," the stranger suggested pointedly.

Jarod's head shot up as the stranger spoke Dana's name. There was no time for this now, he thought. He reached into the truck and gently lifted her into his arms. He closed his eyes for the briefest second, overwhelmed to have her back then he carried her into the house.

June gasped at the sight of Dana being carried into the house and Annie put a comforting arm around the woman.

"Annie, call an ambulance and tell them to get a move on it." Jarod directed over his shoulder as he carefully lowered Dana onto the couch.

"Dana, what happened?" Jarod asked her, trying to keep his voice unhurried and easy.

She remained silent, looking briefly around the room, from one person to another.

Jarod took a deep breath.

"Do you know where you are?"

"No," she whispered in a small voice.

"Where are you hurt?"

"My head hurts and my shoulder... and...." Dana's eyes grew bright with tears. "Who am I?"

Jarod ran his hand over his face.

"It's okay," he said soothingly. "You're not lost, you've had an accident. Your name is Dana Northington and this is where you work and live."

The stranger had followed them into the house and now stood in the corner of the room, Jarod deliberately ignored his unexplained presence.

[134]

"We've called an ambulance," he continued in the same steady tone as he looked to Annie and she answered with an imperceptible nod of her blond head. "In the meantime, we're going to try and make you more comfortable, okay?"

He turned to June, noting her stricken expression. He spoke to her softly. "June, we must have some ice packs, and see if we have something I can use as a makeshift sling." She hurried away in search of the items he needed.

He turned back to Dana. She sat silently on the couch. Trembling, she lifted her hand to her face and wiped a tear from her eye. She looked so vulnerable. Jarod fought a growing sense of powerlessness.

June soon returned and Jarod gently placed ice over and under the injured arm, he then secured the arm in a sling in an attempt to protect it from any unexpected movement. He placed a hand on Dana's knee. "Try not to worry, we're going to take good care of you. June and Annie," he pointed the two women out to Dana, "are going to sit with you for a bit. Try not to move until the ambulance gets here, okay?"

Jarod walked over to where the stranger stood quietly watching.

"Can you come with me?"

He motioned the man into the hall.

"Do you mind telling me who you are and what you happen to be doing here?" Jarod's tone was low but commanding.

"Sure," the stranger responded agreeably. "My name is Sonny Barton, and you must be Dana's boss, Jarod Kingsley," Sonny paused. After receiving no confirmation from Jarod, he continued. "I was coming to see Dana. We were supposed to meet, but when she got there her horse spooked."

Sonny closely watched Jarod digest this information. He shook his head. "God, the horse just went crazy. I stopped my truck, but it was already too late. Dana was on the ground by the time I got to her."

"Dana was going to meet you?" Jarod asked the man, incredulous. Dana had never once indicated to him anything of the kind. "How do you two know each other?"

Sonny could not believe his good fortune. He'd put his money on the chance that Dana had kept their past to herself and it looked more and more like he was right. Smelling victory he was hard pressed to keep his expression unchanged. He had one final hurdle to cross and then the prize would be his.

"We were engaged to be married." Sonny brazenly imparted the news as he savored the moment. A complete look of shock passed over Jarod's face.

"I was the reason Dana came to New Mexico," he continued with his account. "She was heartbroken when I foolishly broke off our engagement. It didn't take me long to realize what an idiot I had been." Sonny looked distraught. "I came here to make things right, to beg her forgiveness and to take her back," he said convincingly. "She told me she had never stopped loving me. I couldn't believe my luck." Sonny's voice caught on his words. "And now this happened."

From the corner of his eyes Sonny was delighted to note Jarod's stricken look of anguish. Jarod abruptly turned his back on the man and walked into the living room.

"How's she doing, June?" Jarod asked.

June gave him a small shrug, not knowing what to say.

Sonny brushed past Jarod and quickly knelt before Dana, tenderly taking her free hand in his. "It'll be okay, princess. The medics will be here soon." He lifted her white hand to his lips and kissed it.

June's eyes opened wide as she watched this display of affection, she quickly looked to Jarod. He ran his hand through his hair and shook his head.

He could feel his world falling out from under him.

The ambulance finally arrived at the ranch. Annie hurried outside and directed the medics into the living room. They did a quick examination of Dana and took down what information they could, then carefully moved her onto a stretcher, preparing her for transport.

"We'll be taking her to the Santa Fe General," one of the medics informed them. "If one of you would like to ride with us?"

Sonny immediately stepped forward. "I'd like to go with my fiancée," he announced.

The group was stunned and Jarod was the first to recover his composure.

"We'll follow," he said curtly.

He walked over to the stretcher.

"Dana, I know you're frightened," he spoke to her quietly as he gently stroked her hair. "Sonny will be with you and June and I will be right behind. We'll get you better," he assured her as he nodded to the medics. "Drive safely."

He watched Sonny climb into the back of the ambulance beside Dana and then turned back to Annie and June.

"Annie, please give June a hand to pack a few things. We'll probably be spending the night in Santa Fe. Then you can let everyone know what's happening," he said, noticing Ben and Kent still anxiously waiting in the yard. "Don't take long," he added, unable to help himself.

The trip to the hospital seemed endless. The strain Jarod was under was obvious to June and she remained silent, keeping her worries and her questions to herself, not wanting to add to his distress.

As he masterfully negotiated the roads, Jarod was deep in thought. Everything was beginning to make sense: the party, the kiss, Dana's continual pulling away. What a fool he had been, he'd misunderstood her actions and completely misjudged her reasons.

Yesterday he had literally pushed her against a wall, in between a rock and a hard place, pressuring her to tell him something she was too afraid to say. He recalled the episode painfully.

Whether she got her memory back or not, he'd lost her either way.

Jarod glanced across at June. He could tell she was trying to keep up a brave front for his benefit, but he knew her too well.

"How are you holding up?" Jarod asked, concerned.

"To be honest," June paused. "I'm worried about Dana...and you."

He reached over and squeezed her hand.

They'd arrived at the hospital.

June and Jarod entered the emergency and soon discovered Sonny pacing back and forth in the hallway. Dana had already been admitted into the emergency room and Jarod hated the fact that he would be forced to turn to Sonny for news of her condition.

"Is there any change?"

"The doctor is examining her now, but no, there is no change. She traveled well, considering."

It was Jarod's first opportunity to take a good look at the man. He was of average build, maybe a few years younger than himself. He was well-dressed, polished and he had all the telltale signs of a man who spent most of his time indoors.

So this is what Dana had chosen for herself, Jarod couldn't help but think, unconsciously measuring the man against himself.

"I want to see her." Jarod glared at Sonny as if daring the man to stop him.

"Be my guest," Sonny shrugged his shoulders. "I can't even get in to see her," he said with emphasis, making sure the barb hit its mark. "The doctor said no one goes in until he's done checking her out. So we wait."

The two men stood facing each other.

June reached for Jarod's arm and led him toward some vacant chairs.

"I know this is tearing you up, but we must wait. Come and sit with me, Jarod."

Jarod hesitated stubbornly, looking from June's pleading face to the empty chair. Drawing a deep breath he finally relented and sat down.

Time passed slowly.

Sonny resumed pacing the floor, frequently looking up at the clock on the wall.

Jarod sat forward with his elbows resting on his knees and rubbed the weariness from his eyes. There was nothing more tiring than sitting and waiting. Every so often, June would run her hand across Jarod's broad shoulders.

The pacing continued.

"Would you just sit down!" Jarod irritably snapped at Sonny, instantly regretting the outburst. He had to get a grip on himself, he thought. He needed some answers.

He stood and walked over to the admitting desk.

"Dana Northington came in here by ambulance a while ago," he spoke with authority. "I'd like to know her condition."

The elderly nurse raised her eyes from her paperwork. "Are you family?"

"Yes," Jarod boldly lied.

"Just a minute, please." The nurse disappeared behind a door and when she returned she was followed by a female doctor.

The doctor approached Jarod.

"I understand you're related to Miss Northington. We've sent her for an M.R.I. and we won't know the whole picture until we get those results. She's had a serious fall, which you are probably already aware of." She referred to the chart in her hands. "She's suffering a number of injuries: a mild concussion, a faint hairline fracture to the left shoulder joint and some bruising, not to mention the loss of memory which is our greatest concern at this point." The doctor looked at Jarod.

"In any event, I've transferred her upstairs for observation, pending the test results. She won't be going home today, that's for sure. I'd like to be able to spend more time with you, but that just isn't possible. It's a zoo in here today."

"When can I see her?"

The doctor checked her wristwatch.

"As soon as the test is completed, in fact she may already be in her room. That would be on the second floor, I don't remember the room number, I'm sorry." The doctor turned about to leave when she was struck by an afterthought.

"Listen, amnesia can be quite traumatic for the patient, as you can well imagine. Try not to overwhelm her."

"Thank you, Dr...."

"Jenkins."

"Dr. Jenkins. Oh, and doctor, I want the very best for her. Money is no object."

"I understand." The doctor turned and hurried back into the treatment room.

He walked back to June, who was now standing and explained to her what the doctor had said. "Where's Sonny?" Jarod asked looking down the hallway.

"He got tired of pacing the floor and went for coffee," June answered, clearly unimpressed.

"Listen, June. Do me a favor. I'm going up to see Dana. Don't say anything to Sonny just yet, I'd like to have some time alone with her first."

"I understand, dear. Give Dana my love."

Jarod bent and kissed June's cheek.

"I really appreciate having you here with me," he told her.

"You'd better get going while you can." June gave Jarod a gentle shove in the direction of the elevators.

The elevator doors opened onto the nurses' station where Jarod inquired about Dana's room. He paused outside her door for a second and took a deep breath before entering.

Dana was lying on her back in the bed, dressed in a blue hospital gown, her arm in a sling. She was pale and as she turned her head towards Jarod he could see her expression was troubled and anxious.

She saw the blond haired man with the clear blue eyes was back again, standing hesitantly in the doorway and she made a feeble attempt at humor.

"Ah, a familiar face." She smiled bravely.

Her spirit touched him. She looked so out of place in these surroundings. Like most men, Jarod had a strong aversion to hospital rooms.

"Hi." Jarod spoke quietly. "How are you feeling?"

"It doesn't hurt too much."

She studied the man carefully, searching for a point of familiarity. He was tanned and muscular, dressed in jeans, his shirt opened at the collar and his sleeves rolled up. He wore a watch, but no other jewelry; no chain, no ring. Her eyes rested on his bare hands for a minute, then she looked back up to his face. She had no idea why, but there was something about him that made her feel calmer.

"How do I know you?" Dana asked.

She hungered for a history, or at least a point of reference where she could begin to fill in the chasm of emptiness in her head. The doctors had already told her to be patient, but that seemed more than impossible.

"I'm Jarod Kingsley," he said, pushing aside the feeling of awkwardness he felt introducing himself. It was difficult to know how to begin. "You've been in New Mexico, working on my ranch for a few months. You work with the horses and you live in my house. Originally, you're from Maine and your parents still live there. We will phone them for you, later." There was so much he wanted to tell her and yet so little that he felt he could say. He waited, allowing her to absorb the information, letting her form her own questions.

Dana's pale face remained absent of recognition as she regarded him. Eventually she spoke again. "Tell me about who I really am. What kind of person am I?"

"Oh, Dana. I don't know where to start." He looked into her wide turquoise eyes, her question had taking him aback.

She waited, expectantly.

He organized his thoughts and when he spoke, there was tenderness in his voice. He chose his words carefully.

"Dana, you are a series of contradictions. You are brave and strong, sometimes even fearless, yet you are also one of the most gentle and caring women I've ever met. You're always willing to give but loathe to take. You're proud and gifted at what you do and you have a unique sense of humor." He smiled briefly, lost in thought. Jarod pulled up a chair and sat beside her bed. "Does any of this help?"

"I like the sound of myself the way you describe me." Unguarded, her words were spoken with innocence and Jarod was struck by their pathos. She was quiet for awhile, thinking.

"What about the other man? The one with the dark hair, Sonny."

Jarod experienced a sense of irritation. He suddenly felt the temptation to take advantage of the situation and portray Sonny in a less than favorable light and he was immediately ashamed.

"I don't know much about Sonny. He's from Maine. You were engaged to him before you came to New Mexico." Jarod answered as truthfully as he could.

"So am I engaged to him now?" Dana asked, alarmed.

"Honestly, I don't know."

A doctor walked into the room, closing the door behind him and Jarod immediately rose from his chair.

"Well, how are you doing, Dana?"

"The same, I guess," she responded.

The doctor nodded and looked at Jarod.

Jarod held out his hand and introduced himself, briefly explaining Dana's circumstances.

The doctor nodded again in understanding.

"I'm Dr. Webber," he introduced himself. "The good news is Dana's test results showed nothing out of the ordinary. There are no serious complications resulting from her accident other than the fairly minor injuries that we were already aware of. Other than being sore for awhile, you'll be fine Dana. I'm sure you must have a lot of questions?" The doctor had an understanding manner.

"When will I get my memory back?" Dana's frustration was apparent in her tone.

"As far as we can determine, there is no physical reason for your loss of memory and that's a good sign," the doctor spoke reassuringly. "This is where you will learn if you're a patient person or not." He smiled at Dana. "The thing with amnesia is that there are very few hardfast rules. Your memory could come back very soon or it may take longer. It could come back in bits and pieces or all at once. I know it's very frustrating. In the vast majority of cases like yours, it's a short term condition. I feel very confident about your prognosis." His words were encouraging.

"The trick in here is not to try and rush things." Dr. Webber looked meaningfully at Jarod, who nodded his understanding.

"What made this happen to me, why?"

"Typically amnesia is caused by injury and/or trauma. You took quite a fall and even though everything appears to be fine, your head suffered an insult."

"Doctor, is there anything we can do to help her regain her memory?" Jarod interjected.

"A man of action I see," the doctor said inoffensively. "Actually, that is a good question and yes, there are some things you can do. Introduce Dana to pictures of her past, stories, that kind of thing. Oddly enough, her senses might trigger a memory, what I mean by that is: a strong fragrance, a certain piece of music perhaps or a favorite food."

Jarod couldn't help but smile at the doctor's last suggestion.

The doctor continued. "Like I said before, the trick is not to go crazy ramming all kinds of information at Dana all at once. Let her take things at her own speed."

"How long will I be in hospital?" Dana asked.

"I want to keep you here for observation, for a minimum of twenty-four hours. Now during that time we will closely monitor you. That is purely a safeguard to make sure we haven't missed anything. Should you remain stable and I see no reason otherwise, you might be released as early as tomorrow.

I'd strongly advise some quality follow-up care of course, and you will have to take care to protect that shoulder of yours, which should heal fine on its own, but I firmly believe you will be more comfortable and fare better in familiar surroundings; for all the reasons I've already mentioned. Well, they might not exactly be familiar to you yet, but that will come."

There was a brief pause.

"If there is nothing else for now, I have some other patients to see." Dr. Webber brought the consultation to an end. "I've ordered Dana something to eat and then I want her to get some rest." He spoke firmly, directing a look at Jarod.

"Thank you for your time, doctor. I will be leaving shortly."

"That's fine." The doctor reached for the door handle and left.

Jarod turned back to Dana. "June sends you her love."

He straightened the sheet on her bed, putting off the time when he would have to leave.

A nurse briskly entered the room, carrying a tray of food. She placed the tray on a stand and rolled the stand to the bed, adjusting the height for Dana. "Can I get you anything? Are you comfortable?"

Dana assured the nurse that she was fine and the young girl left.

She lifted the silver cover from the dish and stared at the pitiful rations before her, frowning.

"I'm starving and look what they send me," she lamented, her bottom lip falling into a generous pout.

Her look of dismay warmed Jarod's heart and he grinned.

"Thank God June's not here to see this," he laughed. "We'll get you home soon enough, Dana. I hate to leave you here. I'm going to leave a number where I'll be staying, in case you need anything, just ask a nurse. Get some sleep, I'll be back tomorrow." He squeezed her hand and left the room.

Jarod paused in the hallway, searching for a quiet spot. He walked over to a secluded corner and reached for his cell phone from his pocket. First he called and booked three rooms at the hotel where he usually stayed when on business in Santa Fe. Next he phoned the ranch to update everyone on Dana's condition. After talking with Annie, Jarod paused briefly then decided to place a call to a private airline he'd used in the past and he booked a flight to Maine for Wednesday.

[143]

Before making his way back downstairs he stopped at the nurses' station and left instructions along with his hotel number.

As Jarod stepped off the elevator he spotted June and Sonny almost immediately. With a certain amount of satisfaction Jarod quickly realized that Sonny was fuming.

"I couldn't get in to see her," he told Jarod accusingly. "Why? 'Sorry, sir, she already has a visitor.' And then the doctor was in there. You were in there the whole time."

"Sorry," Jarod said simply. "I just happened to be there when the doctor showed up." He shrugged his shoulders.

"Well, how's she doing?" Sonny asked Jarod, still far from being appeased.

"Dana is pretty much the same. The doctor expects her to make a complete recovery. He couldn't say when that would happen exactly, but if nothing goes wrong, she may be going home tomorrow."

"Thank God," June uttered.

"Sonny," Jarod politely addressed the man. "I think I should phone her parents and let them know what's happened. Do you have their number?"

"Of course, I know them well. I think it's best if I tell them, don't you agree? Just like I should've been the one upstairs with Dana and the doctor. It was my place..." Sonny began again indignantly.

Jarod impatiently cut him off.

"Listen to me. You're in New Mexico now and that makes it my place. That includes anything else you may think you have claims to. You lost any rights you had the minute you broke off your engagement to Dana. Don't make the mistake of believing you can just walk in here right now and we'll all just get out of your way." Jarod stared at Sonny with controlled anger, his square jaw tight.

"If you love her as much as you say you do then start acting in her best interests," Jarod warned as he paused, collecting himself.

"And I suppose you picture yourself as being her best interest," Sonny returned hotly.

Jarod's eyes narrowed. "If you want to make that phone call, you'd better do it now," he ordered Sonny in a low voice.

Sonny stormed down the hall to the public phones.

Jarod ran his hand over his eyes and turned to face a silent June. "I'm sorry," he apologized to her.

"Don't be, I'm proud of you, Jarod. It's the first time today that I've seen you listen to your heart. The things you said needed to be said." June had a knowing look in her warm, dark eyes.

Jarod looked away and changed the subject. "I've booked three rooms at the hotel. I want to stay close by, if that's alright with you?"

"I think it's best we stay in the city," June agreed.

"We'll go as soon as he's done." Jarod pointed his head towards Sonny who was busy at the telephone. "You must be hungry and tired."

When Sonny returned, his manner was more subdued.

"I got through to Dana's parents. Her mother was ready to jump on a plane and come down here, but I managed to persuade her it was best to wait." Sonny's tone was ostentatiously courteous.

"Jarod, I apologize for my behavior. I guess we're all a little on edge. I had been so looking forward to meeting you. Dana's told me you're a great boss. I can understand how you must feel. It's true, it is your place, your employee, your horse. I can see how you would feel responsible," Sonny said with a great show of sympathy.

Jarod stared mutely at Sonny, wondering how it was that this man had crawled out from under a rock in the desert somewhere and leeched himself onto Jarod, bleeding away his sanity. There was no way of shaking him loose. He was like a burr under Jarod's shirt, always itching. It was hard to believe he'd known him for only a few hours; it was not easy to dislike someone the way he did Sonny, in that short a space of time.

"I've booked hotel rooms for us all, so if you're ready, I'd like to get June settled in. It's getting late." Jarod was genuinely worried about June. It had been a long, trying day for her as well and her features were showing the strain. He placed a protective arm around her shoulders.

"I'll catch a cab later," Sonny informed them.

Jarod gave him the name of the hotel. He and June were making their way to the car when Sonny called to them, running to catch up with them.

"Jarod, before you go, I just wanted to say you were right about something else, too. I hope we can get along, you know, like you said. For Dana's sake." He extended his hand towards Jarod.

Jarod viewed the man's gesture of cooperation with skepticism.

"Fine," he replied, reluctantly shaking Sonny's hand.

Jarod poured himself a stiff shot from the bar in his hotel room. He was waiting for June while she freshened up before they would go down to the hotel dining room. He knocked the drink back in one smooth motion, relieved to be away from the hospital, relieved that Dana would be alright and relieved to be rid of Sonny, at least for the time being.

He took off his shirt and walked into the bathroom. He lowered his head under the tap allowing the cold water to pour over it for a while before reaching for a towel and vigorously rubbing it dry. He didn't need a mirror to prove that he looked exhausted. A lot had happened in the last two days.

He donned a fresh white cotton shirt. Jarod considered having a second drink before going to get June, but decided against it. There would be plenty of time for that later, he thought.

Throwing on a jacket, he went to see if June was ready.

The elevator doors opened and Jarod guided June toward the hotel dining room. A waiter adroitly seated them and handed them their menus.

"It will be wonderful to see someone serving you for a change, June." Jarod said pleasantly, attempting a lighter vein of conversation.

Another waiter approached their table.

"Can I get you something from the bar?"

Jarod looked to June, but she declined the offer.

"I'll have a bourbon, straight up." Jarod made his order and the waiter left them.

There was a moment of silence before June spoke.

"You love her, don't you?" June's words came easily but with belief. She'd thought as much for quite some time and being witness to Jarod's actions that day had only served to deepen her certainty. Her expression was soft in the dimmed lighting of the room.

Jarod leaned back in his chair and a sardonic grin broke through his stressed features.

"Yes, I do," he admitted simply. "Even though I've tried not to... from the beginning it wasn't right. I'm her employer, that in itself made it wrong, but there was more to it." He tried to explain. "Dana always held back, she never really let me in and I suppose I get that more now with Sonny arriving at the ranch."

[146]

Jarod paused as the waiter placed his drink before him.

They were alone once more.

Jarod drew a deep breath. He had privately struggled with his feelings for months and it now felt good to unburden his troubles.

"I could never quite understand her and Dana never once mentioned anything about Sonny." Jarod shook his head in disbelief. "Yesterday I told her I loved her." He looked away recalling the incident in the barn. He emptied his glass. "Anyway, none of that matters now. She's in the hospital and Sonny's here... I don't know what's expected of me at this point."

"Do what you know is right, what you've always done. Follow your heart." June looked directly into Jarod's eyes. "Dear boy, things are not always what they appear to be. Dana wanted very much to talk to you this morning, but she never got the chance. Dana's not herself right now. She's in a very vulnerable position and she needs someone to look out for her. I don't trust that man, Jarod."

The waiter appeared, discreetly offering his menu suggestions. Jarod and June both selected from one of the house specialties.

They ate in silence and when they were done, Jarod ordered a coffee for himself and a tea for June.

"June, unless something changes, I'll be flying to Maine Wednesday morning. The doctor suggested that photographs from Dana's past might help encourage her memory. At the same time it will give me the opportunity to meet and talk to Dana's parents face-to-face. I'd like to find out more about Sonny." Jarod's distaste for the man was evident.

"Anyway, I'd be returning late that evening. Do you think you'd be alright on your own for the day?"

June nodded her approval of his plan. "I think that's a good idea, but hopefully it won't be necessary by then. Of course we'll be fine for the day."

"Well, I think it's time we turn in. We'll see what tomorrow brings." Jarod attempted to make his tone more positive.

Jarod charged their meals to his hotel room and they made their way upstairs.

After seeing June safely to her room, he returned to his own and decided to phone the hospital. He received news that Dana's condition remained unchanged and she was sleeping comfortably.

Wearily, he pulled off his boots and began to get undressed. He sat on the edge of the bed, slowly considering the things June had said to him that evening. She had always had the gift of reading his emotions, of understanding his dreams and his disappointments.

She was right, he could not be sure of how Sonny fitted into the picture and until Dana was able to speak for herself it was useless for him to draw any conclusions. He would have to be patient, and he refused to be railroaded by Sonny.

He yearned to be back home away from the impersonal hotel room, with Dana safely under his roof. He longed for things to be the way they used to be.

Jarod made his way to the bathroom and turning on the water, he stepped into the shower. Raising his arms, he flattened the palms of his hands against the wall and leaned forward into the pounding spray. He welcomed the steady force of the steamy water as it hit across his shoulders and cascaded down his back, slowly eroding away the day.

- Chapter 12 -

The corridors of the hospital were alive with activity as Jarod made his way to Dana's room, having left June in the cafeteria. He entered the room to discover Sonny seated at Dana's bedside, her slender hand clasped in his.

"Good morning." Jarod hesitated. "Am I interrupting?" He was once again reminded of the awkwardness of the situation.

"No, of course not," Dana answered pleasantly.

Sonny remained silent, glancing only briefly at Jarod before returning his attention to Dana.

"Darling. I'll leave you now and go get something to eat. I'm sure you'll be in good hands with Jarod." Sonny bent and gently kissed Dana's forehead. The two men nodded to each other as Sonny left the room.

Jarod walked over to where Dana lay. Her color was better today, but he found her entire being emanated an aura of fragility.

"So, Dana, are you feeling any better today?"

"Yes and no," Dana managed a faint smile. "I feel pretty stiff. I'm sore in places I didn't remember I had." Dana directed Jarod a clever look. "That's supposed to be funny," she pointed out.

For a second, Jarod thought he recognized his Dana. He grinned and nodded. "I guess I'm a little slow on the uptake this morning."

He stood over her and she looked up to him, waiting, neither one knowing what to say next.

The reality of things returned.

"I'm worried about you. This has to be hard on you. How are you really feeling?" Jarod asked, his voice low.

His concern touched Dana. There was so much going on inside of her and it felt like there was no one on earth she was able to share it with, just faces upon faces of strangers. Like a blind person abandoned in unfamiliar territory, she was left to try and figure out how the ground lay. She had been hoping that maybe by today things would be different, but nothing had changed.

Her eyes grew moist.

"I feel empty and frustrated. I've tried so hard to catch even a glimpse of something or someone familiar, but there's nothing." Dana turned her head away in angered defeat. Her free hand had been fidgeting with the covers of her bed and it became suddenly still. "I'm nothing," she added in a voice so small that Jarod was barely able to hear.

Jarod reached out to her and gently stroked her hair.

"Dana," he spoke quietly. "I highly doubt there was a time in your life, either past or present, that you were ever looked upon as 'nothing'. Right now, you're not able to feel just how much you are loved and cared for."

Hearing the depth of emotion in his own voice, Jarod felt oddly the trespasser and he pulled back his hand before continuing in a more formal tone.

"Everything will work itself out before you know it. I promise you."

The door opened and Dr. Webber entered in the same calm manner he had a day earlier. "How is my patient today?"

"I'm feeling okay," Dana answered noncommittally.

"That's good to hear." Dr. Webber placed his hands in his lab coat pockets. "I've been fairly busy this morning. I've spoken to your nurse and I've reviewed your chart. Medically, I find no reason to keep you here, if you prefer to be home. Mr. Kingsley and I have already spoken earlier and he has assured me that he has already contacted someone who is ready and able to provide home care. As I said yesterday, I feel very confident about your case and about the measures Mr. Kingsley is willing to provide." Dr. Webber paused for a moment.

"I also feel you will progress better in your own environment, surrounded by people and things that you once knew, but I want to make certain you understand that you may choose to spend a few more days with us. Your room is available and that is an option for your consideration. We want to make this transition as easy as we can for you. Don't feel pressured to decide right away, think about it and I'll stop in later." Dr. Webber turned to leave.

[150]

"Doctor," Dana's voice held a new determination. "I don't need to think about it, I'd like to go...back to the ranch."

"Okay then, I'll go and get the paperwork started. The details concerning your release will be taken care of by...?" Dr. Webber held out an open hand.

"I'll take care of everything, if that's alright with Dana?" Jarod offered.

"Thank you," Dana agreed.

"Fine. I'd like you to try and rest and get something to eat before your trip home," the doctor advised. "We'll wait till sometime after lunch to discharge you. I'll be back this afternoon just to give you a brief checkup before we send you home." Dr. Webber smiled reassuringly at Dana. "I'll also give you my card, I'll want to set up an appointment for follow-up, or if you prefer I can give you a referral."

Once again Dana was reminded of how dependant she was. She had no idea if she already had a doctor, or how far away the ranch was. She turned to Jarod.

"Do whatever you think is best," she told him simply.

Jarod nodded his assurance and the two men left.

Once Jarod was done tending to the matters relating to Dana's discharge, he went in search of June. He found her in the waiting room, where she sat patiently with a closed magazine in her lap. He sat down beside her.

"Well, the good news is we'll be able to take Dana home sometime after lunch."

"That is good news. I'm anxious to see her. How is she doing?" June looked relieved.

"She's doing pretty well, all things considered," Jarod assured June, patting her hand. "Have you seen Sonny anywhere?"

"He was here a minute ago. He said he wanted to phone Dana's parents, somehow he knew about Dana being released and he wanted to let them know how things were going." June stood and tidied her hair. "It will be good for us all to be home."

They caught view of Sonny making his way down the corridor towards them. He was casually dressed in a pair of khakis and a striped polo shirt. He greeted them.

"I've spoken to Dana's parents, they were very happy I called," Sonny told them affably. "They continue to insist they should come, but I explained to them it wasn't necessary. As soon as Dana is feeling a little stronger I'll be bringing her home, so they just need to be patient for a couple of days." He continued to smile amiably, realizing full well the impact his words must be making on Jarod and June.

Jarod remained composed.

"I think we'll take things a day at a time, Sonny." Jarod's voice was thoughtful as he considered his position and remained firm. "Dana will not be going anywhere until she has her memory back. I don't think she is in any shape right now to make major life changes."

Sonny's smile did not waver.

"I beg to differ and I don't see how you arrive at the assumption that Dana going back home to her parents with the man she loves constitutes a major life change." There was a subtle hint of ridicule in Sonny's tone.

Jarod's eyes narrowed as he drew in a deep breath. It continually amazed Jarod how Sonny had the uncanny ability to cause him to question his own motives, to sidetrack him. Jarod realized it was going to be another long day if he allowed himself to lose sight of what really mattered and that was Dana's welfare. This endless wrangling was beneath him.

"Well, I think we should all be very grateful that Dana's accident was not more serious than it was. The doctor expects her to regain her memory rather soon," June stepped in speaking quietly, taking both men by surprise. Her common sense broached no argument. "Sonny, if you've managed to wait for her this long, a few more days is not going to hurt you. Let's see how Dana copes with the trip to the ranch before we start travelling her across the country." She looked at Sonny with sober disapproval, not unlike a mother reprimanding an errant child.

It was a look Jarod was already familiar with and he was pleased to note that it had the same shaming effect on Sonny as it had had on himself the few times June had chosen to exercise it.

"Now, let's use this time productively and try to prepare to make this transition as pleasant and as smooth as possible," June ordered and as far as she was concerned, the matter was settled.

Jarod was deep in thought as he negotiated his vehicle along the seemingly endless stretch of country road. They would soon be back at Kingsley Ranch. The thought occurred to him how ironic this was for Dana. It would be her second trip along this span of road, yet she would be looking at it with the same newness as the first time, the day she had come to work at the ranch.

That was the day he had first laid his eyes upon her, standing in the doorway to his office.

He'd raised his eyes to a beautiful picture, a tall, slender woman with rich glowing hair and enchanting, brilliant eyes that lit her ivory face. From that day his world had changed. This elusive creature had brought a curious desire and wonderment to his existence.

And like the blood that flowed through his veins, she had become an unconscious part of him and he could not imagine his days or his nights without the possibility of her.

His eyes strayed to the rear view mirror to where she sat beside the ever attentive Sonny and Jarod's tender recollection took a nosedive into harsh reality.

It was with a sigh of relief that he finally parked the car in front of the main house.

June was the first to speak.

"Mr. Barton, if you'll just give me a hand with the bags, I'd be more than happy to show you to the guest bedroom, where you will be staying while you're with us," she said pleasantly.

Sonny hesitated. He was not overly pleased with June's arrangement, obviously contrived to give Jarod and Dana time together alone; but he held his tongue and reluctantly agreed, following the woman into the house.

Jarod opened Dana's door and helped her out of the car. She stood for a moment, silently staring out over the rugged landscape. She took her time, slowly studying her surroundings. Her gaze rested for a while on the big house before she turned to face Jarod, holding her injured arm which still hung in a sling. When she spoke, the simplicity of her statement only served to underline its value.

"You and I are friends."

They were not the words that Jarod had expected.

"Yes, we are friends." Jarod paused, unsure of what he should add to that. "We care about each other," he told her honestly, unwilling to complicate things for her.

She nodded, her detached gazed curious.

"And Sonny?" Dana's eyebrows creased in concentration. "I've been trying to put things together in my mind, things that people tell me. I don't understand...if Sonny and I are engaged to be married and we both live, or lived," she corrected herself, "in Maine, what am I doing here, in New Mexico? I mean, why would I come here if I was to be married?"

It was the essence of what had been troubling Jarod since the accident, the vague irritation that something made no sense, that there was a piece of the puzzle missing, a vital piece that would bring the entire picture into focus. With a memory or without, Dana was an astute thinker and Jarod was inwardly impressed.

"Actually, you have never spoken of Sonny in all the time you were here, so I'm afraid I don't know the answer to that question...yet," he added. "I'm going to find out what I can, but for now our primary objective is your recovery, I don't want you worrying about things. You need rest and relaxation, speaking of which, we should get you settled in your room." Jarod kept his tone light as he guided her into the house.

"One thing I am certain of is how much you enjoy June's cooking. So after I introduce you to your nurse and you are comfortable, we'll get some real food in you." He brought her up the wide staircase to her room where he left her in the capable hands of Juanita, the private nurse who had arrived at the ranch earlier that day.

Once back downstairs, Jarod retreated to the privacy of his office. He sat forward in his easy chair with his elbows crossed over his open knees, his hands clasped together.

In the quiet of his office Jarod did some soul searching. He mentally questioned the motives behind his actions; like his insistence to bring Dana back to the ranch, his dislike of Sonny, even the issue of who should be relaying information to Dana's parents. Some of it was trivial, some of it was not, but Jarod and Sonny seemed to be constantly butting heads. It was impossible to know where to draw the line between reason and defiance.

What was it Sonny had said about his and Dana's engagement? Who had broken it off and how had they come to reconcile? So much had happened in such a short period of time, it was difficult to keep the facts straight, Jarod mused. Could the whole thing have happened the way Sonny had described it?

Jarod was only too well aware how neatly it would serve his own end to doubt Sonny, to paint him as a suspicious character, and it would be easy enough to do; but to whose benefit? His own. He stared out through the open window, lost in thought.

Was his judgement ethically sound or was he just selfishly biased?

There was a knock on the door.

"Come in." Jarod sat back in his chair as Sonny entered the room. "What can I do for you?" Jarod asked patiently.

"I just wanted to let you know that Dana is resting comfortably. She says she feels best when I'm with her, so I thought it would probably be best if I spent the night in her room," Sonny said in casual fashion, eyeing Jarod. "You know, on the cot of course."

Jarod raised an eyebrow slightly.

"I've hired a nurse to do that." Jarod countered, his patience wearing thin. "Regardless of your past and I emphasize the word past, Dana does not remember you. You are a stranger and I would never allow a stranger to spend the night in her room. Dana needs some space and I will insist that she gets it. The doctor was very specific that she should not be pressured." Jarod stood as if making his point clear.

"Look, Jarod, for some reason you seem to have it out for me," Sonny feigned injury. "I only want what is the best for Dana, she's the reason I came to New Mexico to begin with. She will get better and we will be married, whether that makes you happy or not." Sonny discerned Jarod's discomfort, secretly relishing his small victory.

"Whatever," Jarod spoke levelly. "In the meantime, while Dana is under my roof, I'm responsible for her well-being and she will not be pushed."

"Yeah, right. We're under your roof all right and whose choice was that? Not mine. And who are you to make all these decisions regarding her well-being? I forgot, her employer, that's it." Sonny struck back heatedly snapping his fingers in the air. "Well I didn't realize she was still on the job. Listen here, Boss man, you'd better start looking for a new stable manager, because you've crossed the line between work and play." Sonny stabbed at the air with a pointed finger and strode out of the office.

Jarod stood staring blankly at the space Sonny had occupied before his grand exit, struggling for self-control. He would be feeling a lot better about the whole episode if the very same thought had not already occurred to him.

He closed the office door behind him and headed for the kitchen.

"Juanita's already eaten and Mr. Barton has taken a meal upstairs for himself and one for Dana," June announced, smiling at Jarod. "You go have a seat in the dining room and I'll be in with your supper in just a moment."

"If it's all the same with you, I'll eat in here." Jarod pulled up a stool at the counter. "The company is better."

"I've made some of Dana's favorites," June explained over her shoulder as she turned towards the stove. "I'm hoping maybe her taste buds will help to jog her memory." June chuckled to herself. "I suppose that sounds rather silly."

Jarod smiled fondly at her, unable to help himself.

"No, actually the doctor said something to that effect. You're a good woman, June." Jarod took hold of the coffee mug June had placed before him.

"Wednesday can't come soon enough," Jarod sighed, thinking aloud. "I want to speak to Dana's parents personally, to explain things to them and reassure them. It seems irresponsible of me not to have done so already. And I'll feel a lot better to have a third party's input on this whole engagement thing. Some things need to be clarified." Jarod ran a hand through his hair.

June watched him thoughtfully. Sonny's presence was an awkward addition to an already trying situation. The last couple of days had sent them all scurrying for some kind of stability.

"You are doing everything you possibly can for their daughter and as parents, I believe that is what they would appreciate the most," June comforted him as she reached for his hand. "We'll pray for patience and guidance and everything will happen as it was meant to be. Wednesday will come and you will be able to talk with her parents face to face and they will be able to see for themselves the fine man that you are. Maybe you can bring them back with you."

Jarod nodded his head in agreement at the proposed plan.

"I don't like leaving you on your own while everything is upside down like this. I should talk to Ben about spending the day at the house, to give you a hand with the extra work load." Jarod grinned. "I'm sure he would be delighted with the prospect of showering you with his undivided attention for a few hours." He teased her as he ate.

"Now, Mr. Kingsley, that's quite enough!" June blushed. "I won't be needing any help. I've been running this house for years and I'm quite sure I can hold things together for a few hours."

"Alright," Jarod relented. "I get your point. But in all seriousness, if you need something, anything, I want you to promise me you will call Ben, right?"

"Fine, I promise. Although I honestly can't see what you think that coot can do that I couldn't take care of myself." June straightened her plump shoulders as she patted her hair.

Jarod continued to smile.

"Well, June. This has all been a wonderful distraction, I must say." He stood. "I'm going to check in on Dana and Juanita and then I'm going to turn in. I bet you'll also be looking forward to your own bed tonight? I'll see you in the morning, sleep well." Jarod kissed June on the cheek and departed from the kitchen.

Once upstairs, Jarod found Dana's door ajar. He gently rapped on the thick wooden frame.

"Come in," Dana called from inside the room.

Jarod entered her bedroom and immediately noticed that Dana was alone.

"Where is your nurse?"

"After Sonny left, I asked Juanita if she would mind giving me some time to myself." Dana's features were drawn. "I know people mean well and I should be more appreciative, but sometimes I become quite frustrated listening to a litany of things that I know nothing of. In a way I feel quite isolated from everyone and sometimes it's easier to just be alone and not keep up the pretense that there is..." Dana paused, searching for the right words, "a mutual connection going on, if you can understand what I mean. It's all pretty one-sided."

"Well, I didn't mean to disturb you, I'll come back another time." Jarod made a motion to leave. "I just wanted to be sure you were comfortable."

"Now I've scared you away," she said contritely, a small smile lifting the corners of her warm mouth. "Please stay and sit with me." Dana straightened up in her bed as she motioned Jarod to a nearby chair. "You should force your company on me for hours, at least, and insist on telling me about every awful thing I've ever done." Dana laughed softly, her head tilted to the side.

It was a picture Jarod had caught only glimpses of in the past. Aside from the obvious, Dana was different. He tried to put his finger on it, and then it came to him; with Dana's memory gone, so too was her ever present shield of reserve.

Jarod accepted the seat. "I won't stay too long. You've had a big day."

He looked around the room. It was the first time he had been in that room since Dana had come to live at the ranch. He was not especially surprised to find that there were few personal effects; Dana had always been curiously private about her life. There were barely any clues to Dana's past other than a minimum of trinkets and a beautiful photograph of Dana riding horseback. He assumed it was on her horse, Pepper. He turned his attention back to her.

"So do you find your room to your liking? Is there anything you need?"

"The room is beautiful, certainly much prettier than the one in the hospital," Dana grinned, seeming more at ease away from the professional efficiency of the hospital. "I don't think I need anything, but thank you for asking. And you were definitely right about June's home cooking. My meal was delicious. Juanita is very attentive, but really, I'm not an invalid. Apart from having amnesia, I'm quite well and she can hardly be expected to help me with that." Dana made a face.

"Actually, lying in bed like this only serves to make me stiffer," Dana protested. "I'd rather move around a little."

"I'm glad you enjoyed your supper and maybe tomorrow we can try taking you out for a short walk around the grounds, before the sun gets too strong," Jarod suggested.

"That would be wonderful," Dana agreed. "It's too bad about my shoulder," she grimaced at the sling. "It would feel so good to ride. I know how. I guess it's like driving, I know how to do that too." Her

[158]

delicate chin jutted upwards the way it always did when she had that air of daring him to disagree with her.

"Well, maybe we'll save the riding part for another day," Jarod advised, being careful to not let his surprise show in his voice. He silently wondered what else she could remember.

"I'm going to send Juanita in and I'd like her to spend the night on the cot," he put up his hand, forestalling Dana's objection. "It's just for a couple of nights and I'll sleep better, knowing she's with you. You haven't even had the chance yet to familiarize yourself with the layout of the house. If anything happened during the night, or you needed something you wouldn't even know where to go."

"Okay, okay," Dana conceded in amusement. "You make it sound like a labyrinth. How complicated can it be?"

"That's enough out of you," Jarod said with mock sternness. "I'm going to send you back to the hospital." He stood.

"Good night, Jarod," Dana said demurely.

He realized it was the first time she had called him by his name since her fall. He smiled to himself as he left Dana's room.

It suddenly occurred to Jarod that Sonny was nowhere to be found and he was not quite sure if he felt more concerned or grateful for that fact.

He stood in the shadows, the night air was cool enough for this time of year, but he was oblivious to the climate. If he never laid eyes on this Godforsaken dust bowl again, it would be too soon.

He'd had his fill of cowboys and he'd never really cared for the smell of horseflesh to begin with, the big dumb beasts.

The people at this bloody Kingsley Ranch were as thick as thieves, he thought with a sour taste in his mouth. They were their own little mutual admiration society, tripping over themselves with their out-dated codes of conduct.

Kingsley, he snorted, a damn freak of civilization; King of the Yahoos. He smirked and began to chortle at his own joke. Like he couldn't see what that blond haired bastard was up to! His rage continued to gain momentum.

He spat on the ground and even though it was too dark to see, he knew the dry earth had already greedily soaked up his spittle.

"That's the last you'll get of me!" He swore aloud. He was growing weary of this game. It had been amusing in the beginning, but it was no longer. Tomorrow, he would make his final preparation. It was time to bring his sweet baby home.

Jarod made his way downstairs. The smell of coffee and bacon lured him into the kitchen just in time to overhear Sonny asking June what Jarod did for a living.

"I have several different business interests," Jarod answered for himself as he turned and smiled at June. "Good morning, everyone."

Jarod pulled up a chair at the table. "I hope you slept well," he directed towards Sonny. "Have you had breakfast yet?"

"No, actually I was waiting for you. I thought we might talk."

Jarod's face remained pleasant, though the idea of a chat with Sonny first thing in the morning hardly warmed his heart.

"So what will it be, Sonny? Do you want to discuss my business ventures, the weather, the horses or Dana?" Jarod asked, trying not to sound sarcastic, but not quite succeeding.

Sonny appeared unperturbed.

"Well let's see, I don't have any use for your weather or your horses for that matter," he answered easily enough. "I'm mildly interested in where all this wealth comes from, but I'm probably better off not knowing, so that leaves us with our favorite little subject, my darling Dana."

"Sonny," Jarod began patiently. "I've said all I want to say about Dana." Jarod reminded himself that by this time tomorrow he'd be on his way to Maine.

"Well that's just fine and dandy. I haven't said all that I want to say. I want you to hear me out," Sonny insisted.

"Okay. I'll hear you out." Jarod realized that he was no longer hungry.

"I admit I was a little short-tempered yesterday, but I'm only trying to be helpful. I'm under a lot of stress too."

Jarod failed to see when exactly Sonny had tried to be helpful, but the last thing he wanted to do was antagonize the man.

"It's almost forty-eight hours since Dana's accident and she's doing fine, even the doctor said as much himself. I've been more than patient and

I've willingly gone along with all your uncompromising arrangements. Dana traveled fine yesterday," Sonny almost glowered at June as he said that, "but being at the ranch hasn't helped her to remember anything. This place just isn't important enough to her." Sonny stopped, driving in his point.

Jarod held his composure. His overriding priority was to pacify Sonny and get him to at least agree to wait until Jarod got back from Maine, until he'd had the chance to reassure himself that everything was what it seemed to be.

"I think it's too premature to know that for sure. I think we need to give Dana just a few more days," Jarod proposed reasonably, stalling for time.

One thing he did know for sure was the thought of the possibility of Dana leaving forever was more than he could bear and he wasn't ready to let her go until she was able to tell him so herself.

"The doctor said she'd do better in familiar surroundings and that's all the more reason that I should take her home, where she belongs," Sonny argued with confident purposefulness.

Sonny's suddenly rational manner had done more to undermine Jarod's convictions than Sonny realized. Dana was getting better with each passing day and within no time Jarod would no longer have any valid objections to keep her from leaving.

June could pray for patience and guidance if she was so inclined, Jarod was praying for a miracle.

"Dana will decide for herself when she's ready." Jarod said with an air of finality. "Without any undue influence from anyone, including yourself. I'd like to remind you that you are a guest in my home." Jarod warned with quiet emphasis, and he left the house before Sonny had the chance to say anything more.

Jarod had been meaning to take a trip to the barns and he decided that now was as good a time as any. Jesse Dog followed him down the laneway, happy for some company. Jarod stopped and reached down, patting him for a moment.

"You miss her too." He spoke to the golden dog.

The big dog rubbed its head into Jarod's hand affectionately, wagging its tail.

They arrived at the barns, where Jarod came upon Ben.

"It's a fine morning, Jarod. Good to see you out and about, how's Dana?" Ben abruptly stopped his work and leaned his pitchfork against the post, his worn face lined with concern.

"I think it'll be easier if we get Annie, Kent and Adam before I get into all that," Jarod suggested. "We can meet in the tack room."

"I'll get Adam," Ben agreed and he made his way in the direction of Barn Two.

Within minutes the group had assembled in the tack room, Annie sat on a trunk while the others stood, and the atmosphere in the room was solemn.

"First, let me apologize for not making it here yesterday. I won't bother making excuses," Jarod took a deep breath before continuing. "Dana is home, as I'm sure you all know and as luck would have it, the only real physical damage from her fall seems to be a very slight fracture to her shoulder."

"And her memory?" Annie jumped in anxiously, unable to help herself.

"I don't recall exactly what I told you on the phone," Jarod addressed the girl. "But no, she still doesn't remember anything."

"Poor wee thing," Ben said.

"Now, the doctor said everything is fine. They performed some tests and there's no physical damage to her head, so he fully expects her memory loss to be short termed."

"But that makes no sense," Kent quickly cut in. "If she didn't hurt her head in the fall, why would she have amnesia?"

Kent's words caught Jarod's attention immediately. Jarod had not considered that question with everything else that had happened. It was just one more thing that he couldn't explain.

"I don't know," Jarod replied honestly. "From what I could understand, amnesia is not a clear issue. It can happen for a number of reasons. We don't know how she fell." Jarod shrugged his shoulders, shaking his head.

"Well, this is quite the thing." Ben rubbed at his unshaven chin. His words mirrored the thoughts of the entire group. "So, what do we do now?"

Jarod leaned back against the wall.

"Like I said, the doctor is very optimistic, so that's the best news I can give you. I'll probably be bringing her by later and I know you'll all make her welcome; just try to resist overwhelming her. Remember, from Dana's point of view, this will be the first time she's meeting you all. I can tell you from my own experience, you may find it awkward, so I wanted to prepare you."

"Oh, my God," Annie whispered. "I hadn't even thought about that."

"It will be good for her to be amongst the horses." Adam spoke for the first time. "Their spirits are free and Dana understands their language. My people have a strong belief in such matters." He made a motion to leave.

"There is one other thing," Jarod paused, unsure of how much he should say or how much Annie already knew. He looked at the people before him and realized they were the closest thing to family that he had and he decided to lay his cards on the table.

"There is a gentleman here. His name is Sonny Barton and he's supposed to be Dana's fiancé, or ex-fiancé," a weary look crossed Jarod's face. "I don't know very much about that either," he added, noticing the questioning looks on some of their faces. "Well, I guess that's about it."

At Jarod's cue they began to filter out of the tack room.

"Ben," he called to the older man. They moved together into the barn office.

"What's the problem, Jarod?"

"What isn't?" Jarod sighed, feeling at a low point. The morning had so far had been less than easy.

"I have to be gone tomorrow for the day and I'm not comfortable leaving June alone, with all that's happening. I'd like you to keep your eyes open. Check in on her once or twice without making it too obvious."

"That is one proud woman," Ben agreed admiringly. "I'll take care a' things. So what do you think about this guy, Sonny?" Ben wasted little time on trivialities, going straight to the point.

"I'm trying hard not to form any opinions, one way or another," Jarod confided. "I just can't get over the fact that the whole thing has been so incredible.

That's why I'm going to Maine tomorrow. I need to ease my mind about some things. I just want to be sure the guy is who he says he is. If

Sonny manages to persuade Dana to leave, there is little I can do about it. My position in here is tenuous, at best. Sonny is eager for them to get on with their lives and I guess that's understandable enough," Jarod managed to say the words evenly, masking the pain they evoked. "I don't know how long I'll be able to keep them here."

Ben nodded in understanding. "Husbands and old boyfriends have a way of messing things up."

Ben's comment caused Jarod to wince. Was his struggle that obvious to everyone? "Anyway, I'm going to saddle up Goldrush and go out along the trail, I'd like to see if I can find exactly where Dana took her fall."

"Are you expecting to find something?"

"I don't know," Jarod answered honestly. "Later, Ben. Thanks."

By the time Jarod got out onto the trail, the mid-morning New Mexican sun had already begun to preview the hot, dry day that was ahead. Jarod lifted his hat and settled it further forward, the brim now shielding his eyes from the bright sunlight.

Goldrush moved along at an even paced jog while Jarod thought of Dana just days earlier, riding this very same trail. His mind wandered and went back to Kent's question. If Dana had not gotten amnesia from the fall, then what had happened out here?

About thirty minutes into the trail Jarod brought Goldrush to a halt. Off to the side of the trail a riding cap lay covered in dust.

Jarod dismounted and walked over to it, picking it up and examining its condition, which was perfect.

It seemed unlikely to Jarod that the fall itself could have been traumatic enough to have caused Dana's condition. There was no way Dana had become the rider she was today without having taken a few tumbles along the way and Jarod couldn't escape from it; between Sonny's story, the doctor's diagnosis and what Jarod knew of Dana, the feeling inside of him was that something was still missing.

Jarod studied the area closely but could find nothing conclusive. It had been a longshot at best and beyond a few broken bushes, the land was not giving away any of her secrets.

He wiped the dust off the cap and mounted Goldrush, turning the gelding back in the direction of the ranch.

It took little time to settle Goldrush into his stall and Jarod soon found himself back at the main house. After cleaning up and having some lunch, Jarod happened upon Dana in the living room, curled up on the big couch. Her eyes were closed and Jarod assumed she was asleep.

As though sensing his presence, Dana opened her eyes and looked in Jarod's direction.

"Hello," she said smiling.

"I'm sorry I disturbed you." He stepped into the room.

"I thought you'd be sorry that you broke your promise," Dana told him petulantly.

"My promise?" Jarod paused, completely baffled.

"I've been waiting all morning," Dana told him impatiently, awkwardly sitting up on the couch and running her fingers through her untamed hair.

"Waiting?" Jarod's face suddenly cleared, recalling his earlier pledge to Dana, silently cursing Sonny's interference at the breakfast table. "I was going to take you for a walk this morning. I completely forgot, I'm sorry."

"My God!" Dana cried quietly. "There is an epidemic of forgetfulness around here, that's for sure. Only some of us have it worse than others. That's all right Jarod. You're in good company," her soft laughter fell across the room. She struggled slightly as she slowly got her to her feet. Jarod was immediately at her side but she stubbornly refused his help.

"I'm just stiff, that's all. People have to stop fussing over me." Dana's voice had an edge of irritability in it. She instantly regretted her words. "I'm sorry. I'm not very nice company these days, or maybe I'm always this miserable, heaven forbid." She winced as she adjusted her sling. "I hate having everybody always doing everything for me. Especially Sonny, I know he means well and I can see he really loves me..." her voice trailed off with an audible sigh as she attempted to deal with her frustration.

Jarod wasn't sure what to say, so he decided it was best to say nothing. He just stood patiently, letting her get it out of her system.

"I just like to do things for myself," Dana said finally, as if making a point.

He nodded at her, a smile getting the better of him. "You always did," he said with emphasis.

"Well, you've got me there," she conceded, her humor slowly returning.

"So, would you still like to go for a walk? Maybe we could go straight into the barns, it'll be cooler and definitely shadier," Jarod offered, still smiling. "Have you eaten?"

"Yes, between June and Juanita there is no fear that I'll perish. I don't deserve all this attention."

"Don't worry so much. Come on, some fresh air and a little change of scenery will do you good."

As they stepped out onto the large veranda, a hot gust of wind greeted them. Dana lifted her good hand to shield her eyes and she stepped down from the porch. The wind lifted her long hair, blowing it across her shoulders as the sun played in its waves, turning the deep brown locks to copper.

Jarod caught his breath for a second as he wondered just how many times more he would be allowed to experience this pleasure.

She paused for some time, staring off in the direction of the west trail, her expression arrested in concentration.

Jarod watched her closely. It was the trail she'd taken her fall on.

"Do you remember something?"

"No," she answered slowly. "It's more like I feel something. It's like the wind," she explained as she closed her eyes. "I can feel it surrounding me, it's there and then..." Dana opened her eyes again. "It's gone."

"I think it's a positive sign, Dana."

"I hope so."

They began walking towards the barns, Jesse Dog had joined them and was keeping faithfully close to Dana.

As they made their way, Jarod pointed out the various areas of the ranch and they soon came upon Ben and Adam, leading a mare and foal to an outdoor paddock.

Adam, who was in the lead, was the first to come to a stop.

"Hello, Dana, it's good to see you're looking well."

"G'day, Dana."

Dana caught herself looking blankly at the two men and immediately forced her expression to a smile.

"Hello," she said politely, feeling awkward. She turned to Jarod.

"Dana, this is Ben." Jarod took over the introductions without missing a beat, as if this kind of thing happened every day. "He looks a little worse for the wear, but he's got a heart of gold." Jarod kept the situation light and Ben followed his lead, smiling in return. "And this is Adam, who is the most gifted caretaker I've ever come across."

Dana continued to politely smile at the men, but Jarod could sense her growing tension.

"Dana shouldn't stay out too long her first time around, so we'd best get going. Have a good day gentlemen." Jarod placed a hand gently over Dana's good shoulder and guided her around the horses.

"I'm sorry, Jarod. It's so hard to meet people that obviously know me, but I don't know them. I...I get tongue tied."

"Dana, don't be so hard on yourself. No one expects anything from you and everyone realizes how brave you are and how incredibly difficult this must be." Jarod gave her free shoulder a squeeze before dropping his arm to his side.

They reached the barn door.

"So, are you up to this?"

Dana nodded at him and he pulled open the door for her to pass through.

She stood for a brief second allowing her eyes to re-adjust to the change in lighting. An amazing transformation began to happen. A smile crossed over Dana's face, the first true smile Jarod had seen since all of this had started. Her posture changed and Dana held her head higher, the hesitation in her step was absent as she moved with assurance from one horse to another.

"This is wonderful! I love horses," Dana declared with delight.

"So do I." Jarod agreed as he followed at a leisurely distance, content to watch her enjoyment.

Dana came to a stop at Masquerade's stall. The big mare came to Dana and her refined head quickly found Dana's right hand.

"Why does this horse have a bandaged leg? Is she hurt?"

"This is Masquerade," Jarod explained, joining Dana. "She is probably your favorite and she's also the horse you were riding when you

[167]

took your fall." He watched Dana intently, hoping somehow that the information might trigger her memory, but there was nothing.

"Sonny told me the horse was crazy." She quietly studied the mare. "She certainly doesn't appear that way now. Will she be alright?" Dana asked, looking down at the bandaged leg.

"The injury is a minor one, she'll be fine…just like you," Jarod added. "Where is Sonny? I didn't notice his jeep outside."

"He said he needed some things in town, that he had not been planning to stay this long at the ranch." Dana looked away, unwilling to meet Jarod's eyes. "He wants us to leave," she murmured pensively. "To go home."

Jarod had been dreading these words for days it seemed, mentally trying to prepare himself for their eventuality. It had been in vain.

"How do you feel about that?" Jarod asked her with an outward calmness that he was far from feeling.

Dana lifted her troubled eyes to his, how could she tell him that she felt like she was already home?

"I don't know what I feel," she answered him, feeling overwhelmed. "That's the problem. I don't feel anything for Sonny and the thought of going so far away...it's too much, it all frightens me. I've lost my memory, but there are times when I feel like I'm losing my mind. I don't know what I'm supposed to do and I don't know what to say!" Dana's eyes were bright with unshed tears.

Jarod realized with a wave of cold anger that in spite of his words to Sonny that morning, the man had deliberately ignored Jarod's warning and boldly followed his own agenda.

"Sonny keeps telling me how awful this is for my parents. I feel terrible," Dana rubbed at her temple with her fingers. "He tells me how much it hurts him to see me this way. It hurts me too. I feel like I'm messing up everybody's life."

Jarod was furious now and it took all his effort to remain calm.

"Dana, I'm going to see your parents tomorrow. I'll be able to explain everything to them and if they want to come back with me, I'll bring them to you." Jarod comforted her. "Try not to worry. I'm certain your parents love you dearly. They'll understand, Dana. Please promise me that you won't make any decisions until I get back."

Dana mutely nodded her head in agreement. Jarod's idea made a lot of sense and it helped to lift some of the guilt and the enormous pressure she felt under.

She was looking lost and Jarod suggested that they should return to the main house.

"Please, not yet," she pleaded. "The horses soothe me. I wish I could get out and ride. Can't we stay a little longer?"

"What about if we visit the other barn?" Jarod suggested, artfully diverting her away from the riding horses. "We could take a look at the mares and their foals…but not for long." He emphasized strongly.

They crossed over to the next barn, where they found Annie hard at work tending to the yearling horses. She noticed them as they came in and brushing her hands across her jeans she came to greet them.

"Hi, Dana," she smiled warmly. "It's great to see you getting around," Annie said in a relaxed manner.

Dana nodded at the small blonde girl.

"This is Annie," Jarod explained.

"Have you been in Barn One already?" Annie deliberately tried to choose a light topic of conversation. "We're all trying to keep the horses in condition, so they'll be ready for when you get back to full speed."

"That's great... Annie," Dana answered politely, seeming a bit more at ease. "I can hardly wait. I guess there are some things that you never forget." Dana smiled a little at her tentative attempt at humor.

Jarod stood back, unobtrusively giving the girls some time together.

"The smell of the hay and leather; the sounds, they're all very familiar. I feel like I instinctively know where everything is. I wish I could say the same for my personal life," Dana explained, her words suddenly coming easily.

"I can only imagine, you must feel like the odd man out." Annie sympathized as she made an effort to bridge the gap. "Well, you are not only my boss, you are also a dear friend and I'm just going to look at it like you've gone on vacation. We're still in touch, just differently. It's not everyone who gets the chance to get away from themselves!" Annie laughed softly as she leaned against the stall door.

"I wish it felt as good as it sounds," Dana remarked with a wistful smile, feeling comfortable with Annie.

Jarod cleared his throat and Annie immediately picked up on his cue.

"Dana, I'm so glad to see you in one piece," Annie came over and gave Dana a brief hug, taking care of her arm in the sling. "You're a tough cookie. Anytime you feel like some girl talk, you know where to find me."

"Thank you, Annie. That would be great."

"Well, I'd better get back to work, these guys are big on schedules," Annie nodded at the horses. "I think someone taught them how to tell time."

Jarod and Dana made their way back to the main house. He was happy to see that Dana had responded favorably to Annie's casual manner. Annie had always been gifted at anticipating people's needs and Jarod was grateful that the outing had ended on a positive note.

He was also feeling easier about leaving tomorrow now that he had Dana's assurance that she'd be waiting for him when he got back. His temper flared again as he thought of Sonny and he decided the safest course for everyone involved would be that Jarod deliberately avoid the man.

For the next couple of hours Jarod threw himself into his work in the office. He returned some of the more important calls that had collected over the past few days and he confirmed his flight for the following morning.

Jarod was totally absorbed in his paperwork when he heard a vehicle pull in and then the front door opening and closing. Looking at his watch, Jarod was surprised to find it was nearly six o'clock. He waited for a bit before shutting down his computer and then stood, stretching his arms.

As he left his office, he encountered Juanita heading up the stairs. He inquired about Dana.

"She is in very good spirits, Mr. Kingsley. She is recuperating nicely. Mr. Barton has returned and is with her now. I thought it was best if I gave them some time alone. He cares for her so much, he's always asking her if she needs anything or telling her stories about home." Juanita placed her hand on the railing. "Is there anything else, Mr. Kingsley? I would like to check on her before I go to my room."

"No, that's fine, Juanita. I just wanted to be sure her outing this afternoon had not overtired her."

Juanita started up the stairs.

"Oh, one other thing, Juanita. If you happen to notice, could you let me know when Mr. Barton leaves Dana's room?"

"Certainly, Mr. Kingsley," the nurse nodded and continued up the stairway.

Jarod was drawn by the delicious aroma that exuded from the kitchen.

"Hello, June. Something smells wonderful. I had no idea I was so hungry."

"Hello there. I was just preparing two plates to bring upstairs. How was your afternoon?" June began to ready a large serving tray with napkins and cutlery.

"The afternoon was interesting. Dana once told me that she felt her absolute best when she was amongst horses and after today I'd have to say that was true." Jarod leaned against the counter. "You should've seen her come alive in that barn today." Jarod decided it best to omit the piece concerning Dana's parents and Sonny.

"It sounds like that might be just what the doctor ordered. It's probably very good therapy."

"She seemed very comfortable with Annie as well," Jarod considered for a moment. "Maybe Annie could come up to the house for a while tomorrow."

"I'll give her a call first thing in the morning." June had finished arranging the tray. "I'll just be a moment."

When June returned she prepared two more plates and poured a glass of wine for Jarod, before placing everything on the table.

"I thought I'd keep you company tonight." June smiled at him.

They spoke for a bit of small matters but it was difficult to stay away from the topic that was uppermost in both of their minds. It was June who eventually opened the subject.

"Are you anxious about your trip tomorrow?" She laid her hand across his arm.

"How could I not be?" Jarod paused for a minute as he tried to collect his thoughts. The room was quiet. "I've been so busy making plans and taking care of what had to be done...and from the beginning there's been this thing in the back of my mind that I would get to the bottom of all this, one way or another. I've sort of let that thing just fill me." Jarod ran his hand through his hair and attempted a smile.

"I've been concentrating so hard on the packaging that I've pretty much ignored the contents," Jarod noticed June's confusion. "I'm not explaining myself very well." He searched for the right words. He started over.

"Going to Maine won't change the fact that Sonny's here. It will help to quiet my doubts, but right now, my doubts are all I have. They've saved me from the pain; as long as I can be worried about Sonny, I don't have to deal with the reality of losing Dana forever." Jarod looked away and the room was filled with silence.

June could feel her eyes burn with the tears she refused to let fall.

"For the last couple of days all I've been saying is Wednesday couldn't come soon enough. I could kick myself now. I don't want to go. I don't want to hear about Sonny and Dana's past and their future. I don't want to find out that the truth has been staring me in the face all along. They are in love with each other, and I've just been too vain and too in love with Dana myself to accept it."

"It is hard, Jarod, I know. But this is no way for a man to live." June patted his arm, wishing with all her heart that she could ease his burden. "You will find your way through this. Your strength will not desert you."

There was a light footstep on the stairway and then a gentle rap on the door. Juanita stepped into the room.

"Excuse me, Mr. Kingsley. Miss Dana is alone now, if you'd still like to see her."

"Thank you, Juanita."

Jarod hesitated for a moment, looking at June.

"Go to her," June told him. "Enjoy the time you have," she said quietly behind his retreating figure.

- Chapter 13 -

The aircraft landed smoothly on a small runway just outside of Ellsworth, Maine. Jarod had departed early that morning from his home, nestled in the majestic embrace of the Rocky Mountains and crossed the vast plains of the United States to meet the Appalachian mountain range and come upon the eastern seaboard…Dana's home.

The plane had descended through downy pillows of clouds and deep cobalt blue skies to meet the welcoming green carpet that lay below. For all that Jarod was feeling pressed for time, it was hard not to be captured by its spellbinding beauty, the vibrant green blues of New England.

Jarod turned and thanked the pilot for a safe trip. He disembarked from the private aircraft with his briefcase in hand and made his way to the office where he picked up the keys to his rental car and a map. Opening the latter, he estimated that he would reach Dana's home in under forty-five minutes and the drive should be fairly uncomplicated.

He located the car that he had been provided with and once inside he pulled Dana's resume from his leather briefcase and placed it along with the map, within easy reach.

He had gone over Dana's resume on the plane and he had an excellent memory for details, so at least that much was clear in his mind, it was what was to follow that caused him to pause.

Jarod realized he was wasting valuable time and he quickly turned the key in the ignition, leaving the runway behind him, he continued on his journey.

To say that the last few days had caused him to lose his objectivity would be an understatement. He was a man accustomed to intrepidly dealing with whatever rose before him. His life up to now was easily measured in black and white; matters of the mind that were logically resolved.

The matters of the heart, he was quickly coming to learn, came in various shades of gray.

The mechanical efficiency of his upbringing had left little room for error. With no siblings to divert his father's unbridled efforts, Jarod had learned early in life to become successful at almost everything he did, he had had little choice. His father had insisted on most everything that his wealth could provide and apart from June's warm influence, Jarod had not really felt the absence of love in his life. ..Until now.

Dana had changed all of that.

Jarod reached the small village that was Dana's home. It was a picturesque area with colonial style buildings adorned with wooden hand painted signs. The town offered a simple rustic charm and its properties were neatly squared off by fences and flowers in copious quantities. It was a place where green lawns were trimmed by rolling sidewalks and thick, shady trees were abundant.

Jarod soon discovered the address he was looking for and parked his car in front of a square apartment building constructed of clapboard, immaculately kept and surrounded by a long cedar hedge.

Once inside the building Jarod walked up a narrow wooden staircase and knocked on the door to his right

He heard light footsteps from inside and then the muffled sound of a female voice.

"Who is it?"

"Jarod Kingsley... Dana's employer."

The door was unlocked and opened immediately.

"Is something wrong with Dana?" A young woman stood before Jarod, looking concerned. She had very short auburn hair and hazel eyes and she was casually dressed in a pair of jean cut-offs and a cotton shirt. Jarod couldn't help but notice that she was barefoot and a bracelet encircled her ankle.

"I'm sorry, I expected to find Dana's parents. I just presumed, as this was listed as her home address on her resume." Jarod hesitated.

"I'm Emma. Dana and I shared this place before she left for New Mexico," Emma explained as she opened the door wider and invited the tall man to step inside. "If you're here, there must be something wrong." Emma's expression of worry deepened.

"Dana took a fall last Sunday. She's alright," Jarod quickly assured the girl. "But, as a result of the accident she is suffering from amnesia. It's only a temporary condition, but the doctor suggested that photographs could help her and, really I just wanted to explain things to Dana's parents for myself..."

"This is way too much!" Emma exclaimed in distress. "Please, sit down. This is the kind of thing you see on television, I've never heard of it really happening. I can't believe it."

"I know," Jarod agreed. "All we really know is that Dana went out hacking and her horse spooked. She can't remember people, or what happened to her." Jarod looked around the small apartment trying to visualize Dana living there. "We immediately brought her to the hospital, but thankfully her injuries were really very minor. She's back at home, or at the ranch, I should say."

Jarod noticed a photograph on the coffee table of Dana and Emma in their riding gear. Their arms were thrown over each other's shoulders in casual comradery and their faces were bright with laughter.

"This is too strange," Emma repeated, her voice filled with disbelief. "She can't remember anything?"

"Not yet." Jarod shook his head.

"Wow!" Emma stood. "I'll help you anyway I can, but first let me get you something to drink. Are you hungry after your trip?" Emma studied the man more closely. He was a very attractive man and she couldn't believe Dana had not mentioned that fact to her in her calls.

"No, just something cold, water will be fine," Jarod answered.

Emma returned, placing the tall drink in front of Jarod.

"Do Dana's parents know? I don't understand why they haven't contacted me." Emma sat back down on the couch, her open expression perplexed.

"They've been updated daily and if you wouldn't mind giving me their address, I'd like to see them before I return to New Mexico."

"Of course. I wish I could go back with you," Emma frowned. "My sister is having a difficult pregnancy and I promised her I would help out." Emma looked torn. "I can't believe all this is happening at the same time. Actually, you're lucky that you caught me at home."

"If your sister is counting on you, then you need to be there with her. I'm sure Dana would be the first to insist," Jarod said, trying to ease Emma's burden of choice.

"She's spoken of you a couple of times," he continued. "Which says a lot, because other than that, she's described very little about her past." Jarod shook his head again. "That's why this trip was so necessary. I never really understood her reluctance to do so, but it wasn't my business to pry." Jarod spread his hands before him. "Between what Dana doesn't remember and what I don't know lies a pretty blank page. It's kind of hard to help her like that."

"So, Dana's never told you anything?" Emma asked, not really surprised. She carefully studied the man before her as she weighed her obligation to her friend against the circumstances they were facing. "Well, I can help you out there, at least. I suppose I should start somewhere near the beginning." She pulled one leg up beneath her as she settled back on the couch.

"Dana was just a hardworking, fun kid who loved horses when I first met her. It didn't take long for any of us at the stable to realize Dana's natural talent and her open-ended desire to learn. Within no time she was competing and winning against the best of them, including myself." Emma smiled at the fond recollection. Her hazel eyes filled with mischief and dimples played along the corners of her mouth.

"Anyways," she continued, colloquially. "Dana's parents eventually bought her Pepper and that's when Dana's life really started to come together. People all over the country were starting to stand up and take notice of the pair that were ruling the New England show circuit. We all just knew it was only a matter of time before the Selection Committee would be contacting her." Emma pursed her lips and blew softly into the air.

"She was so cool about it, like so what? She never allowed any of it to go to her head. She was always just herself." Emma paused, her impish face becoming sober.

"Then she met Sonny... who would've guessed?" Emma ran her small hand through her short unkept auburn hair, leaving the odd piece standing straight up on end. "Dana's life had been so planned... like, we all knew where she was going. Then Sonny just walked into her life and everything got twisted."

Emma came to a stop as she stared unseeingly at the wall.

Jarod felt like time had come to a standstill. Instinctively he knew that this was the moment he had deliberately sought out. He dared not to move or speak.

Emma took a deep breath and turned to face Jarod.

"In the beginning he was wonderful! He was charming and attentive, all the things a girl likes in a guy. They were so happy together." Her face broke into a sad smile.

"It started with little things. Sonny began to get annoyed with all the shows and the travelling every weekend. It didn't sit with him very well, Dana's being in the spotlight so much. He was constantly complaining about all the time she spent training. In the very beginning I think Dana thought his possessiveness was flattering. It was part of the package of all the attention he showered on her. She really didn't have a lot of experience with men, but I started to get worried. Sonny took care of her like she was a princess, but he wanted her in his castle. He didn't want her going anywhere without him and he didn't like her talking to anyone. It got to the point that he was jealous of the time she spent with me, for crying out loud!" The girl stood, almost beside herself and suddenly realizing that she wasn't going anywhere, she sat back down.

Jarod could not believe what he was hearing.

"Anyways," Emma said again. "They were arguing almost all the time, nothing was ever enough for him. Dana would try to give him the stars and he'd turn around and demand the moon. He was impossible, you have no idea."

Jarod was suddenly certain they were talking about the same Sonny, he knew all too well.

"The final straw came with the notice from the Selection Committee regarding Dana's being longlisted for the team. Sonny blew a fuse." Emma carefully picked up the photograph from the coffee table. She ran a finger over the glass and then replaced it where it belonged. When she looked back up at Jarod, tears were brimming in her eyes.

"They called her here... early in the morning. Sometime before morning feeding, Pepper had sliced a main artery in his foreleg. We managed to get to the barn while Pepper was still alive...barely. It was an awful sight, there was blood everywhere. I've never seen anything like it and I hope I never see it again. The vets were there already..." Emma shook her head slowly.

"Dana just dropped to her knees, in all that blood. She lifted Pepper's head unto her lap, sobbing. She insisted..." Emma cleared her throat and drew another breath. "She insisted on staying and she ordered the vet to put Pepper out of his misery." Emma wiped the tears from her eyes.

"We had quite a time trying to get her out of there after...after everything was finished. I don't even remember how we got home. But we were barely through the door when Sonny phoned. He told her, 'Everything was fixed and now they could be happy again'."

There was silence in the small room.

For a moment Jarod refused the impossibility of Emma's narration.

"What the hell are you trying to tell me? That Sonny killed Dana's horse!" Jarod could feel the color leave his face. "Did anyone call the police?"

"Of course we called the police," Emma said wearily. "But knowing something and proving it are two different things. There was no evidence," she shrugged. "They regrettably informed us there was nothing they could do and no charges were ever laid. That's when we first began to understand just how dangerous Sonny could be. We never knew where he was, but it always felt as though he was somehow watching. Dana wasn't just afraid for herself," Emma emphasized her point. "She was afraid for anyone or anything that touched her. That's about the time that she came across your ad and the rest you basically know."

As Jarod listened to Emma, the frightening possibility of what she was saying began to unfold in his mind. A cold terror gripped him.

"My God, Sonny is in New Mexico at the ranch posing as Dana's fiancé." Jarod looked into Emma's wide eyes. "I need to make some calls."

Emma mutely pointed Jarod to the phone, but he already had his cell in his hand.

He immediately got in touch with the local authorities in New Mexico, then he called the small airport and ordered them to ready his plane.

"Who's been phoning Dana's parents?" Emma asked, her pale face grim.

"Sonny," Jarod replied. His square jaw was tight as he held the cell phone to his ear. He shook his head in exasperation. "I've never talked to them personally. Damn!" Jarod snapped his phone shut. "No one's picking up at the house."

"You've got to get back there! I'm telling you, don't underestimate Sonny. He's crazy." Emma and Jarod looked at each other in an unspoken understanding. "I'll take care of Dana's parents, you keep that girl safe. Call me as soon as you can."

"Thanks for everything, Emma," Jarod told her as he ran down the steps.

Jarod pulled open his phone again and tried dialing the number to the stables without success. He slammed the steering wheel with his fist, his knuckles white, as he put the car into drive. It would take hours before he'd get back to the ranch! Those hours might as well be years, he thought, feeling completely powerless.

Dana woke. She looked around the pretty green bedroom and sighed out loud. It was the third morning and still nothing had changed.

Carefully she sat up in bed and attempted to stretch. Her body was still stiff and a little sore but gradually it was getting less and less so.

She walked over to her bedroom window and pulling the lace curtain aside, she peered outside. Jarod's car was already gone, he was on his way to see her parents. She pressed her eyes shut and willed a picture to appear, but it was useless.

How could a person not remember their own parents, she wondered in frustration? She really had had her fill of trying to be patient and again she felt engulfed by darkness she could not see through.

She went over to her dresser and picking up the photograph there, she carried it back to her bed. She sat amongst her pillows with the picture before her and tried to relax.

Shutting out the sounds around her and pushing away her worries, she studied the photograph carefully for a few minutes and then closed her eyes. It was an action shot, with the horse midway into a jump. Its muscular form was tensed, virtually suspended in midair and the sun was shining upon them.

In her mind she attempted to complete the jump. She could hear the hooves as they pounded the ground and the sounds of lots of people.

They were in the show ring. Dana's heart began to race and she could feel her fingers automatically tighten around the imaginary reins.

Her bedroom door opened and Juanita came into the room.

The image she had creatively brought to life disappeared.

"Beunos dias, Miss Dana. Are you feeling well?" The nurse briskly went to the closet.

For some inexplicable reason that Dana could not understand, she hastily covered the photograph with a pillow.

"I'm fine," Dana answered shortly, feeling embarrassed by the nurse's sudden intrusion.

The nurse began laying out Dana's clothing and running a bath. Dana climbed out of the bed and silently replaced the picture on the dresser.

"I'm able to do these things, Juanita," she told the nurse from the bathroom doorway.

The nurse straightened up.

"Miss Dana, I have to earn my keep," she answered with a bright smile, unperturbed.

Dana sighed again in resignation.

When Dana finished her bath and was dressed, she returned to her bedroom to find Juanita and June engaged in pleasant conversation. Her breakfast was waiting for her on a stand beside the chair and Juanita held her sling in her hands. Dana could feel her irritability once again beginning to mount and she struggled to conquer her growing sense of frustration. "Good morning, June," she greeted the older woman with a smile.

"Good morning, dear. I've just brought up your breakfast, you should eat before it gets cold."

Dana sat down without protest.

"Mr. Kingsley suggested last night that you might enjoy having Annie come by later, maybe she could have lunch here?" June asked. "I think it would be fun for you to have a little company."

"I think that is a great idea," Dana agreed politely as she began to eat. It seemed to her that the two women were hovering over her and she tried to accept their good intentions in the spirit that they were given.

"Well, I'll give Annie a ring at the barn and I'll fix that up. I'd best be getting back to work. Dana, if you need anything, you know where to find me." June gave her a motherly smile and left the room.

"It is going to be a beautiful day," Juanita conversed idly as she made up the bed.

"Really, Juanita. I don't understand why Jarod is having you stay out here, so far away from everything. I'm doing much better. It's really quite unnecessary," Dana said as she finished her breakfast and pushed away her tray.

"Miss Dana, Mr. Kingsley is only trying to do what he thinks is best," the nurse replied placidly as she began a quick examination of Dana. She posed the same short series of questions as she had done each morning.

Dana patiently accepted the nurse's administrations, knowing it was childish to argue any further.

The nurse prepared to put on the sling.

"Please, I don't want that on," Dana's frustration finally got the better of her. "It's a nuisance and it pulls on my neck," she complained.

"But, Miss Dana..."

"I'm just going to sit in my room for a while, quietly," Dana added with emphasis, a hint of sarcasm laced her words. "I'm not intending to fall out of the bed or bump into any walls. I promise."

"Very well," the nurse conceded. "We'll give you a little break from the sling." Juanita gave Dana a sympathetic smile. "I think you would enjoy a little break from me as well, hmm?"

Dana felt immediately contrite as she dropped her glance to the floor.

"What about if I go visit my aunt this morning, she lives not far from here, and I will be back before lunch?"

"I'm sorry, Juanita. I didn't mean to be so difficult."

"I understand. There is no need to be sorry, my aunt will be delighted to see me." Juanita smiled cheerfully at Dana before continuing. "It is never easy for an active person like yourself to be treated like an invalid. You have a strong character, Miss Dana. Never apologize for such a thing." The nurse gave her a gentle pat on her arm and departed from the bedroom.

She appreciated the nurse's intuition and the kindness of her words. Dana soon heard Juanita's car as it drove away.

She arranged her pillows on her bed and choosing a couple of magazines, she sat back to enjoy some privacy. As she leafed through the issues, her mind kept straying to thoughts of Jarod. She wondered if he

[181]

was already in Maine, if he was talking with her faceless parents. Maybe they would return with him tonight and maybe once she saw them she would remember them. She hoped so, for both their sakes.

Sonny entered the room, closing the door behind him. He walked over to her bed and kissed her lightly on the lips. "I thought those fussing hens would never leave," he declared as smiled at Dana.

"Good morning, Sonny." Dana had never felt very comfortable with Sonny's displays of affection, but she reasoned with herself that this strange situation had to be hard on him. After all, he loved her and she was the woman that he was going to marry.

"You must be getting fed up with all this attention," Sonny empathized as he regarded Dana.

"A little...but they mean well," Dana agreed, feeling somewhat guilty.

"It's a beautiful day. A good day to start thinking about making some changes," Sonny began, taking her hand in his. "I haven't seen Jarod anywhere and his car is gone."

"Jarod is gone to Maine." Dana was surprised that Sonny didn't know that already.

"To Maine..." Sonny artfully masked his reaction to the news. "That's right, he'd said something like that in the hospital, but with everything else, it slipped my mind," Sonny lied. If that bastard thought he was going to ambush him, he had another thing coming, Sonny thought to himself as the anger inside him grew. How did Jarod dare leave his little treasure? He was nothing but a fool after all, Sonny decided as he schemed. As if Jarod really expected to find them both there when he got back.

"Princess, this is all such a waste of time and money. I know Jarod has plenty of both to waste, but there is no reason for us to stay here. I can take care of you." Sonny edged himself behind Dana and began solicitously rubbing her back. "Hey, no sling today?"

Dana's body stiffened. There was something different in Sonny this morning and for some inexplicable reason she began to grow uneasy.

"I want us to go home," Sonny pleaded softly.

"No," Dana replied flatly. "I promised Jarod we would wait till he got back."

[182]

Sonny's hand arrested in midair as a blinding surge of rage shot through him. He'd had more than enough of Jarod's continual interference. It was time to put his plan into action, but he had one primal necessity that needed tending to first.

"Princess, I've missed you so bad," Sonny leaned forward and lifting Dana's hair, he began to kiss the curve of her neck. "If only you could remember how happy I can make you," Sonny whispered to her as he put his arms around her.

Dana began to tremble. His words echoed in her mind and fragmented images started tumbling through her consciousness, as her past began returning to her.

"You made a promise to me first," Sonny continued, hoarsely. "But, I guess you've forgotten that one. You promised me that you would be mine forever," he scolded her softly as he slid his hand under her shirt. "I've been so patient, Dana, but this is torture on a man."

The pictures were coming rapidly to Dana now, flooding her in cascading waves of sharply defined memories. The pieces quickly fell together, making the picture complete. She remembered everything.

Sonny slipped one hand between her legs and the other across her breasts, deftly lifting her backwards until she was hard against him.

Her panic was almost overwhelming, but she fought hard to remain in command of her senses. She had to think quickly and she had to be very careful.

Dana felt ill and she swallowed hard. "Sonny, wait," she said softly, striving for some control. "Wait…" her breath came unevenly. "I mean, June could walk in on us. She's always checking on me, let me go and make some excuses." There was a ring of truth in Dana's words and Sonny relented slightly.

"You're right. I'm certainly in no condition right now to be talking to June," Sonny whispered in her ear as he pressed his lower body against hers, making his need felt.

Dana closed her eyes, filled with revulsion.

He released her.

"Go make your excuses, Princess. Don't take long. I can't be expected to wait forever."

"It's true. You've waited a long time," Dana managed, almost choking on the words. Not knowing how her legs carried her, she slipped out the door and steadied herself against it. Please God, she prayed, let me get down the stairs.

She ran down the back stairs that led directly into the kitchen, nearly falling into the room. In her urgency, she barely felt the sharp pain that shot through her shoulder.

"June," she cried in a whisper. "Come with me!"

The older woman turned in astonishment.

"Dear child, what has happened?"

"There's no time for that now. We must leave!" Dana hastily grabbed the keys from the hook as she pulled June from the kitchen. June followed in a state of confusion. Something was terribly wrong.

Once outside Dana scrambled to the ranch truck dragging June behind her. Dana ordered June into the vehicle as she awkwardly heaved herself into the driver's seat.

With fingers that were violently shaking, Dana desperately managed to get the key into the ignition and clumsily she turned the truck away from the ranch. She sped down the lane towards the main road, searching for what Dana hoped would be safety.

- *Chapter 14* -

Leaving the main road, Dana put the truck into four-wheel drive and negotiated it over the hard terrain. There was an old abandoned lean-to that she had come across while she had been out riding Paska a couple of weeks earlier. She prayed that the derelict structure would be large enough to shield the sight of the truck from the road.

From this vantage point Dana was able to monitor any movement on the road that led to and from the ranch.

Dana was breathing heavily as she quickly silenced the engine and turned her attention to June. She was stunned by how pale the older woman's color had become.

"Dana, please explain to me what is going on. What are we doing here?" June's voice was barely more than a whisper in the ominous quietness that surrounded them.

"I'm so sorry, June. I didn't mean to frighten you." Dana stopped, realizing how absurd her words must seem. "Sonny is a very dangerous man. Everything he has told you has been a lie, an invention of his own twisted sense of reality."

She kept her eyes trained on the road below them. "We can't go back until I'm certain that it's safe," Dana warned as she rigidly sat forward in her seat.

"Dana, you remember, your memory is back?"

Dana nodded.

A cloud of dust rising from the road was fast approaching. The two women sat frozen, their hearts pounding as Sonny's vehicle sped by them, down the main road.

"Can we go back now?" June was the first to recover her voice.

"Not yet," Dana hesitated, placing a trembling hand over June's.

"Dana, what was Sonny doing here? What did he want?"

"He came here for me," Dana answered, anguished. "I've made so many mistakes." With a small motion she silently wiped a tear from her eye.

"I don't understand what is going on, but I refuse to believe any of this is your fault. You lost your memory, you couldn't have changed anything, dear." June spoke softly, struck by Dana's attitude of surrender.

June's faithful words of comfort only served to deepen Dana's feeling of guilt. If only she had been honest with everyone about her circumstances from the beginning, she thought. This all could have been prevented. Dana sat quietly, trying to deal with the full impact of the events of the past few days. It was too much for her to cope with.

Her thoughts were interrupted by the sound of a siren and within seconds a state trooper car swiftly sped by them and turned in towards the ranch.

Dana took in a deep breath.

"We can go back now."

In measured steps she started up the truck and carefully manoeuvred it back down the ridge.

A worried group awaited them as Dana parked the pick-up in the yard at the house.

Kent and Ben hurried over to the vehicle and opening the doors, they helped June and Dana from the truck.

Dana stood uncertain, protectively holding her arm as the state troopers approached her.

"Are you Dana Northington?"

"Yes," she replied quietly.

"We received a call from Maine, telling us there was a problem here at the ranch." The officer looked Dana over. "Is your arm injured?"

"My arm will be fine," she replied dismissively. "Have you picked up Sonny?" Dana asked, agitated.

"Not yet, Miss Northington. We will need a statement from you. You might be more comfortable indoors," the officer suggested.

"Can't this wait? Dana should rest, she really is in no condition right now." June looked anxiously at Dana.

Annie and Adam had joined the group. Annie rushed over to Kent asking him what was going on. Kent put his arm around Annie as he turned and faced the officers. "What you should be doing is finding Sonny,

[186]

before he leaves the state. Shit. He could cross the line into Mexico." Kent angrily spoke his mind.

"Let's not get too excited," the officer directed him sternly. "We can't just arrest somebody without a good reason. That's why we need a statement."

"We say we got good reason, that should be enough," Ben grumbled, unimpressed with the officers.

Dana could feel the mounting tension in the small crowd surrounding her. She could see the growing anxiety in their faces and she felt responsible for it all.

"Look, it's okay." Dana unsuccessfully attempted to calm everyone. "Let them just take my statement and get it over with," Dana said with resignation, feeling overwhelmed by it all.

Adam signaled their attention to a car that was turning into the ranch.

"Who's this?" the second officer demanded.

"It's my nurse. She went out earlier this morning," Dana explained as she watched the car approaching.

Juanita jumped out of her car. She rapidly tried to make sense of the scene before her. Ben met the nurse halfway and attempted to explain to her as much as he knew.

Juanita broke into the group. "Miss Dana, you should come inside and let me make sure you are alright," she spoke anxiously, protectively taking charge of her patient.

The nurse spoke briefly to the officer in Spanish and led Dana into the main house. Ben, June and one of the officers followed, while everyone else remained outside.

Dana hesitated and stopped in the doorway to the house.

"We should all go in," she told Ben as she looked to the others standing in the yard. "I think everyone should hear this, they deserve to know the truth."

Ben nodded in silent approval.

June was a woman of habit and she comforted herself keeping busy, preparing a pot of tea.

Everyone assembled in the living room, Annie sitting beside Dana on the couch. The officer in charge drew a chair forward and facing Dana, he pulled out a notepad and began to question her. The procedure was lengthy and difficult.

Dana's answers came slowly at first as she struggled to hold her composure. Her words were delivered in a flat monotone as she haltingly responded to the officer's probing questions.

Ben and Kent were barely able to control their frustration, while Adam stood in the corner of the room in silence.

Dana appeared unaware of Juanita's cursory examination as June placed a hot cup of tea before her. She deliberately avoided the faces of those around her as she continued with her notably unemotional account of what had happened.

She was inwardly consumed by fear and guilt. Dana realized as she had withheld the truth for too long and inadvertently she had placed them all in danger. Her silence had left everyone prey to Sonny's schemes and the one thing that Dana knew with certainty was that Sonny would be back.

The officer closed his notepad and squared his shoulders before speaking.

"Miss, I appreciate the ordeal that you've been through, but I don't have any solid grounds to issue an arrest. There is no existing warrant for Mr. Barton in Maine and as far as what's happened here," the officer shook his head, anticipating that his words would not be well received. "From what you've told me, Mr. Barton was invited into this house. There is no question of him using a false identity...other than a misunderstanding about an engagement."

Dana closed her eyes, she'd heard this all before. A tear slid unheeded down her pale cheek. "There must be something," she pleaded.

"We can bring him in for questioning... did he attempt to harm you in anyway?" The officer deliberately rephrased the question he had posed earlier.

Dana's voice was low and quivered as she spoke, her gaze remained on the floor. "He touched me."

"The bastard!" Kent exclaimed under his breath. Annie put her hand over Dana's.

The officer squatted down in front of Dana.

"Perhaps it would be best if we spoke privately," he suggested quietly.

She shook her head.

"How did he touch you?" The officer's tone was patient and unhurried. "Did Mr. Barton force himself on you?"

"Yes... I mean no!" Dana's self-control began to crumble. "I'm sorry, I can't do this!"

She bolted from the couch and ran up the staircase.

She abruptly came to a stop at the doorway to her room. As she stood immobile, staring into her room she began to tremble and a wave of nausea swept over her. She turned away and leaned against the doorway.

Dana startled at June's touch.

"Poor child," June uttered as she put her arms around the girl.

"I can't go in there."

"There's no need to go in there," June comforted her.

Dana raised her head off June's shoulder. Her face was damp and tendrils of hair fell across her forehead. "I'm so sorry."

June avoided the subject as she led Dana to the main bathroom on the second floor. "What you need is a hot bath."

Juanita reached the top of the stairs and turned toward them. Together, Juanita and June tended to Dana, preparing a bath and getting some personal items from Dana's room.

Juanita paused, considering what she had to say.

"Miss Dana, if there is any question about what happened, there are things that should be done, before you wash," she said as tactfully as possible.

"No, it didn't happen." A look of pain crossed Dana's face. "I swear."

"Okay," June said softly. "We'll leave you alone, but we won't be far." She closed the bathroom door.

Dana stepped into the bath and lowered herself slowly into the hot water. Picking up a sponge she generously covered it with soap and carefully began scrubbing away any trace of Sonny's hands.

When she was finished, she dressed and unlocked the bathroom door. She opened it to find both June and Juanita standing in the hallway.

"Come, Chiquita," Juanita led Dana into June's bedroom. She sat the unprotesting girl on the bed, once again checking her pulse and her blood pressure.

"I'm going to give you a sedative, to sleep," the nurse advised as she prepared the medication.

"I'll stay with you," June told Dana as she saw the look of panic in Dana's eyes. "Don't be afraid, child. We'll take good care of you," she said gently.

Juanita administered the medication and then left the two women alone.

June pulled down the covers on the bed, and settled Dana in. She sat on the side of the bed and held her hand.

"Jarod called while you were with the officer and he's on his way. He will be here in a few hours. I know he'd move heaven and earth to be here with you now, if he could."

Dana nodded her head, becoming drowsy as the medication began to take effect.

Jarod entered the room silently, closing the door softly behind him.

He made his way to the bed in the dimly lit room and looked down on the tightly curled figure with the face of an angel. Dana appeared so delicate in the large bed.

The seemingly endless trip home had been hell and now that he was here, he longed to lift Dana into his arms and hold her against himself forever, feeling her safe within his strong embrace.

He ordered himself into a chair, not daring to take his eyes from her as he quietly waited.

Dana stirred and her eyes slowly opened. She looked around the strange room and her gaze fell upon Jarod.

"Jarod," her voice was a low whisper.

He left the chair and came to her. Standing before her, he looked deep into eyes that were pools of pain.

Dana's lip began to quiver and tears welled up in her eyes as she reached out to him.

Jarod sat on the bed and gently took her into his arms. She buried her face in his chest as she clung to him in quiet desperation, sobbing uncontrollably. Silently, he slowly rocked her back and forth, his body encompassing her like a shield.

Her tears gradually subsided and Jarod reached forward and pulling a tissue from June's bed stand, he tenderly dried Dana's face.

[190]

"I'm glad you're back," she told him in a subdued voice as her fingers clutched nervously at his shirt.

"I'm glad you're back, too." A smile crossed Jarod's weary face. "You have no idea how much I've missed you." Jarod ran his hand down the side of Dana's face, his fingers lightly tracing along her jaw, gently lifting her chin.

"I have so much I have to tell you," Dana's voice shook as she met his eyes.

"Dana, I know most of it already," Jarod explained quietly. "Emma told me when I was in Maine."

"Oh, my God! Emma, my parents, do they know?"

"It's alright. Emma knows you're safe. I phoned her as soon as I got back to the ranch and as fate would have it, your parents don't know anything of what has happened in the past few days."

"That's impossible," Dana argued uncomprehendingly.

"It was Sonny who volunteered to phone them at the hospital and I foolishly went along with him," Jarod explained as he felt Dana's body stiffen at the mention of Sonny's name. "It's okay, Dana. Sonny is long gone. You're safe now." Jarod reassured her as he held her tightly.

Dana closed her eyes, feeling the hardness of Jarod's chest against her cheek. She could hear the beating of his heart. She longed to stay like that forever but she had to make Jarod understand. Taking a deep breath, she pulled herself away.

"You can't make the same mistake that I did. He'll be back, he'll never leave me alone." Dana blinked rapidly, trying not to cry again. "It's not just me, you are not safe either. No one is. I should leave here."

"No!" Jarod said abruptly. "Don't ever say that, Dana. I've just gone through the past five days without you and I don't ever want to do that again. I've already hired security. It's safe here."

Dana shook her head, looking away. It was so hard to stay strong. She felt as if her heart was breaking, but she knew she'd brought enough trouble to this house already.

"Do you really see yourself living around security indefinitely?" Dana asked him. "Sonny won't stop until he has what he wants. You, more than anyone, must see that now." she retaliated bitterly. "If I stay here, I will ruin everything for everyone!"

Jarod watched her with a sense of helplessness. He ran his hand over his eyes as he lowered his head. "Dana, from the day I first met you, my life has never been the same," he whispered to her. "I love you. I swear, I'll never let Sonny hurt you again. I don't care what it takes."

Pain pierced through Dana's heart and unable to stop herself she gently pulled him to her.

Jarod cupped her face with his two hands and gently kissed her.

"I know you're frightened and I know how hard you've tried to handle this on your own, but you're not alone anymore, we are in this together. Please, Dana, just let me help you. You don't need to shut me out anymore."

Dana felt the last vestiges of her resolve collapsing.

"The morning of the accident, I was going to tell you everything but I couldn't find you," she explained quietly. "Everything you'd said the day before in the barn made me realize how wrong I had been." Dana ran her hand through Jarod's hair. She continued to speak. "I don't know when it was, that I started to fall in love with you. It just seems like it's always been there. Almost as if since the time that I was a child, I would grow up and meet you." Dana smiled and a tear spilled onto her cheek. "I can't believe how much I've put you through and I can't believe that you're still here."

Jarod tenderly kissed the tears from her eyes.

"I will always be here," he vowed.

"Jarod, this decision involves more than just the two of us. I want everyone to know exactly what they're up against. Look at what June's been through today." Dana pointed out, unwilling to give in without insisting on her conditions.

"Don't underestimate June," Jarod replied. "She's a smart, strong woman."

Jarod looked around the room. "Speaking of June, we could probably give her back her room," he said.

"I... I don't want to go back to my room," Dana shook her head, her face was drawn. "I just can't yet"

Jarod was immediately reminded of what June had repeated to him of Dana's interview with the authorities and Jarod managed to control his sudden surge of rage.

"Listen, you can sleep in my room and I'll sleep somewhere else," he volunteered.

"No, I don't want to put you out of your room. That's not right," Dana refused his offer.

"Okay, we'll both stay in my room. I can sleep on the chair. I promise I'll be the perfect gentleman. I'd rather have you close by anyway."

Somewhat shyly Dana agreed, feeling the same need.

"Come on then, let's get you settled in."

Jarod stood and gently helped Dana to her feet. She was emotionally drained and still a little groggy from the strong sedative as Jarod guided her down the hall to his room.

"Dana, I'm going to bring us up something to eat. I haven't eaten since early this morning and I would imagine it's been pretty much the same for you."

Dana nodded.

"You make yourself comfortable. I'll tell June she can have her room back and then I'll return with some food. I won't be long."

Jarod made his way down the stairs.

Dana slowly studied the room. Unlike her own attractive room, that was virtually absent of any personal effects, Jarod's room was his own.

The two exterior walls were paneled with timber planks and the interior walls were plastered with stucco. A Navaho quilt covered the massive antique, four-poster bed and over the head of the bed an arrowhead collection hung from the wall. It was a quiet, solid room done in deep earth tones and it exuded the subtle fragrance of Jarod's cologne. Dana found it immediately comforting.

She leaned against a dresser and examined the few items that were there, curious to study the photographs of Jarod growing up. Eventually her eyes came to rest on what was obviously a wedding picture of Jarod's parents.

There was a light rap at the door and June entered. In her hands were Dana's nightgown and robe.

Dana was once again bashful and she could sense her cheeks becoming warm with blush.

"Mr. Kingsley asked me to bring some things to you, Dana." Noticing Dana's discomfort, June made an effort to put the girl at ease. "I agree that it is best you stay in here, so I don't want you feeling awkward about it. After all you've been through, we just want you safe and comfortable."

"Thank you, June... for everything." Dana walked over and gave the woman a heartfelt hug. "You've been so good to me, I don't know what to say. A simple thank you hardly seems to suffice."

"Don't be silly, dear." June returned the hug, clearly touched by Dana's overture. "Anything I do for you, I do by choice. You are a very special person and I've become so fond of you. I'm sure there's not a single soul at this ranch that doesn't feel the same way. We are like family here." June kissed Dana's cheek before she turned and left.

Jarod soon entered the room carrying a tray laden with fruit, cheese and a loaf of crusty bread. He carefully settled it on the bed and they both sat.

"I feel like a kid again, eating in bed," he commented as he broke off a piece of bread and offered it to Dana.

"I just had the same experience when June brought in my things."

Dana remained quiet, picking distractedly at her food. Jarod studied her from the corner of his eye.

"Dana, you have a doctor's appointment tomorrow," he gently reminded her.

"I don't see why it's necessary any longer," she began to protest. "My shoulder is healing fine and my memory is back."

"Dana, you probably won't have to go back after this visit," he interrupted her. "Besides, there is something I want to okay with your doctor," he added, catching her attention.

Dana looked at him with curiousity.

"Are you done with this?" Jarod asked, pointing to the tray of food.

She nodded.

"I'm not very hungry after all," she explained.

He removed the tray from the bed and then sat down beside her, holding her in his arms.

"I'd like to take you away for a while. I think you could use some breathing space, a chance to get yourself together without, you know, without all these reminders." Jarod spoke to her softly.

She didn't answer immediately as she thought over his suggestion.

[194]

"Where would we go?" Dana asked flatly, her face expressionless.

"I don't know," he paused considering. "Somewhere completely different. What about Canada? Have you ever been to Montreal?" Jarod's suggestion took her by complete surprise.

"No," she answered slowly, still unconvinced.

"Then that sounds like a good idea," Jarod continued, his plan beginning to take shape. "We could even stop in Maine on the way there, maybe spend a day with your parents. I'd like to meet these wonderful people," he smiled at her softly. "What do you think, would you like that?"

Dana's eyes began to grow bright with tears.

"I miss my Mom and Dad."

"Okay... don't cry, Dana." Jarod gently wiped a tear from her eye. "I think you've shed your share of tears today." He kissed her forehead. "I think with what's happening between us," Jarod made a small motion. "They might be interested in meeting me as well."

Dana offered him a tentative smile. "I think they'd be thrilled to meet you," she agreed as color began to return to her cheeks.

"Good, that's what we'll do then. We'll go to Maine for a day and then we'll head to Montreal and get away from things for a while. I'm looking forward to us spending some time together, just the two of us." Jarod kissed her again then got up and helped Dana out of bed.

"Okay, you can get changed in my bathroom. We need to get some sleep."

When Dana came out of the bathroom, Jarod was standing at the window in a pair of university sweat pants. He turned to face her and both of them hesitated for a moment feeling awkward.

She noticed that he'd already arranged a blanket and pillow on the easy chair.

"I feel awful about this," she told him, staring at the chair.

"Don't. I've slept in worse places than this," he said, making light of the situation.

She couldn't help but notice his masculine form, she had never seen him dressed this way. She quickly averted her gaze and made her way to the bed and climbing in she quickly pulled up her covers.

"Sleep well, Dana." Jarod told her as he leaned over and kissed her forehead before turning off the lamp.

She heard him walk back over to the chair and settle in. Finding her voice, she answered "Good night, Jarod,"

Dana lay in bed for what seemed an eternity, watching the shadows against the wall. The sedative had long worn off and she was no longer sleepy. There was a dull ache in her shoulder and every creak in the house sent her heart pounding. She tossed and turned, feeling restless and apprehensive. She listened for Jarod's even breathing and then she slowly got out of the bed.

Noiselessly she made her way to the bedroom door and carefully opened it, checking down the dark hallway, listening carefully for movement. She listened so intently that the silence thundered in her ears.

"Dana?" Jarod called softly from his chair. He was awake, but he didn't move, afraid that he might startle her.

She turned back into the room, standing motionless in the semi-darkness against the door.

"What are you doing?" Jarod asked her gently as he rose from his chair and walked over to her.

"I can't sleep. I... I thought I heard something," she said in a small voice.

He led her back to the bed and climbed in beside her.

"It's okay, Dana. You're safe now," he soothed her as he cradled her in his arms. "Listen to me. It's one thing for a man to terrorize a woman who is on her own, but Sonny would be a fool to come back now. His game is up." Jarod told her convincingly. He knew she was listening to what he was saying. "Men like that are cowards at heart. You'll see, everything will be fine. I promise, Dana."

He kissed her forehead as she curled up against his body, laying her head into the hollow between his chest and shoulder.

Her delicate fists clutched at the bed sheets as she nodded and he could feel her silent tears fall to his bare chest.

"Shh..." he murmured as he ran his fingers through her hair.

He lay perfectly still, waiting until her hands finally relaxed and her trembling ceased.

- Chapter 15 -

The sun began to rise and the pale traces of light seeping through the window only enhanced the wheat blond streaks in his hair. It occurred to Dana that she had never seen Jarod asleep and that even in sleep his sculptured features and square jaw defined so well the integrity and the strength of the man he was inside.

Dana silently thanked God for having brought her to this place... to him. She buried her face into his chest and breathed deeply, allowing his scent to soothe her soul. Jarod's arm remained loosely draped around her. Dana closed her eyes and cherished the moment.

Jarod woke and looked down at Dana, his arms instinctively tightening around her. His body begged for her and he quickly reminded himself of all that Dana had been through in the past few days.

"Good morning, sweetheart."

"Hi," Dana replied tranquilly, allowing her hand to run the length of his arm and over his shoulder to where it came to rest on his cheek.

Jarod turned his head into her hand and slowly kissed her palm.

"I cannot tell you how many times I've dreamed about waking up like this... with you here beside me." Jarod turned towards her, a smile breaking across his face. "How are you feeling this morning?"

"I'm feeling better," Dana told him, realizing it was the truth. Last night her fears had gotten beyond her reach in the solitary darkness. Daylight managed to dispel those fears and lying within Jarod's strong embrace offered her the promise of a new beginning.

"Maybe you should stay in bed and rest. I can bring up your breakfast," Jarod offered.

"No, I want to get up." Dana shook her head.

"Okay, you can use the shower in here, I'll go down the hall. If you get out of bed I may actually be able to get myself into gear, because as long as you're here with me, I'll never move." Jarod sighed as he reluctantly opened his arms.

After completing his shower and dressing, Jarod returned to his room to find Dana sitting on the edge of his bed in a robe, her hair damp.

"I'm sorry, Dana. I never thought of sending you in a fresh change of clothing. This morning I'll have June pack up your things and move them in here."

Dana stood.

"I was wondering... if you'd come with me now, to my room." Dana looked at Jarod. "I know it's something I have to do and I'm not helping myself by putting it off."

"Of course I'll come with you, if you're sure you're ready to do this," Jarod questioned, adding "Dana, you don't have to do this if you don't want to. You don't have to prove anything to anyone."

"Only to myself," she answered him and he understood.

Jarod intentionally let Dana lead the way to her room, recognizing the need she had to face her demons on her own terms. He knew that this part of Dana's journey into healing would not come easily to her. He wanted more than anything to make her pain disappear but he realized that even if he was able to do such a thing he would be doing her no favor. Sonny had stolen her courage and she was determined to have it back.

Jarod's role in this was only to be there for her and to catch her should she fall.

Dana briefly hesitated in the doorway before entering the room.

Her bedroom was neat and tidy and it was obvious that June had already been there. She looked over to the bed that had been carefully made and then checked over her shoulder. Jarod gave her a reassuring smile, but she could see the uncertainty in his eyes.

She took a deep breath and walked over to her dresser. She was about to open her drawer when her hand stopped and changed direction. She picked up the photograph of herself and Pepper. "To think that Sonny came in here, day after day and looked at this picture... I'm sure it brought him great pleasure." Dana's voice was low. She replaced the photo where it belonged.

Jarod remained still, pushing his hands deeper into his pockets. His heart ached for her.

He noticed her empty expression. It was a look very similar to the way she had appeared to him when she'd had amnesia, and it struck him that it truly seemed to be Dana's way of protecting herself.

"I think he was originally coming to take me, the day of the fall," Dana looked out her window, pensive. "But then, after I was hurt, he didn't know what to do with me," she stopped, momentarily lost in thought.

"That's when it became a game." Dana sat down in the chair by the window and looked up at Jarod. He understood what she was doing, it was as though they had reached a silent agreement between themselves and he knew she must continue.

"I believed him. He seemed so strange to me, but then almost everything was strange to me. He was constantly telling me how in love we were, how happy he made me. He sat in here, hour upon hour, stealing and exchanging as many pieces of my life as he could. As if he hadn't gotten enough of me already."

Dana's hands came together, lying quietly in her lap. Jarod had seen her do the exact same thing before, but he couldn't place where or when. He knew it was another of her many contradictions, an outward sign of serenity that carefully masked her underlying desperation.

"Yesterday," Dana slowly brought herself to look at the bed. "He came in here and he was in such a good mood. I couldn't understand it. I know now, he was planning to take me away. Then, when he knew you were gone, he decided to take full advantage of the situation."

The seriousness of what Dana said hit Jarod like a rock. He could only imagine what might have happened to Dana if she had not regained her memory. He lowered his eyes and ran his hand over his face as he prepared himself to listen through to the end.

"He never had a problem trading truth for fiction. What I wanted or how I felt never existed for him, even when I had a memory. And with none, I was an easy target. He began touching me, rubbing my back and kissing me. I started having these flashes," she shook her head. "No, it was more like pictures jumping around in my mind, like clips out of a movie."

Dana shuddered and Jarod's jaw tightened.

"By the time that everything made sense to me, he already had me pinned against him. His hands were... everywhere," she described lamely.

"I was terrified that he would know. He'd always had a way of knowing things. I think a pretender instinctively recognizes a pretence. I had to get out of the room. I pleaded with him to allow me to make an excuse to June not to disturb us. He had a look of sheer delight on his face and his hands never left my body while he considered if he should let me go or not. I thought my heart would explode out of my chest. I thought he would look into my eyes and know that I knew. But, for once his fantasy backfired on him, he believed what he wanted to believe and he let me go."

The room was silent.

It sickened Jarod to think of what Sonny had done to Dana... of what he might have done.

"Well, I'm sure June has told you the rest," Dana sat stiffly in her chair, her features defiant. "He'll never touch me like that again."

Jarod walked over to her chair and knelt beside it. Gently he raised her hand to his lips.

"I'll never let him near you again."

Dana looked into Jarod's clear blue eyes and wished she could believe him, but she had long since given up on fairy tales and a part of her denied her that wish. She understood more and more what Sonny was capable of and she doubted that anyone would have any control over what Sonny could or could not do.

"You know everything now," Dana said with an air of finality.

She had cleansed herself.

Jarod stood and held his hands out to Dana.

"Let June pack your things," he told her. "You've done what you came here to do."

Dana nodded and reaching for his open hands she stood up. She went to her dresser and pulled out a change of clothing then reached for the photograph and carefully added it to the small bundle. Taking one last look around the room, she turned her back on it and left.

Jarod closed the door behind them.

Once again in the sanctuary of Jarod's room, Dana turned and put her arms around him. Jarod held her close.

"Thank you," she said softly.

"For what?"

"For knowing me so well, for never pushing or asking for more than I can give."

She lightly kissed his lips and then stepped back. "I really think it's time I got dressed. It's going to be lunchtime before we've had breakfast." Dana was anxious for their lives to return to some kind of normalcy.

Jarod seemed to sense her change of mood. "Why don't I run downstairs and let June know we'll be eating shortly and you can join us when you're ready," he suggested.

Dana agreed and he picked up the tray from the night before and left for the kitchen.

At the sound of his approaching footsteps, June turned and greeted him.

"Good morning, Mr. Kingsley. How is Dana this morning?" June inquired as she handed him his mug of coffee.

"Good morning, June. She's amazingly strong." Jarod put the tray on the counter and accepted the cup. "She'll be down in a few minutes, so you'll be able to see for yourself." Jarod smiled.

"I'll be bringing her to Santa Fe this afternoon for her check-up," he explained as he drank his coffee. "June, I'd like to take her away for a few days, a week. I can ask Kent to come and stay at the main house with you and of course the security people would still be here. Do you think you would be alright like that?"

"I don't think you have to worry about Mr. Barton coming after me," she replied stoutly. "I think he had quite enough of me while he was here." June chuckled. "I think the trip will do you both the world of good. Do you know where you want to go?" June asked him as she busied herself at the stove.

"Canada, Montreal to be precise. I thought we could go to Maine for a day on the way there," Jarod answered just as Dana entered the kitchen.

"Good morning, June," Dana timidly smiled.

"Jarod tells me you are doing well, is that true?" June set down their breakfast and turned to pour Dana's coffee.

"Yes, I'm feeling much better." Dana watched the woman as she moved about the kitchen. "Were you able to sleep last night, after all that happened yesterday?"

"I slept just fine, dear. Thank you for asking. It's been many years now since I've stopped looking behind me. I always try to look forward and there's usually something worth looking towards." June directed Dana a knowing nod of her head as she started clearing up.

As they ate, Jarod worked out the details for the trip the next day in his mind.

"Dana, when we're done eating I'll make our flight arrangements, if there's any problems at the doctor's, they can be cancelled. Maybe we could leave early for Santa Fe and do a little shopping, in case you are needing anything for our trip. I know I'd like to get your parents a little something, I'll be meeting them for the first time. I think it would be rather rude to show up there empty handed."

Dana looked at him, touched by his thoughtfulness. Jarod was always so careful to do the right thing.

June stopped by the table, checking on them.

"I think you'll hardly be showing up empty handed. You'll be bringing them the greatest gift of all," June interrupted as she lightly placed her hand on Dana's arm.

"Everyone has been so good to me, I hardly feel like I deserve this," Dana paused, taking a deep breath. "Jarod, that reminds me. If we are leaving tomorrow, I'd like to get everyone together tonight. I still have something I have to take care of." Dana felt the need to face everyone and make sure they understood the situation.

Jarod nodded.

"June, would it be a problem to have the crew in for dinner tonight?" Jarod asked. "Make something simple, we want you there as well."

"That will be fine," she agreed.

"Okay, after I've called for the flight, I'll get a hold of Ben and he can pass the word along." Jarod pushed away his plate. "I suppose I should tell Juanita that she can leave whenever she's ready. Has anyone seen her?"

"She had breakfast just before you came downstairs and she took her coffee on the verandah. I can get her for you. I'm sure she'll be happy to be getting back to her family."

Jarod stood.

"No, that's alright June. I'll take care of everything at the same time." Jarod bent down and kissed the top of Dana's head. "I won't be long," he told her and left the room.

Dana and June exchanged smiles.

"It's been a hard path that the two of you have had to travel." June sat in Jarod's empty chair. "But it's a wonderful thing that you have found each other. It's good to see Mr. Kingsley is himself once again. For a while I was worried."

"I know. There are a lot of things I should've done differently. I've caused him a lot of pain. I guess I was pretty mixed up." Dana stared at the table in front of her before looking at June. "I never meant to hurt him... or anyone."

"No one thinks that, child. Especially Mr. Kingsley," June smiled fondly. "You've quieted the loneliness that has always haunted him. He loves you with all his heart. Some things are meant to be and sometimes people are lucky enough to find happy endings."

June stood back up. "I shouldn't keep you, you'll be wanting to get ready to go to Santa Fe."

After relieving Juanita of her duties, Jarod placed a call to the hospital. He had Dana's appointment changed to an earlier time and warned the secretary not to give any information concerning Dana to anyone. Sonny was aware of the original appointment and Jarod was not taking any chances.

He then considered the flight arrangements. The thought of having Dana's name on a commercial flight list for twenty-four hours seemed to have too many risks involved and he chose to charter a plane to Maine instead. Sonny had shown his talents and unpredictability in the past and Jarod hated the feeling that he could not be too careful.

The second to last call he placed was to the barns. He talked to Ben and explained about the dinner scheduled for that evening. He made another call as well.

Within the hour Jarod and Dana were on their way to the city. Dana was quietly introspective as she reflected on what June had said that morning.

"A penny for your thoughts," Jarod said, noticing her silence.

Dana smiled at him reassuringly. "I was just thinking how nice it would be if people really could stop looking behind them and just focus on their future," she said wistfully.

"I think it's certainly worth a try. Mind you, there are some things you don't want to leave behind."

"No, I know that," Dana agreed, smiling at him.

"Can you do me a favor this afternoon?"

Dana looked surprised. "Of course, what is it?"

"Leave the worrying to me, okay?"

"I'll try," she promised.

They arrived for Dana's appointment in ample time.

Once Dr. Weber had completed examining Dana, he informed them that everything appeared fine. Her memory had returned much the way he had said it would and her shoulder was healing nicely. He could see no reason why a little vacation was not in order. Dana could go ahead with her proposed holiday.

Jarod and Dana stepped out of the hospital and stopped on the city sidewalk.

"Well, I'm glad that's behind us." Jarod said as he stood in the sunshine looking around, mentally planning what they should do first.

Dana enjoyed watching him, he seemed relaxed and confident.

"So, do you feel up to some shopping or would you prefer to go back to the ranch?" Jarod turned his attention to Dana and caught her watching him.

He grinned boyishly and kissed her.

"I think shopping would be fun," she replied, falling in with his obvious happiness. "And I think I liked your idea about bringing some gifts home."

"Okay," Jarod quickly agreed as he settled Dana into the car. He got in as well and nosed the car out of the parking lot, turning it downtown.

Jarod held Dana's hand as they leisurely strolled from shop to shop. They stopped at a little street booth and Jarod purchased a large brimmed straw hat that he placed on Dana's head. He lifted her chin up and carefully examined the effect.

"You are truly are beautiful," he said the words with feeling as he openly studied her face.

Dana was secretly pleased and she demurely dropped her gaze.

They made their way along the busy street and came across a gift shop that specialized in local handmade items and art.

"Can we stop in here?" Dana suggested.

They entered the small shop and Dana browsed through the wide collection of articles. A small painting caught her attention. It was a landscape of New Mexico and it captured the color and the rugged beauty of her new home. It reminded Dana of the wonderment she had experienced when she had looked across the ranch for the first time.

"Emma would love this painting," Dana said decisively.

Jarod motioned to the clerk, who brought the picture down and carried it to the counter.

"Do you see anything here that your parents would like?"

"Hmm," Dana considered, her gaze travelling along the walls to a set of wind chimes almost directly over her head.

"I think those wind chimes would look lovely on my parents' porch," she said turning to Jarod. "What do you think?" They'll be able to think of me every time the wind blows. That sounds corny, right?"

"I think that sounds like you're planning on staying on at the ranch," Jarod said quietly with an easy smile, imperceptibly moving closer to her.

Dana's breath caught in her throat as she realized the implication in his words. She felt her face flush and her body become suddenly warm.

"It does, doesn't it?" Dana replied in a little breath.

Jarod smoothly reached over her head and unhooked the chimes, placing them in her hands. He guided her to the counter and pulled out his wallet.

"I'll pay," Dana objected. "After all, I have a boss who gives me a pretty decent salary and I rarely get the chance to spend it."

"Dana, today is my treat. Indulge me." Jarod paid the bill and they stepped back out into the street.

"You're so full of demands today, Jarod." Dana teased. "First you insist on doing all the worrying, now you want to do all the spending. What do I get to do?"

"You get to pick where we're going to eat. I'm getting hungry."

They settled on a little restaurant and ordered a light lunch.

Dana realized that she was beginning to look forward to their holiday.

"Tell me about Montreal, what's it like?" Dana urged Jarod as the waitress brought their food to the table.

"Let me see, as you must know, Quebec is primarily a French settlement, a province. Montreal is a major city and as far as I could tell, the population is both French and English. It's not unlike here in Santa Fe where most people speak two languages also. I manage better in Spanish though, my French is a little rusty, I must admit." Jarod shrugged and smiled.

"As far as cities go, it's quite beautiful, especially at night. I was there for a few days a couple of years ago on business and I found it quite enjoyable. This trip will mean so much more to me."

"I'm sure that there must be some beautiful women in Montreal." Dana smiled coyly at Jarod.

"There were and I'm sure there still are, but it's impossible to see the stars when the sun is shining."

Dana made a face at him and shook her head. "You're so smooth."

"I thought so." Jarod smiled.

They finished their lunch and made their way to a dress shop.

Jarod stood and patiently waited as Dana picked up a few items that she thought she might need on the trip. Every now and then she would hold something up for Jarod's approval. As he stood waiting, he noticed a delicate cotton dress that was displayed in the store aisle. His eyes kept straying to the dress and eventually he picked it up and carried it to her.

"Do you like this dress?"

Dana studied the item in his arms. It was a long sleeveless dress made of a fine white cotton that was neatly hand-embroidered. The bodice was fitted with tiny pearl buttons and the skirt was generous.

"It's very pretty. Would you like me to try it on?"

Dana took the dress into the changing room. She lifted it over her head and let it fall into place.

Her hands traveled down the sides of her body as she turned slightly to catch the view of herself from behind.

The cut of the dress complimented the curves of her body and its stark whiteness mirrored the intensity of her eyes. It was the perfect fit.

Dana considered showing Jarod the dress but decided against it, choosing instead to surprise him when the time was right.

Dana changed into her own clothes and joined Jarod.

"So, is there anything else that you need?" Jarod asked her.

She surveyed the selection of clothing in front of her.

[206]

"I think I have quite enough."

"Did the dress fit?"

"The dress fit very nicely. Thank you," Dana smiled up at Jarod. "I mean thank you for everything. I'm sure there are a lot of other things you could be doing."

"I want to be doing things like this for the rest of my days." Jarod answered as he helped her with her purchases.

It was mid-afternoon by the time they got back to the ranch.

Jarod followed Dana up the stairs to his room, carrying the parcels.

"You should lie down for a while and rest before dinner," he suggested. "I think I'll start packing. Dinner will probably take up most of the evening."

He strode over to the large closet and pulled down two suitcases from the shelf, placing one on the edge of the bed and the other on the floor.

Dana came over and began sorting the clothes.

"Lie down," he told her as he gently propelled her to the other side of the bed.

"I'll help to pack," Dana insisted.

"Look, I know you hate people doing things for you, but you've been so co-operative today already, just let me do the packing." Jarod grinned at her and then became serious.

"Really, Dana. We've been walking for most of the day and I can see your shoulder is starting to get sore. I've packed so many times I can do it with my eyes shut. Please lie down, you've got a big night ahead of you and I don't want you taking a turn for the worse before our trip."

Jarod arranged the pillow on the bed and sat, patting the mattress beside him.

Dana sat down too.

He took her hand in his as he studied her face. He could see the traces of fatigue under her blue-green eyes and he pushed an errant tendril of hair from her damp forehead.

"Maybe the afternoon was too big of a jump for you," he said, cursing himself. "I'm sorry, I got carried away. I don't know what I was thinking."

[207]

"You were thinking the same thing that I was," Dana said softly. "How nice it was to be where I've always wanted to be, with you. No yesterdays and no tomorrows to confuse us, just now."

There was no need for any more explanations between them.

Dana obediently lay down on the bed and Jarod quietly resumed packing.

June had already brought Dana's things into the room and Jarod efficiently arranged their belongings in the bags as Dana rested against her pillow, watching. A smile crossed his face as he double-checked his work.

"What are you smiling about?" Dana asked in idle curiosity.

"I was just thinking about how natural it is to have your things mixed in with mine, and how much I like having you rooming with me."

"Well, you certainly got the short end of the deal." The words slipped out of Dana's mouth and she immediately began to blush as she struggled up in bed. "I'm sorry, I meant... I..."

"It's okay, Dana. You don't need to be embarrassed." Jarod placed the suitcase on the floor and climbed over the bed.

"I'm sure we've both thought about it and we've both realized that now is just not the time." Jarod put his arm around her. "Our time will come and we'll know when it's right. That doesn't mean I don't enjoy having you here with me. It seems like I've waited all my life for you to walk through my door. I'm in no hurry. I love you, Dana." Jarod lowered his head and slowly kissed her lips.

"You're going to get me crying again," Dana whispered.

Jarod lifted his eyes to hers and saw that she was telling the truth.

"Lay down beside me," he entreated her and she curled into his powerful frame.

Jarod checked the time on the bed stand.

"Get some sleep, Dana. I'll wake you up when it's time to go downstairs." They had a little more than an hour before dinner would be ready.

Annie and Kent were the first to arrive, followed within minutes by Adam and Ben. They had all extended Dana their best wishes by the time they assembled in the dining room.

Dana had already discussed the seating arrangements with June and she now took her seat at the end of the table directly across from Jarod.

Annie, Kent and June sat on one side of the table while Ben and Adam sat on the other.

The conversation remained light and pleasant during dinner as everyone followed Jarod's lead. Knowing what was to follow, Dana felt on edge throughout the course of the meal and when it would become too much for her to bear, she would look across the table at Jarod and draw needed strength from his comforting presence.

Finally coffee was served and the room gradually became silent.

Dana knew it was time.

"I've asked Jarod to arrange this meeting because," Dana swallowed hard as she helplessly lifted her eyes to Jarod. There was a moment of stilted silence and Jarod watched her, mutely giving her a nod. "Because we have a serious problem," she continued slowly. "I used the word we, because no matter how much I wish I could change things, as long as I stay here I believe I'm putting you all in danger."

Dana looked around the table.

"I've made some mistakes. I was wrong to withhold my past from you. And I was wrong when I vainly believed that Sonny would stop after I came here. I had no right to put any of you in jeopardy. I underestimated Sonny." Dana shook her head as she stared at the table in front of her.

"In light of what's recently happened, I have a hard time trying to justify what I've done. I can only tell you how very sorry I am to have put you all in this position." Her eyes locked onto Jarod's as she directed her next words to him as well as the others. "I can't turn the clock back and change what's already happened, but I'm pretty sure that I know a way to prevent anything like it from happening again. I can leave."

Dissention broke out at the table and Jarod held up his hand. "Hear her out. Dana called you all here, because she feels the need to tell you everything. Please listen to what she has to say."

Gratefully, Dana offered Jarod the ghost of a smile.

"Sonny wants me. He is heartless and would think nothing of hurting anyone who stood in the way of that, but really he does only want me. If I stay here I can't predict what he might do to any of you, but if I remove myself from the equation, you could all return to the lives you had before I came here."

Jarod had never taken his eyes from Dana. She was pale and the strain showed clearly in her subdued manner. He was once again astounded by her courage and her determination.

Jarod hated what he was about to do, but he'd given Dana his word and she was right about having them all come together. He stepped in.

"Last night Dana and I talked about this. She was insistent that it was best for everyone involved if she left the ranch. I personally disagree, but the fact remains that Dana was right when she told me it was not my decision alone to make. You must consider what she has said. She knows Sonny better than we do. I don't think we can underline too strongly the point that Sonny is a real threat that none of you should take lightly." Jarod paused, allowing his words to register in their minds.

"On the other hand, you must have all noticed the security by now. They will be staying on indefinitely. I've also hired a very capable private agent to try and track down Sonny's whereabouts."

Jarod studied the solemn expressions on the faces at the table.

"I'm sure you must have questions," he prompted.

"I can't believe he'd go to such extreme measures if you've already broken up. It makes no sense," Annie said bewildered.

"Sonny thinks he loves me, but he doesn't know what love is," Dana explained with forced composure. "In his warped mind, I am his property and he is only taking what is already his."

"Do you really think he'll come back, after all that's happened?" Annie's tone was clearly incredulous.

"He swore he would never let me go. I never thought he'd follow me all the way to New Mexico from Maine," Dana stressed her point. "So yes, I believe it could happen. His anger drives him to incredible lengths." Dana looked at Ben and Adam. "The horses are not safe either," she added quietly, her expression was emotionless and they realized she was running on raw nerve. "I don't know that he'll stop until he gets what he wants," Dana told them.

Kent had restrained himself as long as he could. "I'll be damned if some psycho is going to run you off this place! We're crazy to be even considering it." He looked around the table, confident of support.

"I agree with Kent," Adam replied. "It is time for you to stop running. This man is no match for all of us. There is a reason for you to be here, there is nowhere else for you to go that would be safer."

June nodded in agreement.

Ben cleared his throat, speaking for the first time.

"In my day, we had a simple way'a dealing with a problem like this. New Mexico ain't Maine." Ben spoke with angry scorn. "It's a big place, people get lost, people have accidents. Sonny's outta his element here." Ben stared at Jarod, making his point.

"Well," Jarod said quietly. "I think we've had enough accidents, but I guess we're in agreement."

"Wait," Dana interrupted. "It's fine that the guys all feel they can take care of themselves. I appreciate your bravery, really I do," she said sincerely as she paused and took a deep breath, turning to Annie, who sat to her left. "Kent, look at Annie and tell me you still feel as brave."

The girl had been silent during the heated discussion and now everyone turned to look at her.

Dana continued. "What about our training program? What about our students? What about Sue? She's a fifteen year old girl." Dana stood, her face was white and she was beginning to tremble.

Jarod and Annie both quickly got to their feet and Annie put her arm around Dana.

"We can put the training program on hold, till we get to the bottom of this, Dana. And I'll be very careful, I promise you," she said.

Jarod made his way around the table. Dana was obviously exhausted and again near tears. He addressed the group.

"I'm going to take Dana away for the week. She needs some time to recover. While we're gone, I want you all to think this over very carefully and when we get back, you can let us know how you've decided..."

Annie interrupted Jarod.

"I'm in agreement with the men. I could never live with myself if I turned Dana away." The girl stood firmly. "Dana, I don't want you to go away for a week and be always wondering if you have a place to come back to. This is your home, and if we turned away those in need, it wouldn't be a place for any of us."

The two girls hugged each other and Dana slowly turned and faced everyone.

"Thank you, you've all been so..." She stopped at a loss for words. "I'm so,so sorry."

[211]

Ben stood.

"You got enough on your plate, without feeling guilty. It's not your fault and you're not responsible. The guy is sick," he said with disgust. "We can take care 'a ourselves. You ease your mind on that and get yourself to bed." The old man's face was inscrutable as he clumsily patted Dana's hand.

"Well put, Ben." Jarod had his arm around Dana. "I will not say that I'm surprised by your support tonight," Jarod told them. "But I am extremely grateful. You're welcome to stay and talk as long as you like, I'm going to bring Dana upstairs. Goodnight."

Jarod guided Dana from the room.

He helped her up the stairs to his room and sat her on the bed. She was emotionally spent and silent.

He brought Dana her nightgown and left the room. When Jarod returned Dana had changed her clothing and was sitting where he had left her.

Laying down on the bed and turning off the light, he crawled in beside her.

"I don't know," was all she said as she turned and tucked herself in beside him, exhausted she hid her face in his chest and quickly fell into a heavy sleep.

Dana heard the bedroom door and watched as it slowly inched open. She tried, but was unable to make out the figure in the darkness. The shadow moved to the far side of the bed. Dana narrowed her eyes, struggling to see what he was doing but she was tired and she couldn't make sense of the dark image.

There was suddenly a heavy weight on top of her, pushing the air from her lungs. He covered Dana's mouth with his hand and his face came into focus inches from hers.

Sonny!

Terror filled her as she looked into his black eyes. She struggled against him, searching for Jarod. She looked wildly across the bed that was covered in blood. She began to whimper.

Sonny started to laugh deep in his throat. "Looking for somebody?"

She pounded hysterically at his chest, pulling her head away.

"No!" Dana screamed. "No!"

"Dana!" Jarod gently shook her, trying to wake her as she struggled against him.

Dana's eyes flew open as she looked around her disoriented. She pulled herself up in the bed, staring at Jarod with disbelief.

"It's okay," he said softly as he slowly reached for the light, using his shoulder to shield her eyes. "Dana, are you okay?" Jarod sat before her. "You had a dream."

She was damp and trembling.

"He was here," she argued, her eyes filled with fear.

"No, it was a bad dream," Jarod repeated, shaking his head. He pulled her towards him and held her close within the shelter of his arms.

Dana was breathing heavily and still unsure, her eyes frantically searching the room.

She burst into tears.

"He will come back!" Dana cried angrily, holding her small fists to his broad chest. Her words came in bits and pieces between sobs. "I want it to stop! I can't do this anymore." She collapsed against him.

Jarod folded her slender body inside his tense embrace. For the first time in his life, he knew he was capable of killing someone.

- Chapter 16 -

It was noon by the time that Jarod and Dana arrived at Emma's apartment building. Jarod turned off the engine and looked across at Dana.

"Here we are."

He reached for her hand. Dana was pale this morning. They had passed a long night, but thankfully she had managed to relax to some extent in the plane. They had carefully avoided any mention of Sonny, and as they had put the miles behind them, Dana appeared determined to forget the entire episode.

"So, do we get to go in?" Dana teased him lightly, as her anticipation of seeing Emma for the first time in months came to surface.

"Let's go."

They climbed the narrow staircase to Emma's apartment and Jarod knocked on the door.

Emma opened the door and upon seeing Dana she let go an unbridled scream of joy which Dana quickly returned, the two women falling into a hug.

Emma stepped back, closely inspecting her best friend.

"Girl, I've been so worried about you, you have no idea!" Emma checked Dana up and down. "You look fantastic!" Emma saw no harm in elaborating on the truth. "I can't stand people like you. Come in, sit down."

Emma briefly looked beyond Dana to Jarod, who gave her a reassuring nod.

"Thank you for bringing her home. You certainly look in better shape than the last time I saw you."

"Hello, Emma. This will be a happier visit." Jarod smiled. "I thought I'd bring Dana as a peace offering to excuse any bad manners I may have displayed the last time I was here."

[214]

The two women sat down on the sofa and Jarod took the chair, content to sit and watch them together. It was obvious that they were very close.

"So, tell me all about New Mexico. What's it like there?"

"Emma, you really have to be there to get the full effect. It's everything you could imagine and more. Which reminds me." Dana walked over to the door and picked up the small parcel. "We brought a little something for you."

"You know I just love presents!" Emma exclaimed as she tore the wrapping paper from the frame. "Wow! This is gorgeous." She sat back and admired the painting. "Thank you both."

"That painting is almost an exact replica of the view from our front porch."

Emma was quick to note Dana's choice of words and she looked across at Jarod. It suddenly occurred to her that he was too involved to be just Dana's employer. She saw the way he was watching Dana and instinctively she could sense the obvious connection between the two.

"The landscape is just stunning," Dana was saying.

"Well, not that I've got anything against rocks and trees, but let's cut to the chase," Emma's hazel eyes were full of mischief. "What's the boss like?" Emma was inwardly delighted to watch color spread across Dana's wan face. So that's the way the wind was blowing, Emma thought to herself.

"Emma, you will never change," Dana mockingly complained as she stole a look at Jarod. "Everyone at the ranch has been great, including the boss," she added. "It's a wonderful set up, Emma. You'd love it there. I've started teaching and I enjoy it. I think I'm good at it." Dana looked drawn but happy.

"How's Lindsay? Did she have the baby, or babies?" Dana asked excitedly.

Emma had one leg tucked underneath her and she leaned forward, slapping Dana lightly on the arm, almost losing her balance.

"Can you imagine? Twins! She's due any day now, because the doctor said she'll probably go early. My mom's fit to be tied." Emma giggled. "Hey, you guys must be hungry. Let's order out," Emma suggested.

"You know what would be great? Pizza from that little restaurant on Washington. What do you think, Jarod?" Dana asked.

"Pizza is fine by me. I can go pick it up," Jarod offered, content to give the women some time alone.

Emma reached over and picked up the phone, placing the order. When she was finished she sat back, checking Jarod out more closely. "So, Jarod, have you noticed how healthy Dana's appetite is?"

Jarod laughed and the girls quickly joined in.

"It took some getting used to. You'd never know it to look at her." He stood.

Emma gave him the directions to the restaurant and then Jarod departed down the stairs to his car in the street below.

Emma immediately turned to Dana.

"That is one good looking man! And he is so in love with you. Do you see the way he looks at you? It makes my heart melt. I can't believe you never told me."

"Oh, Emma. It's a long story." Dana ran her fingers through her thick hair, lifting it from her shoulders and then letting it fall across her back. "I was afraid, you know, after everything... anyway, that's all changed now." She smiled at her friend. "You can't imagine how much I love him, or how wonderful he is, to me and also as a person in his own right. He's taking me to Canada tonight, for a few days."

"I'm so happy for you, no one deserves it more." Emma paused, her boyish face suddenly becoming sober.

"I hate to do this, Dana, but what about Sonny? Do you think he's gone for good this time?"

Dana closed her eyes for a brief moment. "You know what, Emma? Let's not ruin what little time I have here talking about Sonny. Things are still too fresh and there are a lot of things I just don't know right now. Someday we'll talk, about everything," Dana promised. "How are my parents? What have they been told about all of this?"

"I don't know if I did the right thing," Emma began to explain. "By the time that I found out, things were pretty wild and I hardly knew what to tell them. And then finally, after Jarod phoned and let me know that you were okay and Sonny was gone, well, I decided not to tell them anything at all." Emma had been fidgeting, pulling on her short strands of hair and twisting her fingers. She now stopped and looked at Dana.

[216]

"You did the right thing," Dana assured her. "There was no point in upsetting them after it was all over with. There was nothing they could've done, anyway."

Dana sat, lost in thought.

"I don't think they could've dealt with it. There was so much that they didn't know to begin with."

The two girls sat silently, remembering the weeks that had led up to Dana finally going to New Mexico.

Emma reached over and patted Dana's knee. "We've got to put this behind us," she said bravely. "Life goes on and Jarod looks like a fantastic guy. I think it's such a good idea for the two of you to get away for a few days. Promise me that you'll try to enjoy yourself," she pleaded.

Dana nodded and smiled.

There was a quiet rap on the door and Jarod came into the room.

"Emma, your directions were excellent. Smelling this pizza has made my mouth water the whole drive back," Jarod joked in his easy manner. "Did you girls enjoy yourselves while I was gone?"

Jarod placed the box on the glass coffee table.

"We most certainly did," Emma said brightly as she got to her feet. "This deserves a toast. I don't care if it's the middle of the day."

She led the way to the kitchenette where she served the pizza and opened a bottle of wine.

They sat down and Emma lifted her glass.

"Dana, welcome back and thank God you are happy and safe."

"Cheer! Cheer!"

"It's too bad you've already made your plans," Emma said conversationally as they began to eat. "We could've gone boating on the ocean. Jarod, have you ever seen the whales? They are quite amazing this year and we could've gone to Bar Harbor for lobster."

"I've already promised Dana a longer visit next time we come," Jarod said agreeably. "Emma, after your sister has had her babies and they are all settled at home, we would love to have you at the ranch. You can come anytime and stay for as long as you'd like. Dana told me you are a very competent rider as well. I may put you to work." Jarod teased with a grin.

"That definitely sounds like a plan. Maybe this winter, I'll be due for some vacation time."

They talked some more about the horses and the program at the ranch which led to Emma and Dana trading some amusing stories about their experiences in riding. Jarod was encouraged to see the strain slowly disappear from Dana's face. The wine and Emma's unfettered exuberance managed to bring some of the light back to Dana's eyes.

Dana looked up at the clock. "Emma, I hate to eat and run, but we really must leave if I'm going to have any time with my parents."

They all stood and Dana hugged Emma.

"I've missed you so much, it's hard to go."

"I've missed you too, girl," Emma replied. "But, I promise I will come and visit. You remember your promise to me." Emma reminded Dana as she turned to address Jarod. "Thank you, Jarod, for bringing Dana here. You have no idea how much this has meant to me."

"It has been my pleasure," he said honestly. "Let us know when you're ready to visit."

As they drove away, Dana turned in her seat as she waved back to Emma standing on the sidewalk.

"Are you sad?" Jarod asked her as they turned the corner.

"No, I had a good time and Emma will come out to the ranch, if you really don't mind."

"Of course I don't mind, Emma looks like a lot of fun."

Jarod stole a sideways glance at Dana, but she appeared untroubled. He grimly remembered how Emma had told him of Sonny's jealousies and his need to control, and he realized it would take some time for Dana to re-adjust to some of the most minor of habits.

"Jarod," Dana began as she directed him through the streets of the quaint village. "Emma didn't tell my parents about... well, you know. And, I never really told them everything from before either."

"Don't worry, Dana," Jarod put her mind at ease, hardly surprised by her confession. "You'll see that I can be very discreet. I'll just follow your lead."

Dana made a motion and they pulled into the Northington's driveway.

She held Jarod's hand as they walked into the house.

"Mom? Dad?" Dana called out.

Dana's mother came rushing out of a back room.

"Dana! My Lord!" Carol held her daughter close, a wide smile breaking over her features. "My little girl is home," she cried out. "This is a surprise, I must say. Goodness gracious, you never even phoned. How did you know I'd be home," Carol gently chided Dana.

"Mom, you're always home," Dana pointed out patiently.

"Still, if I knew you were coming I would've prepared something special. Especially if I knew you were bringing a visitor," Dana's mother stepped back as she motioned to the tall man at Dana's side.

"Mom, this is Jarod Kingsley. Jarod, this is my mother, Carol Northington." Dana formally introduced them to each other, feeling suddenly shy.

"How do you do, M'am," Jarod held out his hand.

Carol accepted it. "I'm pleased to meet you, Mr. Kingsley."

"Please, call me Jarod."

"Then you must call me Carol. So, Jarod," Carol indicated for them to sit. "You are Dana's employer?"

"Mom," Dana interrupted awkwardly. "Jarod is more than just my employer."

If Dana's mother was surprised she kept it to herself.

"Oh, I'm sorry, Jarod. My daughter has always had a habit of not keeping me up on things." Carol smiled at her daughter with affection. "I'm glad to have her home and to have the opportunity to meet you."

"Where's Dad?"

"Goodness!" Carol exclaimed laughing. "As if you need to ask. He's on the golf course with Harold, but he shouldn't be too long," Carol said doubtfully.

"In other words, you have no idea how long he'll be gone." Dana teased her mother and she turned to Jarod. "My Dad's a die-hard golfer, but it's my Mom who is the real sport of the family. She's put up with him come rain or come shine." Dana threw her arm around her mother.

Dana's mother smiled appreciatively.

"There are a lot worse things that a man could be doing with his time," she said.

"Jarod, I forgot the parcel in the car." Dana suddenly remembered the wind chimes.

"I'll go get it," he volunteered and went outside.

"Is this man good to you?" Carol asked Dana as Jarod was gone to the car. "You look thinner, have you been eating?"

"Mom, you always say I look too thin. I'm fine and yes, Jarod is very good to me."

Jarod returned with the attractively wrapped box that he handed to Dana, which she carefully placed in her mother's lap.

"Oh my! You shouldn't have." Carol opened the gift and lifted the chimes from the box. They tinkled musically through the room. "They're exquisite! I'll be able to think of you whenever the wind blows," Carol said sweetly.

"That is exactly what your daughter said when she chose them. If you like, I'd be more than happy to hang them for you," Jarod offered, giving Carol one of his warm smiles and Dana was touched by his efforts.

"How thoughtful of you. I believe there is an empty hook on the porch already, let me see." Carol stood, taking a few steps to the door before she stopped. "No, really I don't want to be a bother."

"It's no bother," he insisted.

Dana playfully nudged Jarod in the side as Carol looked out to the porch, her temptation evident.

"You have no idea what you're getting into," she whispered to him under her breath.

On the porch Dana could only watch in amusement as Carol had Jarod rearrange plants, the chimes and the budgie Petey's cage back and forth on various hooks for what seemed like an eternity.

Dana was reminded of the time before the party at the ranch, when Jarod had patiently followed June through the house, moving furniture and turning over mattresses.

The little parakeet scolded Jarod incessantly, hopping madly back and forth from perch to perch in a frenzy.

"I had no idea such a little thing could make so much noise, it's no wonder you keep him outside," Jarod said finally with feeling.

"Goodness gracious, no!" Carol said, horrified. "He's just getting a bit of fresh air. He's like my little Doberman, aren't you Petey? He doesn't care for strangers."

Dana noticed that Jarod did appear to be properly intimidated by the small bird and Dana casually brought her fingers to her lips, hiding an amused smile.

Carol put her hands to her hips as she surveyed their arrangements.

"That's perfect," she said delighted. "I'll get us some lemonade," she said as she stepped into the house.

Dana came up behind Jarod and hooked her fingers into the loops of his jeans. Standing up on her toes she whispered into his ear. "What did I tell you?"

A wide grin spread across his face as he stood motionless, his eyes never leaving the still squawking bird.

"Next time, we'll buy her chocolates."

Jarod turned and kissed Dana's forehead and they entered the house.

They returned to the spacious living room and sat down. Jarod looked around with interest. The room itself was a testimony of Dana's youth, decorated with a multitude of photographs displaying her life from birth to womanhood.

Carol entered the room with a tray of refreshments. She noticed Jarod's obvious interest.

"Dana was a beautiful child and she's grown into an even more beautiful woman," he said to Carol.

Carol blushed with pleasure.

"Jarod, I'm glad to see that you think so. I hope you're taking good care of her, we were quite nervous about her decision to move so far away." Carol's tone was light, but Jarod suspected that Dana's mother knew more than Dana realized. "Mind you, she's always been willful. It's hardly like we could've done much to stop her."

"I hadn't noticed," Jarod said dryly.

"You should've seen her as a child," Carol continued as she began pouring the lemonade.

"Okay, that's enough out of the two of you," Dana stepped in. "Mom, I don't think we need to be boring Jarod with every stage of my development."

"I wouldn't call them stages, Dana. It's been more like one steady run all in the same direction," Carol chuckled softly.

"On the contrary, Dana," Jarod interjected. "I'm finding this all quite interesting." He teased before turning back to Carol. "You have raised a remarkable woman, you must be very proud."

"Thank you, we are quite proud. We just wish we saw more of her. Speaking of which, how long will you be staying?"

"Mom, we are leaving tonight," Dana said, at a loss to explain why they would not be staying longer.

"You flew all the way to Maine, just to spend a few hours?" Carol stared at Dana in disbelief.

Jarod clearly heard the disappointment in the woman's voice.

"I'm sorry Mrs. Northington... Carol," he corrected himself. "It's really my fault. We are meeting a horse dealer in Canada early tomorrow. There is a horse I've been interested in and I wanted Dana's expert opinion on it. I should've done a better job scheduling things, but the man has another interested party, so we're a little rushed. Dana wanted to stay longer."

Dana had carefully watched Jarod throughout his sensible explanation and apart from one eyebrow that had risen slightly, she gave nothing away. She turned and faced her mother.

"Mom, I promise the next time I come, I'll stay longer."

A car turned into the drive and Carol hurried to the door.

"I hope you had this hidden talent for whitewashing the truth before you met me," Dana's eyes sparkled as she whispered to Jarod. "I'd hate to think it was something I taught you."

The front door closed with a bang.

"You should see me at work," Jarod whispered back as they both rose to greet Dana's father.

"Daddy! I'm so happy to see you!" Dana ran over and embraced her father.

"This is the kind of surprise I like coming home to. How's my baby?" Paul Northington kissed his daughter, obviously thrilled to see her. He was a tall man in his late fifties.

"I'm fine, Dad. Better than fine." Dana took her father's hand in hers and led him over to where Jarod stood. "Dad, I'd like you to meet Jarod Kingsley."

The men shook hands.

"A firm handshake is always the sign of a good man. I'm pleased to meet you, Jarod. Please call me Paul," Paul greeted Jarod openly.

"Thank you, sir."

"Paul," the man with the salt and pepper hair insisted and Jarod nodded his agreement.

"Would you like some lemonade, dear?" Carol asked her husband as she poured his glass, confident of his response.

Paul smiled his thanks to Carol as he accepted the glass and sat down with Jarod. In no time the two men were immersed in a deep conversation over putting techniques and club preferences.

Carol quietly motioned to Dana and the two women made their way to the kitchen.

Dana helped her mother as she began to prepare supper.

"This is good," Carol confided to her daughter. "It will give us the chance to talk."

Dana smiled to herself as she collected the makings for a salad from the refrigerator. Ever since she could remember her mother had always created these little opportunities for them to talk.

As she washed off the vegetables she realized with a sense of happiness that for once she would have the words that her mother had been waiting so long to hear.

"This seems like a very fine young man," Carol began innocuously, as she seasoned the pieces of chicken.

"Next to you and Dad, Jarod is the best thing that has ever happened to me." Dana worked alongside her mother, both of them apparently involved with their tasks.

"Are you happy? Does he make you happy?"

"I used to be so uncertain about a lot of things, Mom." Dana explained as she began to break up the lettuce. "I know it didn't show, I always looked so sure of myself, but being with Jarod, I've learned so much about life... about myself."

"You were always such a strong little girl, but I used to worry about you, sometimes."

Carol placed the meat in the oven and checked the controls. She opened a bag of fresh potatoes.

"Do you love him?" Carol asked as she carefully selected her paring knife from the drawer.

Dana smiled, watching her mother. "Yes, I do, just so much."

"And he loves you?" Carol began peeling the potatoes.

"Yes," Dana replied again.

[223]

"Your onions are very strong," Carol complained as she wiped her eyes.

"Mom," Dana spoke softly. "I don't have any onions."

Startled, Carol finally looked Dana in the eyes.

"It's for real, Mom." Dana reached out and hugged her mother.

"Dana, I'm so happy for you. You can't begin to imagine." Carol enthusiastically returned her hug before stepping away as she tried to compose herself.

"Now, where did I leave my knife?" Carol moved the bag of potatoes that sat on the kitchen counter and they went spilling across the floor, tumbling and scattering in all directions.

The two women looked at each other and burst into laughter.

Paul turned to Jarod in the living room, his eyebrows climbing up his forehead as he made a wry face.

"What on earth are they doing in there?"

Jarod smiled and shrugged his shoulders.

Over supper, the conversation centered around Dana's life and Jarod couldn't help but be overwhelmed with contentment as he watched Dana's eyes radiate with happiness as she described the ranch and the people who lived and worked there.

There had been many times when Jarod had been troubled by the distance that separated his home and hers, but listening to her tonight he understood that New Mexico was where Dana wanted to be.

Today had been a slice of time without Sonny and Jarod had never seen Dana laugh more or move so freely. This is what he wanted for her. This is what he had only been able to catch glimpses of in her before and now more than ever he was determined to find a way to make it last.

After supper Paul helped Carol to clear up while Dana and Jarod made their way to the front porch swing at her parents' not so subtle request.

There was a light breeze carrying in the brisk scent of the ocean air and the chimes Jarod had hung earlier that day released their delicate song.

"I've always loved that unique scent," Dana told him softly. "It tends to catch you off guard, the wind picks it up off the water and if you close your eyes you can almost hear the ocean and feel it's power." Dana tilted her head up and closed her eyes, taking a deep breath. She slowly reopened them, turning to Jarod.

"Try it." Dana's hands lightly covered Jarod's eyes. "Now," she said slowly. "Take a deep breath, let the air fill you."

Jarod obediently did as he was told. Dana dropped her hands from his face.

"Wasn't that wonderful?"

"Yes, it was wonderful. You are wonderful." Jarod smiled down at her as he put his arm around her. He was once again reminded of Dana's gift for finding simple pleasure in the most innocent of things.

"My parents are quite taken with you, which I never doubted they would be."

"They are good people. Your father and I have already arranged a golfing match for our next trip." Jarod laughed quietly.

"It's odd. I've never really seen you away from the ranch. I've never thought of you doing things like golfing," Dana said as they gently swayed on the swing.

"Executives love golfing. A lot of deals have been made on the golf course. Then in university there was football, basketball, by the way, I am proof that white men can jump," Jarod joked with her. "What about you, Dana? Other than the horses, did you have any interests or hobbies? When we were at Emma's before, she mentioned boating."

"I love sailing. When I was very young, I remember my parents bringing me to the ocean. I could sit for hours just watching the sailboats go by. They all looked so carefree skimming across the water, travelling in the breeze. Once I started riding though, there was really very little time for anything else. That was my choice, that's the way I wanted it."

Carol and Paul joined them on the porch.

"So, how do you like Maine, Jarod?" Carol asked as she sat down. Paul lit up a cigarette.

"Actually, we were just planning our next trip," Jarod answered politely. "It seems that I'm missing out on quite a few enjoyable pastimes like golfing and boating."

They conversed pleasantly on the porch for a little while longer until Jarod sighed audibly and Dana knew it was time to go. They slowly got to their feet.

"Not so soon," Carol pleaded.

"You don't have time for an after-dinner drink?" Paul suggested.

"I'm sorry. I'll take a raincheck on that though. The fact is, if we don't get a move on it, we will miss our flight." Jarod held out his hand to Paul.

"I'm sorry, Mom, Dad. We really do have to go. I love you both and we'll make it up to you, next time we come." Dana hugged and kissed her parents.

"Jarod, you take good care of our daughter, she's all that we have." Carol held his hand for a moment.

"I will do that." Jarod lightly kissed Carol's cheek. "It's been a pleasure meeting the both of you," he said sincerely. Jarod turned to Dana. "Are you ready?"

She nodded her head and taking their leave, they headed to the airport.

- Chapter 17 -

The next morning Dana awoke to the unfamiliar sounds coming from the busy city street below.

They had arrived at their destination Montreal, very late last night and by the time they were settled in their hotel suite they were more than happy to call it a day.

Dana checked the clock by her bedside and was astonished to discover it was close to noon. She had slept soundly through the night and that sudden realization brought a welcome smile to her sleepy face.

She heard the shower running and knew that Jarod was in there preparing for the day ahead of them. Dana pulled herself up in bed and stretched and yawned. She lazily rubbed her eyes then made her way across the thickly carpeted floor to the closet. She stood there for a moment considering what she should wear and finally selected a camel colored two-piece outfit of crisp linen. It was a simply cut tunic blouse that fastened from behind accompanied by a mid-length skirt.

Dana carried the ensemble into the second bathroom. After showering she dressed then swept her hair up into a loose knot and applied a light dusting of color to her eyes and cheekbones. She stood back from the full length mirror to survey her appearance. She smiled once again, pleased with the results.

Dana returned to the bedroom to find Jarod already dressed in jeans and a sky blue Oxford shirt and walking over to him she tousled his damp hair. "You were ahead of me this morning," she said to him, smiling.

He stood and held her away from him. "I didn't have the heart to wake you."

Jarod studied the woman before him. The color of her outfit complimented the gentle honey tan of her skin. Her vibrant eyes were sharply etched by dark, curling lashes, her lips soft and lush. He drew a deep breath. "You look lovely," he told her simply.

"Thank you." Dana gently turned her back to him. "I'm not able to reach my top buttons. Would you mind?"

Jarod lifted his hands to the back of Dana's slender neck and fastened the top of her blouse. Her subtle fragrance lightly greeted him as he bent in towards her.

Unable to resist, he kissed the nape of her neck before stepping back.

"So," he said. "How do you feel about a walk and a late lunch?"

"I think that would be fun." Dana nodded her head in agreement. "I'm looking forward to seeing what this city has to offer. I was looking over a few of the pamphlets in the lobby while you were registering last night. Montreal is a city of diverse culture, it should be interesting."

"That constitutes as cheating," Jarod teased her. "Dana, I want this trip to be full of surprises. So I want you to stay away from the tourist literature." He put his arm around her.

"Montreal also has some of the finest restaurants in the world," Dana chided him.

"Oh, now the truth is revealed," Jarod laughed as he guided her to the door. "Come on, let's check out some of that diverse culture that you were talking about and then we'll see about the restaurants."

They made their way through the busy city streets, hand-in-hand, pausing every now and then to study something of particular interest. Eventually they reached a quieter area where the streets were made of cobblestone and closed to traffic, proudly lined by magnificent stone buildings.

It was a great historical setting. Vendors were set up in the open, narrow streets and the venerable buildings had been cleverly renovated into cafes, bistros and souvenir shops.

Dana stopped at a tall triangular edifice that stubbornly jutted into the crook of two angled thoroughfares.

"Now this is what I call a cornerstore," she pointed out to Jarod with humor.

He nodded with a smile.

"I think I'd like to buy a postcard for June, she really looks forward to getting mail," Dana said thoughtfully as she carefully viewed the selection of postcards before her.

"You're right," Jarod agreed and for a brief moment he was lost in time, remembering how he'd done the same on his travels as a boy. Sending postcards home to June, it was something he had long forgotten.

He looked towards Dana and quietly smiled. "I think she'd be touched," he said.

They made their simple purchase and walked across the little street to an attractive cafe that included an inviting outdoor terrace.

"Bonjour madame, monsieur," a waiter promptly greeted them. Considering Jarod and Dana, he continued in English that was strongly laced with a French accent. "It is a beautiful day, do you prefer to dine outside?"

Jarod looked to Dana, who readily concurred.

The waiter adroitly seated them at a small round table that was topped by a generous, colorful parasol and politely handed them their menus.

Dana opened her menu and began to laugh softly. "Maybe I'll let you order for me."

Jarod opened his menu as well and briefly scanned its contents, grinning.

"I see, it's all in French. Some of this I can figure out for myself, but I'm sure whatever we order will be delicious." Jarod teased, sending Dana a meaningful glance.

Dana playfully shook her head.

The waiter returned and with some assistance, they made their selections and ordered. They ate a pleasant lunch and when they were finished they continued with their sightseeing, admiring the architecture and making a few purchases along the way. Dana caringly selected mementos to bring back with them to the ranch.

They happened to come upon a small park and decided to rest for a while, it was late afternoon and they had been walking for some time.

Jarod was quietly pensive as they sat and Dana turned to him.

"What are you thinking about?"

He flashed her an easy smile. "I was thinking how much I'd like to take you dancing tonight."

"Dancing?" Dana paused, her mind going back in time. "Do you remember the last time that we danced?"

"How could I forget?" Jarod smiled again. "I treasured that memory for weeks." Jarod closed his eyes briefly. "I remember you saying that you weren't much of a dancer."

"I'm a quick study and you're a great teacher," Dana explained with an impish smile. "I'd love to go dancing with you tonight," she told him softly as she leaned against him. "Where will we go?"

"The hotel we are staying at happens to offer a world class dining room that includes live music and a spacious dance floor," Jarod described as he contentedly drank in the pleasure of having Dana resting within his arms.

"When you booked this hotel, did you specifically inquire about that?" Dana stifled a laugh.

"Yes, I did." Jarod answered proudly, grinning.

"I'm very flattered that you would fly me all the way to Canada to take me dancing." Dana turned her face up to his.

He was captured by the spell she cast. Jarod leaned forward slightly as he stared into Dana's smiling eyes. She was immediately aware of the subtle change within him and unconsciously she reached for his hand. Lowering his head to hers, he kissed her deeply, becoming oblivious to the sights and sounds around them. Dana leaned in towards him, her lips responding to his.

Gently, Jarod pulled his head away.

"I love you, Dana," he whispered into her ear.

Dana struggled to her senses, caught unaware by the sudden rise of passion within her. She laid her hand against Jarod's chest as she shyly looked around them. No one was concerned with the romantic couple, everything was just as it was.

She looked at him and smiled tenderly.

"I love you, too."

Jarod drew in a deep breath. "Come on," he said as he helped her to her feet. "We should be getting back."

Dana stepped out of the shower and dried herself. She methodically blew her hair dry, having decided to leave it loose. The sun from the afternoon had brought out the rich copper highlights in her chestnut hair and a gentle color to her cheeks. She sprayed her body with a fine mist of perfume and carefully applied mascara and lipstick.

As she gently pulled the white dress that Jarod had bought for her over her head and smoothed it into place, she felt a flush of anticipation. She found herself looking forward to the evening ahead.

Dana stepped out of the bathroom to find Jarod sitting on the couch, his blond head bent over the local newspaper.

Upon sensing her presence he quickly rose, squaring his broad shoulders. He was debonairly dressed in a sharply tailored suit of navy blue. He looked incredibly strong and handsome to Dana and she stood for a second, etching this picture of him into her memory.

The sight of her took his breath away, as she stood in the doorway with her gleaming hair falling over delicate bare shoulders, the subtle curves of her body not entirely veiled by the fine cloth of her long dress. His piercing eyes grew dark in the soft lamp light.

"Every time I see you, you look new to me," he told her quietly.

A small smile hovered over Dana's lips.

"I was thinking the same thing," she murmured.

Jarod approached her and deftly lifting her face to his, he lightly kissed her soft lips.

"We'll be late for our reservations," he said as a grin spread over his tanned face. Backing away a step, he drew a deep breath and placed her hand over his arm as he led her from the suite.

The dining room was aglow in mellow amber candlelight. The tables were adorned with crisp linens and vases of fragrant summer blooms, the music subdued.

Dana and Jarod were courteously seated at a table by the window, where they could look out over the city below. Jarod ordered a bottle of champagne from the wine steward and then sat back in his chair finding he was unable to take his eyes away from Dana. The glittering light of the candle flame danced in her eyes and elusive shadows played across her warm skin with each gentle movement she made.

The waiter returned and the boisterous pop of the champagne cork broke the silence that had settled over their table.

"Merci," Jarod addressed the waiter as he acknowledged his acceptance of the sparkling liquid. The waiter bowed slightly and left them.

Jarod handed Dana a fluted glass as he raised his own.

"To the beautiful treasure that has come into my life."

Dana lowered her eyes, a soft blush coloring her cheeks. As she sipped at her champagne, her eyes wandered to the dance floor.

Jarod stood and offered Dana his hand. "May I?"

She smiled and placed her slender hand within his. She demurely followed him out to the dance floor where other couples were already flowing in time to the music.

Sliding his arm behind her, Jarod drew Dana within his embrace. He lowered his head slightly as he whispered into her ear. "Do you remember all the rules?"

Her light laughter fell like petals around them.

"I lead, you follow," she replied coyly.

"We'll see about that," Jarod returned with a grin as he masterfully guided her across the polished dance floor.

Dana was aware of Jarod's reserved strength as his muscular form easily commanded her yielding body to the rhythm of the melody. Their bodies moved in perfect unison. Dana placed one hand against his chest and closed her eyes, engulfed by the wondrous magic of the moment. She moved closer into his body and sighed deeply.

The song came to its end and Jarod tenderly kissed her.

"You dance divinely," he whispered in a low voice.

"Only with you," she responded, her smile filled with love.

They slowly walked back to their table. Jarod pulled out Dana's chair and seated her before himself. The waiter returned, refilling their tall fluted glasses as he took their dinner order then departed.

"I've been thinking about when we first met," Jarod spoke quietly. "God, you unnerved me."

Dana smiled, reliving the experience. "The man behind the desk...you were not at all what I expected." Dana shook her head, her eyes alive with amusement.

"Neither were you. I had misgivings about you being able to handle the heavy workload, but as I laid my eyes on you, I knew I would've moved heaven and earth to keep you there."

Jarod looked deep into her eyes as he reached across the table for her hand. "I've never met anyone like you. I knew from that very first moment how special you were and that I would never be the same person again."

The waiter arrived with their meal, silently arranging their plates before them. Dana's eyes had become moist at Jarod's words and she was thankful for the brief interruption. She watched silently as Jarod turned his attention to his plate. Lovingly, she studied every detail about him: the strong lines of his handsome face, the strength of his hands as they moved across the table. She absently toyed with her meal as her thoughts were filled with how blessed she felt to have found him. Her heart ached with tenderness.

"Dana?" Jarod's question broke into her thoughts. "Is your food alright? You've barely touched it."

She looked down at her plate.

"I've been in the moon," she told him softly. "It's a beautiful place to be." Her eyes drifted to the dance floor.

Jarod stood, escorting her once more to the floor.

They seemed to dance endlessly, swept away by the music and the novel awareness of the depth of their love for each other. The slow seduction of being so near to Jarod made Dana heavy with desire. He pulled her in closer and kissed her lips. She had no sense of time or place, she was conscious of only their two bodies, lightly touching together then moving apart as they danced.

"It's getting late," she whispered to him.

Jarod's expression was inscrutable as he nodded in agreement.

Once back in their room, Dana slipped into the bathroom and undressed, wrapping her body in a silk robe. Her fingers trembled slightly as she discarded her jewelry and freshened up. She hesitated before opening the door and looked into the mirror hardly recognizing herself. The iridescent emerald green of her robe reflected the color of her eyes and the color in her cheeks had naturally remained high.

She quietly walked into the dim bedroom.

Jarod stood by the dresser. He had already removed his tie and blazer and was beginning to unbutton his shirt. Her breath caught in her throat as she watched him.

He lifted his head as she entered the room, his hands falling to his side. Jarod remained silent, his eyes never leaving her as Dana slowly approached him in the semi darkness.

[233]

She stopped just inches before him, discerning the wonder in his eyes.

Slowly, she loosened her robe, allowing it to softly slide to the floor.

Jarod watched as it gracefully traveled down Dana's slender body then lifted his gaze to hers. She read the hesitancy in his expression.

"I've never wanted anything more," her voice quivered as she spoke the words to him.

He stepped towards her, his hands slowly reaching out to touch her bare skin. She felt her spirit awaken with yearning as his fingertips seductively traced the curves of her body.

"Dana, you are so beautiful," Jarod's voice was deep with emotion. He cradled her head in his hands as his lips searched for hers. Her body swayed to him and trembled. He swiftly lifted her light figure and carried her to the bed, gently lowering her on to it.

He stood for a moment, his heart pounding deep within his chest, taken by her beauty and filled with a powerful need.

Jarod carefully lowered his body over hers, his mouth eagerly seeking her lips. He kissed her deeply, his body tensed.

Dana undid the remaining buttons and removed his shirt. She turned him onto his back and he silently watched as she finished undressing him.

Wordlessly, he reached up to her and brought her head down to his, kissing her once again with growing ardor. He slowly reached for the lamp.

"No," Dana whispered. "We've been in the dark long enough."

He kissed her eyelids, his passion mounting. He rolled her over and began to kiss her body, his hands and his lips secretly calling to her, flaming her inner fire. Dana moaned in quiet desperation as her body arched to his, pleading to be taken.

Their bodies molded together as one as they made love throughout the night. There was no beginning and no end to their world as they explored and discovered each other. The first signs of daybreak had begun to appear before their hunger was satisfied and sleep finally found them, nestled in each other's arms.

- *Chapter 18* -

The following days passed quickly as Jarod and Dana visited several of the places of interest that the city had to offer. During the warm cover of the night they would come together, celebrating the wonderment of each other's existence.

Jarod closed the car door behind Dana, this would be the last day of their holiday and by tomorrow they would be back at the ranch. Jarod suppressed his mixed feelings as he walked around the rental car and got in.

He pulled a map from the console and studied it briefly.

"Let me see, we'll go over the Mercier bridge and down the 138 to Huntingdon and turn to Port Lewis," he said aloud.

"Where are we going? What's in Port Lewis?"

"I thought it would be nice to get out of the city for a change and get to see some of the countryside here. Not only that, I've arranged for something I thought you might enjoy." Jarod started up the car and turned it into the traffic.

"I don't see how you'll be able to make today anymore special than yesterday or the days before that," Dana said happily, as she settled back in her seat. "This trip has been so perfect." She sighed.

They made their way out of the city and through the suburbs and a quietness settled over the car as Dana also began to think of their return to the ranch.

Jarod stole a glance at her as he drove. He noticed an anxious expression had settled over her soft features, it was a look he had not seen during their entire stay in Montreal.

"Let's just think about today," he said compassionately as he placed a hand over her knee.

"I know," Dana agreed quietly. "It's hard though."

"I think you're going to enjoy what I have planned and we've been graced with perfect skies," Jarod attempted to entice her.

Dana nodded and smiled at Jarod, refusing to allow herself to spoil their last day in Canada.

"You are too good to me."

They leisurely made their way through little villages and farming land, making desultory comments about the rural landscape.

"Where are we going?" Dana asked again bewildered.

"Just a little more patience, we're almost there."

Jarod pulled into the marina and parked the car. "I'm sorry it's not quite the high seas, but I thought an afternoon of sailing would be a nice way of closing our trip."

"I can't believe you did all this. It's been so long since I've been on the water," Dana said in amazement as she got out of the car.

Her enthusiasm was apparent as they walked down to the pier. The lake lay lazily sprawled out before them, lapping rhythmically against the built up shore line, a mammoth pool of perpetual motion contained in voluminous hollow of solid earth.

Dana stood on the edge of the dock, lifting a hand to her brow and scanned the unending horizon. The sun struck the gentle dapples of water, sparkling gaily across its expanse.

Jarod came up behind her, gently laying his arm around her shoulders.

"It's strange," he explained. "When we were sitting on the swing on your parents' porch and we were talking about things we'd done while growing up, it occurred to me that with all the experiences I've had, boating really hasn't been one of them."

Dana turned to face him and smiled.

Jarod's eyes were narrowed against the sun and his manner was relaxed.

"I thought that maybe before we actually go whale chasing across the ocean I should check out my sea legs on something a little more my size," he laughed.

"It's hard for me to imagine anything getting the better of you," Dana said, reaching up to kiss him.

"Why is that?" Jarod affectionately stared into her turquoise eyes. "You managed to."

"Jarod Kingsley," Dana scolded him as she suddenly burst into laughter. "I feel like I've just been compared to being sea-sick. Maybe I should test your swimming ability first." Dana gave him a gentle shove in the direction of the water.

Jarod easily regained his balance and eyed her with a grin. "Don't worry, I can swim just fine. Right now I'm wondering what I can do with all this excess energy you seem to have and there are a few things that come to mind." He directed her a pointed look as he boyishly cocked his head. "Come on, let's find our boat."

They made their way down the planked walkway, passing by a selection of boats that were gently rocking back and forth, moored in their berths.

A tanned stocky man in his mid-forties approached them, extending his hand.

"Monsieur Kingsley?"

"You must be Jean-Luc?"

"Yes, I am Jean-Luc. I have everything ready for you." Jean-Luc indicated with a wave of his hand as he led them to a large sailboat docked at the end of the wharf.

"She's beautiful!" Dana exclaimed as she lightly stepped onto the boat's deck.

"Ma fille, wait until we get her out on the lake and we open her sails. C'est magnifique. Have you sailed before?"

"A few times," Dana answered their guide amiably with a smile.

"I will bring her out and after I will give you the navigation, eh?" Jean-Luc smiled broadly. "The jackets are there," he casually pointed to the life jackets, shrugging his shoulders. "You don't need them now. It is a beautiful day."

Jean-Luc started up the small engine and navigated the craft out onto the open water.

Dana and Jarod were comfortably seated against the bow, with the vessel's large sail fully extended over them, sheets taut against the wind.

"How did you find this place?" Dana turned to Jarod, filled with curiosity.

"I asked the concierge at the hotel and he called over one of the clerks. As it turned out, Jean-Luc happens to be the clerk's best friend's father. The clerk said it was an easy drive, only an hour or so from the city, so here we are."

Dana settled down across the wide seat resting her head against Jarod's thigh, staring up at the deep blue sky above them.

"Montreal is an island, and we could've gone sailing along the canal there as well," Jarod told her softly as he played in her hair. "But Isabelle recommended the lake. She told me it would be quieter in the country and I'm glad we came here."

"So am I, it's nice." Dana reflected on their holiday. Each day had brought with it something new and Jarod had unobtrusively filled every moment with some simple pleasure and Dana came to understand the power of love. It was not where a person went or what it was they did that so much made their time extraordinary, it was who they had to share those moments with that made all the difference.

A smile of contentment crossed Dana's features.

Jarod bent down and kissed her forehead.

"I think Jean-Luc wants you to drive." Jarod nodded towards the man who was motioning to Dana.

"You don't drive a boat." Dana admonished Jarod with a smile as she straightened up and made her way to the older man.

Dana stood alone at the wheel while Jean-Luc tended to the mast. Jarod leaned back against the padded bench, bringing his hands up behind his head.

It was peaceful on the open water and Jarod watched Dana as she conversed with Jean-Luc, listening intently to his instructions, laughing lightly at his jokes. Her face was untroubled and happy.

Jarod was acutely aware that Sonny's name had not once come up during their trip and at first the thought had pleased him. Dana had been through so much, he could only begin to imagine what life must have been like for her and in a way he had succeeded almost too well in taking her away from all that.

Now he was beginning to have second thoughts. His eyebrows creased in concern as he sat forward in his seat.

There were a lot of grave issues that they had deliberately avoided during the last week. Dana had been so convinced of Sonny's eventual return, almost as if she seemed to accept his presence as her destined fate. At the ranch, she had resolutely attempted to make them all aware of the dangers they might face at the ranch should she stay. They had not talked about any of that.

Jarod shook his head. That kind of belief didn't disappear. He knew it was inside her still. Jarod was once again in awe of Dana's courage and strength of character. This week had not been shadowed by worry or fear.

Tomorrow he would be bringing her back to the ranch with an entire list of restrictions, it was another conversation they had not had.

Jarod's jaw tightened as he contemplated his options and found they were few. The authorities had been virtually useless in all this. Jarod had been discreetly checking in with the detective he had hired and as of last night, Sonny still had not been located.

He grimly recalled the meeting at the ranch house the eve before their departure and Ben's parting words ran repeatedly through his mind, seeming more credible to Jarod each time.

Dana squatted before him crossing her arms over his knees, looking into his dark face.

Jarod saw her concerned expression. He remained silent. He had never found the right time or the right words during their holiday, because he had been unable to bring himself to break the magic that they had shared together.

"Jarod," she said softly. "You have done everything you possibly can do." Dana looked to the shore. They would be there soon. She took a deep breath. "I'm tired of running and I'm tired of hiding. I don't want to give him that power anymore. If we always live in fear of what may happen tomorrow then we've given him everything."

Dana's words were brave but Jarod realized that she had not called Sonny by name.

He nodded and covered her hands inside his and kissed her.

Jean-Luc brought the boat into dock. They rose and thanked the man for the afternoon as Jarod paid him and soon they were on their way to the city.

They had traveled a little while when Jarod noticed his gas gage was low. He pulled off the highway in the little village of Ormstown and filled up the car. He turned to Dana.

"I'm getting hungry. What about you? It's almost an hour before we get back to the hotel. Let's see if there's a restaurant close by."

Dana agreed with the suggestion. The car ride so far had been filled with a heavy silence and a break in the journey would do them both good. Jarod received simple directions from the garage attendant and they made their way over a little bridge to the main street.

They entered the restaurant and ordered from the menu.

"So, how are you feeling about going back to the ranch?" Jarod asked Dana as he sat forward in the booth.

"I miss June, I miss everyone. It will be good to see them," Dana smiled at him reassuringly. "Actually, I'm looking forward to going for a ride and getting back to work." Dana felt the truth of her words as she spoke them and a warm feeling came over her.

The waitress brought their meals.

"Work?" Jarod hesitated. "It seems early to get back to work, I think it's too physical."

Dana laughed and answered in a low voice not to be overheard by others. "Suddenly you're worried about physical activity?" Dana arched her brows. "Jarod, you look me straight in the face and tell me that after this week, you think I'm not up to riding a horse."

A grin spread over Jarod's features.

"Alright, you win. We'll go day by day to start with and see how it goes."

Their meal proved to be delicious and by the time they were done eating they were both in a lighter mood.

Jarod and Dana stood at the counter waiting to pay their bill. A tall, distinguished looking man dressed in kitchen whites approached them. He spoke with a European accent that Jarod presumed was Greek. "Did you enjoy your meal?"

"Our meals were excellent. It's a nice place you have here," Jarod answered conversationally as he handed the man his bill and credit card.

The man studied the card briefly before inserting it into the machine.

"Where are you from, Mr. Kingsley?"

"Actually, we're from New Mexico. We're in Montreal for the week and we were out at the lake today, sailing."

The man held out his hand and smiled. "I'm George. I'm glad you found my restaurant."

Jarod shook the man's hand and smiled at Dana. "Dana and I are quite impressed with the area. The lake was beautiful."

"If you enjoy water and boats, it's a shame you just missed the regates, the boat races. Also, there are the canal locks not far from here. It's quite the thing to see in operation."

"Unfortunately, we're heading home tomorrow," Jarod replied.

"That's too bad. Next time you come by this way, stop in and see me. It seems like a quiet area, but we have lots to see and do." The man handed Jarod his transaction to sign and returned his card.

"We'll have to do that, if we're ever by this way again."

"Well, have a safe trip home, Jarod," George said with a grin as he tapped his fingers against the counter. "I may not remember your names the next time you stop in, but I never forget a face." The man saluted them and headed back to the kitchen.

The lights of the city welcomed them as they crossed over the bridge onto the island.

"Dana, if you are not too tired, there is one more spot I'd like you to see. I know it's getting late..."

"I'm fine, it's not too late." Dana looked down at her casual attire. "I should change my clothes."

"It's not like that, don't worry. You're dressed fine." Jarod drove through the city.

"This is Mont Royal," he explained as the car climbed the upward streets. He found the parking area. "It's not far."

Jarod opened her door. He put his arm around Dana as they walked along a quiet, wooded path. They reached a vantage point that looked over the entire city.

Cloaked by the velvet darkness of the night, standing on the top of the mountain, they looked over the broad expanse of dancing lights.

"It's like being above the stars," Dana uttered in amazement.

"I wanted this to be the way you remember Montreal." Jarod pulled Dana back against him, his arms sheltering her as he kissed the top of her head.

"I'll never forget any of this," she vowed solemnly.

Reluctantly, they knew it was time to go.

[241]

At the hotel suite, Dana stared at the empty suitcase on their bed. She should start packing in order to be prepared for their morning flight. She was looking forward to returning to the ranch, but she couldn't shake the growing fear inside her.

She walked to the window and looked out. The feeling had been slowly building throughout the day.

Would she ever be safe? Would he ever tire of her and leave her alone?

She turned back towards the room. She stared at the door to the suite, willing him to come through it right now, to find her now and for whatever was going to happen to happen and be over with.

When he came back the next time, he was going to be in for a surprise, she thought fiercely. She was going to fight him with everything she had. He'd taken all that he was ever going to get from her.

As they drove down the familiar stretch of road to the ranch, Jarod found himself looking forward to coming home. Their time away had been idyllic, but this was his home, it was a large part of the man he was inside and the place to which he would always came back to.

The joy he felt at finally having someone special to share that with was tempered by the reality that their circumstances were harshly influenced by the unknown whereabouts of Sonny.

Dana had become increasingly silent during the course of the trip and Jarod looked over to her now to find her lost in thought, palely staring before her, unseeing.

He placed his hand over her knee and she startled slightly.

"Sweetheart, there are some things we need to talk about, before we get home." Jarod hesitated, trying to choose his words carefully, anticipating that this was going to be difficult. "I know you'd like for everything to be back to normal, but for a while I think we need to do things differently."

Dana's soft lips drew into a tight line and she turned her head away, mutely staring out the passenger window.

"I know you'll hate this," he continued with grim determination. "It's good for you to get back to work, if that's what you really want to do, but there are some things like the trail riding for example..." Jarod sighed. Dana's silence wasn't helping any.

"I will make things better," he emphasized. "But it's going to take some time. I need to know that you're safe and not running around the ranch all by yourself." Jarod saw her slender hand curl into a tight fist in her lap, it was the only indication he had that she was even listening to him. "Dana, I can't be fighting with you through all of this."

"So what you're telling me is that I can't even walk to the barn on my own. I can't believe that you want me to become a prisoner all over again." Dana spoke flatly to the window, her chin held high.

"Dana, it's just until I get things worked out."

"Get things worked out?" Dana flashed him a look of anger as she uttered a small bitter laugh. "And just how do you propose to do that, Jarod?"

Jarod pulled to the side of the road and with a quick motion he silenced the engine. He could feel the muscle in his jaw tensing and he strove to remain patient.

"Dana, this is enough, I know you're angry, and you have every right to feel that way but…"

"Yes, I'm mad and screaming inside of myself, and scared beyond your imagination," she cut in. "Jarod you can't possibly even begin to understand how I feel. I am trapped, overwhelmed, and so at fault for bringing this all here. I want to live a life where I don't have to be afraid, not only for myself but especially for everyone close to me. I am livid that I have this thing," Her eyes glared at him. "This thing that shadows my every move, it's always there.

For once, I don't want to feel like the victim, I'm sick of being careful, and sick of giving in. I can't believe any of this has happened. I feel so cheated. I worked hard to get where I was with my training and it meant everything to me and Sonny snapped his fingers and everything was gone. And now everything I have with you," Dana's words spilled out in a torrent of rage and despair. "Can't you see? Can't you understand? I feel like I'm standing on a cliff and the view before me is breathtaking, only I can't see the ground beneath my feet. I'm paralyzed and I hate it! I want to have an ordinary life like everyone else, Jarod. Sonny's coming here to New Mexico to find me has really shaken me. I had put so much belief into the desperate hope that I'd finally be rid of him, that he'd let me go. And I was so wrong. Now you're sitting here, calmly telling me what's best for me," Dana shook her head. "Short of me finding Sonny myself and handing my life over to him, I don't know how to fix this, so what makes you think you can?" Dana came to a stop, shaking with frustration.

Jarod stared at her.

The sudden silence in the car was eerie.

"Dana," he said slowly, an uncomprehending look covered his features. "You don't want security because you want Sonny to find you?" Jarod's hand crossed over his face as he shook his head. "I don't understand what you're saying."

"Sometimes I don't understand what I'm saying." Dana looked across the land, her expression empty. "It's the waiting, the never knowing." She took a deep breath and swallowed hard.

"I just feel like... I know inside, if you make it impossible for Sonny to get to me directly, he'll find another way. Someone will get hurt, that's the way he works. You cannot begin to know the guilt and fear I feel for bringing him here." There was desperation in Dana's voice as her eyes began to water. "It could be anyone, it could be you. Jarod, if anything happened to you, I would rather die." Tears ran down her cheeks.

"Oh, Dana." Jarod got out of the car and came to her door. He opened it and squatted down beside her, taking her trembling hands in his.

"We've been through all this before. Everybody knows what's going on and nobody is going to get hurt. You can't live your life like some sacrificial lamb to Sonny. Please tell me you will try things my way, at least for a while." Jarod pleaded.

Dana stared down at the face she had come to love, wanting to believe everything he said.

"I will," she answered him slowly. "As long as you promise me that you will be careful. Jarod, I'm really serious about this. Nothing can happen to you," her bottom lip quivered as she spoke.

"We're in this together. We'll be careful for each other." Jarod released one of her hands and ran his strong fingers gently down the side of the face, wiping away her tears.

"I'm so sorry. The things I said before, they were unfair and hurtful. It's not you that I'm angry with." Dana ran her hand through his hair. "I could never be angry with you. I guess the closer we get to the ranch...." she sighed heavily.

Jarod pulled her from the car and held her tightly.

"Sweetheart, I love you and you can't keep holding everything in. Whether you are happy or sad or angry at me, it won't change the way I feel about you." Jarod took her face in his hands and kissed her. "There is nothing that I wouldn't do for you."

"I know," Dana closed her eyes. "That's what hurts so much."

Jarod held her against him for a while longer before placing his hands on her shoulders and taking a step back.

"June will be waiting for us. Do you feel ready?" Jarod watched her closely.

She met his steady gaze and nodded.

They arrived at the ranch. Dana stepped out of the car as Jarod opened the trunk and removed their suitcases. A smile came to her lips as she looked around the yard. Everything was just as they had left it. Her gaze traveled to the main house to where a stranger stood on the verandah and her expression became sober.

Jarod was beside her aware of the object of her attention as he shuffled the suitcases in his hands. "That's one of the security men," he said quietly.

"I know." Dana let go a sigh of resignation, her expression remained unchanged.

"Come on, let's go inside."

They climbed the wide steps and entered the house.

"June? We're home." Jarod called out.

June bustled into the hallway, greeting them. "Mr. Kingsley, Dana! It's so good to have you both home."

Jarod set down the suitcases and bent to kiss the older woman's cheek.

"June," Dana said as she hugged her with affection. "I didn't realize just how much I missed this place until I saw you."

June smiled in appreciation, her face becoming warm.

"Come into the kitchen," she urged. "I've just made a fresh pot of coffee and you can tell me all about your trip."

"If it's alright with you, I really should check my messages in the office. It shouldn't take too long and then I'll join you." Jarod smiled at the two women. "I'm sure you two girls have plenty to talk about, it'll give you a head start."

"Very funny, Jarod." Dana made a face. "Actually, it will be nice to sit with June for a while," she admitted.

"Alright then." Jarod kissed Dana's forehead and turned into the office.

Dana followed June into the kitchen.

"It feels so good to be home. June, your kitchen always smells so delicious." Dana sat down at the big, worn table and looked across the spacious room.

June smiled proudly and placed a plate of muffins and two mugs of coffee down on the table before seating herself next to Dana.

"Things just weren't the same without you here," the older woman said. "Kent can be amusing, but it's hardly the same. I've missed our little talks together. So, tell me about your trip."

A small smile played across Dana's lips as she began to speak. "Our trip was wonderful, June. First we went to Maine and I got to see my parents and my best friend, Emma. It's the first time I've been away from them that long."

"They must've been thrilled to see you," June said with understanding.

Dana regarded June with her head tilted to the side. "I don't think I ever told you. I know I've thought it several times, how you remind me of my mom. It's strange because in some ways you're not at all like her but I know that staying away from home would've been harder for me if it wasn't for you."

"Why, that's one of the nicest things anyone has ever said to me, dear." June reached over and squeezed Dana's hand.

Dana smiled and paused, sipping at her coffee.

"After visiting my parents, we went to Montreal. Did you receive my postcard?"

"It came this morning, it was nice of you to send it. Montreal looks like a beautiful city."

"It was. We had the best time. It was so romantic." The words escaped unguarded from Dana's mouth and she blushed, lowering her eyes.

"My dear girl," June chuckled softly. "I wasn't always this age. There is no need to be shy. I'm so glad the both of you have found each other. It's good that you went away and had that time alone, together. It does the world for me, to see the two of you happy."

[246]

Jarod walked into the room and poured himself a cup of coffee and joined them at the table, helping himself to a muffin.

"So, did everything go alright here while we were away?" Jarod asked casually, looking back and forth from June to Dana and their sudden silence. "What? Did I interrupt something?"

Dana stole a glance at June then turned to Jarod innocently. "No," she said as she smiled.

"I was just saying how hard it must've been for Dana's parents to let her go. They must've been so delighted to see her," June turned back to Dana. "And what did they think of Jarod?"

"I think they were pretty impressed with Jarod, so that made it easier on them. We promised we'd stay longer the next time we visit."

Jarod nodded. "They seem to be very nice people." He put his cup down. "Well, I have some business in the office that shouldn't be put off..."

Dana sighed. "I should unpack."

"If you want to wait I'll give you a hand," he offered as he stood.

"Don't be silly, I'll give Dana a hand, if you'd just bring the bags up. It's a good excuse to spend some more time with her." June turned to Dana who nodded in agreement.

Jarod brought the suitcases to his room, leaving the women busily engaged in conversation in the kitchen. He smiled as he returned to the office.

He crossed over to his desk and returned two calls then reached for his mail. He leafed through the envelopes and stopped at one that had no return address.

He slit open the envelope and pulled out a single sheet of paper. His face tightened and grew dark as he unfolded the page. The paper was stained with a dry crimson splatter and he read the ominous message scrawled there.

YOU'VE TAKEN SOMETHING THAT WAS NOT YOURS TO TAKE. ENJOY HER WHILE YOU CAN.

"Damn!" Jarod slammed his fist on the desk. He stared before him, consumed with blind rage.

Swiftly he crossed the room and went outside, motioning to the security officer.

"How many men are on duty?" Jarod asked the man in controlled anger.

"Two on each shift, Mr. Kingsley; one for the house, one for the barns."

"Fine, I want an additional man, just for Miss Northington." Jarod narrowed his eyes as he tried to think rationally. "This came in the mail...I want you to take care of it," Jarod ordered as he handed the man the envelope and its message. "Have it analyzed or fingerprinted. Do what you have to do, but let's try to get a restraining order against this maniac!"

"Yes sir," the man answered.

Jarod paused, his sense of reason slowly returning. He checked the man's identification card. "Listen, Frank. Unless I am with Miss Northington, or she is in the house, she is not to be left alone. She's very sensitive about all of this and I'd like the entire matter to be handled discreetly. Do you understand what I'm saying?"

"I understand perfectly, sir. Our staff is very professional. Will tomorrow be soon enough for the extra security?"

"Tomorrow will be fine." Jarod dismissed the man and decided to get some fresh air and try to clear his mind.

He walked down to the paddock and leaned against the railing, absently watching the horses in the distance, deep in thought.

The letter was another grim reminder of Sonny's boldness. Jarod had not expected the man to do something that seemed so incredibly brazen, yet he should not have been surprised as he thought over what he already knew of him. Sonny always had a way of challenging reality. He always had to go back for another bite. He was obsessed and he was dangerous, this man had no fear. Jarod's understanding of Sonny grew as did his apprehension. A restraining order, Jarod laughed at himself in contempt. It was like shaking a fly swatter at a rabid coyote.

He ran his hand over his face. Without warning he found himself questioning his ability to keep Dana safe.

He turned back towards the house and caught sight of Dana in the bedroom window, her back to him.

Jarod knew he would not tell her of the letter. He was uncomfortable with that decision but what purpose would it serve? She knew all too well what she was up against and the extra guard would be there tomorrow.

[248]

Dana was coming down the steps as Jarod entered the house.

"We're all unpacked," she said lightly. "I was just coming to look for you. Dinner is almost ready."

"I went out for a walk," Jarod answered with deliberate casualness.

"Some of us are entitled to that liberty," she teased as she reached up and kissed him.

Jarod looked away and forced a smile, the secret knowledge of Sonny's letter burning at his conscience.

They sat over drinks after supper. As always June had lovingly prepared a delicious meal, but Dana couldn't help but notice that Jarod seemed preoccupied and distant.

"You're looking tired tonight, Jarod," she said finally.

"Am I? It must be jet lag." Jarod smiled at her briefly. "What do you think about an early night?"

"I think that would be a good idea. I want to get back to work tomorrow and I want to be fresh."

"Not too fresh," Jarod proposed as he emptied his glass.

They wished June a good night and went to their room.

Dana crawled into bed, bringing her body in close to Jarod's. She laid her head upon his chest.

"I can feel your heart pounding," she whispered.

"It's calling your name." He opened his arms and drew her into his embrace as he raised himself over her. He closed his eyes, overcome by unbridled desire. Wordlessly, he sought her lips. He was desperate to lose himself inside her, to become as one with nothing between them.

She returned his probing kiss, swept away by his urgency.

There was a hungry intensity to their lovemaking and as they finally fell back exhausted, he kissed her tenderly. Night covered them and he lay in the darkness holding her sleeping body closely. His passion had tempered neither his fury nor his worry.

[249]

- Chapter 19 -

Dana rolled over in bed and opened her eyes. The early morning sun filtered through Jarod's bedroom window casting the room in a pearly light. She fondly studied his face as he lay sleeping and smiled to herself. Gingerly she slipped out of the bed and dressed in her riding clothes. She carefully picked up her riding boots and tiptoed out of the room. Making her way down the long hallway to the back stairway she stopped and put on her boots before going down the steps for breakfast.

"Good morning, June," she said brightly as she entered the kitchen.

"Good morning, dear." June turned from the sink, her expression rapidly changing as she noticed Dana's attire. "My dear girl," she said. "Don't tell me that you plan to ride today."

"June, I'm just going to take out Goliath and really he's safe enough for a child to ride. My shoulder is fine." Dana sat on the stool and picked up the coffee mug June had placed before her.

"It's not just your shoulder that worries me," June said in concern as she hesitated at a loss for words. "Does Mr. Kingsley know?"

"Yes, Jarod knows that I'm going back to work." Dana spoke with a gentle firmness. "I think we've had enough drama around here lately. It's the middle of show season and I have a job to do. I need to do it," she underlined as she tapped a finger to her chest.

June nodded, slowly understanding Dana's decision.

"Is Mr. Kingsley on his way down?" June asked as she held two eggs over the frying pan.

"No, he's still sleeping." Dana felt her cheeks become warm as she remembered the night before.

June appeared not to notice Dana's awkward shyness as she replaced the eggs in the carton and busily began peeling apples for her pie.

"I like to get my baking done early, before the day gets too hot," she needlessly explained and they both tacitly agreed.

Eager to begin her day, Dana finished her breakfast and went over to June. "I'll be careful," she reassured the woman with a smile.

She stepped out onto the verandah to find not one but two security guards waiting there. Dana stopped, taken aback by the presence of the second man who stepped forward to greet her.

"Good day, Miss Northington," the pleasant looking young man said politely. "My name is Tom."

Dana's eyebrow arched slightly as she began to understand his purpose. She sighed.

"Let me guess, Tom," she said with an underlying note of sarcasm. "You have the sorry privilege of following me around all day."

"Yes, m'am." Tom smiled at her disarmingly.

"You look like a boy scout," Dana complained as she looked him over.

"So I've been told. Actually, it's my secret weapon," he replied in confidence, still grinning.

"Well, don't call me m'am. You look too young as it is. I thought you were supposed to be making me feel safe, not decrepit." Against her will, Dana could feel herself warming up to the man. He was not at all what she had expected. "What's he doing here?" Dana pointed to the older large-framed man who stood at the end of the porch, silent. That was what she had expected, Dana thought to herself as she turned her attention back to Tom.

"That's Frank. He guards the house, I guard you."

"You're the one who guards me," Dana repeated, overcome by the irony of the situation.

"Yes m'am."

"Dana," she insisted, unable to hide the smile that came to her lips.

"You will be safe with me, Dana." Tom casually shifted his weight, allowing a glimpse of the revolver he carried to be briefly seen. The movement appeared to be entirely accidental but Dana's smile lost its freshness as she found the introduction was no longer entertaining.

Dana turned away and walked down the steps.

"Well hop to it, Tom. Mr. Kingsley can be quite the tyrant." She made her way to the barn with Jesse Dog at her side.

[251]

Stepping into the barn entrance a third guard nodded to her as he walked outside.

"My God, and I thought we bred horses here!" Dana said tightly under her breath as she turned to glare at Tom.

"Richard," Tom cleared his throat. "He guards the barns."

"Are there any more?" Dana asked tersely.

"No, not on this shift."

Dana narrowed her eyes and took a deep breath. The toe of her boot lightly tapped the barn floor as she struggled to regain the feeling of anticipation that she had awaken to that morning. She looked at Tom who stood quietly a few steps away.

"Don't take it personally if I seem less than thrilled. I hate the idea of someone watching me all the time."

"For whatever it's worth, I'm not watching you. My job is to watch what goes on around you. I don't know if that makes any difference to you, but believe me, it is a big difference." Tom's explanation allowed Dana a different perspective and she nodded, feeling more accepting of the situation.

She entered the recess of the barn just as Annie and Kent were finishing up morning feeding.

"Dana!" Annie called as she put down the bucket in her hands and came over, Kent following in her footsteps. "It's good to have you back." They met together in the barn aisle and Dana and Annie hugged each other.

"It's good to be back," Dana agreed. "How is everything going here?"

She scanned over the horses in the stalls.

"Everything's going fine," Annie explained. "We've been trying to keep up the horses' training programs. Adam has been a real life saver and we've managed to follow their usual schedules pretty closely without the students coming in." Annie spoke in her unhurried manner, her round face content.

"Well, except for Masquerade, we haven't done anything with her since..." Kent stopped himself short, catching Annie's sudden look of discomfort. "I'm sorry," he fumbled.

"There's no need to apologize, Kent. Don't worry about it," Dana explained to them both. "I don't want everyone walking on eggshells around me. So, how is Masquerade?"

[252]

"She's fine. We just figured it would be best to leave her for you, for a lot of reasons," Kent finished.

Dana walked over to the mare's stall.

"Hi, baby."

The horse came to her and Dana stroked her awhile before slipping a halter over the horse's head and leading her out onto the cross-ties.

"I'm sorry, girl." Dana ran an opened palm down the horse's gleaming neck. She then carefully ran her hand over each of the mare's legs, paying particular attention to the foreleg that had been injured in the accident. "She seems sound. How is she moving on it?" Dana looked up to Annie and Kent.

"She's been great on it since about three days ago," Kent replied.

"Good." Dana nodded as she straightened up and brought the horse back to her stall.

"Well, we'd better get finished cleaning up," Annie said, offering. "If you need anything..."

"No, I'll be fine. You guys go on with what you were doing."

Dana stepped into the office and briefly reviewed the horses' files. Nothing out of the ordinary had occurred during her absence and everything appeared to be under control in spite of the fact that the students' training program had been discontinued for the time being.

Dana had been hired to manage this barn and to undertake the teaching program and she sat for a moment, deep in thought as she considered the ramifications of her circumstances. She had come to enjoy the teaching aspect of her work and she knew her students' training progress was being seriously compromised and the show schedule in disarray. At this point they had already missed two important shows.

She sighed as she shut off the computer and returned to the barn, where she immediately caught sight of Tom. One hurdle at a time, she thought to herself as she carried her tack to the cross-ties.

Slowly, she walked from stall to stall checking all the horses. She reached Goliath's stall and led the horse out and saddled him up. Her eyes drifted to the wide open doors at the end of the barn.

"Hey there, big guy. It'll be the riding hall for us today." She turned the horse and led him into the arena.

Dana mounted and put the gelding into a working trot, eventually moving into serpentines and circles before bringing the horse back to a walk.

"Good man." She stroked his neck before putting him into a canter. It felt so good to be riding, Dana thought to herself as she felt her concerns fall away.

She worked on lead changes for a bit, which the big horse responded to easily then she turned Goliath into the ring on the diagonal and jumped the two fences that had been erected there. She slowed him back down to a walk and noticed Jarod leaning on the arena doors, smiling.

"Good morning, Jarod." Dana rode over to him.

He wanted to tell her that she shouldn't be jumping but decided against it, preferring instead to be grateful that she had chosen to stay in the arena. "You looked great out there. How does it feel? How is you shoulder holding up?"

"Fine." Dana dismounted. Jarod opened the door for her and she led Goliath back into the barn.

"I can cool him down for you," Annie suggested as she walked over to them.

"No, that's okay. I'll do it, thanks." Dana stripped the horse of his tack. "Do you feel like walking with me?" Dana invited Jarod.

"Sure." Jarod noticed Tom was about to follow Dana out of the barn and he directed him a dismissive nod.

Outside, the temperature was beautiful and the billowing clouds streaked across the deep blue sky. Dana and Jarod walked side by side with the big gelding following.

"Jarod, what are we going to do about our student program and the show schedule?" Dana took the opportunity to approach Jarod with her concerns. "Everyone was progressing so well and we're registered in most of the season's shows. It's a big setback for the ranch and the students as well."

"I thought you'd be content with just getting back to riding. I should've known better." Jarod said slowly as he looked across the distance to the strong jagged mountains. "Everything has its time. There will be more show seasons. For now, things are on hold. Day by day, remember? Do you like Tom?" Jarod tried to change the subject.

"I'm not a very big asset to this operation," Dana pointed out, refusing to be sidetracked.

"But you're essential to my operation." He turned to her and grinned. "Look, there's Adam." Jarod indicated, relieved by the man approaching them.

"Dana, Jarod. Did you have a good trip?"

"Wonderful! And you all seemed to have done a great job here while we were gone. I wanted to thank you," Jarod answered.

"Annie was telling me you have been filling in quite a bit with the riding, it really helped them out," Dana said gratefully.

"You had the horses in peak condition. It was only a matter of keeping it up." Adam adjusted his hat. "I really enjoyed Paska, that mare has a lot of spirit. It was good to put my hand in, but I'm glad that you're back." Adam looked towards the paddock.

"I was just about to bring Serenity and the mare into the barn. The filly is looking great. Stop at the barn when you have time and see her. Dana, if you need any help with the training schedule let me know."

"Thanks, Adam. I may take you up on that."

Adam nodded and made his way to the paddock.

Dana and Jarod walked companionably for a few more minutes cooling down the black gelding before returning to the barn.

Once there Dana stopped and looked to Jarod.

"I want to try Masquerade this afternoon. She seems fine and no one's been working with her."

"Dana..." Jarod began.

"Jarod, I don't think I ever mentioned this, but Masquerade had nothing to do with my taking that fall. I passed out while I was still on her. The horse was doing so well, I hope that none of this has damaged her confidence. I've put a lot of work into that horse."

Jarod deliberated over this new piece of information as he weighed his concerns.

"Okay," he relented. "But I want to be there the first time you take her out, that way you can use the outside ring if you prefer." Jarod recognized that Dana was back in her element and he admitted to himself that it was just what she needed.

"Well, can I take her out now, before the sun becomes any stronger?"

Jarod smiled at Dana. He knowingly shook his head. "Go ahead and get her ready. I'll put this guy away."

It was not long before Jarod was leaning with his arms crossed over the top rail of the outdoor ring, watching Dana as she prepared to mount the tall bay mare.

Ben joined Jarod on the rail. The mental image of Masquerade catapulting into the yard without her rider on the day of the accident was still vivid in the older man's mind.

"You think that's a good idea?" Ben said in an aside, his face lined with worry.

"You try and stop her." Jarod frowned. "I think she's feeling useless enough already."

Ben nodded in mute understanding as Dana pulled her stirrups down and calmly mounted Masquerade. The mare snorted lightly.

"It's alright, big girl."

Dana gave the mare a fairly loose rein and put her on the rail at a walk. Within minutes Masquerade's gait had begun to relax. Dana shortened her reins and her legs urged the horse into a trot.

Jarod could never tire of watching Dana ride. She had a unique ability to shut out everything around her except the horse, knowing every movement as it happened. From where Jarod stood the entire process was a thing of beauty.

Dana kept the session short and deliberately decided not to jump the mare at all. Jarod could tell by her expression as she cooled the horse down that she was happy with how it had gone.

Ben offered to bring the horse in and Dana and Jarod decided to break for lunch.

They were sitting over coffee when Dana looked across the table at Jarod.

"What are your plans for this afternoon?"

"Why? Are you trying to get rid of me?" Jarod smiled as he teased her.

"No, not at all. I just feel like I've been monopolizing all your time. I know you have a lot to catch up on."

"I have a pile of work waiting for me at my desk. I was thinking that maybe you'd like to give everyone the gifts you picked out for them during our trip," Jarod suggested.

[256]

"That's an idea. Don't you prefer it if I waited for you?"

"No, you go ahead. I'm going to lock myself in my office."

"I should catch up on some of my office work too," Dana agreed. "I'll give Empire a work out in the hall..."

"Take it easy. I don't want you wearing yourself out today." Jarod rose from his chair and came over to kiss her. "Save some energy for me tonight."

"I don't think that will be a problem," Dana assured him with a quick smile.

Jarod went to his office and Dana collected the souvenirs from their room and left the house.

"Let's go Tom." She laughed as she started down the steps of the verandah. "Mr. Kingsley is in quite the mood today."

Dana's afternoon passed quickly. Everyone seemed pleased with their gifts and although Empire's session had been slightly off, it was nothing too serious and now she rubbed her eyes as she turned off her computer.

"Enough of this," Dana said aloud as she stretched and walked into the barn. She said goodnight to everyone and with Tom following at a discreet distance, she headed back to the main house.

Jarod's office door was open but the room was empty. Dana made her way to the kitchen.

"Hi, June. How was your afternoon?"

"Fine, dear." June answered from the stove without turning.

"Do you know where Jarod is? I thought I should let him know I'm in."

"Mr. Kingsley left a little while ago. He said he had some business to take care of and for you not to worry if he was late."

Dana began to feel unsettled.

"I don't understand why he didn't come to tell me himself at the barn," Dana said as she thought aloud. Her uneasiness grew. "He's been so... June, look at me. Was there anything else?"

June turned and faced Dana. She appeared worried and Dana knew something was definitely wrong.

"June, you're not telling me everything. What happened?" Dana insisted.

"I don't know that anything happened," June answered, her expression doubtful. "He received a phone call and left shortly afterwards. I don't know, he wasn't himself." She frowned. "He seemed almost offhand, too much so." She paused, noticing the look that had come over Dana's features.

"I'm sure I'm making too much of this. It's just an old woman's imagination getting carried away." June went over to Dana and put a comforting arm around her. "Sit down dear. I'll prepare your plate."

"I'm sorry, June. I think I'll just go upstairs. I'll wait till he gets in. You'll call me if there's anything?"

"Of course, dear."

Dana kissed June's cheek and left the kitchen. She slowly made her way up the stairs. Where was Jarod? She found the possibilities frightening.

- *Chapter 20* -

Jarod parked his car to the side of the motel and cut the engine. He picked up the pair of gloves from the console and pulled them on.

He stood out of the car and the detective rapidly walked over to meet him.

"He's in #14," the man informed him.

Jarod looked at the man and nodded curtly. "I'll take care of this myself."

He left the man and purposefully made his way to the room and rapped on the door.

"What? The voice was unmistakable and Jarod answered. "Management."

"What now?" The voice repeated irritably.

The door opened slightly and Jarod forcibly kicked it inwards, sending Sonny heavily to the floor. Jarod stormed into the room.

"Get up!" Jarod bent, and grabbed Sonny by the shirt, pulling him into a standing position. "I said get up!" He shoved Sonny hard against the wall, holding his arm across his neck.

Sonny attempted to speak.

"Don't say a word. Don't even breathe too loud." Jarod commanded lowly between clenched teeth. "You have no idea how close to the edge I am right now." Jarod leaned his weight into his arm. "How much I want to kill you."

Sonny choked for air as he struggled to free himself. Jarod threw the man's head forcefully back into the wall.

"This is the plan. You are going to get out of New Mexico tonight, and I mean tonight. You will never show yourself anywhere near this state again. You will never go near Dana or anything close to her. Do you understand?"

Sonny's bulging eyes blinked in response.

"If you so much as step on a flower she likes, I swear with God as my witness, I will kill you. Do you understand me?" Jarod pushed on Sonny's neck as the man's face turned a hideous purple.

Sonny nodded.

Jarod released his hold then slammed his fist into Sonny's jaw. He collapsed to the floor.

"You remember what I said," Jarod threatened as he stood over Sonny's gasping form. "Go near her again and you're a dead man."

As Jarod turned to leave he saw a laptop on the desk. Picking it up, he strode from the room.

The detective stood outside the door.

"Is there anything you'd like me to take care of Mr. Kingsley?"

"Let me know when he crosses the state line and find out what's on this." Jarod ordered as he handed the man the laptop and left him.

He quickly got into his car and drove away, certain that if he stayed any longer he would finish what he had started.

His rage gradually dissipated as Jarod drove back to the ranch. He had been only a hairbreadth away from killing the man in that hotel room. He knew without the slightest doubt that he had been capable of carrying it through. He could've crushed the life out of Sonny with his bare hand and that knowledge brought him a grim satisfaction.

For the first time since all of this began Jarod felt in control, he had the upper hand. Now he could only hope it was enough.

He arrived at the ranch and got out of his car, flexing his hand. The pain in his fist gave him a strange sense of pleasure.

Jarod climbed the steps to the porch where Frank came to meet him.

"Mr. Kingsley. I thought you would want to know that the preliminary tests have come back on that letter. The envelope was covered with prints which is to be expected, but the letter itself showed only one set which we must presume are yours."

Jarod nodded.

"As far as the paper itself goes, it's your typical five and dime brand. There really was nothing extraordinary, other than the staining which was some type of animal blood."

Jarod rubbed at his eyes. It had been a long day. He bid the guard goodnight and entered the house.

"Thank God you are alright!" June exclaimed as she hurried towards Jarod. "We've been worried."

"June, I told you I would be late," Jarod explained as he kissed the woman's cheek. "How's Dana?"

"She's upstairs. She was upset and wouldn't eat dinner." June shook her head. "Where have you been all this time?"

"I'll tell you everything tomorrow. You should be getting some sleep. Everything is okay. I'd like to go check on Dana, are you alright?" Jarod asked compassionately.

"I'm fine, now that I see you're home and safe," June answered, somewhat calmer.

Jarod climbed the staircase and quietly opened the bedroom door. Dana lay in the large bed, curled on her side into a tight figure, still dressed in her riding clothes.

Dana sensed movement in the room and her body bolted upright. She looked up at Jarod with anxious eyes. He came and sat beside her on the bed, putting his arms around her.

"Where were you? Are you alright?" Dana's expression was a mixture of concern and relief.

"I'm fine," Jarod shook his head and smiled. "I left for a couple of hours and between you and June...you shouldn't worry so much." He kissed her gently. "Though I must admit, it's very flattering."

"Don't give me that," Dana reproached him. "You still haven't told me where you were. What about that big speech about us taking care of each other? Why didn't you come and tell me you were leaving?" Dana tried to make him understand. "Imagine how you would be feeling right now Jarod, if the shoe was on the other foot?"

"I'd be going out of my mind with worry." Jarod gently brushed the hair from Dana's forehead. "You're right and I'm sorry I've upset you."

Jarod stood and taking Dana's hands in his he pulled her to her feet.

His lips softly explored the gentle hollow at the base of her throat. Dana felt her desire stir. "I hate it when you're upset," he said deeply, continuing to kiss her. "Especially with me."

[261]

Dana's body quickly responded to his touch as he persuasively drew her in closer.

"Can't we let this go until the morning?" Jarod's hand lightly caressed her as it traveled with unhurried deliberation down her back.

Dana's arms reached up behind his shoulders and she brought his mouth to hers. "We can let this go for now," the words escaped her in a whisper as she ran her fingers through his hair. "But in the morning..."

"I know, Sweetheart." Jarod answered her as a confident grin slowly crossed his face. "What about if you join me in the shower and I can apologize to you properly."

Dana no longer felt like talking as she followed Jarod without protest into the bathroom.

Jarod slowly opened his eyes the next morning to find Dana lying quietly beside him already awake.

"I love waking up like this," he murmured as he reached for her.

"Jarod, we need to talk," Dana spoke quietly.

"It's not exactly what I had in mind." Jarod rubbed at his eyes as he sat up in bed. "What's wrong, Sweetheart?"

"I think you should tell me." Dana's worried eyes fell to Jarod's swollen and discolored hand.

The phone rang beside the bed and Jarod picked it up, lifting one finger to Dana as he watched her and listened to the caller.

"Good. Thank you." Jarod hung up the phone.

"Jarod, this is really starting to bother me. Strange trips, a swollen hand and mysterious phone calls, something is wrong and now is not the time to start keeping secrets."

"I'm sorry, Dana. I didn't want you to worry last night. I would've told you then but I didn't think it was a good idea and actually it was better that I waited for that call." Jarod kissed the top of her head.

"I told you that I hired someone to track Sonny." Jarod pulled her towards him as he settled back in the bed. "Well, he finally located Sonny late yesterday and I went to talk to him."

"You went to talk to Sonny?" Dana was incredulous. "Oh my God."

"No, Dana. It's okay. That was the detective now on the phone. Sonny has left the state and if he knows what's good for him, he won't be back."

Dana sat up and turned a white face to Jarod.

"You promised me that you would be careful." Dana's voice shook as she stared once again at Jarod's hand. "You did more than just talk. I don't even want to think of what could've happened to you. Oh, Jarod. How could you have?"

Jarod was immediately struck by the note of disappointment in her tone. He had not expected this reaction from her.

"Dana, I was careful. The detective was there," he attempted to ease her worry. "I was never in any danger."

"How do you know, Jarod? Did you even stop to consider it? Would it have changed anything in the end?"

He stared at her silently, unable to answer her right away.

"I would've gone anyway," he said finally.

She nodded slowly. "Now do you understand what I was trying to explain to you in the car? The thing about finding him and facing him, whatever the risk?" Dana stared him straight in the eyes.

Jarod's silence was answer enough.

"What did you say to him?" Dana asked slowly.

"I explained to him that he would be much better off anywhere but New Mexico and apparently he agreed."

Dana sat quietly thinking. "Is he really gone?"

Jarod watched her, thinking how innocent she looked at that moment. "Yes, he's gone."

Dana lay back against her pillows finding it hard to believe it was really over. She looked up at Jarod and she knew he would be a formidable opponent to Sonny. If Sonny had left New Mexico, he had to have been scared, maybe scared enough to never come back.

It was the first time she felt that it could be possible.

Jarod lay down beside her and traced his fingers across her shoulder. Dana caught his hand and turning it over she tenderly kissed his open palm.

"You have no idea how much I love you," she whispered.

"Oh, Dana. I think I do."

[263]

Jarod's lips lightly teased her mouth as he slowly undid her nightshirt exposing her supple body to the gentle rays of the morning sun and before they were done, Dana knew she would never be without this man in body or soul.

It was well into the morning before Dana arrived at the barn. She immediately saddled Paska and began to work.

Having eaten a late breakfast, she continued through lunch, deciding to finish the horses' files which she had begun yesterday. She was in the midst of updating Empire's file when Annie knocked on the frame of the open office door.

"Are you busy, Dana? I can come back later," the girl offered as she turned to leave.

"No, that's fine. Come in," Dana invited.

"It was nothing really. We just haven't had much chance to talk and I wanted to make sure you were doing alright." Annie spoke as one friend to another.

"Come in and sit down. I'm due for a break from this monstrous computer. It tires my eyes when I look at it for too long." Dana smiled as she pulled two sodas from the small fridge and handed one to Annie.

"I was just worried about you," Annie continued as she sat down and popped the drink open. "You came in really late this morning and went straight to work. I thought maybe something was wrong or you could use a friend to talk to." Annie's expression was of genuine concern.

Dana's cheeks grew warm with blush as she recalled the reason for her tardiness that morning.

"Annie, I'm doing much better and I should've told you so myself. I guess I'm still in the habit of keeping things to myself, I don't want to be doing that anymore."

"Do you remember the night that we all met up at the house? You were so brave, after you left I felt terrible for you. I wasn't sure that you would actually come back, I just wanted you to know how happy I am that you did."

Dana was touched by Annie's words.

"That night was really rough for me and if I looked brave I certainly wasn't feeling it." Dana looked across the desk at Annie. "I'm just feeling a lot stronger now and I couldn't have become that without all

[264]

of you. Things have changed, you have all helped me in more ways than you will ever be able to understand and Jarod, well..." Dana smiled.

"I remember the night of the party," Annie smiled, her eyes sparkling. "It was a very special night for me and I think it was a special night for you, too. I remember the way you both looked when you danced together."

"Jarod is a very special man." Dana paused, her face radiant. "Anyway, that's enough about me. How are your plans coming along for the engagement party and your wedding? Maybe I can help you with something?" Dana offered.

"We're planning on a spring wedding," Annie smiled and then hesitated. "We haven't thought too much about the party. Now doesn't seem like the right time to be planning for something like that."

"I can't speak for Jarod, but I think it would be wonderful to have something to celebrate. Things are not as dire as they seem. I would feel awful if I was the cause of your not going ahead with your party." Dana was not sure what she should say or how Annie really felt about having a party under the circumstances. "What about if you talk to Kent and I'll talk to Jarod. Between all of us we should be able to come up with something that everyone is comfortable with."

"Okay," Annie agreed as she stood. "I'd better get back to work. I'm glad we had the chance to talk."

Annie left the office and Dana sat back in her chair. She felt better than she had for a long time. Her eyes caught sight of the show calendar and it made her aware that she was to have ridden Paska the following weekend.

Dana ordered herself back to work at the computer. When she talked to Jarod about Kent and Annie's party she would bring up the show schedule as well.

Dana finished up her files and walked into the barn to find Ben admiring Jarod's swollen hand.

"I got a couple'a those in my day. Hope it was well spent."

"Hello, gentlemen," Dana said pointedly, catching the two men off guard.

"G'day, Dana. I saw you working Paska this morning. That horse looks as fit as a fiddle." Ben spoke proudly as he turned to Jarod. "That mare's got heart, Jarod. Dana has her ready to go."

Jarod stopped brushing Goldrush for a moment and looked at the two as he measured the impact of Ben's words. He was well aware of how much Dana wanted the mare to finish the show season and he briefly considered the notion that they were conspiring together towards that end.

"Dana has done an excellent job with all the horses," he said noncommittally, continuing to groom his horse.

"You know, Jarod," Dana jumped in. "After the call you received this morning, there really is no reason Paska can't go to the show next weekend. It's not too late, we still have a chance to pick up the points we need." Dana's voice began to pick up enthusiasm. "What Ben said is true; the horse is in excellent condition. Adam has done a great job with her while I was off and really we've only missed two shows at this point."

"Whoa, Whoa!" Jarod exclaimed with a smile as he held up a restraining hand, eyeing Dana and Ben.

He unhooked Goldrush from the cross-ties and led him back to his stall as he weighed the situation over, trying to remain objective. He latched Goldrush's door and turned to face the pair.

"If you really believe that you're up to this, I can't see why you shouldn't go." Jarod spoke evenly. "But," he added with emphasis. "Dana, I still want you to be careful and we will only be bringing Paska." Jarod made his point clear as he smiled.

"I know, one day at a time." Dana returned his smile warmly. "That's all I'm asking for."

"This time," Jarod said under his breath as he started to laugh.

Dana felt her self-confidence coming back to her in bits and pieces and she relished the feeling. She quickly gave Jarod a hug and then hugged Ben, who seemed pleasantly startled.

"You won't be disappointed. I really think Paska stands a good chance at the state championship."

"Good man, Jarod." Ben nodded at the younger man approvingly and Jarod once more had the fleeting impression that he had been smartly ambushed by the pair as Ben winked at Dana and strode out of the barn. Ben had never been a match for a pretty face, Jarod thought as he shook his head in amusement.

He checked his watch.

"We should be getting back to the house," he suggested. "June is still not pleased with me over last night and I don't want to add being late

[266]

for dinner to her list of grievances." Jarod laid his arm lightly across Dana's shoulders and guided her out of the barn.

They leisurely made their way up the lane and nodded to the guard as they entered the main house. After washing up and changing they went down to the dining room where they found June busily setting the table.

"Good evening, Mom." Jarod kissed the woman's cheek. "You are looking lovely this evening." Jarod flashed her a charming smile.

Dana restrained a laugh as June directed Jarod a reprimanding look.

"Don't you even think for a moment that I don't know what you're up to, young man." June brushed her hands across her apron. "Now, you both have a seat, dinner will be just a minute."

June left the room and returned shortly with their meals. As she laid Jarod's plate before him on the table she noticed his hand for the first time. "What have you done here?"

"It's nothing, it was an accident," Jarod said lightly.

"An accident?" June's voice was disbelieving as she frowned. "When you are done eating, we should put some ice on that." June looked critically at Jarod as if about to say more.

"If it will make you feel better I'll do that as soon as I'm done eating," Jarod interjected quickly. "My food is getting cold," he said, exasperated with the entire affair as he reached for his fork.

"I'm starving," Dana added with feigned innocence as she attempted to divert June's attention. "It looks wonderful, June."

"Hmm. Enjoy your supper and Mr. Kingsley don't forget," was all June said as she left the room.

"That was touch and go," Dana whispered as she smiled.

"Don't laugh," Jarod chided her with humor. "June always knew when I'd gotten into trouble. It's like she's clairvoyant or something. She kept me on a straight line," he said affectionately.

"I've never seen this side of June." Dana remarked, bemused. "You are getting the cold shoulder treatment."

"It's her equivalent to a slap on the fingers, no pun intended. She'll be her old self tomorrow." Jarod grinned once again as he poured a glass of water. "If you think that's bad, you should pay more attention to Tom."

Dana was confused. "Tom?"

[267]

"The man avoids me like the plague and he barely looks at me when I talk to him. I don't thinks he's very good at his job. We should consider replacing him with someone who's a little more experienced. I really question his abilities in a true crisis."

"Jarod," Dana's voice was contrite. "I think I should explain... Tom seems to be very good at his job, I mean once you get past his appearance, that's true. But, I've..." Dana paused. "Well, actually I think I'm a little to blame. I kind of told him you were a tyrant."

"A what?"

"A tyrant... well, a pretty moody tyrant, at that." Dana's eyes sparkled with mischief.

Jarod stared at her in amazement.

"I don't know why I did it." Dana cleared her throat and started again. "That's not really the truth. Initially, I really resented the whole idea of having a personal bodyguard and it was my own way of... of..."

"Slapping my fingers?" Jarod finished for her.

"I'm so sorry," Dana said as she broke into a laughter.

"You look sorry." Jarod grinned as he shook his head. "I guess we won't be letting go of Tom. Dana, you never cease to surprise me. Every time I think I have you figured out..."

"I know. Are you upset with me?" Dana asked meekly.

"I want you to promise me that you will never change, that you will always keep me guessing."

"That's a tall order, Jarod Kingsley."

"I think you have enough spunk to fill it." Jarod lifted her hand to his lips. "So besides destroying my reputation what else have you been doing today?"

Dana thought back to her earlier conversation with Annie.

"Annie came to see me in my office this afternoon. She's so sweet, she wanted to make sure I was okay."

"Annie is very fond of you. The poor girl was really upset when you were hurt."

"I know. She told me that she had been worried that I wouldn't come back to the ranch."

"I hope you told her that I plan on keeping you deliriously happy." Dana smiled.

"Not in so many words, but I think she knows."

[268]

They had finished eating and Dana rose from her chair and went to the kitchen carrying their plates. She returned with an ice wrap and pulled her chair close to Jarod. She carefully lifted his injured hand and placed it into the wrap.

"Jarod, when Annie was in the office, I was asking her about her engagement party. They haven't made any plans." Dana waited for Jarod to say something but he remained silent. "They've been engaged for a while now and if there's going to be a party, well, it should happen soon enough. I mean, usually you like to time it to fall somewhere during the engagement period." She showered Jarod with a charming smile before becoming more serious.

Dana lowered her head and a lock of hair fell forward. She absently tucked it behind her ear. "I know a lot has been happening, but now things are fairly stable. I think we could all enjoy a celebration. I would feel terrible if I was responsible for them missing out on something so special."

"This is obviously very important to you." Jarod's statement came out as more of a question.

Dana lifted her wide eyes to his. "Yes."

"I don't know. It's one thing to be responsible for the safety of a few people, but we're talking about a big party here. I agree that the situation has improved but..." Jarod shook his head. "It's still not a guaranteed thing, Dana. Do you think we're being fair to everyone involved? I can stay open minded about this but I want us to be reasonable." Jarod spoke calmly as he attempted to have Dana look at the entire picture.

Dana sat for a moment deep in thought as she considered the validity of what he had said.

"I want that too. Jarod, what about if we scaled things down a bit. If it was just all of us and Kent and Annie's immediate family, then the number of people would be considerably less and everyone would be pretty much aware of the situation. I just think it's a shame to drop the party entirely."

Jarod took his time before answering.

"I'll talk to Annie and Kent tomorrow. We should be able to work something out. If they agree with the idea then we'll try and set a date and you girls can work out the details. It's true, we are due to celebrate some good news around here. This engagement party means a lot to me as well."

Dana leaned forward and softly kissed Jarod. "It will be a wonderful night."

- Chapter 21 -

Dana placed one booted foot on the bottom rung and folded her arms across the top as she leaned in closer to the rail. A warm gentle breeze tugged at her light cotton shirt as she rested her chin on her tanned arms.

Serenity, delighting in her ever strengthening power, would run at full speed to the end of the paddock coming to a dead stop on her hind legs only to realize that her mother had not followed. The black foal would then bolt upright into the air, turning on her hind legs and gallop proudly back to the mare.

This process had now been repeated five times but the mare refused to be enticed by the filly's boundless energy as she grazed, indifferent to her offspring's entertaining antics.

Dana laughed quietly to herself as she watched on with growing amusement.

Her days rolled one into another, gradually lying across a stretch of time where life was good. Dana could feel its effects as it came over her tranquilly and every now and then she would catch a glimpse of her past self...the way she had been before Sonny had become a part of her life.

She looked over to where Jarod was busy repairing the rail at the far end of the paddock. The mere sight of him caused Dana's breath to catch in her throat and send her heart fluttering. She had come to understand this kind and noble man more than she understood herself at times and loving him was the completion of the part of herself that had been absent until now.

As if reading her thoughts Jarod lifted his head to her and suddenly grinned. He straightened up and walked over to Dana. His body lightly brushed against hers as he joined her at the rail.

"What are you looking so thoughtful about?"

[271]

Dana gave a small shrug of her shoulders as she smiled. "I'm just happy," she paused. "That seems so simple, it must sound silly."

"I don't know. It works for me." Jarod leaned over and kissed her. "What do you think of your filly?"

"She is quite the athlete. One day she will be flying over fences. I think you would be wise to consider keeping her for your competition program," Dana answered as she watched Serenity gallop across the paddock.

"Dana, I really did mean your filly," Jarod repeated with quiet emphasis. "It's time for you to have your own horse again. I know she'll never replace Pepper and she's not meant to. She's about growing and the future. I signed her papers over to you last week, not long after we returned from our trip. I was just waiting for the right time to tell you."

Dana turned wide eyes to Jarod. "Are you serious?"

She stood silent for a moment in amazement and then wrapped her arms around him, giving him an enthusiastic hug. "Jarod, she is such a beautiful gift. Thank you!" Dana started to laugh as she turned back to the filly who was now greedily nursing from its mother. "I never thought about getting another horse of my own. She's so perfect!"

"You were equally excited the day she was born," Jarod grinned, recalling the event. "Last week Adam and I were beginning to work on the fall sale and which foals we would be keeping. Well, Serenity's name came up. Adam believes this filly was meant for you. I had to agree with him. Once she is weaned, you can move her into Barn One." Jarod knew without a doubt that giving Dana the filly was a much appreciated gesture. Her reaction had not been the series of protests that he had almost expected.

It warmed his heart to watch her now as she silently looked on to the picture before them. Somehow Dana's joy filled him, giving him a sense of purpose and he thought how happy he could be spending a lifetime making it so.

"I could easily pass my whole day here," Dana said with a smile. "But, I have a horse show tomorrow that I need to be preparing for." She reached up and kissed him. "You are so thoughtful. I don't know if you realize how much this means to me."

"I love you, Dana." Jarod held her tightly for a moment before releasing her. "Come on, I'll walk with you to the barn. I have to see Ben about some equipment that's not working properly."

They turned back to the barn where Jarod quickly found Ben and left with him to check the hay elevator in Barn Two.

Dana immediately made her way to Paska's stall and brought the mare out onto the cross- ties.

Annie was hard at work in an adjacent stall and she stopped for a minute, her short blond head barely visible over the dividing wall.

"Hey, Dana. How's your afternoon going?"

"Great, and yours?" Dana began brushing down the horse.

She wiped her forehead with the back of her arm as she made a wry face. "As well as can be expected. Empire is such a beast in his stall. I thought I'd give it a good turning out while he's outside."

"It's a big job. I bet you're glad you're almost done," Dana casually bantered from across the barn aisle. "Annie, would you like to get together Sunday afternoon? It's only a week away until the party and I thought if you weren't doing anything, we could go over the final details you know, make sure everything has been taken care of."

Annie stepped out of Empire's stall and rested the pitchfork against the beam.

"That sounds like fun," she agreed, her face breaking into a dimpled smile. "Do you want to meet here in the office or should we get crazy and go into town. We could make a day of it, go for lunch," Annie suggested as she removed her work gloves. She looked over her shoulder and nodded her head to where Tom stood. "We could bring him with us, he must be getting bored hanging around here day after day."

Dana lowered her voice slightly so she would not be overheard. "He's coming with me to the show tomorrow, thankfully without the uniform. I've almost gotten used to him around the ranch but I'm still a little uncomfortable about going out with him...maybe we could just meet at the house on Sunday."

"Sure," Annie said agreeably. "That's fine, Dana. Well, I'm going to watch Kent while he finishes up with Empire and let him know I'm done with his stall. So, maybe I'll see you outside?"

Dana nodded and Annie headed out of the barn.

Dana saddled Paska and led her out to the same ring that Kent was working in. She stood with Annie and quietly watched as Kent manoeuvred Empire over a series of jumps. Whatever problems that Kent had had in the past with Masquerade, he had definitely worked out with Empire. The chestnut gelding responded to Kent with an easiness that Dana had previously not seen in the horse. Kent had markedly improved his ability, both as a rider and as a trainer.

When he had completed his course, Dana entered the ring and mounted Paska, joining the other horse and rider.

"I've had a difficult time with Empire on the in-and-out. You rode through it beautifully Kent." Dana acknowledged as she trotted Paska along the rail, warming her up.

"He takes a lot of leg going into it. This guy keeps you on your toes, he's a fun ride." Empire was now trotting alongside Paska. "So, Dana, are you looking forward to the show tomorrow?" Kent asked, bringing Empire to a walk.

"I really am. Say, would you mind watching us have a go around while you're cooling down Empire? Let me know how we look."

The next forty-five minutes were spent completing a variety of jumps that Kent strategically set up in the ring while Annie cooled Empire.

The mare performed flawlessly and Dana knew they were primed for tomorrow's event.

When they returned to the barn Dana meticulously groomed Paska before putting the horse back into her stall. She then found the mare's tack box list and packed the trunk while Kent and Annie did the four o'clock feeding.

Dana closed the trunk lid and sat down on it as she contemplated the braiding of the horse's mane and tail. In the jumper division it was a matter of choice and although it was a tedious job, Dana had always preferred the smooth line the braids gave to the horse's overall appearance. She laughed silently to herself as she realized that she went through this debating process before each show only to end up doing the same thing every time. Dana stood and reached for the mane comb and the elastics.

Bringing Paska back onto the cross-ties she started to work. Dana found the repetitive exercise of braiding to be soothing, requiring little conscious effort and her thoughts soon drifted to Serenity.

The tragic loss of Pepper had left a gaping hole inside of her. Jarod had been right that Serenity would never replace what Pepper had meant to her, but as with her first horse, Serenity was a gift given in love. As she had stood against the fence earlier that day she had experienced the same thrill as the day her parents had brought her to see Pepper.

She recalled Serenity's birth and the wobbly little filly as she first attempted to stand. At the time Dana had felt that the foal represented her own new beginning at Kingsley Ranch.

The barn was suddenly quiet now, all that could be heard was the sound of the horses contentedly munching on their hay.

Kent and Annie had gone for supper and Dana was alone in the barn. An uncontrollable shiver ran through her and she quickly looked to the barn doors where Tom stood on guard.

It was hard to put everything behind, Dana thought to herself as she smiled, reassured by Tom's presence. She flexed her fingers that were beginning to cramp and continued on with her task.

She was on her last braid when Jarod walked into the barn. His shirt and jeans were virtually covered in oil and perspiration and a huge, dark smudge streaked across the side of his face and cheek.

Dana burst into laughter, helplessly lowering herself to the nearby trunk, overcome by the unexpected sight.

"If only your hot-shot business associates could see you now!"

"That's enough out of you!" Jarod ordered with mock sternness. His blue eyes seemed incredibly light against the black stain on his face. "I could've just bought a new elevator, but no. I figured I was Mr. Fix-It and full of sheer abstinence, I spent most of the afternoon on top of that thing under the glaring sun and do you know what?" Jarod asked as he looked at her with disbelief.

Getting to her feet, Dana remained speechless, hardly knowing what to say.

Jarod grinned at her and shook his head. "Monday, I'm buying a new elevator."

She stifled a laugh as she stepped back from Paska and surveyed her job. Satisfied with what she saw, Dana unhooked the mare and led her back to her stall.

"So, are you finished in here?" Jarod asked her as he dismissed Tom.

"Yes, I guess I'm all done."

"Good." Jarod stepped towards her.

"Don't even think that you are getting anywhere near me, looking like that," Dana warned as she withdrew a step, shaking her finger at him.

"We'll see about that." Jarod made a sudden move to catch her and Dana slipped by him and took off on a run. She was halfway to the house before Jarod caught her in his arms.

"You are terrible!" Dana laughed softly as he held her close.

"No," Jarod denied as he smiled invitingly at her. "I just know it will be a lot more fun cleaning up with you than without." He kissed her forehead. "Come on, I'll wash your back."

They walked arm-in-arm towards the house.

Dana's class was scheduled for the mid-afternoon and they arrived at the horse show the following day with time to spare.

The air was dry and hot as Jarod and Dana stepped down from the truck.

Tom approached them. "Good afternoon, Sir. I've checked around the grounds, everything seems to be fine." Tom stood awaiting instruction.

"Everything is fine, Tom." Dana interloped. "We're in the middle of a horse show, not a war zone." She directed Jarod an irritable look.

She had become accustomed to Tom following her about at the ranch, but this would be different. Dana suddenly felt his presence to be awkward and even though he was casually dressed in jeans, it did little to dispel her sense of embarrassment.

"Tom, if you don't mind to accompany our little ray of sunshine to register her horse, I'll unload Paska while you're gone." Jarod reached over and kissed Dana's cheek. "Remember, you are supposed to be enjoying yourself today."

"I am and I will." Dana returned with an exaggerated smile.

The registration office was close by the barn and Dana and Tom were back within minutes. Jarod had just latched Paska's stall door shut when they entered the barn.

"Did she travel well?" Dana asked.

"She traveled just fine," Jarod assured her as he filled Paska's water bucket. "How long before you ride?"

Dana looked at her wristwatch. "My class is in about two hours. I should be mounted a half hour before that."

Jarod gave the mare her water then turned his attention back to Dana. "Let's go get a bite to eat," he suggested. "Tom, keep an eye on the horse and our tack. Would you like us to bring you back something?"

"No, Sir. Thank you, I've already eaten."

"Alright then." Jarod slipped his hand into Dana's and they walked out of the barn and leisurely made their way across the show grounds. "I don't envy you having to wear a riding jacket under this sun." Jarod pulled the brim of his hat lower as he looked over to Dana.

"It's going to be a scorcher," she agreed.

As they walked, Dana found herself unconsciously searching for Monica. Undoubtedly, Monica would be exhibiting in Dana's class later on and Dana mentally scolded herself for the petty thoughts that she entertained towards the woman.

A man of Jarod's height and age approached them with an outstretched hand.

"Jarod, buddy! Long time, how are you?" The man greeted him with open friendliness.

"Warren, by God! How have you been?" Jarod shook the man's hand.

"Great. It's been awhile."

"Warren Foster, I'd like you to meet Dana Northington." Jarod introduced the two as he put an arm around Dana's shoulders.

"I'm pleased to meet you, Dana.' Warren flashed Dana a welcoming smile as he shook her hand.

"Likewise."

"Warren, horses were never your thing. What brings you here?"

"Can you believe I have a daughter showing her pony for the first time? We aren't getting any younger."

"Dana, Warren and I know each other from way back." Jarod explained as he turned back to the man. "So how many kids do you have?"

"Two. What about yourself?"

"I guess it would be a good idea to get married first," Jarod returned with a grin as he gave Dana a sidelong look.

"That would help." Warren agreed with a laugh. "Playing the field is a lot of fun, but once the right one comes along..." Warren looked at

Dana suggestively. "You wait till your turn comes, Jarod. I can see you with a couple of kids glued to your leg."

"I'm looking forward to those days," Jarod admitted.

"Well, talking about kids, I'd better get a move on. Tracy's waiting for me."

"Warren, we should get together sometime. It would be nice to meet your wife. I really mean that, give me a call." Jarod gave Warren his card.

"Sure thing. I'll do that." Warren tipped his hat and hurried over to a young girl in breeches who was waiting impatiently.

Jarod and Dana made their way to the expansive food tent and found an empty table.

"You are very quiet. Is there something wrong?" Jarod asked as he watched Dana.

"No," she responded quickly. "It's just I've never really thought about children," she paused. "You will make a wonderful father."

"You think?" Jarod looked thoughtful. "It would be one area of my life where I would like to believe I could do better than my father did. That sounds terrible, my father was not a bad father... he just could've used a little more insight, I guess." Jarod squeezed her hand. "Hey, let's eat. It'll be time for your class before you know it."

They had just begun their light meal when Dana spotted Monica making her way through the crowded tables.

"Jarod, darling." She bent and kissed his cheek as he rose from his chair.

"It's good to see you, Monica."

She turned and faced Dana. "Now, let me get it right this time, it's Dana?"

Dana forced a polite smile.

Monica pointedly regarded the empty chair before her and waited.

"I'm sorry," Jarod said quickly. "Would you like to join us?"

"Why, thank you. I'd love to join you," Monica accepted the offer and Jarod seated her.

The day was rapidly becoming hotter and Dana was suddenly conscious of the sweltering air.

"Would you like to have a bite to eat?" Jarod graciously offered.

"Heavens, no! I can't stomach food before a jump," Monica declined as she briefly glanced at Dana's plate. "I like going into my events a little hungry. Dana, I see we will be competitors in about an hour," the small blonde spoke pleasantly, but the overt significance of her words were not lost on Dana.

Jarod watched with amusement as Dana's eyes narrowed. Her chin rose ever so slightly and he recognized the look. Surprisingly, she remained silent.

Monica turned her attention back to Jarod. "So, you've brought back that horse you picked up at the racetrack." Her charming smile belied her cutting remark. "You always did love a challenge, Jarod."

"That I do," he responded easily.

"I see you've been absent from the last few shows," she continued. "This won't be favorable for your chances at the championship. Dana, have you been ill?" Monica ran a hand over her breeches, brushing away a smudge of dry dust.

"I took some time off," Dana answered vaguely.

"Time off during the height of show season?" Monica arched a sculptured eyebrow. "You are so fortunate to have such an extraordinary employer."

"You have no idea how very extraordinary he can be," Dana pointed out with a toss of her head as she stood. She had had enough. "I'll be looking forward to our competition. It'll be interesting to see how Carter performs against the race horse today." Dana turned and walked away.

Jarod also rose to his feet.

"Monica, I'm sorry to leave but I really must be going. If I don't see you before you ride, good luck." Jarod made his exit and caught up to Dana, placing an arm around her slender waist.

"You shouldn't let her get to you like that, really she can be quite entertaining," he offered complacently.

"Entertaining? That's a polite way of putting it." A smile slowly broke over Dana's face. "She's a witch and you enjoyed every minute of it." She accused him, laughing.

"Was it that obvious?"

"No, you're quite the poker face." She responded dryly, giving him a playful shove.

[279]

"Hey! Take it easy, save your strength for the ring," Jarod warned her with an open grin.

"I've got enough strength for both you and the ring, don't worry."

"Well you should, after packing away all that food," Jarod shot at her as he broke into unrestrained laughter.

"Don't you start," she threatened him, her eyes sparkling with mischief in the strong sunlight.

They turned towards the barn.

"The course is probably up. Do you want to walk it now or do you prefer to change first?"

"I think I'll change first and get Paska ready, as long as you don't mind holding on to her while I go over the course." Dana considered her plan of action as she began her preparations for her meet.

"I'll tack the mare for you while you change," Jarod readily obliged.

Within fifteen minutes, Jarod stood holding Paska's reins as he watched Dana walk the course. She stopped for a moment at the sixth jump and stood there in her sleeveless riding shirt with her jacket neatly folded over her bent arm, carefully contemplating the jump. Jarod had also noticed how tight the turn into the fence would be and he knew they both saw it as a problem. Dana looked from the fifth to the sixth jump one last time and moved on and finished walking the course.

Jarod joined her as she left the ring. Dana wiped the tiny beads of perspiration from her brow with the back of her hand.

"Paska is going to be earning her keep today," Dana smiled optimistically as she put on her jacket then her helmet and gloves. "I should start warming her up."

She placed a gloved hand briefly over Jarod's before taking the reins from him.

"Dana..." He wanted to tell her that he had changed his mind, that he had been crazy to agree to this in the first place, it was too soon after her fall but as he watched her mount he knew it was not his decision to make. This was Dana's domain. "Never mind," he said.

By the time it was Dana's turn, two-thirds of the class had gone through and only one horse and rider had completed the course cleanly.

Dana's number and name were called up on the loudspeaker. She entered the ring and bowed her head to the judge. Out of the corner of her eye she was aware of Jarod moving to the ringside for a better vantage point.

She turned her attention inward to a place where only her own interpretation of the course existed: her, the horse and the jumps. With an instinctive sense of confidence, she put Paska into a light hand gallop. She boldly rode the course from fence to fence, vigilantly measuring Paska's strides. They cleared the fifth fence and Dana sharply turned Paska into the sixth, masterfully commanding the horse's powerful form using her seat, legs and hands to direct the mare through the tight jump with Paska swiftly answering Dana's split-second instructions. They cleared the sixth fence without mishap and finished the remainder of the course.

Dana listened intently as they exited the ring. The loudspeaker announced her faultless execution of the course.

She made her way around the outer rim of remaining competitors and caught sight of Monica astride Carter. Her mouth was set in a tight line as she stared straight ahead. Her number was called and she moved Carter forward and entered the ring. Dana knew from personal experience the added pressure that Monica had to be feeling at this moment. It was imperative that she complete a clean round.

Dana had already dismounted by the time Jarod reached her, his enthusiasm was apparent. "Well done, Dana!"

"The next round will have to be faster," she warned him. "I was worried about time penalties coming out of this one." Dana loosened Paska's girth and waited to watch Monica's performance.

As Monica cleared the jumps leading to the fifth, her skillful technique was obvious, the horse and rider's movements strong and exact. Dana could feel her body tense as they approached the critical fifth and sixth combination. Carter's massive form would be working against the pair in the narrow maneuver. If Monica chose to pull the horse in too tightly there was a strong possibility that they could tumble. Dana held her breath as the pair cleared five and then six successfully. Monica had chosen the safer route and had given Carter a wider berth, the extra stride costing them crucial seconds in their time.

"Time penalties," Jarod said as he stood beside Dana. "She should finish in the ribbons."

"That number six is putting a lot of people out of the running." Dana looked to the sky. The wind had begun to pick up, swirling red dust around their feet. Mercifully the temperature had dropped a little as the clouds moved in blocking the relentless sun. "It looks like rain."

"Hopefully it will hold off until you're done." Jarod looked towards the clouds.

"I should be bringing her back." Dana tightened Paska's girth once more and remounted.

Jarod laid his hand on Dana's thigh. "Good luck in there. Ride careful." He squeezed her leg gently and let his arm drop.

There were to be only two competitors in the jump-off, with Dana riding second.

She watched as the first competitor entered the ring. He would set the pace for Dana on this shortened course. Dana was grateful to find that the fifth and sixth jumps had been moved in the ring and the altered design featured a style that Paska habitually performed well in.

Her competitor rode the course expertly in a time of 34.1 seconds.

Dana rode into the ring at a trot and once again respectfully acknowledged the judge before taking up a canter on a circle, crossing the start line on a strong hand gallop. Speed always excited Paska and Dana worked at keeping the horse focussed on the fences ahead of them.

They were on their last jump when Dana heard the sound of Paska's hind hoof tapping the rail. She let the mare go into a strong gallop and crossed the finish line. Almost afraid to look back, Dana turned her head to the direction of the jump. The rail stood in position, firmly resting in its cups. She drew a deep breath and listened for her time: 33.4 seconds.

She left the ring with a smile of deep satisfaction. Dana dismounted and was loosening Paska's girth when she felt Jarod's arms close around her waist.

"Congratulations, Sweetheart. That was a fantastic ride!"

Dana turned to face him and he kissed her.

"Thank you," she said smiling. "I thought we dropped the rail. When I turned to check it I almost didn't believe it was still standing."

"It's too bad Ben wasn't here to see it. He would've been proud of his little race horse," Jarod said, still grinning.

She nodded in agreement. "We needed this show to stay in the points." She led Paska into the ring for the last time to collect her award. It felt great to be back in competition.

Dana looked up towards the now menacing black sky as she met Jarod at the exit gate of the show ring. "Jarod, do you think we should be worried about that?"

His eyes followed Dana's. "Just to be on the safe side I think we should get loaded and be on our way."

Dana untacked and bandaged Paska while Jarod began loading their gear. Tom stood close by keeping his eyes trained on the hectic activity surrounding them. People were moving through the barns, checking on their animals and their equipment. Strangers congratulated Dana on her success as they passed by. There was a general sense of uneasiness as everyone contemplated the possibility of a storm.

The drive home would take approximately two hours and the thought of Paska in a horse trailer on the road made Dana increasingly unsettled. She had experienced how unpredictable the climate in New Mexico could be.

"Dana, don't worry. We will be travelling ahead of the storm." Jarod assured her as he tracked the passage of the clouds filling the sky like angry blisters of silvery smoke.

They drove home with Tom following behind them and Dana nervously checking the side view mirror. As Jarod had predicted, they managed to keep abreast of the storm. They turned into the ranch just as it began to pour.

"I'll get Paska out of the trailer, you should stay in the truck," Jarod advised as he turned off the engine.

"I should see if anyone needs help," Dana suggested strongly.

"They will already have brought the horses in." Jarod jumped out of the pick-up and ran behind it. Within seconds he led Paska into the barn.

The incessant clamor of the rain as it hit the truck roof was deafening and Dana opened the door and sprinted into the barn behind them.

"I want to check her, Jarod." Dana explained to him. "She wasn't even cooled down properly at the show grounds."

Jarod nodded as he tied Paska on to the cross-ties. "Okay. I'm just going to make sure everything is alright in Barn Two."

Dana removed the bandages from Paska's legs as Kent approached her.

"How did it go? Did you get your class in before this?" Kent pointed to the barn roof that had suddenly become a percussion of metallic raps.

"We were extremely lucky," Dana told him as she lightly rubbed the mare down. "Paska won her class and we managed to make it home before the storm broke."

"Way to go, Dana. Congratulations!" Kent tapped Dana's shoulder and went back to work.

Dana straightened up and reached for a lead rope. She hooked it onto Paska's halter and unclipped the cross-ties.

"This will have to do, girl," she spoke soothingly to the agitated mare and for the next fifteen minutes Dana led Paska up and down the long barn aisle, loosening her up before putting her into her stall.

Dana ran into Annie as she latched the stall door. "Sorry if we were in your way just now, but the riding hall must sound like a hard rock concert," she apologized with a grin.

"That's okay. We were almost done anyway. Actually we're just waiting for it to let up some."

The two girls turned into the tack room.

"I hear you had another win in the ring today, Dana. That's great."

"I'll say. I needed this show to stay in the running for the championship."

"Well, you've done a lot of hard work since you've come here. It would be nice to see you reap your rewards," Annie said as Jarod entered the room, the shoulders and back of his shirt were soaked.

"It's starting to ease up a little," he said as he shook himself off. "Ben and Adam have closed up Barn Two."

Kent joined the group in the tack room and Jarod looked around. "Why don't the two of you join us for dinner at the house? We can celebrate Dana's win today." Jarod put his arm around Dana affectionately as he regarded the other two.

"Sounds great. What do you say, Annie?" Kent looked to Annie.

"Well, there's not much more we can do here," Annie answered agreeably. "I think that sounds like fun."

"Alright, it's a plan. Just let me give June a ring at the house and let her know what's going on. If you want to, you're more than welcome to spend the night. There's no point travelling in that rain if you don't need

[284]

to." Jarod went into the barn office and returned shortly. "June's waiting for us, so I guess we're all set."

"My car is right beside the barn, why don't you just leave the truck here for the night?" Kent suggested.

They closed Barn One and drove up to the house in Kent's car.

June greeted them at the door, her round face creased in a smile. "This is such a good idea," she said as she enthusiastically welcomed them. "Supper will be ready in about half an hour. Kent, Annie, I'm so glad to have company. What else can you do with this rain?"

They moved into the living room where Jarod opened the bar. "Kent, make yourself at home while Dana and I get out of these clothes."

"Annie, do you need a change of clothes?" Dana asked.

"No, my raincoat took the worst of it. I'm fine, I'll just wash up a bit downstairs."

"Okay, we'll be back in a few minutes." Jarod and Dana left to freshen up and get out of their damp clothing. When they returned they found Annie and Kent relaxing on the sofa with their drinks.

Kent immediately got up. "Jarod, bourbon? Dana?"

"I'll just have a glass of red wine. Thank you, Kent."

Dana and Jarod accepted their drinks from Kent and everyone sat down. Jarod raised his glass in a toast. "To Dana's win and to the upcoming engagement party."

"Cheers."

"This evening over dinner we can talk over the arrangements for the party next weekend and make sure everything is in order," Jarod suggested as he sat back in his chair.

"Dana and I were going to do that tomorrow, but it would be much nicer to do it as a group," Annie agreed with a smile.

June entered the room.

"Dinner is ready in the dining room," she informed them.

"I hope you set a place for yourself," Jarod insisted.

"I've already eaten, Mr. Kingsley."

"Well, you can have a small bite with us." Jarod rose and put his arm around the older woman. "You can have a glass of wine and sit and visit with us."

They made their way to the dining room table where the food was laid out waiting for them. The lights were turned low and candles adorned the long table.

"God, June. This looks wonderful!" Annie exclaimed as they took their seats.

"Thank you, Dear. Oh my! I forgot the bread rolls." June turned towards the kitchen as Jarod gently stopped her.

"I'll get the rolls."

They sat and leisurely dined, talking over the show and Paska's performance and they discussed some of the details concerning the much anticipated party.

The rain continued to fall outside the softly lit room.

Dana and Jarod had previously decided to give Annie and Kent a few days off beginning Wednesday and they took this opportunity to tell them about the arrangement. Normally their days off did not coincide and Kent and Annie were delighted by the generous gesture.

The evening was enjoyable and relaxing and as they all eventually made their way upstairs to their respective rooms, Dana felt a wave of happiness overcome her. Everything somehow finally seemed right.

- Chapter 22 -

The week leading up to the party proved to be a hectic one. In addition to the final preparations for the upcoming event, Dr. Winslow had been to the ranch to administer some of the horses' annual inoculations and more importantly, Dana had shown Paska at another exhibition and although it had not been a flawless performance, it had been adequate enough to place Paska in the lead position for the running of the State Championship in her division.

It was a demanding yet rewarding time for Dana. She threw herself into the heavy schedule with unrestrained vigor, concentrating on her future and resolutely turning her back on the darker issue of her past. The security at the ranch was the only obtrusive reminder of what had happened and Dana found herself increasingly able to ignore its presence.

Annie and Kent had been absent most of the week, appreciating the time off that Jarod and Dana had offered them and everyone else pitched in to help shoulder the extra work load, including Jarod.

The barn seemed unusually empty with Annie and Kent gone. Dana decided to begin the noon feeding a little ahead of time.

"Hey, I thought that you were going to wait for me." Jarod entered the barn and immediately began to open a hay bale.

"I think I can handle a feeding or two on my own." Dana answered him with a grin as she brushed the hair from her forehead with her hand. "You were in here so long this morning, I just thought you'd be pretty occupied catching up with your office work," she said with understanding as she began to do the grain.

Dana had spent countless hours adjusting the feed program to suit each individual horse's particular needs and she now carefully measured the tailored recipes into corresponding feed pails. Dana was satisfied with the results she had achieved. The horses' gleaming coats, their increased strength and stamina were all positive signs that her efforts had not been in vain.

Dana and Jarod quietly worked alongside each other and when they were done, she walked up to him as he stood at Goldrush's stall.

Placing her arms around his waist she lifted her chin onto his shoulder. "Are you going to have enough energy left to dance with me tonight?"

"Tonight, today and tomorrow," he vowed as he turned to face her. "With music or without." He took her in his arms and humming smoothly under his breath he began to dance with her up and down the barn aisle.

Slowly, they came to a stop and Dana lifted her upturned face to kiss him.

"I love you, Jarod Kingsley," she said softly as she stared deeply into his eyes, her heart filled with a peaceful joy.

"If this is a prelude to what I should expect tonight, I can hardly wait," Jarod spoke with a quietness. He lifted his strong hands to her delicate face and returned her kiss.

They turned and made their way, arm-in-arm, to the house.

June, wearing a large sun hat, was busy in her immaculate garden and she greeted them as they approached. "I've laid out your lunch for you," she explained with a smile before turning back to her work.

"Don't stay out here too long," Jarod advised her and she nodded, waving them on.

They entered the house and washed up before going to the kitchen to find a cold lunch awaiting them, just as June had promised.

Dana poured two tall glasses of iced tea from the pitcher as they sat down to eat.

"Adam and Ben have offered to do the last feeding, so we should be able to finish up in the barn by four," Jarod said as he accepted the glass of tea from Dana.

"We're already short staffed as it is," Dana answered with a worried frown. "I know it's a kind offer but I feel guilty, it seems unfair. After all, they're also going to the party tonight."

"I know, that's pretty much what I said, but they insisted. Apparently Adam's girlfriend is going to be arriving a little late so he has extra time and Ben said he was in no rush." Jarod shrugged his shoulders.

"I told them we'd help but they refused. Don't worry so much, Dana. They want to do it."

As Dana ate her lunch she heard Tom's footstep outside on the porch. She stole a sidelong glance at Jarod and decided to bring up the issue of the security at the party.

"I was thinking," she began slowly. "Maybe we could give Tom the night off." Dana hesitated as she noted Jarod's slightly raised eyebrow. "Really, it's not necessary for him to be following me around all night. I'll be surrounded by people and you'll be there. I think the ground's security will be more than enough," Dana explained with growing confidence. "Jarod, it will be embarrassing for me to have him there. I don't want to put a damper on the entire evening."

"I'm not comfortable about cutting back on security tonight," Jarod said as he considered the situation. He watched her as she nodded not protesting and her unexpected quiet acquiescence touched his heart. "Look, I can put Tom on the front gate, how's that?"

She nodded once again with a small smile.

"Dana, I wanted to ask you, what do you think about coming with me to Houston for a few days next week?" Jarod asked casually as he helped himself to seconds.

"Houston?"

"I have a deal that's been in the works for months and it's at the signing stage. I have no choice but to go, and there are a few other things I'd like to take care of while I'm there," he mentioned as if an afterthought.

It was not the first time that it had occurred to Dana that Jarod must be foregoing some of his responsibilities. How much of it was a matter of choice, she did not know. Whenever she had tried to bring the topic up Jarod had always cleverly changed the subject.

"With all that's happened...well, I have a lot of work ahead of me, trying to salvage what I can of the training program and the show season." Dana reached over placing her hand on Jarod's arm. "I know you've been avoiding talking about this but I can figure some things out for myself. I understand you have work to do, Jarod. Don't you think I've noticed it's been almost a month since your last business trip?"

They sat for a moment in silence, each of them choosing not to force the conversation any further, preferring to say less than to say more.

June stepped into the kitchen and removed the wide-brimmed hat from her head.

"The caterers have just arrived," she informed them as she tucked her working gloves into the hat and put them away. "I told them they could start setting up in the same area as the last time. Is that okay?"

"That's fine, June." Jarod stood. "I'll go out and see if they need anything." He stopped in the doorway and looked back to Dana with a persuasive wink. "Think over the Houston thing, I think we would have a good time." Jarod turned and left before she could answer him.

Dana shook her head and smiled as June poured herself a glass of tea and sat at the table. Her face was warm and red.

"June, you shouldn't be working outside this time of the day," Dana remarked as she looked at June fondly.

"I know, dear. I didn't mean to stay out, I was just getting a few tomatoes and peppers. Once I got out there, well, the time just flew." June picked up a napkin from the table and ran it across her damp brow as she smiled. "You must be looking forward to the party tonight," June continued. She noticed how much more relaxed Dana seemed over the past few days. The long days of sun had blessed Dana's clear skin with a gentle honey tan and her long dark hair was burnished with rich copper highlights. It thrilled her to see the girl at peace with herself.

"I've grown very fond of both Annie and Kent. It's heartwarming to think we will be formally celebrating their engagement tonight, together as a group," Dana replied, aware of June's affectionate scrutiny.

"Love is a wonderful thing." June sat quietly, lost in thought.

Jarod re-entered the room.

"It's starting to look like we're going to have a party out there. The tents are already up." He turned to June. "They wanted to know about using the kitchen for something, I thought it was best to check with you first."

"I'll go and see what they need." June rose in her usual good humor. She patted Jarod's shoulder as she passed him on her way out.

Dana also rose and began to clear the table.

"Jarod, did you ever wonder how come June never married?" Dana asked as she set the dirty dishes in the sink.

"I guess. I don't know, June's June. What's brings this on?"

"I guess it's all this party planning. June's such a sweet lady, she has so much love to give. I wonder if she has any regrets?"

"June is very happy. I think you just want to get everyone married off," Jarod teased her and he saw her suddenly blush.

Dana hastily changed the subject. "So, are we still going to take that ride you talked about this morning?"

"Sure."

They made their way back to the barn, getting Masquerade and Goldrush ready.

The day was beautiful and as they cantered across the open range, Dana felt as though they were kindred spirits roaming free in the vast scope of the untamed countryside that surrounded them. Between a fathomless blue sky above and the red, hard earth below existed nothing but themselves.

They welcomed this enjoyable reprieve from their demanding schedule, but eventually they realized it was time to turn back towards the ranch. Jarod and Goldrush pulled in beside Dana on Masquerade and the riders slowed their horses down to a walk, cooling them off as they unhurriedly returned home.

Jarod eyed Masquerade walking confidently on a loose rein. "That's a new horse. It's unbelievable how you have brought her along."

"Masquerade only needed to learn it was alright to trust again." Dana ran her hand down the mare's neck.

Dana's innocent words struck Jarod. He looked over at her, understanding now why the mare had become so important to her, why Dana had become so attached to Masquerade and had refused to give up on her.

"Like you," he stated in a level voice.

"Like me," Dana agreed and smiled. "Now Masquerade and I both feel safe and loved."

"Out of anything I have within my power to give you Dana, that is what I want most for you."

After arriving back at the barn, they dismounted and untacked the horses, returning them to their stalls. Dana joined Jarod in the tack room where he was hanging up Goldrush's bridle.

"Jarod." Dana walked over to him and lifted her eyes to his. "I just wanted you to know, you have given me much more than safety and

[291]

love. When I first came here I was just a shadow of a person. I was running from everything and I was terrified. For the first time in a long time, I feel like I know myself again." Dana took his hand in hers. "Everything has changed for me. I have so much that I am grateful for and it's because I have you in my life. You have given me back a future." Jarod bent and kissed her forehead.

She ran her hand down the side of his square jaw. "Come on," she said. "Let's get the feeding started with. I'm really looking forward to tonight."

"Listen Dana, why don't you go on up to the house and get some shut-eye? You've been working out here all day and you could use some rest before the party. I'll finish up here with Ben."

Dana protested and Jarod laughed as he pushed her out of the tack room and through the wide barn entrance. "Come on, little girl. You've been carrying a heavy load for the past few days with Kent and Annie gone. I don't want you falling asleep at the table tonight," he insisted with a grin.

"Alright," she capitulated. "I'm outta here."

Jarod watched as Tom followed her to the house then he turned and got to work.

Once he was done feeding he gave Ben a nod.

"We'll see you tonight, Ben."

The old man tipped his hat and smiled and Jarod made his way across the busy yard towards the house. The large tent was in place, the tables and chairs set up and service people were scuttling back and forth, beginning the finishing touches to the festive decorations. Jarod noted with satisfaction that Richard and Frank were keeping a vigilant eye on the proceedings.

He stopped and talked to Frank briefly about the evening ahead and the change he wanted regarding Tom's duties. Assured that everything was under control, Jarod entered the house and turned into his office.

He switched on his computer and sat at his desk, pulling up the file on the upcoming merger and as he abstractedly stared at the figures on his screen, his thoughts turned to Dana. Sighing, he turned the machine off. His mind was not on his work today. He made a few calls and then booked a suite in one of Houston's finest hotels.

Jarod stood and crossed the room to the large window that overlooked the yard where things were rapidly taking shape for Kent and Annie's celebration tonight. In a couple of hours, he would be toasting their future happiness and their desire to share the rest of their lives together.

A smile crossed his face. He had never really thought of marriage before Dana. It wasn't that he had disallowed the idea, there just had never been a reason before now, but there was no question in his mind that Dana was the one. He couldn't imagine his life without her.

Jarod walked back to his desk and pulled open the top drawer, removing a small velvet box that rested there. It seemed so delicate sitting in the palm of his large hand. He carefully opened the box and stared at the beautiful ring within. The solitaire diamond set in an antique rose gold band glittered up at him. It was perfect for Dana, he thought to himself as he smiled once again.

He carefully closed the ornate box and replaced it in the desk drawer. He had waited this long, a few more days wouldn't hurt. To ask her now would be an inconsiderate intrusion into Kent and Annie's own special celebration.

He had to find a way to persuade Dana to accompany him to Houston without her becoming suspicious. He had it all planned out in his mind and he wanted it to be a perfect and complete surprise.

Jarod checked his watch. It was time to start getting ready. He went upstairs to find Dana asleep on the bed and he stood for a minute before easing his body down beside hers and reluctantly waking her.

She stirred, moving closer to him. "Hi. Is it time to get up?" Dana asked in a drowsy voice.

Jarod lifted the hair back from her face and kissed her forehead. "I'm afraid so, Sweetheart."

She rolled onto her back and slowly stretched. "This is so nice, I don't want to move. If this party was not in honor of Kent and Annie and if you were not the host, well...I think we would definitely be late." Dana directed him a suggestive smile and groaned, pulling herself away from him and out of the bed.

"I feel so abandoned," Jarod sighed as he looked across the empty expanse of bed.

Dana walked around the bed and bent over Jarod, slowly kissing him. She whispered to him. "That will have to do for now. I promise I'll make it up to you later." She straightened up. "For now, we need to get ready."

Dana showered and began to dress for the party. She chose a shoulder-less, shimmering fitted dress of midnight blue splashed with a warm, tropical print that she had purchased during their stay in Montreal. She swept her long hair to one side and fastened an orchid hair clip in place before stepping back from the mirror to survey her appearance. The vividly contrasting colors of the dress were appealing to the eye. It was a style that attractively lent an exotic flavor to her usually conservative appearance, leaving Dana in a festive mood.

She added just a touch of makeup and a spritz of perfume before stepping out of the bathroom.

Dana found the bedroom empty but it was obvious that Jarod had already showered and changed. She glanced at the bedside clock and realized it was almost time for the party to begin so she decided to go downstairs.

She had just started down the wide staircase as Jarod walked through the front door.

He noticed her immediately as she paused in the stairway and as he stared up at her, she smiled.

"Dana, you are truly stunning. I've never known a woman more beautiful." Jarod's eyes never left her as she made her way down the steps.

He took her hand and brought it to his lips before carefully tucking it inside his arm. "Unlike the last party we attended, this time I no longer have to mask my feelings for you. It was torture to have you so close…so far away." Jarod looked down at her, smiling.

Dana blushed with sudden shyness, realizing this would be their first formal appearance as a couple and the thought filled her with pleasure. She reached up and kissed him.

"Shall we get going?"

Dana nodded with a smile.

They stepped out onto the verandah.

Quite a few of the guests had already gathered. Laughter and the gentle clinking of glasses could be heard coming from under the tent.

"Annie and Kent, their parents and a few other people have arrived. Annie was looking a little nervous, she was asking for you," Jarod explained as he escorted Dana towards the small crowd.

They spotted Kent and Annie and made their way towards them.

"Annie, Kent! Congratulations!" Dana gave them both a warm hug. "I hope tonight is perfect for you."

"Everything is so beautiful, Dana. You look gorgeous!" Annie's face was flushed with happiness. "I can't believe you went through all this bother for us. Thank you, Jarod."

"It was not a bother at all. It was my heartfelt pleasure, Annie." Jarod smiled magnanimously at the girl before turning his attention to Kent, placing a hand against his shoulder. "What do you say we get these lovely ladies a drink?"

"I think Annie could use one, she's been jumpy and teary-eyed all day." Kent affectionately teased his fiancée.

"Kent, I have not," Annie denied as a tear welled up in her eye. "My God! I don't know how I'll ever get through the wedding," she confided to them as Kent handed her a tissue, sagely shaking his head.

"We'll just make your veil out of this stuff here."

Annie laughed softly as she accepted the tissue and dabbed her eyes.

The men left and Dana took Annie's hand in hers.

"You look radiant, Annie. Try not to be so nervous, you are surrounded by people who love you. Enjoy your evening. This is your night." Dana squeezed Annie's hand before letting it drop.

"You're right, Dana. It's silly, I know, but I'm not used to being the center of attention."

"I know, but we're all the same people you see every day, we're just dressed up and we're all so happy for you. Why don't you introduce me to your family?"

Annie led her friend under the large canopy to a small group of people.

They were in the midst of introductions when Jarod and Kent returned with their drinks.

Kent wrapped his arm over his elder brother's shoulder. "I'm just letting everyone know ahead of time. I'm not anything like Dave here."

"No, he's a lot worse!" Dave countered with a laugh that was very similar to Kent's. "Although, I must say Kent has a heart of gold and it seems to have been won by little Annie."

Everyone toasted the young couple.

It was quite a group. Annie was the second of four fair and quiet daughters that all appeared to have taken after their mother who was an attractive, small statured and reticent woman. Annie introduced her sisters in a sing-song cadence: Julie, Laurie and Sadie. Dave attended with his wife, Felicity. Kent's parents and older sister were unable to attend. They lived out of state and would only be coming to the wedding.

Adam and his girlfriend Leanne had also joined the group as had Emily and her husband, Samuel.

Dana noticed June and Ben standing off to the corner of the tent and by June's expression, Dana could tell that Ben must be up to his usual tricks. Jarod followed Dana's gaze to the seemingly mismatched pair and he shook his head and grinned.

"If you'll excuse us," he said politely to the group as he placed his arm around Dana's waist and they walked over to Ben and June.

"June, you are looking magnificent, as always." Jarod bent and kissed her cheek. He looked over at Ben and laughed quietly. "I see you agree!"

"Sure do. June is one fine lookin' woman," Ben acknowledged with enthusiasm.

A waiter approached Jarod and spoke with him briefly. Jarod nodded his head and the man left.

"If I might have your attention, please." Jarod waited a moment for everyone to become quiet. "If everyone would be seated, I've been informed dinner is ready. Enjoy your meals."

Unlike the previous party at the ranch, smaller individual tables for groups of six had been set up under the tent. Kent and Annie sat at the first table with Dave and Felicity and Annie's mother, Barbara.

Dana and Jarod sat down with Ben, June, Adam and Leanne while the remainder of the guests occupied the other tables.

Waiters were busy filling champagne glasses as each table prepared a toast. When it became Jarod's turn he stood for a moment facing the young couple.

"I have had both the pleasure and the privilege of knowing Kent and Annie for some time now. I wish you both the very best that life has to offer you and may your love be the compass that guides you through all your years, unerringly toward each other. Congratulations!" Jarod drank from his glass and sat back down as everyone clapped.

"That was very touching," Dana said softly as she put her hand in his.

"You think?" Jarod kissed her cheek lightly, his eyes smiling.

Everyone began to eat and during the course of the meal the conversation was easy, frequently interrupted by laughter. Some members of the couple's extended families were present along with a few of their friends.

The sky surrounding the tent was now a deep ebony and once more the front yard was brought to life by strings of tiny lights that generously sprawled overhead, twinkling invitingly. As they finished their meal, Jarod ordered a round of Spanish coffees for their table and they sat back and relaxed as the music was turned up. Everyone stood and clapped as Annie and Kent walked onto the dance floor.

In grand fashion, Kent bowed to Annie and kissed her hand before sweeping her into his arms. Annie smiled bashfully, her round face blushing and they slowly began to dance to the soft music. They made an attractive pair and Dana smiled to herself as she sat back in her chair.

Jarod quietly watched her, Dana's eyes were radiant and the faintest of smiles remained on her generous lips as she stared out at the dance floor unaware of his attention. It filled him with a sense of serenity to be able to see her this way.

She turned and caught his expression. Neither of them spoke as their eyes held each other. Words were unnecessary.

They were abruptly interrupted by the sound of more clapping. The song had come to its conclusion and Kent and Annie were leaving the dance floor.

"Would you like another drink, Dana?" Jarod asked attentively.

"No, I'd rather wait a bit." Dana pushed away her empty glass. "Annie and Kent look so happy. It's a wonderful thing you did for them, having this evening."

"If I remember correctly, this event is only taking place at the insistence of a certain beautiful woman that I happen to have a marked weakness to denying."

Dana dropped her eyes as her lips parted in a slow smile.

"You are very smooth tonight, my darling."

"I thought I was always pretty smooth," Jarod returned with a confident grin as he stood and held out his hand. He made an imposing figure, his tall muscular shape sharply clad in a fine white dinner jacket that contrasted handsomely against his strong, tanned face.

"Dana, dance with me and make me a happy man."

Dana accepted his hand and willingly followed him onto the dance floor. Jarod brought his free hand to the small of her back as she met his steady gaze.

The world dropped away from them as they effortlessly gave themselves to the music.

Jarod kissed her forehead and Dana moved closer into his embrace, surrendering to the movement of their bodies and the sensation of his presence enveloping her.

"I'm looking forward to falling asleep every night with you at my side and waking each morning, your body lying next to mine," she whispered in his ear as she lay her head upon his shoulder.

Jarod's arms tightened around her in response. "A lifetime of dancing together."

They danced silently and when the song reached an end Jarod bent and kissed her tenderly, holding her face within his hand. Dana felt like they were alone under the stars.

Jarod slipped his hand into hers and led her across the dance floor over to where Annie and Kent stood talking with one of Annie's sisters and Darren. They joined in the conversation for a few moments before Jarod turned to Dana. "Dana, if you wouldn't mind, I promised a dance with June."

"Of course. It'll give me a chance to freshen up." Dana smiled. "Enjoy yourself."

Jarod ran his hand through his sun-streaked hair and slightly loosened his tie. "Don't be long," he teased her with a grin.

"I won't."

Jarod gave her a kiss and walked over to where June was pleasantly engaged chatting with Barbara.

"Ladies, forgive me for interrupting, but..." he offered June his hand. "I promised this dear woman a dance."

"Mr. Kingsley, you are too kind," June responded, much flattered.

"I'll bring her back," Jarod promised to Barbara, who smiled her agreement as Jarod guided June to the dance floor. He enjoyed these quiet moments with June. She had always been the closest thing he had ever had to a mother and he loved the woman as one.

She looked up at him as they danced. "I was watching you as you danced with Dana earlier. It is easy to see how genuinely you feel for each other. It makes me very happy." June smiled. "It is time that you found someone to love and to return that love. Dana is a wonderful woman."

"It's never been like this," Jarod confided to June. "I can't even begin to describe this feeling. It's as if the sun has broken through the clouds, she warms my life and I see everything differently now." Jarod gave an embarrassed laugh. "I sound like a school boy."

June regarded him affectionately. "It lightens my heart to see you so happy, Jarod."

Jarod looked at the older woman, suddenly remembering what Dana had said to him at lunch. "June, you would've made a fine wife and mother. It's not too late for you to find happiness."

"Jarod Kingsley, I have found happiness. You should know that better than anyone," June insisted. "I did have a love. Sadly it was not meant to be, but he left me something precious, something I will treasure always." June looked at Jarod meaningfully as she squeezed his hand.

The song ended and Jarod hugged June briefly. "I'd always wondered as much," he said to her quietly.

"What is given in love is never lost," June sighed with a smile.

They returned to the table to find Barbara quietly sitting alone.

Jarod quickly searched the small crowd and seeing that Dana had not yet returned he politely insisted that Barbara honor him with a dance. The woman meekly accepted his offer, pleased by his thoughtfulness.

Jarod and Barbara danced and as the melody slowly faded away Jarod caught sight of Ben approaching them.

"Thank you for the dance, Barbara."

"You're entirely welcomed," Annie's mother answered as Ben reached them, a grin widening across his weathered face.

"Ben have you met Annie's mother, Barbara?" Jarod asked the man as he introduced them to each other.

"How'd you do, m'am."

"Ben works with us here at the ranch, Annie must've mentioned him?" Jarod smiled knowingly at Barbara.

"I believe she has, yes." Barbara looked at Ben curiously.

"You have a fine young daughter, Miss Barbara. She's a hard worker, that's for sure and her young man is too. He'll make you proud." Ben said with charm as Jarod watched on amused. Obviously Ben was enchanted with the quiet woman and Jarod could not help but smile at Ben's irrepressible behavior. "I guess I'll leave you in Ben's capable hands, Barbara." Jarod excused himself and made his way back to Annie and Kent. "Annie, Dana's not back yet?"

"She's just gone to the house," Annie glanced in that direction. "I don't know how long she's been gone." Her answer was uncertain. "Do you want me to go and check on her?"

"No, that's fine. I'll go up." Jarod left the tent and made his way to the house, entering just as the phone began to ring. He sighed at the distraction and turned into the office. "Hello?"

"My, my. A king who answers his own phone. What luck!" There was a sneering chuckle on the line. "Is your throne feeling a little hot right now, Jarod?"

"Sonny!" Jarod spoke sharply as his hand tightened around the receiver. Panic rose inside of him as he tried to listen for sounds of Dana within the house.

"Clever man. This time I'll do the talking so you just shut up and listen. I have something here from your little kingdom. She's a little tied up right now, but so far she's still in one piece."

Jarod hastily removed his jacket, he could feel his pulse racing. "Sonny, if you so much..."

"Hey! Remember...I'm doing the talking. Open your mouth again and you'll be talking to a dead phone...among other things. Now listen here, the three of us are going to play a little game."

There was a slight pause and Jarod ran his hand over his ashen face.

"The first rule is that if you screw up on anything...one player gets removed from the board. Understand, Kingsley?"

Jarod closed his eyes and held his tongue.

"You're a quick learner, Kingsley." Evil laughter filled the line. "Now, you are going to come and join us. Don't think about being a hero," Sonny warned him in a menacing tone. "You come alone and unarmed. Your princess eagerly awaits you and she's counting on your complete obedience. You screw up and the lovely damsel perishes. It's a fairly simple game."

There was another pause on the phone and Jarod could do nothing but wait for Sonny to speak.

"I think you understand the stakes. Don't waste any time getting to the barn. I'm all out of patience these days."

The phone went dead.

-Chapter 23-

Dana watched helplessly as Sonny slammed the phone down. She had prayed the security guard at the barn would have helped her, now his motionless body lay sprawled across the floor of the tack room.

Sonny had called Jarod and Dana was only to aware of what Sonny's intentions were, he was about to get the revenge he had been seeking all this time. Dana struggled in another futile attempt to free herself from the wide tape Sonny had used to bind her wrist and ankles to the chair. Her heart was pounding so hard she felt it would explode.

"Sonny," she pleaded "don't do this. You don't want to do this."

He remained mute pacing behind her with the only sound coming from his feet as they hit the floor heavily.

"Sonny, please, you have me, I'll go with you, I'll do anything. Jarod has nothing to do with any of this." Dana attempted again her voice broken "I can make you happy."

Dana had barely finished the last word before Sonny's hand flung out and slammed into her head with force. He came around to face her.

"You lying whore!" he brought his face in close to hers as he bent down in front of the chair and slowly ran the long silver blade of a knife down her cheek letting the tip rest on her chin. Dana swallowed hard frozen in fear.

"I did everything for you, it was never enough, was it Dana?" Now you and that blonde bastard are both going to pay."

"You want to act like a whore, I promise you before this night is over you will feel exactly like a whore, and when you are begging for me to end it, I'll use you all over again." He stared at her, his expression crazed. His free hand ran down her open neckline finding her breast, "I should almost let Jarod live long enough to watch it all, then he can see you for the tramp you are too."

Dana closed her eyes, "Sonny I am telling you, Jarod means nothing to me, I was using him. C'mon Sonny let's leave this place now, please" she begged her cheeks wet now with tears.

Sonny smiled at her and his features softened, "I loved you so much Dana" and then suddenly he struck her again, her head snapped to the side, Sonny sprang upwards and went behind her chair "You are a lying whore."

"Sonny," Jarod's voice cut through the room, he stood at the open doorway.

"Jarod, get out of here, he is going to..."Dana screamed the words frantically but stopped as Sonny pushed the blade of the knife against her neck, this time she could feel the razor sharpness against her skin.

Jarods eyes found Dana's. She was terrified and he quickly looked away not wanting to add any fuel to Sonny's inferno. He turned his attention to Sonny who now looked like a madman, his eyes huge filled with rage.

"I am here Sonny. You have what you want, let Dana go."

"The bitch stays," Sonny replied.

"Sonny, you love her. You don't want to hurt her." Jarod tried to keep his voice calm as he moved in closer.

"You move one inch closer and I'll slice this bitch's throat right now" Sonny yelled back at him.

"OK, OK, I'm not moving" Jarod was quickly assessing that reason was not going to be an option and that he had to get Sonny to move away from Dana before things escalated any further.

Sonny raised Dana's chin with the tip of the knife, "Tell him what I want Dana, tell him!" he screamed frantically.

Trembling, Dana looked up towards Jarod, her face white "He wants to..."she shook her head as tears silently continued down her cheeks.

"Look, Dana here seems to have lost her ability to speak. Suffice to say she will be busy for the rest of the night," Sonny ran her hand across her damp face. "It may not be what this princess is used to but it will sure be a learning experience for her, I'll make sure of that." Sonny looked at her with pure disgust and laughed.

"Sonny" Jarod's voice commanded, "You said you wanted me. Stop hiding behind a little girl. You're holding the knife, I'm waiting. For once in your life be a man."

"Don't push me or I'll end this for her right now," Sonny threatened.

"I thought you wanted to keep her for later. You want me, let's do it!" Jarod raised his voice.

"Shut up, I make the rules here" Sonny glared at Jarod.

Jarod realized his next actions were not without risk but he was not about to let this go any further, if he was going to get control of any of this he had to lure Sonny away from Dana.

He drew in a deep breath, "You know what Sonny, fuck you. I'm not playing!" Jarod's voice filled with disrespect as he turned to walk away.

Jarod heard Sonny lunge towards him and Dana shriek as Sonny plunged the knife deep into his shoulder.

Jarod grabbed Sonny with his uninjured arm and threw him over the bodyguard's body out on to the barn aisle. Sonny's body landed roughly onto the cement floor.

Sonny scrambled to stand back up but Jarod was immediately on top of him, his force and weight forcing Sonny's body downward.

They fought violently half way down the barn floor their bodies rising and falling over each other with Sonny stabbing Jarod deeply one more time before Jarod could free the knife from Sonny's grip. Jarod was now bleeding profusely and he could feel his strength abandoning him.

Jarod pressed Sonny firmly against the barn wall knowing he would not be able to hold him for much longer. He slowly pulled Sonny down with him as his strength weakened. Jarod looked up at the stall latch and grabbed for it while keeping Sonny pinned under him. Jarrod's fingers found the latch and opened the stall door. With one final burst of power he heaved Sonny into the stall just as his world went dark.

*****

Jarod parked his car in front of the small New England cemetery. He looked towards the delicate bundle of flowers that sat on the empty passenger seat and he gently picked them up.

It somehow only seemed fitting to Jarod that the frigid early winter air accompanied him as he walked in silence from grave to grave, reluctantly searching for the one name.

Then he came upon it. The large charcoal tombstone looked far too impersonal to be hers, yet unmistakably DANA NORTHINGTON was deeply engraved into the dark granite.

Jarod suddenly felt as though his shirt was too tight. He loosened his tie and undid the top button of his shirt. He lowered agonized eyes to the mound of earth before him, his jaw tightened. Minutes passed before he finally raised his head and read the name again.

Jarod closed his eyes to it, willing it be different. He could see her so clearly, smiling, her delicate chin raised ever so slightly in that teasing way she had. He opened his eyes back to the harsh reality of the silent, solid granite that faced him. Hesitantly he approached the tombstone.

He did not want to be in this place. He had been drawn here by something he couldn't understand. He stood by the headstone for some time before dropping to his knees. He lay the bundle of flowers down and held an open hand out, slowly tracing over the letters of her name.

"Dana, it wasn't supposed to be like this." The breeze caught the words from his mouth, carrying them away. "We should have had forever. I don't know, Dana." Jarod rubbed at his eyes and swallowed hard. "I don't know about anything...I don't know how or why I'm supposed to go on without you." He ran a cold hand over his face. "I am so sorry, Dana. I promised I would keep you safe, I was sure… I was so wrong. I would do anything to change this, it should be me..." Jarod stared unseeingly at her grave.

He lowered his hand to the hard earth and dug a small hole into it. Reaching into the pocket of his coat, he removed the delicate ring, brushing it lightly against his lips.

"I wanted you to have this with you, Sweetheart."

The pain inside of him was unbearable as he placed the ring into the ground and carefully covered it.

"I'll love you always," he whispered in a staggered breath.

A strong wind swiftly picked up, bringing with it the distinct fragrance of the ocean.

Impulsively, he closed his eyes and breathed in deeply. He could feel her. She was there inside of him, around him, embracing him. In that moment he was filled by her warmth....and then in an overwhelming stillness, she was gone.

*****

Jarod moaned inaudibly as he woke and through what seemed like a thick fog his eyes slowly adjusted to the brightness. Gradually between the sounds and smells he became aware that he was in a hospital.

He began to focus more clearly and Jarod caught his breath as he looked down to find Dana's head lying softly on his bedside. The cemetery had been something born from his mind and he thanked God she was here with him. His hand reached out to stroke her hair needing to touch her and he smiled, his heart filled with gratitude and love.

Dana raised her head at his touch, "Jarod," her eyes quickly filled with tears.

"Shhhhh, no more tears Dana," he gently wiped a stray one from her bruised cheek, "I'm so sorry Sweetheart." He was glaringly reminded of how differently this all could have been. Jarod attempted to heave himself upward, a sharp pain went through him and he laid his head back upon the pillow.

Dana stood and bent over him, lightly kissing him. "It was really serious Jarod, for both you and the guard at the barn. For awhile they didn't know, but the doctors say you are both going to make a full recovery. It will just take a bit of time." She placed her hand gently on his chest. "I love you so much, if this had ended any other way. If Tom hadn't found us when he did, I don't know....."

"Dana, everything is going to be alright now," Jarod smiled, "although I really do think we've both probably have had our fill of hospitals." Jarod closed his eyes for a moment, still feeling heavy from the effects of the medication, then he looked at Dana solemnly, "and Sonny?"

"Masquerade.....Sonny is dead." Dana answered quietly as she tucked her hand into Jarod's. "She must have been feeling threatened by the fighting and when you pushed Sonny into her stall she panicked. Ben says she is doing fine."

Jarod nodded and rested once again. He considered the irony to how Sonny had met his death. At the time he had no idea it had been

Masquerade's stall he had pushed Sonny into that night. In the end Jarod's conscience was clean; he had done what had to be done.

Jarod looked up at Dana, his blue eyes warm and reassuring, "It's over," he squeezed her hand tenderly. In that moment he realized Dana would at last have what he had always wanted most for her...she was safe.

Dana pondered feeling somewhat incredulous. Jarod's words seemed so simple. Silently she reflected over everything that had happened to reach this point. What it had cost to so many. It almost seemed unimaginable that she was now finally free. Free to live this new life she had forged for herself here in New Mexico alongside Jarod.

Dana had come to this place out of necessity; it truly had become her home out of love.

She looked poignantly at Jarod, bit by bit an expression of hope broke over her weary features as she smiled, "You're right, it really is over."

In so many ways Dana's life was just about to begin.

Made in the USA
Columbia, SC
08 March 2018